"What really happe..."

"It is all in the report, Captain."

"Is it?" Mironova mused. "So you found Captain Spock's burial tube and discovered he was alive. How, exactly? Brushed the giant microbes off and felt compelled to take a peek at what ought to have been a moldering corpse? Or did he knock on the lid like a vampire? Sit up and ask for breakfast?"

Saavik broke eye contact, looked down at her hands. "Not precisely."

There was a very long silence. Mironova seemed satisfied.

"That's all I'm going to get from you, isn't it? You're discreet; I like that. All the same, if I weren't short-handed, I'd throw you back in the pond. But if you must go back out again this soon, this promises to be a very tame mission. You're correct; I do need a science officer. And my civilian scientist needs a babysitter. You'll do just fine in both capacities."

Before Saavik could ask what she meant, Mironova stood up abruptly, causing her to do the same. The interview was apparently over, and Mironova had made her decision. Based on *what* precisely, Saavik did not know.

"Right, then. We're cleared to leave orbit in three days. Welcome aboard, Lieutenant!"

STAR TREK®

UNSPOKEN TRUTH

Margaret Wander Bonanno

**Based upon *Star Trek*
created by Gene Roddenberry**

POCKET BOOKS

New York   London   Toronto   Sydney

Pocket Books
A Division of Simon & Schuster, Inc.
1230 Avenue of the Americas
New York, NY 10020

This book is a work of fiction. Names, characters, places, and incidents either are products of the author's imagination or are used fictitiously. Any resemblance to actual events or locales or persons, living or dead, is entirely coincidental.

First Pocket Books paperback edition April 2010

POCKET and colophon are registered trademarks of Simon & Schuster, Inc.

For information about special discounts for bulk purchases, please contact Simon & Schuster Special Sales at 1-866-506-1949 or business@simonandschuster.com.

The Simon & Schuster Speakers Bureau can bring authors to your live event. For more information or to book an event, contact the Simon & Schuster Speakers Bureau at 1-866-248-3049 or visit our website at www.simonspeakers.com.

Cover art by Doug Drexler

Manufactured in the United States of America

10   9   8   7   6   5   4   3   2   1

ISBN 978-1-4391-0219-0
ISBN 978-1-4391-7320-6 (ebook)

For Marco,
where ideas begin

HISTORIAN'S NOTE

The main events in this story take place in 2286 (ACE), concurrent with the interstellar Probe's incursion in the Sol system seeking humpback whales and the command crew of the *Enterprise* facing charges of the theft of that starship (*Star Trek IV: The Voyage Home*). It also relates events of Lieutenant Saavik's early years on Hellguard, the planet where she was found as a child by Spock (*Star Trek: The Pandora Principle*).

Prologue

———

The lizard writhed against the blade. The movement was mere reflex; the creature was already dead, pinned to the cactus it had been crawling on. More than a decade out of practice, Saavik's eye was still keen, her hand unerring, the speed with which she'd thrown the knife rendering it all but invisible until it struck home.

Reaching carefully between the deadly spines, she retrieved her prize. Pulling the small carcass free of the weapon that joined her present to her past, she wiped the blade clean on the hem of her robe and then, out of old habit, began with the lizard's head: bit it off cleanly and, her eyes unfocused and glinting with a primeval strangeness, methodically began to chew.

Minutes later, except for trace DNA on the knife and a slight rise in Saavik's metabolic rate as she digested after a long fast, it was as if the lizard had never existed. Saavik would continue to hunt the night through, then seek shelter from the sun's brutality during the day, even as she waited for her larger prey to come to her. Then she would do what she needed to do.

Her path, it seemed, had come full circle. If she had thought a life in Starfleet would protect her from her past, she had been mistaken. The soft-spoken, methodical young officer with the brilliant mind, the impeccable manners, the near obsession with rules and regulations was long gone. Her garments in tatters, her once luxuriant hair a snarled, dusty mass, dirt embedded in her nails and ingrained in her skin, a feral gleam in her eyes, she had regressed completely into the nightmare she had known as a child.

She might have left Hellguard, but Hellguard had never left her.

One

———

Captain's Personal Log, Science Vessel Chaffee, Galina Mironova in command. Twenty-eight days ago, we made orbit around Vulcan with the intention of restocking and getting our final orders for what was to have been a simple mission—a month or so of cataloging rocks and trees on an out-of-the-way world in the Deema system. That was before a spacefaring Probe looking for whales came marauding through the quadrant on its way to Earth and effectively grounded all nonessential missions until we got sorted out. Better late than never, we are finally cleared for departure, but now I'm short a science officer. Or perhaps not. Today I interview one Lieutenant Saavik, whose reputation precedes her.

If I were impressed with surfaces, I'd hire her on the spot, but I was a scientist long before I was a command officer, and consequently I've a tendency to treat each mission like a chemistry experiment. The proper mix of reactants is essential. We're a small vessel with a handful of crew, little more than an extended family, and everyone has to get along. Sibling rivalry is to be frowned upon, but a little friendly competition can yield the best results.

• • •

Mironova stopped writing her personal log in her head and pretended to study Saavik's service jacket on her desk screen, though she'd committed the important parts to memory before the young Vulcan officer had arrived.

Stop being clever or you'll trip over your own metaphors! she cautioned herself. *Bottom line, you want someone sober, sane, and unshakable to balance your lead civilian scientist's peccadilloes, and here she is sitting across the desk from you. Get on with it!*

"Ordinarily, Lieutenant, I'd refuse your request," Mironova said. "What happened on Genesis had to have been traumatic, yet you've taken no leave time in which to process those events, despite Command's rather strong suggestion that you do so."

"There were extenuating circumstances, Captain," Saavik pointed out.

Mironova looked up sharply, expecting sarcasm but finding only Vulcan logic.

"Yes, bloody Probe! Half the quadrant's busy cleaning up after the damned thing, which leaves me without a science officer. And since you're not only one of the best candidates for the job, you're here instead of halfway across the quadrant participating in the cleanup, and Starfleet has debriefed you and deemed you fit, I'm strongly tempted."

Even as Mironova studied the Vulcan, Saavik was studying her. Mironova hailed from the Iadara Colony, as her crisply accented Standard suggested. The colony's proximity to Cardassian space had rendered its inhabitants tough, resourceful, and not easily rattled. Slim and slightly smaller than average height, Mironova gave the impression of being taller than she was. Her silver hair was cut to military precision, her tone and manner were no-nonsense, and her gray-green eyes could be penetrating, but the occasional twinkle suggested she was not averse to a bit of fun when the occasion warranted.

She'd met Saavik in the *Chaffee*'s transporter room in person, rather than having a junior officer escort her to the ready room, then had to order her to be seated in the single chair on the other side of the desk. Saavik sat, but at attention, her posture ramrod straight and inches from the back of the chair, resisting the urge to compare Captain Mironova's taste in decor with the late Captain Esteban's.

Chaffee was an *Oberth*-class vessel, a sister ship to the *U.S.S. Grissom*. *Perhaps*, Saavik thought, *it had been unwise to request an assignment on a sister ship so soon after the loss of* Grissom *and her crew.*

Mironova might have been thinking the same thing. She found the look in the young Vulcan's eyes unsettling.

"You seem in an awful hurry to get out of Dodge," Mironova suggested, keeping her tone light.

"It is my understanding, Captain, that *Chaffee* is cleared for departure in three days' time—"

"—and you're so eager to go off cataloging rocks and leaves on a dull little planet in a newly charted sector that even the fact that your crewmates from *Enterprise* and the entire planet Earth along with them nearly perished hasn't slowed you down."

"With all due respect, Captain, I have been stationed on Vulcan for almost four months, assisting Captain Scott with the refit of the Klingon vessel *Bounty*—"

" '*Bounty*'?" Mironova frowned.

"I believe Doctor McCoy was being ironic."

"Yes, he would be, wouldn't he?" Mironova said wryly. "But, to the point, Command granted you extended personal leave once *Bounty* left Vulcan, leave that you did not take. Forgive me if I keep harping on that, but the Probe's been talked to, Lieutenant, everything's back in its proper place, yet here you are requesting reassignment when you ought to be lying on a beach somewhere instead.

"Screen off," the captain said crisply, her chin in her hands, elbows on the desktop, as she searched her would-be science officer's face for something that wasn't in the record.

"So here's everybody else breathing a sigh of relief and remembering to stop and smell the roses, and then there's you. Running toward or running from, Lieutenant?"

"*Que sera, sera*," Amanda had said as they stood together at the foot of Mount Seleya and watched the *Bounty* bank and turn and disappear just to the left of 40 Eridani, as if swallowed by its corona, an omen Saavik's Romulan forebears might have found portentous. Saavik herself had dismissed such a superstitious notion for what it was by running through her mind the equations that made it possible for a vessel designed to look like a living thing to propel itself into space with far less effort than the bird it strove to emulate. Amanda's words had disrupted her reverie.

"I do not understand, Mother," Saavik said.

" 'Whatever will be, will be.' "

The human had turned away from the vista of the valley floor, striding purposefully up the path to the waiting aircar that would return them to ShiKahr, eager to get out of the sun before it rose much further in the sky. Saavik considered taking her elbow to assist her on the incline, but Amanda was still light on her feet despite her age and the thin atmosphere and needed no assistance.

"You're understandably concerned about the trial," Amanda said as the air car lifted off in a spray of red Vulcan dust, and she set the autopilot to the correct altitude and direction. "But there's no point in fretting about it. What can either of us do? Certainly not feel guilty for not accompanying them."

The crew had stood up for her. Saavik thought there must be some way she could reciprocate.

"She's a Vulcan!" was Doctor McCoy's argument to the powers that be as soon as his head cleared from the *fal-tor-pan* and before someone decided to ship her off on enforced leave or transfer her to another ship. "Work is therapeutic for them. Besides," he'd added, giving Scotty a mental poke in the ribs, "Mister Scott tells me he needs her expertise."

"Aye!" Scotty had piped up. "That Klingon ship's guidance system is a rats' nest. The lass would be instrumental in the refit. Don't know how I'd manage without her, frankly," he'd finished lamely, never a good liar but earning points for sincerity.

"She might also be able to help us reintegrate Spock's *katra*," McCoy had thrown in as a last desperate ploy, and even Starfleet Command couldn't argue with that.

Yet after granting her permission to help with the refit, Command had balked at her request to accompany Kirk and his crew back to Earth. Saavik was not implicated in the theft of *Enterprise*, it was argued; her testimony about the events on Genesis was all that was needed, and she had a promising career ahead of her that ought not be overshadowed by any association with Starfleet's chronic miscreants.

Still, as *Bounty* was preparing for departure, she had all but abandoned her years of Vulcan discipline in a moment of sheer Romulan impulsiveness when Admiral Kirk took her by the shoulders and said, "Saavik, this is good-bye."

She wanted to plead with him, *Let me go with you, Admiral! I have seen Spock wandering the highlands—confused, bewildered, lost. Like you, Admiral, I owe him my life, and like you I cannot bear to see him this way. I know it's against regulations, but at this point, does that matter? Let me help!*

Instead, she had clenched her jaw, wrenched her control into place, and replied as calmly as she could, "Yes, Admiral," and, as much to distract herself as him, told him how bravely his son had died. Let him learn about the protomatter from others; he would not hear it from her.

Was it possible to contain so many unspoken truths and roiling emotions and still walk upright? She had turned on her heel, crisply, professionally, prepared to make a dignified exit, walk away without looking back, and suddenly *he* was there.

What else was there to say but, "Good day, Captain Spock. May your journey be free of incident"?

If she'd had a human heart to break, the puzzlement on his face (*Have we met before? Do I know you?*) would have broken it. But she was nothing human, and no one, not even her mentor—especially not her mentor, though the being before her might be only a shell of what he once was—would ever see her shame.

Yes, she had wanted to go with them. Yes, it troubled her profoundly that she could not. And now that they were on their way, Amanda was reading her mind, something she had been able to do, even with her limited telesper skills, since Saavik was a child . . .

Oh, you precious thing! Amanda had thought at the first sight of the little bundle of arms and legs with her mop of unruly curls and eyes that had seen what no child should ever see. It was all she could do to keep from gathering her into her arms and holding her close.

Instead, her hands clasped nonthreateningly in front of her, the human had inclined her head and allowed herself the smallest of smiles, before saying very softly, "Vulcan honors us with your presence, Saavik. Welcome."

Spock had spoken to his mother weekly during the

extended leave in which he'd attempted to foster his foundling himself. The other Hellguard refugees had been relegated to a facility in the far reaches of one of Vulcan's polar regions, far from mainstream sensibilities, their arrival unannounced except to those whose kinship had been established, and who might choose to claim their own. Most would not.

Saavik's refusal to submit to an antigen test to determine her ancestry (having attained more than seven years of age—the first stage of adulthood by Vulcan standards—she was permitted to make that decision for herself) meant that if Spock had not claimed her, she would have remained at the facility until her education was complete and a suitable occupation found for her. Not a tragedy, considering where she'd come from, but Spock had had other plans for her.

The time he had been able to spend with her had been sufficient to replace her hypervigilance with something resembling control. They had worked together to transform the pidgin RomuloVulcan she'd spat at him at first with the rudiments of conversational Vulcan, though she still often tangled her syntaxes. He had taught her to read and to study—easier, given her insatiable curiosity, than teaching her to wear shoes and not gulp her food. But when his leave time was up and he had to return to duty, Spock had known where to turn for assistance.

All things considered, he had managed remarkably well, Amanda saw. The child was clean and well fed, though the ravages of the starvation years were still evident in her coltish appearance—small for her age, all arms and legs, ribs visibly rising and falling, a little too fast, beneath the practical clothing. (Starfleet issue? It was completely unadorned. That would be remedied shortly.) She wore shoes, though clearly unhappily; Amanda could see the small toes curling and uncurling restlessly inside them, as if she couldn't wait to cast them off.

Her chestnut ringlets had been cropped to a practical few inches in length all around, forming a soft aura around an elfin face which, as Saavik was studying her own feet when Amanda first spoke to her, seemed from this angle to be little more than cheekbones and a sharp little chin.

It was hard to find a Vulcan child who wasn't aesthetically pleasing. But this one would stand out even among this most beautiful of species.

All of this flashed through Amanda's mind in the breath or two between her words and Saavik's answer.

"Hon-or is mine," the child said carefully, as if she had rehearsed it for the entire journey here. Her voice was husky—naturally so, or was that fear? For a moment longer Saavik studied her imprisoned toes. Then her chin came up, and her overlarge eyes met the human's, unblinking. "Lady A-man-da."

From that day forward, the bond was forged.

"I know you wanted to go to Earth to show your support. So did I," Amanda said now, more than a decade later, as the air car rose and set course automatically, turning in a slow arc until Mount Seleya vanished from view, only its desultory plume of smoke rising languidly above the surrounding mountains. At this speed, they would be at the outskirts of ShiKahr in a little more than two hours. "But the trial is closed to all but essential personnel, and we'd only be in the way." When the girl said nothing, she added, "I'm listening,"

Saavik thought of how to frame the words.

"The trial seems . . . unjust," she began carefully, but then the words tumbled out of her. "It is true that Admiral Kirk violated Starfleet regulations, and for that he should—objectively—be punished. Yet the outcome of this . . . illegal action was a dual good. It prevented the Klingons from potentially using Genesis as a weapon, and it restored Spock to life."

"Moral choices are black and white only in theory, Saavik," Amanda suggested.

"So I have observed."

The car skimmed on in silence for a time, above modern cities and ancient ruins. Saavik considered her future.

Starfleet had not reassigned her. Instead Command had reiterated its suggestion, little short of an order, that she take extended leave, including either counseling or a course of meditation with the Vulcan savants, which, in view of her heritage, was considered an acceptable alternative.

But the last thing she wanted, after what had transpired on Genesis, was anyone else's mind—human or Vulcan—poking about in hers. She had temporized, asked if she could wait until the trial was over to make a decision, and in light of the unusual circumstances, Command had acceded.

What would happen to her once the Federation Council reached its verdict was as uncertain as that verdict itself.

"They'll be all right," Amanda said.

Saavik frowned. She did not necessarily share her foster mother's confidence in either the future or the wisdom of the Federation Council. Spock would no doubt have said something about the universe unfolding as it should. At least, the Spock who had been her mentor would have done so. The Spock who had greeted her aboard *Bounty* just before its departure had looked at her without recognition. The Spock she had known might be lost to her forever.

Que sera, sera, she thought, yet, "How can you be so certain?" she asked.

"Because everything you've mentioned will be weighed into evidence. Besides"—Amanda did not so much as try to repress a smile—"you have to concede that the crew of *Enterprise* have the best possible advocate on their side."

Sarek had been a different kind of presence in Saavik's young life. While Amanda was there to ease the nightmares and tolerate her sometimes regressions into the small child she had never been allowed to be, his influence was more subtle, Saavik's approach to him more oblique.

His study door was never closed, and often when he was away—and he was away frequently—she would tiptoe inside and, not touching anything, look at the awards, the artwork, the volumes of law and polity and linguistics and music and a dozen other subjects available on his personal computer and in a few antique paper books. When he returned, he seemed to intuit somehow that she had been there, and if he caught her hovering in the doorway, he would say without glancing up, "You are always welcome."

There was no question she could ask that he would not answer, and until she decided she was too old for such behaviors, she often sat at his feet, simply watching him work, listening to him speak to the leaders of planets she knew only as dots on a starmap about subjects she couldn't begin to understand. And when she sometimes caught a brief glint of something affectionate in his hooded eyes—quickly extinguished, of course, and deniable if questioned—she basked in it for days.

Amanda was warmth, comfort, safety; Spock was challenge and role model; but Sarek was wisdom. She'd have died for any or all of them.

So when it was clear that the repairs were almost done and the Federation Council's summons must be answered, Saavik had left Mister Scott to putter about in *Bounty*'s engine room without her for a day and returned to ShiKahr to say her farewells. She found herself lurking in the doorway like a hesitant child as Sarek prepared to depart for Earth well ahead of Admiral Kirk and the crew in order to speak in their defense. Even with his back to the door, he sensed her presence and, out of habit, said, "You are always welcome."

"Father . . ." She had rehearsed her words carefully. "I came to bid you a safe journey and . . . hope for an optimal outcome."

"Had you not, I would have sought you out," Sarek said, slipping the brief he had prepared into a small carry case, along with the research materials he would study on the journey. Anyone else might have relied on the onboard computers, but the ambassador wanted his references to hand. "We have some unfinished business, you and I."

She had been dreading this since she had first come to live on Vulcan, but all the more since Genesis.

Her arrival on Vulcan at the age of eleven had presented a dilemma: She had not been betrothed in childhood as was traditional. But there were always a few casualties during the *kahs-wan,* leaving some eleven-year-olds unbonded, and tradition allowed for that. After a suitable period of mourning, it was deemed appropriate for families whose child had been widowed by a mate's demise on Vulcan's Forge to approach each other and form new bonds.

Amanda had put the kibosh on the notion as soon as Sarek suggested it.

"It's too soon, husband! Little more than a year ago she was still a wild thing. She has so much to learn! Surely it can wait until she's older."

"I agree the circumstances are unusual, my wife, but if a suitable mate is not found for her—"

"—she will be free to choose her own, well before she needs to."

"To leave such a thing to chance is not only illogical but dangerous. There is a reason that childhood betrothal is our way."

"Of course," Amanda said lightly. "After all, it worked so well for our son!"

Whatever else Sarek might have intended to say, there was no argument to counter that. He had simply waited until Saavik was preparing to leave for Starfleet Academy and broached the subject then. As an adult, he explained, she would have more discretion than she might have had as a child. He would screen several potential candidates from suitable families, and as soon as she had graduated and before accepting her first assignment, she would be free to choose from among them. Well aware of the tradition, grateful for all that her foster parents had done for her, Saavik had agreed.

Once again, as if toying with her, circumstance—the "minor training cruise" and Genesis—had intervened. And now here she was, wondering how that circumstance might affect her future. She could not meet Sarek's eyes, but found herself instead studying the intricate and familiar patterns of the carpet, remembering the feel of the pile beneath her fingers as a child, stroking it, never having seen a carpet before, marveling at its softness and how the patterns moved like grass when she touched them.

"Untoward circumstance need not endanger tradition," Sarek said gently, erasing a universe of doubt. "Upon my return, we shall do what we intended to do before."

Before. Could it be that simple? Saavik found she had been holding her breath and remembered to breathe again.

"Yes, Father," she said, trusting him in this as she did in all things.

Why, then, as she helped him into his travel robe and watched him stride purposefully down the corridor toward the waiting air car, did she experience a shiver of dread?

She had not even had the presence of mind to ask if he had preselected any candidates for her to consider ahead of time, perhaps some personal histories to peruse, some holo-images to study, some family lineages to consider. That thought had not occurred to her until after he was gone, and she dared not trouble him with her trivial concerns while he was immersed in the Council's preliminary hearings, much less during the trial.

Damn! she thought, remembering just in time not to say it aloud in Amanda's presence. Sarek would have arrived on Earth by now, *Bounty* would follow. The future was as unreadable as ever.

The air car adjusted altitude over whatever terrain they traversed, from flat desert floor to jagged foothills to lush agricultural valleys and serene urban clusters, compensating for the other vehicles sharing its airspace as well. Saavik tried to take comfort from Amanda's words. Surely there was no better advocate for her crewmates than Sarek of Vulcan.

"Indeed," she said at last, daring to hope for that much at least, and trying not to think of what would transpire once the trial was over and Sarek returned home.

Neither woman spoke again until the familiar parkland ring surrounding the city of ShiKahr passed under their wings, and they were almost home.

"In any event," Amanda said as the car slid beneath the familiar portico and powered down, "there is nothing you or I can do while we wait but keep ourselves occupied. I have a conference to prepare for. And you? What will you do now?"

In all the time she had assisted Mister Scott during the refit, she hadn't considered any alternatives. She had no thought now except to await the outcome of the trial.

"Perhaps a course of study, a time of meditation, travel?" Amanda suggested much later that day as they walked in the garden after the evening meal. The desert beyond the city ring had plummeted into darkness with a sharp drop in temperature; the stars in the moonless sky were so bright it seemed one might almost reach up and touch them. The breeze carried scents of cardamom and sandalwood, and the far-off cry of a *le-matya* was answered by the echo of a nearby temple gong announcing an ancient tocsin preserved by ritual more than a thousand years after the war it commemorated, lest Vulcans ever forget their violent past. "At least a sojourn at one of the shrines, to gather your troubled thoughts."

"I have no need," Saavik said softly but with determination.

There was a stubbornness to the set of her jaw that Amanda recognized all too well. The sister planet T'Khut skirted the horizon, casting just enough light so that the shadows from the trees overhead played across Saavik's face, reflecting the shadows behind her eyes.

"Saavik," Amanda said carefully, "I know that you, at least as much as Admiral Kirk and the others, were instrumental in saving Spock's life. I do not need to know more to know this much."

Mercifully, Saavik thought. What was there to be said about *Pon farr,* especially the circumstances under which it had occurred on Genesis?

"Can I not do something for you in return? I can speak to the savants at Amorak. A place can be set aside for you."

"Mother—"

"At the very least"—Amanda cut across her objection with a smile—"go and enjoy the hot springs."

This evoked a bittersweet memory, and Saavik might have smiled. When she was a child, running water had fascinated her. She would stop and stare at the numerous fountains that graced the streets of ShiKahr, the play of the sunlight on the spray as fascinating to her as it might have been to a toddler. The urge to dabble her fingers in the water proved almost irresistible. The desert hot springs had been an indescribable luxury to someone who knew what it was like to live in filth so ubiquitous one no longer remembered what the skin beneath the layers of dirt looked or felt like.

To recapture that sense of wonder, to be alone with one's thoughts, perhaps to find the courage to uproot and confront the traumatic events of her very first deep space mission—Spock's death, the destruction of *Grissom* with the loss of all aboard, David Marcus's unethical conduct and his violent death, the possibility that they all might have died on Genesis, the bizarre effect of discovering the reborn Spock as a small child evolving into adulthood by the hour, and her need to help him through the throes of *Pon farr*, Spock's ultimate rebirth through *fal-tor-pan* and the possibility that his mind would never truly be restored . . .

The trilling of a pair of mating lizards in the nearby shrubbery cut through the maelstrom threatening to engulf her, and she gathered herself. She could not continue in this way without respite.

"I shall consider it," she said at last.

But with the dawn came word that an alien probe was cutting a swath across the quadrant, silencing comm on planets and deep space stations, leaving ships in its path adrift without life support, heading toward Earth. The trial of the *Enterprise* Seven was set aside in this time of crisis, and Saavik reported immediately to Starfleet HQ Vulcan even before the official summons came. Meditation, and the hot springs, would have to wait.

Or perhaps be forgone altogether.

The crisis was over, the crew of *Enterprise*, even without *Enterprise*, having once more saved the day. The trial had ended just as Amanda had predicted it would: Spock was safe, and Sarek was on his way home. Now all that was left was quite literally the mopping up.

Saavik remained at her post, assisted by a Denobulan by the name of Lieutenant Eyris, in charge of contacting Federation worlds that had been in the Probe's path, determining what assistance they might need and how critically, cross-referencing with any available vessel, Starfleet or civilian, that could be dispatched from unaffected systems with the needed supplies. Eyris didn't need much sleep, but Saavik's ears were beginning to ring from fatigue, overlapping multiphasics at various frequencies, and orders being shouted across the command center itself.

Despite the background noise, she heard Captain Mironova before she saw her, shouting into a personal communicator ("Because all the official channels were overloaded, weren't they?" she would explain later) at someone apparently doing the same at his end.

". . . bollocks, if you ask me. A day later and we'd have been en route to Deema III and fare-thee-well, but now we're stuck here. Asked Command to let us out of spacedock to go help or at least get out of the way, but they've effectively told us to stay put . . . Yes, darling, I know, but that's what they've told me . . ."

"O Captain, my Captain!" Lieutenant Eyris said merrily. "Galina Mironova, shy as a Klingon on prune juice."

"Your commanding officer," Saavik supplied, recalling that Eyris was science officer aboard *Chaffee*.

"The same." Eyris nodded cheerfully. "We were assigned to preliminary geological and biological survey on Deema III. Resupplying when the Probe put all ships in Vulcan space on standby. Mironova's been in an uproar ever since. She seems to think if she keeps yelling, Command will release her ship just for the sake of the silence."

"Yet you seem unperturbed by the delay," Saavik suggested.

"I can't go with them now, anyway." Eyris sighed. "I've been summoned home. Family issues."

Saavik knew better than to ask. The interrelationships of Denobulan extended family members were more complex than the calculation of *pi*, and no Denobulan ever said no to family.

"Want to keep my seat warm for me?" Eyris asked, and Saavik gave her a puzzled look. "It's a short mission. Interim science officer, until I get this family *mishegoss* untangled."

Que sera, sera, Saavik thought. The universe would unfold as it should.

Several days later, sitting across the desk from Mironova and as uneasy as she was with some of her questions, Saavik understood why the captain was asking them. An *Oberth*-class vessel was little more than a science lab with warp nacelles, with a small crew complement and accommodations for a handful of civilian scientists, living and working at close quarters because the labs took up most of the ship. Their missions took them to unexplored and often uninhabited regions far from aid or support, and the crew needed to be self-sufficient, able to get along with one another and to work synergistically. Captain Mironova wanted no surprises. She seemed to be doing her utmost to tell Saavik she was not needed.

"The mission parameters are within my areas of expertise," Saavik said carefully, hoping she sounded persuasive, "and the opportunity to study an unexplored planet—"

"There are plenty of unexplored planets, Lieutenant." Mironova wasn't buying it. "Skip this one, there'll be another along next week. Off the record, I think you're being pursued by ghosts, and you're trying to outrun them. You're apt to find that they travel at warp speed.

"Let me level with you, Saavik. I've read the official report on Genesis; everyone in the Fleet has. How you and Doctor Marcus followed a mysterious energy reading that turned out to be a reborn Captain Spock, Klingons killed your crewmates, hunted you down on a planet that was destroying itself beneath you, Admiral Kirk and *Enterprise* came to the rescue—all very heroic and larger-than-life, which of course anything involving James T. Kirk is apt to be. But it's what isn't in the report that interests me more, particularly as it relates to you. I've known a few Vulcans in my time."

Saavik waited for the inevitable questions and wondered how she would answer.

"What really happened on Genesis?"

"It is all in the report, Captain."

"Is it?" Mironova mused. "So you found Captain Spock's burial tube and discovered he was alive. How, exactly? Brushed the giant microbes off and felt compelled to take a peek at what ought to have been a moldering corpse? Or did he knock on the lid like a vampire? Sit up and ask for breakfast?"

Saavik broke eye contact, looked down at her hands. "Not precisely."

There was a very long silence. Mironova seemed satisfied.

"That's all I'm going to get from you, isn't it? You're discreet; I like that. All the same, if I weren't short-handed, I'd throw you back in the pond. But if you must go back out again this soon, this promises to be a very tame mission. You're correct; I do need a science officer. And my civilian scientist needs a babysitter. You'll do just fine in both capacities."

Before Saavik could ask what she meant, Mironova stood up abruptly, causing her to do the same. The interview was apparently over, and Mironova had made her decision. Based on *what* precisely, Saavik did not know.

"Right, then. We're cleared to leave orbit in three days. Welcome aboard, Lieutenant!"

Two

—

To someone who has known dire need, the sights and smells and sounds of a typical Vulcan market could be all but overwhelming. Saavik was here on the eve of her departure to purchase the ingredients for a special dinner—a peace offering, really. Amanda had been disappointed with her decision to ship out again so soon but knew her well enough not to try to talk her out of it.

The first time she had come here as a child, she had clung to Amanda's hand and dug in her heels.

"What is it, dear?"

"Staring!" the girl said, jutting her chin at the passersby moving among the stalls in the open-air market, some of whom had indeed glanced at her with passing curiosity, if only because they had not seen her with the ambassador and his human wife before. "Staring-not-staring!" she clarified.

Amanda had smiled and squeezed her hand; she knew exactly what she meant. Vulcans never *stared* per se, but they had a way of looking while not looking, and she knew it well.

"They're admiring you," she said. "Appreciating you and how well you carry yourself."

The girl had glanced up at her skeptically, her sullen expression deepening.

"Besides," Amanda continued, "it's not really you they're staring at. It's me."

The expression on Saavik's face verged on serious disbelief now. Only the little bits of decorum Spock had managed to teach her—most of them having to do with not blurting out whatever was on her mind the instant it occurred to her—coupled with a deep respect for Amanda kept Saavik from speaking.

"You don't believe me," Amanda said lightly, looking off into the distance to keep from smiling. How young this one was, in spite of everything! "That's understandable. You can't know what it's like to be a human on a Vulcan world."

Saavik considered this. "Don't know what it's like . . . to be human . . . anywhere," she decided finally.

Amanda beamed at her. "Then you do understand!"

Even more confused, Saavik studied her feet in their unaccustomed sandals—less uncomfortable than shoes, in any event. Amanda leaned down to whisper to her.

"I'll tell you a secret. When you feel them not-staring at you, hold your head up. Walk proudly, as if to say, 'Thank you for appreciating me.'"

"But—"

"Will you at least try?" Amanda asked.

The girl nodded and allowed Amanda to lead her into the crowd.

Having observed this exchange in silence, Sarek had finally trusted himself to speak. "My wife—?"

"You're about to say you'd have handled this differently?" Amanda asked playfully.

"It would never have occurred to me."

• • •

As an adult, Saavik experienced only a twinge of memory as she noted the glances of a few passersby who did not cut their eyes away in time. She returned those glances mildly, eyebrows arched only slightly—less than a challenge, more than passive acceptance—then set about buying the ingredients to prepare a special meal for herself and Amanda that, she hoped, would take some of the sting out of her abrupt departure.

Her thoughts were as tranquil as they could be under the circumstances. At 0600 tomorrow, she would report to the *Chaffee* and, she told herself, the chronic unease she felt (*Spock is safe, Sarek is safe, the crew of* Enterprise *is safe, Earth is safe* her constant silent mantra) would dissipate. She would be back in uniform, have a set schedule and specific duties to perform, her life ruled by a chronometer, not by the passage of sun across sky, the very model of Vulcan decorum, accepted as a Starfleet officer and a valued member of the science team. No one would stare-not-stare at her where she was going.

A planet did not have to be a Hellguard or a Genesis to be alien and potentially dangerous. Planets were not safe for her—not now, possibly not ever. On a ship in deep space, she would have the structure she craved.

The market was busy as always. Although it was a simple matter to replicate everything one ate from the essential nutrients without ever leaving one's residence, and even if one wanted fresh ingredients, one need only order them delivered to one's doorstep, there was something about choosing them by hand, appreciating the colors, the textures, the aromas, selecting the individual fruits and vegetables and spices, seeing the various grains and tubers weighed out and saying, "No, not that one, but this one, and three of those, rather than two, and a pinch more of this and less of that . . ."

And thus was she occupied, her mind in fact almost tranquil, when he spoke to her.

Would I have known you? he wondered. *If they had not told me where to find you, would I have recognized you after all this time?*

Yes, he thought, *the eyes. I'd have known you by the fire in the deep dark pools of your eyes, no matter how much the rest of you has altered. Can I accomplish what I have been sent to do? Have I any choice?*

She did not recognize him at first. The context was wrong, for one thing. For another, he did something no Vulcan would do—called to her by name.

"Saavik? It *is* you. I dared not hope—!"

She spun around before she remembered where she was. To cover her indiscretion, she allowed two *yonsavas* to tumble from her market basket, using the excuse of retrieving them from the cobbles to disguise the abruptness of her movement.

At least, she managed to retrieve one of them. The second rolled to his feet, and he stooped to pick it up and present it to her. Covering his own indiscretion as well?

His hair, she remembered, was curly like hers, another aspect of her appearance that caused Vulcans to stare-not-stare. On Hellguard he had worn it tied back with a thong and halfway down his back; now it was cropped close and combed over his brow in the Vulcan fashion. His pale eyes with their thick fringe of lashes were the same, as were the two crushed fingertips on his left hand. Without those clues, would she have seen the hollow-cheeked, gangling boy within the handsome confident adult who had spoken her name?

"Tolek," she said, finding her voice as the fingertips of his good hand brushed hers when he handed her the bruised fruit and she returned it to the basket. "I had not thought to see you again."

"Nor I you." His voice, which the last time they had spoken had been reedy with a starving boy's arrested adolescence, had grown deeper with adulthood, pleasant to the ear. "Is there somewhere we can talk?"

The truth of Hellguard was that the Romulans had abandoned their eugenics experiment gone awry and left its outcome to fend for themselves on that barren and inhospitable world. The myth that grew around that truth was that a horde of feral children had somehow survived from toddlerhood through intertribal war and cannibalism until a Vulcan science team rescued them. As with most myths, this one was both oversimplified and grossly exaggerated.

In fact, when the Romulans departed, they left everything behind, including stores of food that the children, ranging in age from perhaps two or three up to the cusp of adolescence, had doled out fairly in the beginning.

The eldest took charge, seeing that the youngest were fed first, as they had been trained to do in the communal facility where they'd been warehoused—fed, sheltered, taught the rudiments of language, subjected to a regimentation that governed every waking moment and often spilled over into their dreams.

But as supplies dwindled and it was clear that the adults who had heretofore controlled every aspect of their lives were not coming back, there was hoarding, theft, the formation of loose alliances conspiring to steal back what had been stolen from them, outright brawls in defense of the shrinking stores. These alliances evolved into tribes staking claim to territory and waging guerrilla wars where not a few died. Those who were wounded were often abandoned, and if their bones were picked clean afterward, none could say if it had been by the opportunistic insect life that swarmed out of underground burrows with nightfall (What had they fed on before there were Romulans? Saavik wondered to this day) or by larger, bipedal scavengers.

Why should children be expected to have any more compassion in time of war and famine than adults?

She recalled with painful clarity the first time she encountered the world beyond the walls.

Was it possible to rear children in a completely enclosed environment, without any awareness that there was a world beyond the classrooms, the corridors, the dorms, the refectory and the exercise hall, the domed atrium where a few trees struggled toward the light, the recreation hall where propaganda films were shown nightly, the only form of entertainment permitted? Of course it was.

Preflight civilizations had cloistered segments of their population with varying degrees of success. Children had come of age on space stations and multigeneration ships without ever feeling the sun on their faces, the breeze in their hair. The Sundered who left Vulcan had done this, and theories abounded that the journey had somehow marked the Romulan soul for all time, imbuing the Vulcan passion for freedom with an even greater ferocity.

Some who come of age in enclosed environments choose to extend that lifestyle into adulthood, safe in the familiar. Many in Starfleet were such "lifers," more comfortable within the confines of a vessel than beneath the open sky. But the majority preferred to plant their feet on real soil and watch the stars pass over their heads, hungry for something embedded at the genetic level that no artificial environment can satisfy.

Perhaps some few have had their hermetically sealed world snatched away from them to find a Hellguard beyond the threshold, but there is no record of such, at least not within the Federation.

In the dorms late at night, there were rumors of a world beyond, the regimented speak-when-spoken-to silence broken by the more rebellious regardless of punishment. Children will be children, in spite of the adults who attempt to dissuade them.

"Must go *somewhere*, them," Tolek insisted, meaning the proctors who supervised them, some who disappeared ("on leave," whatever that meant) for brief periods, others going away and never coming back. The numerals on his uniform (loose-fitting dun-colored unisex jumpsuit, the child's date of birth, genotype, and optimal breeding matches emblazoned in a string of numerals on the breast pocket, marking each child at all times for the adults' convenience) specified that he was one year and seventy-three days Saavik's elder. "There must be other places."

Saavik, six years old and possessed of the universal omniscience of all children at that age, had rolled her eyes at him.

"Course they do, stupid head!" she'd scolded in the patois they spoke among themselves, no matter how often they were punished for it. "They has their rooms where they lives."

"Not just *rooms*, drool-baby. Other places," Tolek insisted. "Away. Outside."

"Outside?" Saavik had repeated, too loud. The two were crouched in an air duct between the male and female dorms, one of their secret hiding places, with no guarantee, judging from the scratches on the walls (coded messages from one child or group of children to another), that they were the only ones who frequented it. They listened for a moment to what might have been the scuff of jumpsuit-clad knees crawling toward them but decided it was only the flutter of their hearts. In any event, she lowered her voice. "What means 'outside'?"

Tolek tapped lightly on the metal floor. "Walls are insides and outsides. Where do proctors go when they go away?"

Saavik thought about it, came up with nothing, scratched one shin, and shrugged. "Sleep, maybe?"

"Sleep!" Tolek shook his head, pitying her youth and innocence. "Can't sleep forever. There's outside. Maybe even *away*-away."

Saavik looked at him blankly.

"Where does food come from?" he prompted her.

Now she knew he was teasing her. "Machine, dummy. Babies know that!"

"But where does machine come from?" Tolek demanded. "And clothes and shoes and en-ter-tain-ment?" Even as circumscribed as their knowledge base was, the propaganda films struck the brighter ones as nonsense. "En-ter-tain-ment is other places. Where?"

This one Saavik could answer. "Romulus!" she said smugly, though she had no idea where that was or even what it was. Another complex of buildings like the one they lived in? A garden, perhaps, nicer than the atrium? She'd heard the word "planet" but had no context for it. All she knew about this mythic Romulus was that it was where they'd been told, from the time they first learned to speak, that the more fortunate among them might be permitted to visit someday if they were very, very good.

Saavik and Tolek had parted soon after that, crawling back along the ducts to their respective dorms, and she lay awake most of the night listening to the sighs of the other girls sleeping in the long rows of cots, wondering.

She was still wondering two years later when the adults abruptly disappeared.

•   •   •

At first the children had kept to the regimen, the eldest taking the place of the proctors, overseeing meals and exercise and bedtimes, though they made no attempt to maintain the schoolrooms, and they released the handful of the recalcitrant confined in solitary for crimes real and imagined. Volunteers oversaw the laundry and housekeeping chores and prepared meals, just as they had when they were assigned to by the proctors. But when the food in the refectory ran out, and after a lot of disagreement about whether they should or shouldn't, some of the bolder ones disabled the locks and broke into the larder.

When the food in the larder ran out, someone remembered the kitchen staff talking about other storage areas on the grounds. It was time to put Tolek's theory to the test and step Outside.

The first time they did so—Saavik among the youngest in the party, driven by curiosity and perhaps a desire to prove Tolek wrong—a lifetime of skirting the proctors and sneaking about at night held them in good stead. It was night when they ventured beyond the portal they'd been told all their lives was off-limits. Not that other children hadn't tried it in the past, but when they did alarms went off, and punishment was swift and often permanent. Transgressors were never seen again, and while the youngest comforted themselves with the thought that they were merely in solitary or sent to another dormitory, the elder ones narrowed their eyes and said nothing.

But with the proctors gone, so were the alarms. In recent days there had been power outages—there was no one left who knew how to maintain the generators—and places and things that had heretofore shrieked at anyone who ventured too close without proper authorization now sat silent, vulnerable. A handful of the braver children dared to push open the tall double doors and found starlight.

Desert as far as the eye could see, shifting sand and scrub and the distant cries of *things,* a few scraggly mountains in the distance, and a coolness in the air that was deceiving. Still, it was all so alien to children who had never before been outdoors that they clung together as a group, Saavik bringing up the rear, and skirted the high walls of the complex where they had lived all their lives, one hand holding on to the wall as if the ground might shift beneath them or swallow them up, until they found the outbuildings where the stores were kept.

That wasn't so bad! Saavik thought once they were safely back inside, bragging to the less brave about how they'd found "enough food to last forever."

But even that began to run out eventually. And when the power failed permanently and the atmospheric controls that kept the compound temperate no longer functioned, the heat of the planet's twin suns burned their confidence away.

How could light be so hostile? Some of the fairer-skinned children—possessors of rare recessive genes mutated in the milder climes of the homeworlds once the Sundered left Vulcan—literally died of sun exposure. The rest built up a gradual resistance, but one learned to seek shelter as long as there was sunlight and, despite the dangers, to move about only at night.

One learned the hard way which plants were edible, which not, which somewhere in between—fruit or leaves deadly, roots tough but digestible. One learned to trap rodents and small reptiles, and not to turn one's nose up at eating insects, grubs, worms, anything. Stagnant water might make one's gut rumble and swell, but it was better than no water at all.

The youngest and the weakest often simply *stopped,* lay down in the dust, and didn't get up, their breath growing shallower until it ceased, their matted hair and ragged scraps of clothing the only things that moved in the arid breeze and heat shimmer beneath the unforgiving suns. If there were instances of cannibalism then, none of the survivors ever spoke of it, regardless of the intensity of questioning. Years later, a poem titled "Communion" entered the public consciousness; it spoke of feeding on a dead friend as the ultimate expression of love. Its authorship was never determined, its point of origin obscured, and it was brief enough to suggest it might be pure fantasy, or addressing some other tragedy, but the survivors of Hellguard knew.

When Saavik was of an age to undergo the Vulcan *kahs-wan,* the ten days in the desert that marked passage into adulthood, she learned to her fury that Spock had made a request she be permitted to forgo the ritual on the Forge, arguing that she had already endured far more in surviving thus far. The requirement was waived. Saavik was outraged and said as much.

"Could have done it!" she shouted, fists clenched, stamping her feet, falling back on the clipped cadences of Hellguard when she was upset. She hadn't been this angry with Spock since that first year. "Deaf, blind, hobbled, survive better than sissy Vul-cans!"

It had been a bad week at school, whispers behind her back, half-muttered insults spoken just beyond arms' reach. If Spock was visited with déjà vu, he did not allow her to know it.

"No doubt you could," he had acknowledged dryly. "However, I had a more arduous challenge in mind for you."

This piqued her curiosity.

"You bring it, I do it."

She was less confident once he'd told her.

"I have spoken to the savants at the Temple of Amorak," he said. "They would be receptive to your pursuing a course of study with them while your peers explore the rigors of Vulcan's Forge."

It was not the first time they'd discussed this. Given the gaps in her education, Saavik had not been schooled in the telesper techniques that were second nature to most Vulcan children by the time they were her age. While both Spock and Sarek had taught her the rudiments of mind-meld and self-healing, any attempt to fill in the missing pieces of her memory were resisted more mightily than wearing shoes.

For one thing, she did not wish to know whether her Romulan heritage might have weakened her innate esper abilities. Discovering that her skills were weak would be yet one more shame to countenance. For another, there were too many things she did not wish to remember.

Heretofore Spock had not pressed the point. One thing he had learned about her was that, young as she was, she was almost his match in stubbornness. This time, he had hoped the tradeoff in not having to undergo *kahs-wan* would appeal to her.

Instead, her jaw tightened and she glared at him.

"If I refuse? No Academy?"

It was as if, despite the nurturing, the embrace as a coequal member of Spock's family, she still mistrusted her good fortune, still expected to be cast aside.

"Have I at any time suggested such an outcome?" Spock asked long-sufferingly.

"You think it."

"And you know this without a mind-meld? Fascinating."

The glower deepened.

"Know this, Saavik-*kam*. When it is time, I give you my pledge that I will sponsor you at the Academy. It may seem illogical to you that I promise this so far in advance, but it is as a token of my faith in you that I do so."

"I . . . I do not understand."

"Such is my confidence in you and your innate abilities and your sense of honor that I can logically promise you my patronage. However . . ."

Even if she had been able to find the words to respond to this, she did not have time to speak them.

". . . before Vulcan had logic, it had curiosity. We have as a people driven ourselves to extraordinary lengths—often to the sacrifice of life itself—in our insatiable desire to *know*."

This gave her pause. History spoke of *tharavul*, Vulcans who had had the telepathy centers of their brains excised in order to gain permission to live and work inside the Klingon Empire. Spock himself had once risked blindness in order to study a parasitic creature that had taken over his nervous system, simply because he had never encountered its like before.

As she cast about for something to say, some argument to counter this, Spock said, "To lack curiosity about any subject, Saavik-*kam*, is to be less than fully Vulcan."

That made her angry. It wasn't fair, and they both knew it. At the cellular level she would not, could not, ever be fully Vulcan, and for her mentor, of all people, to accuse her of something that was not her fault, something that others had decided before she was even conceived . . . It was a trick, a test of her reasoning abilities, something he'd challenged her with throughout the years since they'd saved each other's lives. And who but the half-human Spock himself had more right to challenge her?

Nevertheless, at the age of eleven, she had held fast. She would not retrieve those lost early memories, did not want to remember. The few events she did remember clearly were unsettling enough.

• • •

Among themselves they referred to it only as the Place. What else could it have been called? Surely not an orphanage, for at first only some of them were half orphans, and at the time, given the scraps of education provided them, they would not have had the words even for that. Words like "mother," "father," "family" were not included in their vocabulary.

When they were old enough to eat solid food but not yet old enough to feed themselves efficiently, they were seated at a long table where they could watch the door at the end of the room, waiting. Saavik could recall even now the rumble of hunger (long before she understood the meaning of *real* hunger) and vague aromas simmering up from huge vats in the next room, as the small ones, perhaps thirty of them, waited silently— outcries of any sort earned a sharp slap—for the proctors to appear.

One proctor pushed a trolley containing dull metal tureens filled with bland foods of a universally nondescript neutral taste, texture, and color. Another proctor took each toddler's hands in turn and held them down on the tabletop as a third spooned something into each waiting mouth, open like a bird's, then moved down the row to the next child. When they reached the end, the three would trundle the cart back to the start of the row and deliver another spoonful.

The method was tedious but equitable. The children were seated in different positions in the row with each meal, so that no child was always fed first or last. After each spoonful, the spoon was carefully dipped in a sterilizer, because even the scores of immunizations the children had been given from birth could not anticipate the stray viral infection that might run rampant in such close quarters. The one-spoonful-at-a-time ritual satisfied hunger and gave each child the chance to digest slowly before the next spoonful, and to learn patience, all at the same time.

Their hands were held down to keep them from grabbing at the spoon themselves. There must be order, efficiency, nothing so inconvenient or time-consuming as messy self-feeding. Any child who resisted—refused the next spoonful, expressed a dislike for whatever was on the spoon, had the effrontery to spit it back—was fed no more at that meal. The children learned quickly.

By the time they were deemed old enough to feed themselves, to march in single file into the refectory and sit silently at the long tables with their hands in their laps until they were given the signal to begin, the sheer freedom to move one's hands and eat what one wished in the order one wished to eat it made some of them almost giddy. But there was also the matter of eating everything on one's plate before someone else snatched it away when the proctors weren't looking.

Rumors abounded that some few of the eldest were permitted to eat with the proctors, where they were taught proper table manners and even allowed to speak, but no one Saavik knew had ever seen it happen. The adults abandoned Hellguard soon after, and she never learned if it was true.

Her other memory was about the doors.

Doors between places opened and closed automatically. But the doors to cupboards and other storage places had to be opened and closed manually. From the time they were old enough to walk, the children were responsible for keeping the doors closed. To take something from a cupboard, usually that day's identical-to-yesterday's jumpsuit, and leave the door so much as ajar for more than the few seconds necessary, was to incur at least a scolding, at worst a dangerous retribution.

It was how the tips of Tolek's fingers had been damaged.

Beyond that, there was only sameness, one day indistinguishable from the next. Day meant the lights were bright, night meant they were dimmed. Every activity—eating, sleeping, exercise, instruction—occurred at regulated intervals in between. None had ever felt rain on their faces, grass between their toes; none had ever seen the stars.

For most, it meant acquiescing to the sameness, blending in, becoming indistinguishable from one's peers. For others, it meant defiance, however inward—expressing it outwardly had too great a cost—a defiance that said, *I am I, and you will not change that!*

Saavik was among them. So was Tolek. In a different reality, their childhood bond might have grown into something else, the genotype emblazoned on their jumpsuits forbidding it notwithstanding.

A human would have called it a girlhood crush. In the context of Hellguard, it had other dimensions. The crushing came when Tolek told her they could never mate.

What, in their universe, did they understand about mating? At their age the urge lay dormant, inchoate, but somehow they knew it was there.

"Explain!" Saavik had all but shouted when Tolek told her. They were sprawled in the artificial soil in the atrium, after a rather violent game of kickball in which they'd both been eliminated, by design. The adults insisted on a certain amount of vigorous exercise, especially for the older children, in addition to daily chores like laundry and scrubbing floors and preparing meals, in order to siphon off some of their energy. Saavik and Tolek had played badly in order to be eliminated from play and have some time to talk.

She was over seven years and he was nearly nine by now. Within a matter of weeks, everything they knew would be taken from them.

"What means we can't mate?" she growled at him, fists clenched, ready to hit if he didn't tell her. She'd hit him before, and he'd held her wrists and laughed until she'd started to laugh too. She adored him. "What means?"

"See this?" Tolek pointed to the last string of numbers on the pocket of his jumpsuit. "They don't match yours. You look for a male with the same numbers. You can have each other when you're older. Or someone else, if you get to go to Rom-u-lus."

"Don't want someone else!" She'd pouted. "Want you."

He'd shrugged. "Can't." He thrust his chin in the direction of one of the senior proctors, supervising the kickball game and out of earshot. "*They* decide."

Saavik uttered a string of curses on "them," feeling her heart break. "Run away," she suggested.

She hadn't expected Tolek to laugh. "Oh, so *now* you believe in 'away'!" he taunted her, and she had hit him then, flailing with her fists so he wouldn't see her weeping. They'd rolled around in the dirt with him gripping her wrists and laughing helplessly until the proctor separated them, cuffing them sharply about their tender ears, and both forfeited dinner that night.

A few days later, Saavik was assigned to kitchen duty, lugging piles of plates from the storage pantry to the refectory, laying them out methodically on the long tables. The plates were heavy and she could carry only a few at a time, which meant many trips. Why she couldn't have access to one of the trolleys the proctors used (she had asked and been told not to be impertinent) was only one of innumerable because-we-said-sos. During one such trip, balancing the heavy crockery in both hands and tipping the cupboard door shut with one foot, she hadn't managed to close it all the way.

The kitchen proctor was a particular martinet, perhaps because she was very young and, save for the sigil on her uniform, might have been mistaken for one of the children herself. She scanned the long rows of cupboard doors, seeking flaws by habit, spotted the open one, and swooped.

Before she could finish saying, "Number 8390923, you have left the cupboard door ajar!" someone raced past her and slammed it shut.

"Closed!" Tolek announced, out of breath, hands

behind his back, leaning against the cupboard to hold it shut, his tone smug.

It was the smugness, no doubt, that earned him what happened next.

The proctor grabbed him by the arm and swung him around. He was almost as tall as she and no doubt stronger, but he knew better than to resist.

"Is it?" she hissed, her face inches from his, shaking him, her nails digging into his arm. "Let us be certain, shall we?"

Still holding him firmly, she opened the cupboard with her free hand, swinging the door wide, eyebrows raised. Saavik was never entirely clear about what happened next.

Perhaps Tolek tried to close the door a second time, to defy the scenario the proctor seemed determined to create in order to bring retribution down on Saavik. Perhaps the proctor meant to make an example of him as a warning to Saavik, or a way of forcing her to watch someone else suffer in her stead.

All she remembered was the look on Tolek's face as she realized that two of his fingers were caught in the door, and the proctor was leaning all her weight on it, holding it closed.

His jaw was clenched, eyes clamped shut, his face a mask of pain, but he made no sound. Then, his fingers crushed, the pain no doubt near unbearable, he forced his eyes open, blinking away tears and fixed them, pale and accusing, on his tormentor. She recoiled inadvertently, releasing the door and his hand. Virid blood spurted from mangled flesh and severed capillaries, spraying all three of them.

"Fortunate it wasn't your entire hand!" the proctor sneered, but her voice was shaky. "Report your carelessness to the infirmary at once! And *you*!" She grabbed Saavik by the hair at the nape of her neck to keep her from running after Tolek, shaking her. "Not a word to anyone, or what happens to you won't be an accident!"

Neither was this! Saavik thought, but she bit back the words.

Tolek wore his damaged fingers as a badge of honor thereafter. The flesh healed eventually, leaving livid scars, but the nerves were damaged and he had lost all sensation in the fingertips. Nevertheless, he managed to survive, as Saavik did, learning to hunt in the desert when the time came.

Whatever memories she had of that time, Tolek was always there.

Now here he was in the marketplace in ShiKahr, well nourished, grown to adulthood, his hair, close-cropped and tamed in the Vulcan fashion, already graying at the temples, his pale eyes holding memories neither wanted to examine too closely. Nevertheless, the memories came flooding back, suspended almost palpably between them. Saavik pushed them away, focused on the now, wondering why Tolek hadn't had his fingers regenerated. It was only one of innumerable questions she would like to have answered.

He asked if they could have tea together, sit at a small table in a public place where the murmur of other voices, he hoped, would prevent them from being overheard.

"By whom?" she asked, but he had cut his eyes away from hers—less perceptible than a shake of the head to anyone who might be watching—and did not elaborate. It was their secret meetings in the air ducts all over again.

She had intended to return home with her purchases immediately to prepare the meal, but only because she could think of nothing else to do before she beamed aboard *Chaffee* on the morrow. It was still midafternoon. Surely she could afford a little time for someone who had once been the most important person in her universe.

Tolek paid for the tea and asked her if there was a particular type of sweet she favored. This question, considering their shared background, startled her as it would not have if asked by anyone else. She tried not to think of small animals killed and devoured raw, roots grubbed up with the dirt still on them, insects squirming against the tongue even after one bit their heads off, and told him he could choose.

Tolek chose two *plaberry* pastries, rich with fruit and still warm from the baking ("I can never get enough of these," he explained almost apologetically), and Saavik followed him, carrying the tea, to a table in the center of the plaza, though she would have preferred a spot near the greenery at the edges. Still, if Tolek was concerned that they were being watched and listened to . . .

He arrange the utensils on the tabletop as they'd been taught. Her years with Spock's family had helped her learn to relax at mealtimes, sit up straight instead of hunched over her plate, but where had Tolek been in those intervening years? She saw him consciously stop himself from guarding the plate with one hand out of old habit, lest someone snatch it from him.

"This was no chance meeting," he said after a brief exchange of pleasantries during which he pointedly gave her no information about himself, and she was too constrained by propriety to ask. "I sought you out."

"For what purpose?"

"To warn you," he said succinctly. "Before they murder you too."

Three

Saavik's impulse was to blurt out "Who? Why? How do you know?" But what was the logical question to ask first? All she could think of to say was, "Have you gone to the authorities?"

"The authorities!" Tolek echoed her, and they were back to being children again, he always the older and wiser. "The authorities have examined the three dead and concluded that they died of natural causes."

Saavik barely managed to control a flash of anger at being patronized here, now, after all this time. "I have no knowledge. You will have to explain from the beginning."

Tolek reached into a pocket to produce a device no larger than his thumbnail. Activated, it projected a holo-image in the center of the table. "Do you remember Rajek?"

As the image solidified, Saavik noticed that it was visible only from certain angles, specifically from where she was sitting. If she shifted her position in the slightest, the image disappeared. Even as she was tempted to ask about the technology, she called to mind a stocky boy of about her own age and—the identicode on the uniform pocket more visible at first than his face— from the same mate-cohort.

At least he had been stocky the second-to-last time

she'd seen him, going off over the horizon with a pack of the strongest boys . . . to hunt, they'd said, but no one asked what. The last time she'd seen him, being helped onto the Vulcan rescue ship, too weak to walk, the natural bulk of his frame had only accentuated his deprivation. His ribs seemed more pronounced than anyone else's, the muscle wasting more obvious.

The tiny holo's presence pulled Saavik back to the present. The figure that had materialized in the center of the table, no larger than the palm of her hand, was of a prone figure in the rigor of recent death, an older version of the boy Rajek, his face and body filled out with adulthood and good nutrition, but the attitude of death suggesting that the end had been violent.

Rajek's image was replaced by two others in turn, a slender female with silk-black hair, and another male with pronounced Romulan brow ridges who would never have passed for even part Vulcan. Their facial expressions seemed less agonized than Rajek's, but they were no less dead.

"Metana and Lerius," Tolek said, though he knew Saavik remembered them. Metana had been one of her dorm mates; Lerius had often been paired with her during exercise drills. Tolek pocketed the small device as soon as he'd said the names. "These I know of. There may be more."

Again Saavik didn't know what to ask first. How had Tolek come by this information? How did she know, in light of her recent experience with *Kobayashi Maru* scenarios real and imagined, that this wasn't some sort of trap?

"Would you like to know the official cause of death?" Tolek asked into her silence.

Saavik sipped her tea, holding tight rein on her thoughts. "Doubtless you will tell me."

Tolek did not so much as lean toward her, yet his voice and manner became somehow more intimate, more urgent. They were back in the air ducts again, in danger if they were caught.

"A committee of healers examined the bodies and concluded that all died of 'unknown cause or causes, believed to be natural barring evidence to the contrary,'" he said carefully. "The one report I was able to read—Lerius's—indicated an absence of external force or internal toxicity. There were no marks on the body, and the most detailed molecular scans revealed no poisons, no foreign objects, nothing but multiple organ failure. In other words, he simply died, in the way one might expect an elder of great age to die. The only hypothesis anyone could offer was that the deprivation of our early years might have caused some sort of accelerated aging, but not all of the healers agreed on even that much."

"Certainly it is true that what we endured on Hellguard took a certain toll on even the strongest of us," Saavik reminded him, thinking of the many nutritional supplements and the several regen treatments she had needed following her rescue.

"Of course!" Tolek said abruptly. "But as soon as the first healer made that statement, another healer disagreed. His argument was that if early deprivation were the cause, the younger rather than the older survivors would have been more profoundly affected, just as they were on Hellguard. His hypothesis was that our genetic 'admixture'—his word—was the cause. In other words, he considers us congenitally defective. Both were overruled by a third healer, who said—"

" 'Put two Vulcans in a room, and you initiate three arguments,' " Saavik said thoughtfully. "Something Spock, my mentor, would say . . . used to say," she added over Tolek's bemused look.

Would she ever know that Spock again?

Again, Tolek did not so much as sit back in his chair, yet he seemed to be distancing himself from her.

"In short," he said, "Vulcan authorities do not know the cause of death and do not wish to pursue the matter further." He gulped the rest of his tea, then indicated with an eyebrow that he was going to get more, and did she want anything more?

Saavik shook her head, waiting patiently until he returned to their table with tea and a second pastry before she asked, "How have you come to know all of this?"

"Lerius and I became close in the . . . camp." Saavik had never heard this particular word for the place where all of the survivors but she were at first repatriated. "Even after his family took him in, we remained in communication." Saavik noted that Tolek gave no indication of whether his own family had claimed him. Why had she not attempted to communicate with him during all these years? It was a question she could not answer, and the lack of answer disturbed her. "He had a kinswoman who did not accept the official explanation for his death. It was thought I could be of help."

He devoured the pastry and gulped the second cup of tea, barely tasting it.

"Why you?" she asked, expecting him to tell her he had some specialized expertise that might refute the healers.

"Because she couldn't think of anyone else. I know what you're thinking," he said so intensely Saavik wondered if he was reading the thoughts behind her eyes, or if he simply knew her too well, even after all this time. "I'm no one. A minor clerk in an adjudicator's office in a minor city you've never heard of. Who I may or may not be has nothing to do with this."

Saavik's tea had gone cold, but she sipped it anyway. "And you came to me with this because . . . ?"

"Because you and I were once close, closer than I with Lerius," Tolek said, and for the briefest moment Saavik wished for that closeness again, no matter the adversity that had forged it. "And I wanted to warn you."

"Warn me to . . . beware of death by unknown cause or causes?"

"Vulcan wishes we had never existed!" Tolek said, remembering at the last moment to keep his voice down despite the sea of murmur that surrounded them in this public place. "They wanted to leave us to die on Hellguard. Vulcan will not be satisfied until we are all dead."

Saavik remembered all too well lurking near the Vulcan landing party's tent where that argument had transpired. She didn't need to understand the words to hear the disdain in the voices arguing to leave the children where they were. Only one had stood in opposition and eventually changed the others' minds. That one was Spock.

Still, once consensus had been reached, the children gathered and rescued and fed and clothed and healed of their physical suffering if not the psychological consequences of their ordeal, and thereafter brought to Vulcan, educated, most of them integrated into whatever families chose to claim them, was it logical to start killing them?

Was murder ever logical?

While she thought it through, Tolek had been absently capturing the last crumbs of his pastry on the tip of one finger and licking them off. When he was finished, the plate was so clean it might never have been used.

"I have no doubt many on Vulcan wish we did not exist, but I cannot believe a Vulcan would murder."

Now he held out his hands, damaged and whole, in a plea for reason.

"What other explanation is there? The deaths were reported, and supposedly investigated thoroughly, then dismissed with remarkable alacrity as 'unexplained.' It is that alacrity which concerns me."

Saavik frowned and pushed aside the remainder of her pastry, her appetite gone. Without a word, Tolek placed her plate on top of his and began to eat.

It is a wonder, she thought, *that he does not move about among the empty tables devouring everything the other patrons have left unfinished!*

"You are suggesting a cover-up," she said.

"At least a desire to make the matter go away."

"Each of the deaths occurred on Vulcan?"

Tolek nodded. "The ones I know of, yes."

"Do you believe there may be more?"

"Unknown at present." He had finished the last pastry and was once again retrieving the crumbs. "I intended to contact all of the survivors, but I have come up against the unassailable wall of Vulcan silence. And now I have come to you."

Saavik raised an eyebrow. "To warn me, you said."

Tolek sighed. He had been unable to hide anything from her when they were children, either. "And to ask for your help. As a member of Starfleet, you have access to resources for which I cannot get clearance. I thought that the two of us together . . ."

He left the thought unfinished, the silence filled with a dozen memories—of the time he'd helped her fight off an ambush by three other feral children, of the time they'd shared the last of the dried fruit she'd hoarded from the storehouse, even though they both knew there would never be any more, the time they'd diced for the last of the lizard eggs, and he'd let her win.

That is not sufficient reason to trust him now! something said. *You do not know who he is now, what he has become, whether what he has told you is true or even partly true. Do not let sentiment cloud your judgment!*

She found herself scanning the plaza, studying the faces of the passersby, seeing more import than usual in the stare-not-staring of a few. Was it only sentiment that made it seem as if she and Tolek were alone in the midst of this crowd, isolated by their difference, more kin to each other than to anyone else here?

If she had not been heading offworld tomorrow, she might not have made the decision she made next.

"Give me access to all of the data you have gathered so far," she told him, explaining that she was off on a short-term assignment, though giving him no more detail than that. "We will remain in subspace communication while I am away. I make no promises, but I will see what I can do."

"Thank you!" he said, a glint of something like hope in his pale eyes for the first time.

She retrieved her market basket and gestured to him to remain seated. Somehow it seemed necessary to make this appear as nothing more than a casual encounter. The stare-not-staring seemed intensified. More than ever, she was grateful to be leaving Vulcan.

"Live long and prosper, Tolek."

The slight twist at the corner of his mouth suggested he had little faith in either prospect. Nevertheless, he managed to reply.

"Peace and long life, Saavik."

She turned away before she could see him reach across the table to finish her half-drunk tea.

Even before the Sundering, many Vulcans had ceased to eat animal flesh, and over the millennia they had developed an ability to absorb nutrients exclusively from plant life.

Uncertain what this near-silent and profoundly malnourished half-Romulan child might need, however, Spock had taught her how to use a food slot, giving her free rein to choose whatever foods her body craved, and when the child came to live on Vulcan, Amanda had done the same. There would be time to discuss the philosophical reasons why even synthesized "meat" formed of basic protein molecules was something a Vulcan would philosophically refuse. As she grew to maturity and understood those reasons, Saavik had gradually adapted to the Vulcan way, so that by now the taste of even replicated meat was a distant memory.

The house was empty when she returned from the market, and she immediately repaired to the kitchen, where she laid out her ingredients in their colors and abundance, and began to wash and pare and chop and season, in the hope that this simple task would occupy her hands and leave her mind clear.

Instead, she found herself thinking of lizard eggs . . .

They had been playing dice for the last of the food.

There had been six of them at the outset. They had watched the first impatient few leave the compound in the beginning, never to return. Gone feral, or gone to dust? No one knew. But she and Tolek and the others had waited until it was clear that the adults were gone forever and, improvising carry bags for water and the last of the food from the storehouse, they'd split up into small bands of the most able-bodied, leaving the weak and the very young to languish in the echoing compound with promises that if they managed to find enough, they would bring some back for them.

Thus a band of three males, three females, all within a year or two of the same age, set out together, instinctively collecting sharp stones for throwing or pounding, moving silently. Saavik stayed close to Tolek. Six began the journey, but one died a few nights later after blundering into a strangle-vine and choking to death before the others could cut her free, and there was conflict almost at once between the three who wished to cover her with rocks out of deference and the two who argued it wasn't important, because if they found nothing else to eat they would have to come back here, because there was no sense in wasting fresh meat.

Unaccustomed to desert travel, they would forget where the cairn was. Only Saavik would stumble on it quite by accident months later, desecrated, the bones scattered, cracked to get at the marrow by creatures that had used stones, not teeth, and anyway she knew by then that there was nothing larger than a lizard native to this world.

But that was long after the night of the dice—polished, pretty things, probably left behind by one of the adults in their haste to flee—and no one asked how the elder of the two surviving girls knew how to use them, but she taught the others and they played, because except for roots and insects, the hunting had not been good. But they'd found a cache of lizard eggs just as the suns were coming up, meaning they would have to seek shelter soon.

Nine eggs, five hunters. Someone would have to make due with one. They diced.

When there were three eggs left and it was Tolek's throw, he fumbled at the last minute and threw a loss. Saavik was the only one who saw he'd done it on purpose; the others were already retreating, sucking the ends out of their eggs, licking spatterings of yolk off filthy fingers. Grabbing the two eggs he had left her, she tried to go after him, to share one, but he cursed at her and stormed away, disappearing into the heat shimmer—she thought, for good.

Seeing him again in the marketplace on Vulcan, surrounded by such largesse but still licking the crumbs off his plate and then hers . . . why hadn't she at least thanked him for saving her life back then? Was her promise to help him now in what she thought a fool's errand thanks enough?

"Did she believe you?" T'Saan asked as soon as Tolek appeared in her office. V'Shar operatives were not known for wasting time on pleasantries.

"My story was accepted," Tolek replied. "There was just enough truth in it to make it plausible."

"I am constrained to disagree. What you told her was entirely true. You simply neglected to mention that Lerius's kinswoman was an operative for the V'Shar. And as any Vulcan can tell you—"

"—there is no such thing as the V'Shar," Tolek finished for her.

"Indeed. Unpleasant truths are best left unspoken. You will continue to supply Saavik with the data she requested. The rest will be up to her. I know—" She raised one hand in a gesture her mentor T'Pau was noted for, but T'Saan wore it more gently than the old aristocrat ever had. "Your concern for her safety is noted. You are as protective of her today as you were when you were children, and we have taken that into consideration. It was no accident that we arranged for you to contact her just prior to her departure on a Starfleet mission. The predator we seek is not aboard her vessel."

"If you know that . . ." Tolek began, as frustrated with the entire mission as he had been from the moment the V'Shar had recruited him. If it weren't for his concerns for Saavik, he'd have refused, and T'Saan knew that, just as he knew she was using his emotions to her service's advantage.

"It is sometimes simpler to know who the suspect is *not* than who he or she—or they—might be."

Tolek sighed. "When Saavik's mission is completed . . ."

"It is our hope that we will have made an end of this."

It was the best answer he was going to get. "Then I shall have to perform my part with greater alacrity," he said, resigned.

Amanda made note of the depth of the silence as she and Saavik ate together that evening but did not remark on it. Saavik's girlhood silences had been profound and often lasted for days.

"Are you certain you need to leave again so soon?" was all she said.

Saavik had made no mention of her encounter with Tolek in the market. His reappearance in her life had seemed less real than the heat shimmer in which he had vanished on Hellguard, leaving her holding two lizard eggs. Add him to the resonances of Genesis and everything else that beset her, and he seemed even more ephemeral. Let Amanda think she was merely preoccupied with her assignment on *Chaffee*.

"It is essential that we return to normalcy as quickly as possible."

" 'We'?"

"Earth, Starfleet, the Federation . . ."

"You?"

Tolek wasted no time in sending Saavik every fragment of data he had collected on their three dead comrades. Though she should have been sleeping, she read through it all but could see no correlation among the three dead. Each had been adopted, with whatever degree of reluctance, into their Vulcan kinship group, but except for the friendship between Tolek and Lerius, there appeared to be no points of contact among the three or between them and any of the other survivors thereafter.

She was not alone in wanting to put that part of her life behind her.

There were no connections or even similarities among their professions. Rajek had gone into business with a distant cousin, Metana had been pursuing a degree in microbiology, and Lerius, like Tolek, had worked in the public sector. Whatever they might have shared in interests, hobbies, avocations, travel, dreams, or desires was not contained in the records. Were they also haunted by what they had been through? Did they guard their plates while they ate to keep some unforeseen foe from snatching the food away? Did any sudden hissing sound remind them of the lizards whose bite was fatal? Did they dream?

Unknown, unknown, unknown. The only data beyond these sketchy biographies were contained in the medical records, and there was as much similarity in death as there had been difference in life.

Saavik read carefully through each medical chart. Age, height, weight, blood type (all different), medical history, known family history, genetic predispositions, separation of mitochondrial from nuclear DNA to determine which parent was of which subgroup . . .

She stopped. Similar data were contained in her own medical chart, data that she steadfastly refused to access. If she were to die, that which she refused to know in life would be known only to medical personnel after her death.

Why was she so resistant to that knowledge now? It was not logical. She was a scientist, fascinated by knowledge in all its forms, except for this.

The answer she would not allow herself was that if she ever learned her parents' identities, even to this extent, she would be forced to hate one of them. Hatred was even more illogical than denying oneself knowledge.

Or so she told herself as she continued reading the autopsy reports. As Tolek had told her, all three had died of multiple organ failure, of the kind that might perhaps cause a frail Vulcan elder to simply fade away in the twenty-fifth decade of life, but to the best of her knowledge there was no precedent for it happening to an otherwise healthy Vulcan in the twenty-fifth *year* of life.

Something she had once overheard on *Enterprise,* about radiation from a comet causing rapid aging among some of the crew who had beamed down to a particular planet, caused her to search out the logs from James T. Kirk's first five-year mission. But as far as she knew, none of the three Hellguard dead had left Vulcan since their repatriation. Could there have been some similar form of radiation on Hellguard? If so, why had it affected these three and not others?

Hellguard no longer existed, and that sector lay within Romulan space. Tolek had been correct. She would need more information, information that she could obtain through Starfleet files that he would not have access to. But there was nothing more she could do tonight. With less than three hours before she was due to report to *Chaffee,* she allowed herself to sleep, and dreamed.

"Oh, no, you don't!" Captain Esteban said. "Regulations specifically state, 'Nothing shall be beamed aboard until danger of contamination has been eliminated.' "

"Captain," she suggested, "the logical alternative is obvious. Beaming down to the surface is permitted—"

"—'if the captain decides that the mission is vital and reasonably free of danger,' " Esteban finished the thought.

"Captain, please, we'll take the risk," David Marcus interjected. *"But we've got to find out what it is."*

Saavik would never know what made her add, *"Or who."*

Esteban looked at her strangely. *"We're not here to chase ghosts, Lieutenant. Continue scanning. The answer is no."*

Why had she said that? If not for that emotional outburst, would Esteban have said yes?

She was running down the corridor toward Grissom's transporter room, wresting a phaser from the security guard stationed outside the door to prevent her from beaming down. She could hear the child sobbing, the sound growing fainter and fainter as he grew weaker and weaker . . . until the sobbing was drowned out by the screams of a half-Romulan child whose hand had been slammed in a door . . .

She bolted upright, gasping for breath. *Spock was alive, Tolek had not cried out . . .*

It was only a dream. There had been many, beginning on the journey home from Genesis. Nightmares about what might have happened if she and David had not persuaded Captain Esteban to let them beam down to investigate the mysterious life-form reading. About what might have happened if they hadn't found the child Spock before he froze to death. About what might have happened if she hadn't known enough about *Pon farr* to save him. About every point along the time line at which she might have failed. She would wake, drenched in sweat, jaw clenched, grasping at the shreds of logic to remind herself that none of it was real.

Running toward or running from, Mironova had asked her. She hadn't had an answer.

At least she had made no sound, she thought, slipping out of bed and into the shower, trailing tendrils of the dream in her wake. She had learned considerable discipline since the night terrors that had awakened her in childhood, screaming and inconsolable until Amanda arrived to hold her, soothe her, assure her that she was safe.

Grateful that the sky was lightening, she dressed quickly, running her fingers through her wet hair without combing it—it would dry quickly in the desert air—intending to slip quietly out of the house before Amanda awoke. They had said their farewells the night before—the human sensing that this was what she wanted—and in her current state of mind she couldn't bear to see the concern in her foster mother's eyes.

As she buttoned the flap of the red uniform tunic over the white turtleneck and examined her attire in the mirror to be certain all was in order, was the figure looking back at her the model Starfleet officer—calm, controlled, prepared for all contingencies—or someone whose turmoil was barely concealed beneath a veneer of civilization?

Four

———

Captain's Personal Log, Galina Mironova recording. The children are fighting already. Our civilian scientist Doctor Mikal joined us three days out, and the games have begun. Having had the duty of escorting Mikal on several missions previously, I'm familiar with his antics. Like all Tiburonians, he's brilliant enough, but he's also a bit of a showboat.

As anticipated, he and Lieutenant Saavik have already locked horns over both the important things and the most trivial. The contrast in their respective methodologies, I am hoping, will result in optimal data gathering and a successful, if noisy, mission . . .

"They're nothing but intelligent worms," Doctor Mikal said dismissively, the multiple earrings in his overlarge ears jangling as he tried out all the chairs in the small briefing room until he found one he liked.

"And that in itself does not intrigue you?" Saavik asked as the rest of the science team trickled in and they waited for Mironova so they could begin. "That with neither limbs nor digits, sight nor hearing nor any sense other than touch and, it is presumed, some level of esper skill, the Deemanot have constructed entire cities that suggest a level of civilization—"

"Worms!" Mikal repeated, but with a winsome smile.

Not for the first time, Saavik wondered why the Tiburonian had bothered signing on to this mission. However, she was beginning to understand what Captain Mironova meant about him.

"He'll tell you he's slumming," Mironova had said as they made rendezvous with the ship bringing Mikal to them. "Truth is, he's been a bad boy . . . again."

Still adjusting to the captain's unusual way with the language, Saavik waited for the translation.

"You'll have researched him by now. Maybe been impressed with the advanced degrees, the scholarly papers, the awards and commendations and visiting professorships. But tell me you're not equally intrigued by what's missing. Conclusions, Science Officer?"

The holos had shown a compactly built Tiburonian male of middle years, bald and tattooed in the tradition of his people, his many-lobed ears ornamented with numerous earrings, no two alike. There was an arrogance in the cant of his head and the quirk of his mouth that detracted, Saavik thought, from the intelligence in his eyes. But Spock would have told her not to be so quick to judge.

Mironova was correct. His education and his credentials were impressive. But there were also unexplained gaps in both.

He held degrees from universities on Earth and Trill but, surprisingly, none from a homeworld noted for its advances in science and medicine. A search of all biographical data indicated that he had in fact been born on Tiburon forty-three years earlier, but no mention of him could be found in any other database until his enrollment in the premed program at Nairobi University at the age of twenty-two.

For every successful expedition, development, or discovery, there was a gap of months or even years. And yet the accomplishments were undeniable: Sepec Awards in biology and mineralogy, a Carstairs Medal in geology, nominee for the Carrington Award two years running, discoverer of numerous species of fungi, lichens, phytoplankton, and even a few complex biota; he'd recently had a conifer found only on Tellar Prime named after him.

"He seems . . . quite accomplished," Saavik said carefully.

"Oh, come on!" Mironova said dryly. "I know you've read the opinions of his peers. The nicest thing they can say about him is that he's an 'intellectual swashbuckler.' He's reckless and temperamental, and he's been sacked from more exploratory missions than you've got fingers. Yet when he's good, he's spot-on, as the awards testify. Still, he has a tendency to go off the reservation, and I'm one of the few in Starfleet who'll still let him hitch a ride. This little expedition is to be his way back into the fold, if he doesn't cock it up. That's where you come in."

Before Saavik could ask what she meant, the familiar hum and sparkle of the transporter had deposited Mikal in their midst.

"Galina Ivanovna!"

He greeted the captain by her patronymic, as if they were old friends. Arms outstretched, he swaggered down from the transporter platform like a pirate, his traditional multicolored robes swirling around his ankles, seized Mironova's hand in both of his and kissed her palm—a Tiburonian greeting, Saavik knew from her research, usually reserved for intimates. He then spun around and, hands on his hips, proceeded to study Saavik with a frankness any other female might have found unsettling.

"They're making science officers not only younger but prettier," he observed in a deliberate breach of several kinds of protocol. "When I heard 'Saavik of Vulcan,' I expected some pickled old prune."

"It is an honor to meet you, Doctor Mikal," Saavik replied primly, hands carefully clasped behind her back. What would she do if he tried to kiss her hand as well? She found herself uncertain, and that disturbed her. "I look forward to working with you."

"That's it?" He feigned seriousness, but the hazel eyes beneath the tattooed brow were merry. "Not even a handshake?"

"Social niceties are in no way essential to the mission, Doctor Mikal," she replied, mindful of intellectual swashbuckling. If she was to be science officer on this mission, it was necessary to set some boundaries at the outset.

Mikal threw back his head and laughed. The sound, like his gestures, was exaggerated, too large for him, and seemed staged. Who was he pretending to be, and why?

"Opinionated as well as pleasing to the eye," he remarked, shouldering the overlarge rucksack of personal belongings that had accompanied him through the transporter and striding into the corridor ahead of the two women as if he knew exactly where he was going. "This will be fun!"

Less than an hour later, he had been first to arrive in the briefing room, even before Saavik, who was to conduct the presentation. After the obligatory introductions to the other members of the science department—four males and two females, a Mazarite, a Fabrini, and four Terrans—and his snide comments about worms, he'd tilted his chair back against the bulkhead, hands clasped behind his head, and winked at Saavik, as if to say, *Go ahead, impress me!*

"Planet Deema III," she began, bringing up the starchart on the monitor in the center of the conference table. Mikal made no effort to lean forward in order to see it clearly. "First charted seventeen-point-three-five years ago but unexplored until now. Its primary is a spectral type G2 star, but with slight variations in hydrogen and calcium . . ."

She brought up an inset that showed a comparative spectral analysis of a standard G2 star and Deema. Again, Mikal didn't move, but Saavik became aware (no need to look up; when one had been prey, one knew when one was being watched) that he was studying her face.

"You're beautiful, do you know that?" David Marcus had asked her once. "Of course you do—you must! Vulcans have a highly developed aesthetic sense, and I can't be the first person to have told you that."

"You are not," she had said, wishing not for the first time that humans didn't set so much store by superficial things. Why compliment one on something over which one had no control?

What was "beautiful," anyway? She had read any number of philosophies of aesthetics, and they had had the effect of rendering her more puzzled than before. There was a time when the most beautiful thing in her universe had been the rainbows formed by coolant slicks on the surface of a puddle near the storehouse where the food had been. She no longer remembered why she had returned to this place, perhaps in the vain hope that some few grains of food might remain, or that lizards could be surprised lurking in the cool beneath the rafters. Apparently there had been ground vehicles parked in the courtyard before the adults left, and one had had a leaky coolant hose.

The puddle, it turned out, had sprung from a long-forgotten water source, a near-empty cistern that exposure to the suns and wind-driven sand had caused to leak, and the water, while stagnant and no doubt teeming with bacteria, was better than no water at all. Saavik's initial impulse had been to slake her thirst, perhaps even drench her hair and body in the dabblings in order to cool herself, but the rainbows had distracted her and, nascent scientist even then, she had been poking at them, trying to determine what they were, swirling them into different patterns, when the sight of her own reflection had startled her so much she leaped backward, like a kitten confronting itself in a mirror.

There had been no mirrors in the compound, but there were shiny things that showed reflections. She knew what she'd looked like then—pale and small and solemn, but also clean and groomed. This . . . thing in the mud puddle was some hideous transmogrification of that child, almost as if it had sprung from the coolant-polluted mud itself, and ought to have been left undisturbed.

A handful of other children had straggled in then, as if the rumor of water from the cistern had drawn them there, and their squabbling over the puddle not only dispersed and refracted reflections and rainbows but roiled the water into mud, undrinkable even by their limited standards.

Disgusted, Saavik had withdrawn into shadow until they were gone, then emerged to smear herself thoroughly with the surviving mud, even rubbing it into her scalp, as protection against the heat of the day. Of course it would dry and crack as she walked, but enough would cling to her to offer some scant insulation. Hideous she might be, but she would carry the rainbows with her.

The years following her rescue had shown her much more flattering images of a tall, well-groomed young woman with large, liquid eyes so dark they were almost black set above high cheekbones in a pale face framed by waves of chestnut hair, a luxuriant cascade to her shoulders when left to its own devices, all but impossible to tame to Starfleet regulation.

Was this beauty? The males of several species had assured her it was. She lacked the objectivity to judge their accuracy and so solved the problem by giving it no weight, and thus no consideration.

Mentally she added Doctor Mikal to the list of males who found her beautiful. To her it meant only an additional dimension of complexity to what she had hoped would be an uneventful mission. She cleared her throat and continued her briefing.

"As its name suggests, the planet is the third from the primary, the first two planets having been scanned from space and found to be virtually devoid of atmosphere, indicating an absence of life-forms past or present, and the two outer worlds being gas giants."

Why had she been thinking of David just now? Perhaps it was only the fact that she had once again been paired with another "brilliant" if unconventional civilian scientist. At least this time there would be no Klingon attack, no planet destroying itself beneath her feet, no child Spock to rescue, no *Pon farr,* just an uneventful scientific survey.

"Deema III is geologically Earth-like, with one notable exception," she went on. "Variance in its axial tilt renders the climate slightly more temperate than Earth's, with fewer extremes of temperature from equator to poles. Tides are also affected, but as we will not be surveying littoral regions, this is of interest only in passing."

The Mazarite—Ensign Graana, Saavik recalled— was dutifully taking notes on a padd, absentmindedly twisting her waist-length ponytail around the fingers of her other hand as she did so, her breather gills lying flat against the sides of her face, indicating that she was relaxed and concentrating. The others listened intently, though any one of them, judging from the personnel files Saavik had perused beforehand, could probably have led the briefing at least as well as she could. Appreciating their attentiveness, she went on.

"Initial orbital surveys indicate extensive plant life, a surprising absence of animal life more complex than bacteria, and the presence of a single intelligent species hereafter designated as Deemanot."

A series of images taken by an orbital probe sent out by the first ship to map this sector appeared on the center screen. The Deemanot at first glance resembled nothing so much as very large earthworms, varying from two to three meters in length and perhaps eighty centimeters in circumference. Eyeless, boneless, they moved by undulating along the ground or balancing upright on the lower third of a body that tapered to two almost identical ends, a layer of slime the only thing that protected them from their environment.

There were murmurs of surprise around the table.

"Imagine how bizarre we would seem to them," Mikal said. "Assuming we were ever allowed to get near them!"

So that was what Mironova had meant about his needing a babysitter, Saavik thought. Left to his own devices, he would have no compunction about violating the Prime Directive in order to add a new species to his résumé.

Not on her watch.

She went on as if Mikal hadn't spoken.

"Global population is sparse, consisting of an estimated ten million inhabitants, concentrated primarily in three central regions." She indicated them on the readout. "Nothing is known about their culture, but their architecture is quite impressive, constructed as it is without tools. The Deemanot build extensive, complex cities, half aboveground and half underground, entirely by ingesting the soil around them and excreting it into a form that, once hardened by exposure to air and sunlight, appears to be as durable as thermoconcrete. Captain?"

Mironova took over from there. "Computer, live feed, sector seventeen, grid forty-three."

For several moments no one spoke, as they observed the Deemanot about their work, ingesting soil that had clearly been refined beforehand to remove rocks and large particles, perhaps by an earlier version of the ingestion they were watching. In a continuous process, the soil passed through their bodies and was egested into carefully planned forms—a wall, an arch, a path—where other workers shaped and smoothed it before moving on to leave it drying in the sun.

"Computer, expand by a factor of five," Mironova said.

The image panned out to encompass an entire sector, perhaps a hundred by a hundred meters, being constructed in the same manner.

"Factor ten and continuous," Mironova said, and the image panned out slowly to reveal winding streets full of ornate and intensely appealing structures as far as the eye could see. Attenuated spires spun out above gigantic wasps' nests and what looked like cross sections of giant ammonites and stairways out of an Escher print going up and down simultaneously in dizzying profusion.

Murmurs of amazement rippled through the briefing room and, undoubtedly, around the bridge and down the corridors to private quarters, off-duty areas, and engineering ("Oh, look at that one!" "Wow, have you ever—?" "Does that coil lead up to that parapet or . . . no, wait, it goes down and connects to that spiderwebby thing . . ."). As biologically primitive seeming and perhaps unattractive to humanoid eyes as the Deemanot might be, their cities were just the opposite.

"Live feed off," Mironova said crisply, then waited until everyone's eyes were on her. "Wanted you all to see that, and feel free to observe the live feed at any time . . . from here. I know it's tempting to want to make their acquaintance in person, but it's not to happen on this mission."

It was at this point that Mikal tilted his chair forward with a bang and stormed out of the briefing room. Saavik looked to Mironova, who shook her head slightly. *Let him go.*

"Perhaps," Mironova went on as if there'd been no

interruption, "if we're all very good and bring Starfleet back some pertinent data about the plant life—
about which Lieutenant Saavik will enlighten us
momentarily—we'll be first in line to come back another
time. Lieutenant?"

Saavik returned to the data the earlier probe had
gathered.

"In addition to limiting temperature and climatological variations, the planet's anomalous axial tilt has
resulted in, for the most part, fewer variations in plant
life than might be expected on a typical Class-M world.

"However"—the readings she pulled up this time
made her teammates sit up and pay attention—"the
original orbital probe picked up traces of some uniden-
tifiable plant life in several regions. Not only are these
flora found nowhere else on Deema III but in these specific regions, but they are unknown anywhere within
explored Federation space."

"Sir? I've seen readings like that before." The eldest
of the team, a grizzled Terran named Palousek, had his
hand raised as if he were in school. "Long-range probes
into the Beta Quadrant recorded similar spectra in the
first systems they approached."

"But what are they doing here?" someone else
demanded. Esparza, Saavik recalled, another of the Terrans, young, argumentative, but also, according to his
file, intuitive and very bright.

Ships' logs and personnel files indicated that the
Terrans liked to think out loud, disagreeing with each
other until they had examined all aspects of a problem and drawn conclusions. It was as valid a scientific

method as any. Saavik glanced in Mironova's direction and the captain nodded, as if to say, *Let them have at it!*

"Maybe someone from the Beta Quadrant came bearing gifts." This was Jaoui, youngest of the Terrans, and surely another female Mikal would have found beautiful, Saavik thought, if he'd stayed around long enough to notice her. Her voice was calm, but her pale eyes flashed with fire whenever she argued a point.

"Or just tracked them in on their shoes!" the last of the Terrans, Cheung, said dryly, her otherwise pretty face drawn into a mild sneer.

"Yes, but the distances involved—" Esparza began.

"For us, maybe," Jaoui cut across him. "There are far more advanced species that could have—"

"But why?" Cheung demanded.

"Could be something else entirely," Palousek said calmly, refusing to raise his voice to their level. "Just because the readings *look* like something from the Beta Quadrant . . ."

"They could as easily be the result of distortions or artifacts in the atmosphere," Ta'oob, the Fabrini said, speaking for the first time.

This went on for some minutes. Then Ensign Graana had a question. "Are there visuals from the surface?"

"Negative," Saavik said, and the rest of the team simmered down and paid attention. "The orbital probe was able to gather unusual spectral readings but without ground-level detail."

"And that's why we're here," Mironova interjected, making it clear that discussion was at an end. "We're to locate and collect these oddities, catalog and study them. That's in addition to standard geology and biota surveys. Thank you, Saavik, I'll take it from here."

Mironova pulled up a series of topographical maps.

"Currently it's the dry season in Biome 1." She indicated a vast expanse of open grassland, dotted with occasional volcanic outcroppings. "You all know the drill. Set up a base camp and measure out a perimeter of one day's walk, then work inward until at least one specimen of every rock, soil type, and growing thing inside the circle has been bagged, tagged, and beamed up to ship's labs. We've a cross section of biomes in other terrains and climates in which to do the same. No jungles or tundra, but plenty of mild weather, and enough variety to entertain everyone, I hope. Fleet's given us no specific timetable, so with luck we can gather up a sample of every weed and daisy that long-range scans tell us doesn't belong there and try to figure out where it's from and how it got where it is. Any questions?"

Silent shakes of the head indicated there weren't any. Mironova looked pleased.

"Engineering tells me we should make orbit in three-point-four-days' time. Anything occurs to you in the interim, you bring it to me. Until then, light duty, play nice, and first round at end of shift is on me. Dismissed."

Laughter and chatter drifted down the corridors from the mess hall every night, reaching Saavik's acute hearing as she oversaw the labs, often taking over a shift from a grateful crew member in order to have a lab to herself.

Not surprisingly, the loudest voice was Mikal's, though he had some competition from Esparza, who was known to sing Klingon arias when he was in his cups. Tonight's rendition of "Melor Famagal's Lament" had been Saavik's cue to bus her dinner dishes and slip away unnoticed. They would make orbit sometime tomorrow. She had work to do.

She had promised Tolek she would use the ship's library computer to search out serial killings and unexplained deaths among Vulcan populations in a given age cohort over the previous decade. The task might have been daunting to a less thorough individual, but Saavik approached it as she did all things, patiently and meticulously, and with the assistance of the most complete database in the Federation.

If she was disturbed by the sheer varieties of unnatural ways a Vulcan could die even in this most civilized of times—shooting, stabbing, strangulation, poisoning, burns, falls, vehicle accidents that might not have been accidental, and the most elusive Unknown—she gave no outward sign. She scanned countless documents seemingly without tiring, her expression remaining serene regardless of the horrors flitting across the screen.

At the end of each shift, she sent her findings to Tolek via subspace, for whatever use he might make of them. Not surprisingly, she had not yet found a correlation with the three deaths he had described to her.

"That's because you still don't entirely believe they were murdered," Tolek said.

They were on a live feed, most likely the last until her mission on Deema III was complete. His tone was lighter than it had been when they'd met face-to-face, almost teasing, as it had been when they were children. Before Saavik could protest that her approach was both logical and objective—as he knew she would—he asked, *"What about the Heliopolis murders?"*

Despite the plethora of material she had scanned thus far, Saavik's recall was almost instantaneous.

"Negative. The victims were all female, and all were stabbed. The ten killings were later correlated with serial killings on several other worlds, beginning on Earth almost four centuries ago, and culminating in the destruction of a being identified as Redjac."

"You see why this is helpful?" Tolek said, a mix of fascination with the study itself and disappointment in its results evident in his tone. *"All I had access to was the name 'Heliopolis' and some docudramas whose content was mostly supposition. That level of detail is not available outside of Starfleet files."*

Logical, Saavik thought, since the last in the series of murders occurred aboard a Starfleet vessel, and there had been some official concern at the time about potential copycat killings. What particular twist of mind, she wondered, compelled anyone to want to commit such crimes?

"I've read through everything you have sent me thus far . . ." Tolek was saying. Ambient light in the lab on night shift came only from the readouts and specimen cases. The voice in Saavik's earpiece was inadvertently intimate, almost secretive, resonating with their childhood meetings in the air duct. *"And I continue to try to make contact with the other survivors. There*

seem to have been no further deaths beyond the initial three. I had thought to communicate with the others, as I did with you, and suggest they undergo medical examination."

Saavik frowned. "For what purpose?"

"To eliminate the possibility that some might also be undergoing the beginnings of the multiple organ failure that killed Lerius and the others," Tolek said, but Saavik knew him too well, even after all this time.

"And also to bring the plight of the dead to the attention of the general public," she suggested dryly.

"Well . . ."

"Which might have the effect, if they were in fact murdered, of alerting the killer or killers to our awareness. Is this necessarily a good thing?"

She waited for him to consider the possible ramifications. "I hadn't thought of that. Again, this is why I need your help. But what if the killer is already stalking another victim? Do we not have an obligation to warn the others?"

"Warn them of what?" Saavik asked, not for the first time. "Perhaps we have found no correlation among the three deaths because there is no correlation to find."

There was a long silence. Finally Tolek said, "You may be correct. Forgive me, but I cannot shake this . . . intuition. At least on Hellguard one could recognize the enemy in the sun, the predators, the hunger. Here it is like being pursued by shadows. And you are the only one who understands . . ."

Suddenly aware that she was not alone, Saavik

waited for Tolek to finish his thought. At the same time, she rotated her chair a few degrees to the left to give herself a wider view of the lab behind her. A glimpse of multicolored Tiburonian robes told her all she needed to know. She wondered why he was eavesdropping, even as she wondered if his overlarge ears were as sensitive as her own. When she glanced away from the comscreen again, he was gone.

"Tolek," she said, "once we reach our destination, I can continue to send you data packets sporadically, but live communication—"

"*—will be impossible*," Tolek finished for her. "*I understand. Pity. I've enjoyed our reacquaintance. And while I'm grateful you're offplanet and safe from this predator, I also look forward to your return.*"

As Saavik wondered what to say to that, he added, "*May your journey be safe and your mission successful*," and logged off before she could say anything by way of farewell to him.

"Boyfriend?" said a familiar voice behind her.

Startled, she leaped from her chair, in full Romulan attack mode, and it took more than a veneer of Vulcan civilization to keep her from lunging at his throat. So he had continued to lurk even after she thought he was gone! How dare he?

"Sorry!" Mikal said, hands raised defensively, stepping back out of range of her ferocity. "I meant no harm. I'd forgotten your species bonds in childhood . . . and I should probably shut up now."

"Indeed!" she said tightly. "Is there a purpose to your presence here?"

He tucked his hands into his flowing sleeves and bowed his head, looking almost sheepish.

"I just wanted to invite you to join us. You spend all your free time alone and—"

"—and I am content to do so." She had toggled off the screen displaying the data she'd sent to Tolek, but not quickly enough.

"Serial killings?" Mikal asked, apparently able to sight-read almost as quickly as a Vulcan. "Unusual hobby."

"It is research," Saavik snapped, glowering.

"And I've made you angry again. *Noli me tangere.* I'll try not to bother you again."

He was gone in a flurry of robes and rapid footsteps. Saavik had been concerned about how she was to follow Captain Mironova's order not to let him out of her sight. She had not anticipated having to hold him at arms' length for the entire mission.

Mironova had watched Mikal slip out of the crew lounge, even as she had watched him flirt with every female crew member since he'd come aboard. Only Saavik had not reciprocated. Mikal had that effect on women, she knew. Her own memories were far enough in the past for their sharp edges to have worn away, and whatever feelings she retained toward him now were more maternal than romantic. It was the motherless child about him that had attracted her to Mikal in the first place, and she'd learned too late that it was not enough.

Saavik, she was confident, would be impervious to such emotions.

Mironova found herself grown too quiet in the raucous merriment of the crew lounge, and ordered another round of drinks to mask her mood.

The Scotch was warm at the back of her throat, but her mood remained.

T'Saan had given Tolek specific instructions not to contact her directly unless the matter was urgent. As he was about to go far afield to track down the remaining survivors, he took the risk.

"I should like to cease communication with Saavik even before her return," he said. "I am not confident our communication is secure even on Starfleet frequencies. The meeting in the marketplace could have been ascribed to chance, but for us to meet again—"

"—*would be far more natural than for you to suddenly sever all connection after such a fortuitous encounter,*" T'Saan said with a touch of impatience. "*You came to us, remember. You may as easily depart.*"

"You used me," he suggested, coolly but not without rancor, "and compelled me to make use of Saavik." That he was complicit in that usage—he hadn't mentioned to Saavik that Lerius's kinswoman was a member of the V'Shar, or that it had been he who approached her, not the other way around—he left unspoken. "Starfleet could as easily have given us the data we needed without implicating her."

"*You forget yourself. For one, there is no 'we.' You are not a member of the V'Shar . . .*"

". . . except when you find me useful."

"Kroykah!" she said, and he subsided.

"*Do not overestimate your importance or mine, or even that of the V'Shar,*" T'Saan said after a very long silence. "*There are some things that must appear to out-worlders as being less significant than they truly are.*"

"In other words, the V'Shar does not ask Starfleet for favors."

"*Precisely.*"

Now it was Tolek's chance to be silent. T'Saan waited. She knew from long experience that he had further concerns.

"I am, as you have pointed out, not one of you. Therefore I am not skilled at concealing my intentions. Can the V'Shar provide me with cover as I complete this final phase?"

"*You want a trained operative at your back, in the event you are followed?*"

"Precisely."

T'Saan's answer surprised him. "*No.*"

"I see. So I am expendable?"

"*Not entirely. But the thought that you might be will teach you greater caution.*"

With that she terminated the connection. Tolek found he was shivering, though not from cold.

She's betrothed, you idiot! Mikal castigated himself as he hurried away from the lab, furious with himself for being caught lurking. *They all are in childhood. Her husband, future husband—what does it matter either way?—is who she spends her evenings talking to while you're carousing with the crew. It's clear she's devoted to him, and it's wrong for you to even think what you're thinking! Why can't you content yourself with Graana or Jaoui or even Cheung for all her sarcasm or any of the other unattached females aboard, or for once just be professional? Why must you always want what you cannot have?*

He knew the answer as he knew himself. His early life had taught him painfully that what was out of reach was by its very nature that much more desirable. But was that the only reason he couldn't get Saavik out of his mind?

Curse Galina anyway, for replacing that giggly and entirely too accessible Denobulan Eyris with this solemn, unattainable elf-queen with the haunted look behind her eyes!

And curse yourself, you posturing buffoon! he thought, *for thinking you ever had a chance to be anything more than that to the likes of her . . .*

Five

——

They watched on the live feed above one metropolis as a group of Deemanot went about their daily lives on the planet below, greeting each other, if one were to judge from their posture as they met in passing, stopped their wormlike creeping to raise themselves, using the clitellum as a kind of temporary foot, and touching their eyeless faces to each other (sniffing, kissing, communing telepathically? Impossible to tell) before going their separate ways.

"*This* is what we should be studying, Saavik, not rocks and trees," Mikal said, not for the first time. "There are ways of studying indigenous populations without being detected. I know—I've done it!"

"And yet you requested this mission, knowing that first contact was expressly forbidden," she pointed out.

"Rapamycin," he said cryptically, then began his data gathering. "Scanning Biome 1. Predominantly perennial grassland interspersed with eroded volcanic outcroppings. Grasses are fed by groundwater year-round, and preliminary scan suggests several hundred varieties . . ." For the first time since he'd beamed aboard, he was all seriousness. "Volcanic stria should provide easy access to a range of mineral and soil varieties across the planet's life cycle."

At her station, Saavik was gathering meteorological data. *Perhaps,* she thought, *last night's outburst was not such a bad idea after all!* "Temperatures in Biome 1 ranging from a high of thirty degrees Celsius daytime to a low of seven point two at night. Present temperature, twenty-two point two degrees.

"Rapamycin," she added, following his train of thought in spite of herself. "An immunosuppressant drug, used centuries ago to prevent organ rejection following transplant."

"First discovered by chance as a microbe in the soil of a tiny island in the Pacific Ocean on Earth. One of those phenomena that are stumbled on by pure chance and end up saving countless lives. *Taxus brevifolia* is another. A humble little yew plant that turned out to be a primitive but effective cancer cure."

Somewhere during this exchange, the lift had deposited Mironova onto the bridge, dressed in a practical field uniform and carrying a mug of strong tea. She slipped into the center seat and listened, pleased that her experiment—call it catalysis, symbiosis, synergy—was working.

"You are suggesting that perhaps the anomalies noted during the initial long-range scans of Deema III . . ." Saavik began.

". . . could be something that exists nowhere else, might be something that could save lives or be the basis for an unforeseen technology, and could end up being named for one or both of us," Mikal finished, idly spinning in his chair. "I see another Carstairs Medal on the horizon."

Saavik quirked an eyebrow. Such things were of no interest to her. "Which you would expect me to share with you?"

"Not necessarily."

Saavik made note of the unnatural silence on the bridge, as if everyone including the captain were listening to their exchange. She concentrated on her scanners.

"Biome 1, continuing. Typical foliage presenting. Native varieties to be expected in a veldt, including low scrub, several species of acacia, and over one hundred varieties of flowering grasses. However, orbital scan reveals none of the anomalous plant life found by initial probes to be present in roughly seventeen percent of the region . . ."

Mikal was scowling at the scanner. "The initial scans showed peculiar mineral deposits as well, but I'm not seeing any now."

"Unusual mineral readings could be explained by meteor showers or other space debris," Saavik suggested.

"So could the plant life," Mikal conceded. "Spores hitching a ride on the space debris."

"Which might have evolved into unusual flora on the surface."

"Granted. But plant life might have found the environment inimical and died off. Rocks don't just pick up and walk away."

Mironova had finished her tea. She cleared her throat. "Time to get some dirt under our nails and find out."

• • •

The breeze made a sound like bells. With nothing to impede it over broad expanses of flat land, it blew continuously but softly. The light from the planet's Sol-like star was warm, the atmosphere temperate and clear, with a slightly higher oxygen content than that of Earth, invigorating. Rainbow-hued flower banks, self-segregated by color and variety, interspersed with the occasional low-growing and wind-shaped shrub or tree, extended as far as the eye could see. Despite the region's being deep into its dry season, there was running water, in the form of an icy rill bubbling between banks deep cut into the rock bed and bordered with the surprise of mosses and lichens.

"Odd!" Mikal commented, on his hands and knees taking samples. "Those didn't show up on the orbital scans."

"Perhaps they are so sparse that our instruments didn't register them," Saavik suggested, studying her tricorder. "However, they are indigenous."

"These are not the anomalies you're looking for," Mironova said.

"There also shouldn't be running water this late in the season," Mikal grumbled. "Riverbed should be mostly mud."

"Unless," Saavik proposed, scanning a distant outcropping, "it is fed by an underground stream."

"Tastes better than recycled water, anyway," Mikal said, dabbling his fingers in the stream and sampling it.

Saavik made a mental note to double-check the med kit for antimicrobial sera. The landing party had been immunized against every known bug, but their mission here was to isolate *unknown* phenomena, even if they ended up in someone's digestive tract.

Ensign Graana was overseeing the assembly of a field shelter in the lee of a thirty-meter-high outcrop, an ancient volcanic upthrust, to judge from the degree of erosion, forced upward at an oblique angle several million years before.

"Good choice of location," Mikal announced, studying the outcrop, which was striated like a layer cake. "There are about three million years of history in those layers. And I for one intend to backtrack that stream and find the fountainhead. Ensign Graana, would you care to accompany me?"

He took her hand and tucked it into the crook of his arm before she could respond. The vestigial gill slits in front of her ears blushed pink, but she did not protest.

"Good thing we're far enough from any of the Deemanot cities to keep him out of at least one kind of mischief," Mironova remarked as they strode off, studying Saavik for any possible reaction, but there was none.

Mironova had been gathering wildflowers, mostly for their aesthetic value, as the others fanned out to begin their exploration. For a moment she held them to her nose and inhaled, sighing happily, then got back to being captain again.

"You're officially in charge down here, Lieutenant. But don't expect Mikal to pay you any mind. Your job is to manage him so he doesn't realize he's being managed, but as long as he's not a danger to himself or the landing party, keep an eye on him but leave him to his own devices. Carry on."

The team beamed down daily and set to work, each staking out a grid within which to gather specimens to bring back to the shelter, often several times daily, from dawn till dusk. From deep-core readings to the microbes on a blade of grass, using ship's sensors, tricorders, fine tools, and often their bare hands, they weighed and measured, gathered and assessed, sifting soil samples, separating rock samples, carefully lifting plants from the soil without damaging their roots.

Each evening they returned to the shelter to catalog what they had collected, discarding some specimens, beaming others aboard for further study in the ship's labs.

"Basanite," Saavik recited, taking a chunk of gray-green rock from Esparza and placing it under the spectroscope. "Collected from—"

"—level 47A, section 114c of the volcanic upthrust," Esparza supplied, not a little smitten with Saavik and always too eager to please.

"Indicating feldspathoids, plagioclase, and augite, as well as olivine, ilmenite, and magnetite," Saavik reported, handing it back to Esparza, who almost dropped it in his nervousness but finally managed to set it in a container that Jaoui had already labeled. Jaoui sealed the container and placed it on the pallet to be beamed up, while Esparza handed Saavik a densely grained light-gray rock with flecks of darker gray, black, and pink, grinning fatuously when she glanced up and made eye contact.

If she noticed Jaoui and Mikal smirking at Esparza's puppy love, Saavik gave no sign.

This is what you wanted, she reminded herself. *A routine assignment without challenges or crises, methodical, meaningful tasks, duty, order, discipline . . .*

"Marble," Mikal guessed about the new specimen.

"Carbonatite," Saavik corrected him, her gaze focused on the specimen despite his insistence on hovering just over her shoulder. The specimen in question had cost him dearly; he'd taken a tumble down an escarpment in his eagerness to pry it loose, sustaining more bruises to his ego than his person. "Containing in order of magnitude: phosphorus, niobium, uranium, thorium, copper, iron, titanium, barium, fluorine, and trace zirconium."

"Are you sure? I pulled that out of an alkalic intrusion on level fifty-three. I could have sworn it was marble."

"Angularity of the clasts suggests carbonatite," Saavik replied, studying the readout.

"You wouldn't be disagreeing with me for the sake of disagreeing?" Mikal teased.

Saavik looked up from the readout. "Geochemical analysis confirms."

She handed the specimen to Jaoui, who was now smirking at Mikal; Esparza had gone off to find more specimens.

And so it went.

Mikal seemed somewhat less irritating now that they

were downplanet and working every day. Perhaps the
vastness of a wilderness devoid of other complex life
was a better setting for the overlarge personality contained in his compact body, but Saavik found his presence off at a distance in her peripheral vision, flirting
with Ensign Graana, lecturing the younger members
of the team on the nuances of their craft, entertaining
them during breaks by weaving flower wreaths and
cavorting along the top of the volcanic ridge, the sunlight reflecting off the tattoos spiraling along his hairless brow less unsettling than at close range.

By contrast, she was the consummate professional,
and the team respected her for that. She gave few orders,
confident that these young scientists knew what they
were doing, and found those orders obeyed with alacrity. No one presumed to the familiarity they enjoyed
with Mikal, who as both civilian and self-assigned class
clown earned their respect for his credentials, but their
fellowship in exchange for his.

The windswept silence was often punctuated with
sounds of idle chat and floating laughter wafting over
great distances to her sensitive ears. Saavik had hoped
it would be possible to learn to live out under the sky
again. Why, then, did she feel uneasy?

*"Because, as humans are wont to say, 'It's lonely at the
top'?"* Spock suggested.

She could not be certain when these conversations
had begun. The dialogue she and her mentor had sustained from the earliest days when they were primarily exercises in proper grammar, coupled with ideas

to challenge her fears and ever-boiling rage, had continued in her mind after Spock's death and since his "resurrection," as it seemed impossible to sustain these conversations with the ghostly, puzzled Spock who had greeted her with a bemused lack of recognition just before *Bounty*'s departure.

But had they begun even as the awful truth wafted up from *Enterprise*'s engine room as the ship sped away from the blossoming destruction of the Genesis device, or later? Try as she might, she could not recall.

She could see herself, as if from a distance, standing at attention as the coffin slid down the torpedo rack to the sound of bagpipes (all but excruciating to Vulcan ears, yet somehow appropriate), but could not recall what she was thinking at the time.

She did recall a moment—a flashback, humans called it—when she had heard the whimpered distress of the boy-Spock on Genesis and realized what the problem was ("It is called *Pon farr . . . Pon farr . . .*"), the face of her mentor superimposed over the evolving face of this troubled, primitive being, and she had almost recoiled (*I cannot do this, though I must. It is not proper, yet if I do not, he will die . . .*). But duty had won out, and she had done what needed to be done. But where was her mind at the time? And what about the times in between, and since?

She could not recall.

Forgetting was not something she did as an adult. It was not something, as a Vulcan, she should have been able to do. To her it signaled a part of her other heritage, and as such it was anathema.

She could not remember. And the not-remembering infuriated her. Perhaps that was why she filled those mental lacunae with conversations she might never be able to have in actuality.

Was it truly lonely at the top? She turned the thought over as she might a palm-sized rock, examining it until, *It is logical,* she concluded. *Fraternization between officers and crew is discouraged, therefore it is possible to seek companionship only among one's fellow officers, and the captain of a ship must be the most alone of all.*

And yet that is not what you fear.

Was it only wishful thinking, or some manner of delusion, that rendered Spock's voice so clear, as if he were actually here and speaking directly to her?

She realized for the first time that she had neglected to inform him of her whereabouts. Throughout her adolescence, and especially during her years at the Academy, his weekly subspace messages had sustained her, helped her control her anger, her frustration at the spoiled and immature humans surrounding her, her exasperation that things could not move faster so that she could get out into space where she belonged.

Why had she neglected to tell him she had taken another assignment? Was this another of those lacunae? What was causing them? The same mix of guilt and bewilderment that had her hearing his voice in her mind?

"Fear?" she repeated. If she spoke aloud, what of it? The others were scattered all over the grid; no one could hear her.

It is I, Saavik-kam. You need not dissemble. It is not the solitude you fear but your own innate gifts.

"That is not correct," she said stubbornly. "I have never shied from my gifts as scientist and—"

—leader?

"I do not wish to lead, except as I do now, as a scientist guiding a small team of fellow scientists. Surely the model of your own life is such that—"

I served as balance to an innate leader such as James T. Kirk. My path is not yours, Saavik, nor should it be.

Saavik banked down a sudden flare of anger. Was this madness, to argue with someone to whom one owed one's life, someone who wasn't even here?

"While your advice is always welcome, Captain Spock," she said formally, "it *is* my life! I will live it as I choose!"

At that moment a shadow fell over her in the late evening sun, Ensign Esparza lugging a laden specimen bag back to the shelter, reminding her that she was not alone and that if she had been speaking aloud, it was past time to stop.

Alone but not alone, not alone but lonely? Subjects for future contemplation, which reminded her that between the work downplanet and her research for Tolek, she had been neglecting her meditation.

Perhaps all of it was as simple as that. Perhaps she should have taken Amanda's advice after all. Too late now. But there were ways to meditate while one worked, flamboyant tattooed distractions notwithstanding.

• • •

Two specimens of rock remained. Giving the others permission to beam aboard for the night, Saavik reached past Mikal to retrieve the first.

"Microfibrous chert," she announced as the spectral analyzer completed its first pass and she reset it for a second to confirm. "As with all of the other sedimentary rock we have collected, it shows no indication of animal fossils. This, coupled with the complete absence of complex life-forms, suggests that it is possible to hypothesize the Deemanot may in fact be the only animal life-form on the planet, though the small range of the sample makes the hypothesis inconclusive . . ."

Mikal sighed. "It's getting dark. Time to pack it in for today."

The shelter had its own light source, and there were rations and sleeping bags if they wanted to spend the night. Mikal, Saavik surmised, didn't want to miss the first round of drinks in the off-duty lounge. Or perhaps some other form of recreation.

She could not know that in fact he would have preferred to stay here all night with her, studying the way the tendrils of her hair, straying out of the practical clasp she had bound them in, arranged themselves against the whiteness of her delicate neck, and the thought made him wonder if he could trust himself.

"There is one sample remaining," she insisted, misreading his impatience, taking a perverse enjoyment in making him wait. "It may explain the anomalous plant life detected by the long-range probes."

He sighed again. "It is odd we haven't found any unusual specimens at ground level yet. I'm wondering if the whole thing wasn't a fluke."

"A fluke?"

"Scanner error, something in the atmosphere that distorted the readings. We should have found *something* out of the ordinary. Maybe this will be it."

It was heavy, dense, dark in color, and smooth in texture, almost as if it had been polished, as indeed it had, by forces so powerful they could not be duplicated by any human endeavor. It was a chondrite—a meteorite, in lay terms—a stray chunk of rock from the time the universe began, broken free of an asteroid or comet, or perhaps tumbling through space on its own for billions of years until the planet's gravity had drawn it in, the atmosphere burnishing it as it gathered speed and struck the surface, embedding itself in the surrounding rock, an alien come from another place, as were the two intelligent beings who studied it.

Saavik's suggestion that it and its brethren scattered all over the planet following perhaps millions of years of meteor showers might be responsible for the anomalous life-forms their orbital scanners had detected might not be as strange as it sounded. One of the earliest theories of the origin of life was that it had been transported from other galaxies on such stray alien things. If any of the chondrites the science team gathered over the next several weeks showed evidence of even the most primitive life-forms, and an evolutionary progression could be found between those life-forms and the plants they had yet to identify, they would solve one mystery—and create another.

But while the chondrite contained all of the expected components of interstellar dust, metal droplets and silicate spherules embedded in a fine-grained matrix of predominantly iron ore, repeated scans showed no trace of life.

Now it was Mikal's turn to reassure Saavik. "There'll be others. We'll solve this." His voice drifted off, and there was a faraway look in his eyes. "And maybe my sins will be forgiven . . ."

He seemed to be referring to something other than the metaphorical toes he'd stepped on in order to earn this assignment, but Saavik did not pursue it. Sealing the chondrite into the final container and setting it on the pallet, she signaled the ship to beam it, and them, aboard.

There was a subspace text from Tolek waiting for her in her quarters, with detailed accounts of contacts with the other Hellguard survivors, sometimes successfully, sometimes thwarted by the inalienable Vulcan right to be left alone.

Saavik filed this message with the others and sighed. Perhaps when he had run through the entire roster and found no more deaths, Tolek would abandon his quest, and at least some of her unease would abate.

As a scientist, she had to admit that the three deaths were puzzling, yet Vulcan healers with far more expertise than she had performed exhaustive tests and concluded that they were the result of an inexplicable but not unnatural cause. Any attempt to obtain more data than Tolek had already given her would hit the unbreakable wall of Vulcan privacy.

It was not a lie to keep the truth to oneself. But how many unspoken truths had obfuscated Vulcan history, truths that might seem small in their concealment but that, over time, could aggregate into larger, more damaging untruths? Was it only humans who subscribed to the concept of "little white lies"? Not for the first time, Saavik wondered how a "minor clerk in an adjudicator's office" had managed to acquire as much information as he had.

Had she allowed their childhood bond to obscure the fact that she knew nothing about what Tolek had become in the intervening years? Could she trust him? And if not, was any of his story true?

Her final thought as she slipped into sleep that night was, *I still owe him one lizard egg . . .*

She dreamed.

Hellguard, hunting in the early morning hours before the suns came up, when the false dawn yielded some light but as yet none of the vicious heat. Crouched behind a rock, facing into the light so that she cast no forward shadow, she was stalking a night-crawling millipede hurrying toward its underground burrow before the sunlight struck and killed it. The creature was the length of her arm, its body mostly liquid; ingesting it would keep her hydrated for several days. As it scurried along the ground,

*and she stood to fling one of her collection of throwing
sticks, what she saw made her drop the stick and shrink
into herself in horror.*

*Tolek, sprawled on the desert floor, skin blackened and
blistered, teeth drawn back in a rictus of death. It was her
fault, for letting him go off with only one lizard egg.*

The sound of her own hoarse cry woke her, bolt upright,
staring into the almost dark of her starlit quarters, the
sound of the impulse engines, the atmospherics purring softly, regulating airflow, temperature, every aspect
of life controlled, comfortable, safe.

Saavik threw aside the bedclothes, enjoyed the
softness of carpet beneath her bare feet, ran her fingers through the tangled mass of her hair, feeling the
prickle of sweat on her scalp. She stepped into the sonic
shower, savoring the simple pleasure of cleanliness,
order, predictability. Would she ever take these things
for granted?

She brushed her hair until it gleamed, slipped into
one of the several field uniforms lined up in the wardrobe, absently chose for breakfast the first thing that
came to mind from a thousand entries in the replicator.
To be clean, fed, and sheltered, to have duties to perform and know exactly what the day would bring was
all she asked.

Not until she emerged into the corridor, uniform
impeccable, demeanor to match, did the resonances
of the dream retreat to the darker corners of her mind,
never gone, merely at bay. Today was to be their last day

in the grassland, a final survey of the plant life before they moved camp to Biome 2.

Despite their meticulous gathering and cataloging, they had not found a single anomaly either on the ground or under constant daily scans.

"Where in the hell did they go?" Mikal demanded of no one in particular, turning to the four points of the compass, tricorder set to maximum range, then in gradually decreasing radii until he was glowering at the grasses beneath his feet. He'd pored over the long-range scans for hours, comparing them to the daily readings, mystified.

"Still nothing, Galina," he said into the communicator in his other hand. "Even the microbes are ordinary, and there's no complex animal life at all, nothing that might have moved out of range. Unless some of the plants have feet."

"*You mean like the pseudolichens of Piscine V?*" Mironova reminded him, laughter in her voice. "*Oh, that's right, they had fins . . .*"

"You didn't think it was funny at the time!" Mikal said testily.

"*Not when one bit me, no. But when you fell facedown in the mud trying to catch it . . . Right,*" she said, becoming serious again. "*Last day in Biome 1, children. Make it worth your while. Chaffee out.*"

"Super!" Mikal grumbled, shouldering his collecting bag and striding off toward one of the last unstudied grids, close enough to be seen and well within communicator range, but far enough away to offer solitude, which suited Saavik perfectly. She set to work on her own patch, grateful for the silence.

Repeated short-range scans here had found no mammals, no birds or reptiles or fish, not even insects. Subterranean scans revealed numerous varieties of annelids, ranging in size from tiny threadlike creatures to some ten to fifteen centimeters in length, possibly the primitive ancestors of the Deemanot, busily aerating and fertilizing the soil. The plants, in the absence of insects, were either self-pollinating or relied on the wind. There wasn't so much as a gnat or fly to be found anywhere. Saavik didn't mind at all.

She'd flung the sharpest of her throwing sticks with practiced accuracy. It knocked the lizard off the ledge where it had concealed itself, breaking its back. In the time it took her to scramble over the rocks to retrieve it, a swarm of flies had already gathered, though the lizard was still breathing feebly. Smashing its skull with the first rock that came to hand, she'd had to fight off the flies repeatedly, raising another of her childhood's unanswered questions. How did they survive? What did they feed on when there were no dead lizards—or children?

The memory lasted less than a second before she shoved it back into the engrams where it lay waiting, impossible to erase, even as she wondered, *Why?* She had successfully repressed the childhood memories for years. Was it only Tolek's reappearance in her life that brought them forward now? As her hands worked methodically, gently scooping under the roots of one specimen after another and placing them in her collecting bag, her mind would not be still.

She had chosen this grid last because it was far from the water sources and the soil was thin. As a consequence the plants that grew here were more usually found in desert rather than grassland. She had hoped that might reveal some anomalies, but instead she found only the ordinary, as if any plant could be considered ordinary.

Plagiobothrys nothofulvus, salvia columbariae, common name chia, *chaenactis stevioides,* make note of the white flowers, be mindful of the spines . . .

The cataloging occupied only a portion of her mind, but she persisted.

Abronia villosa, also called verbena, both attractive and fragrant, *fabaceae,* subspecies *sophora flavescens, echinops gmelinii* or thistle, edible and medicinal, *artemisia scoparia* or wormwood, *thymus gobicus,* purple-flowered mint, fragrant, sweet tasting, excellent for tea . . .

Six

_____

Saavik's first morning on Vulcan, Amanda had found her in the garden just before dawn, crouched in a flower bed, scrabbling in the soil with her fingers. The human trod softly, but the child sensed her presence and spun around like a cornered thing. There was dirt around her mouth, and her jaw worked on something that crunched audibly.

"Was there nothing in the kitchen that pleased you?" Amanda asked, sitting on one of the numerous stone benches arranged along the sinuous paths, careful to make herself as small and unthreatening as possible. "I know Spock taught you how to use it, and the names of many of the foods it can make for you."

The child spat the root she'd been chewing—a species of _apiaceae_ native to Vulcan that Amanda had cultivated for its delicate, lacy flowers, not its edibility—into the dirt, inelegantly wiping her chin with the back of her hand. Clambering to her feet, she looked about her in the increasing light at the order and beauty of the many plantings Amanda had nurtured over the years, and though she had never seen a garden before, sensed that she had done something wrong.

"Not eat these?"

"We do not," Amanda said gently, keeping her voice

neutral, implying no judgment, simply a need to impart information. "You're right, some of them are edible. But we do not eat them." _

"Why?"

"Because we don't need to."

"Why they're here, then?"

"Because they're beautiful. And some of them have lovely fragrances, don't you think?"

She had noted the child's tendency to smell every new thing she discovered—logical in a feral child, as were all her behaviors in the context she'd come from.

That first day, while Amanda observed, she had walked along the carpets and the polished floors on her tiptoes, moving lightly from room to room, touching everything gingerly as if it might attack her, but touching nevertheless. Her overlarge eyes gleamed with curiosity. Her manner was contained, though the flare of her nostrils indicated she might bolt like a fawn at the slightest unexpected sound or movement. And whenever she touched an object—a vase, a chair, a wall hanging, the padd on which Amanda had been reading a novel before she arrived—she also leaned in close and sniffed it.

It would be months before she abandoned the need to touch and smell everything before she found it acceptable. Until then, every piece of fruit had to be rotated in her fingers in order to examine it from all sides. Then it was squeezed, sniffed, studied to determine whether it could be eaten whole or needed to be peeled. If, once broken into, it had multiple seeds, these were also examined. If their color was too bright, they were rejected as potentially poisonous. As there were no birds or lizards available to test them on, one had to follow one's instincts.

Prepared dishes were also scrutinized, their individual components separated and sniffed, tested with the tip of the tongue and, when it did not swell in protest at hidden toxins, accepted and ingested heartily.

But that would take time. That first day, having examined everything in the main room and finding it safe, Saavik had turned to find Sarek standing beside his wife. The struggle on her face (*Newcomer, stranger, why did I not hear him? Danger? No, Spock said two. Pa-rents. Sa-rek and A-man-da. Safe*) was a wonder to behold.

She managed her introduction to the ambassador as carefully as she had that to his wife, her overlarge eyes meeting his unblinking, as if to say, *After what I have survived, am I to be afraid of you?* Even so, Amanda saw the great weariness in the dark smudges under those eyes. It had been a long journey from the colony world where Spock had sequestered her for a year, and no doubt between excitement and anticipation of the unknown, the child had barely slept.

"Are you hungry?" Amanda asked. First food, then sleep. There was a lifetime for the rest.

The child nodded. Even if she hadn't been, she'd have replied in the affirmative. *When there's food, eat. When you can, sleep. And even when you sleep, be aware!*

Amanda had had the presence of mind to set out the meal beforehand, and while ordinarily a guest was served first, in this very special case her teacher's instinct caused her to take her own portion first and taste it, to show the child that it was safe. Still, though it was obvious that she was famished, Saavik waited until both Sarek and Spock also began to eat before she joined them.

"Don't you see, Sarek?" Amanda said against his later skepticism. "Her reaction was quite intelligent. 'Maybe humans can eat this safely, but that doesn't mean I can.'"

"She thought you might be attempting to poison her?" Sarek made no effort to keep the incredulity out of his voice. They were alone in the privacy of their rooms, the child's inquisitive eyes and ears safely tucked into bed in her own suite of rooms at the far end of the hall.

"Not necessarily. But she did intuit that not all species can necessarily eat the same things. It was a scientist's thought, and quite logical."

Sarek's expression softened. He had originally concurred with his wife that taking this child into their home was the right thing to do. That did not mean it would be the easy thing to do.

"Intuition? A human characteristic," Sarek had remarked. "The child is not human."

"Nor is she entirely Vulcan," Amanda reminded him. Any suggestion that they might have had this conversation before, about another child, was absent from her tone. "We have to make allowances for that. Logically."

"And you are willing to make such allowances?"

"Of course!" Amanda replied. "Aren't you?"

Wisely, Sarek had kept his thoughts to himself for the next little while. Gradually Saavik learned to trust them both, though it would be a long time before she stopped examining every new thing that came her way, sniffing a garment before she put it on, caressing the fabric as if to analyze the very molecular constituents of the fibers with her fingertips, needing to know, learning to trust.

Gradually socialized, she had learned not to engage in these childlike behaviors when anyone was watching, but sometimes when she was alone she could not resist examining some new thing with a more than Vulcan intensity.

And so that first morning in the garden, out of old habit, she had seen what to her was a food source, and perhaps with a further intuition (*Do not disturb the parents. Make no trouble. No matter what Spock says, they may send you away*), she had helped herself, rather than venture into the kitchen. Now that she had thought it through, she felt furtive and ashamed. There was so much to learn. What if she did something wrong? What if they sent her away?

Amanda saw all of this in those liquid eyes and reached out her hand. With no choice but to trust, Saavik took it.

"You and I will go inside and have a proper breakfast," the human said. "Then if you have no other plans, I thought we might spend some time in the garden before it gets too hot. We will teach each other about plants."

And with that simple task, Saavik learned that there was more than eat/not eat, and the scientist flourished.

Mikal's voice shook her out of her reverie.

"I found something," he said, taking a specimen out of his sample bag and crouching down to her level to show her.

She had been sitting on her heels beside one of the numerous watercourses, gathering a sample of what appeared to be a species of *apiaceae* that had particularly long roots, the better to take advantage of the rare dry-season groundwater. For a single moment all of her memories merged, from the time when she had had to live on roots to survive through that precious morning with Amanda in the garden ("We also call it Queen Anne's lace," Amanda had explained. "And wild carrot. The root does taste sweet, so you were wise to want to eat it"), only the first of many. She was holding the delicate flowers to her face to remind herself of the light sweet scent that had sparked the memory. If Mikal had not happened by, would she have taken a bite of the root for old time's sake?

"What is it?" she said quickly, scrambling to her feet to cover her confusion. The sun was over his shoulder, and she would have the excuse of not being able to see clearly what he was holding in his hand.

"Ordinary-looking portulaca," he said. "Something you'd expect to find in this biome, but . . ."

He paused for dramatic effect.

"I don't know why, but something seemed odd about it. I ran the tricorder over it before I put it in the bag. The molecular structure is completely off. It's not from this world, or even from any other known world in this sector of space. I think we've found our anomaly."

"Say again?" Mironova's voice issued from the communicator in Mikal's palm.

"I said, 'We've found our anomaly.'" Mikal scowled at the communicator, a newer model than he was used to, and adjusted the frequency. "It's akin to portulaca. Also known as purslane or moss rose. Low-growing spineless succulent with multicolored flowers—"

"I know what a moss rose is, Mikal," Mironova cut him off. *"I expect you'd find them in that biome."*

"Except we didn't until now, and the molecular structure's wrong."

"Stand by . . ." Mironova said, sounding preoccupied. *"We're showing pop-ups on scanners. All around you, at about the same rate as the initial scans, and in approximately the same locations. I'll be right there."*

"We can just as easily . . ." Mikal began, but Mironova was no longer there. ". . . beam it aboard or send you the tricorder reading," he finished stubbornly into the silent communicator just as the transporter sound came from behind him.

"You could have, yes." Mironova took the small flowering plant from him and ran her own tricorder over it. "But always better to see the thing in situ, isn't it?"

She scanned the area the same way Mikal would,

turning in a slow circle, and Saavik wondered who had taught whom that trick.

"Cabin fever?" Mikal muttered, but Mironova ignored him.

"More of them," she announced, indicating banks of the low-growing succulent where there had been bare ground moments before. "Yellow flowering variety at two o'clock, variegated red and white at seven. And you're telling me this is the first you've seen of them. Explain."

"We cannot, Captain," Saavik replied. "We have studied those grids meticulously and cataloged the majority of them individually and hands-on. Even if they had been dormant, below the surface waiting to sprout—"

"—they'd have shown up consistently on orbital scans, but they didn't," Mikal finished for her. "But the bigger mystery is the molecular structure."

Mironova waved that away. "Might be something unique to this planet. We'll figure that out after we figure out how they disappear and reappear. And what the hell is *that*?"

She indicated a vine that had suddenly appeared from a cleft in the outcropping near the shelter, sprouting intertwining branches as they watched. As if in time-lapse photography, in a few moments it grew to several feet tall, sprouted leaves and silver-blue flowers that, where the tendrils grew into the shade of the rock, gave off a faint phosphorescence.

"That wasn't here before, I swear it wasn't!" Mikal

said, groping for his tricorder, a sense of excitement in his voice for the first time since they'd gotten here. "I would have noticed."

"Confirmed, Captain," Saavik said, watching the thing send runners along the ground, claw its way through the topsoil to form roots, and then branch upward again, showing weeks' worth of growth in only moments and creeping inexorably in their direction, almost as if it sensed their presence.

"Steady!" Mironova said, phaser pulled from her belt and set on stun just in case. "We don't know how big that thing can get or what its intentions are."

" 'Intentions'?" Saavik repeated, but then she remembered how many species of interactive plants had been cataloged in the Alpha Quadrant alone. The spores of Omicron Ceti III, among others . . .

She was setting her tricorder to analyze the phenomenon when Mikal cried out in pain.

The plant had sent a particularly long tendril out to lash at him, as if it did indeed have intentions. Something—unseen spines or perhaps a toxin—had raised a series of angry welts on his arm, almost like second-degree burns. His dignity was damaged as well. Mironova, small as she was, had shoved him aside and fired at the vine. The phaser blast distracted it enough to make it release Mikal's wrist, but neither damaged it nor slowed it down.

Mikal scrambled out of the way just as the twining branches reached the shelter and began weaving their way around the support struts, pulling it down.

"Transporter!" Mironova was shouting. "Get us out of here!"

By the time Mikal was released from sickbay, his burns healed but his ego still bruised, all of the anomalies, from the tame little portulaca to the killer vine, had disappeared. Repeated scans showed nothing growing on the surface that they hadn't already identified and cataloged. Only the crushed and mangled shelter, the churned-up soil around it, and the single moss rose specimen languishing in one of the ship's labs confirmed that they'd been there at all.

"I know what you're going to say," Mikal said when he and Saavik had returned to the surface to survey the damage. "Spores traveling through space. One variety I might believe, but not two."

"Portulaca reproduce by placental seed, not unicellular spores," Saavik mused. "Doubtful they could survive extremes of temperature in deep space."

Mikal stared at her in amazement. "Are you serious? I wasn't talking about the portulaca. What about that . . . that *thing* that sprouted out of the ground in seconds? It was like nothing I've ever seen before, anywhere, and now it's just *gone*."

"Indeed," Saavik said, studying what was left of the shelter. Despite the reassurance of numerous tricorder readings, she wondered if the ground beneath them might open suddenly and produce other untoward and potentially dangerous phenomena. It was an all-too-familiar feeling.

"Damn shame Mironova didn't let me get a piece of that thing before she pulled us back to the ship!"

"To all appearances," Saavik said dryly, " 'that thing' was attempting to get a piece of you."

Together they surveyed the spot where the twining plant had first emerged from the cleft in the rock. Surface scans to deep-core scans showed no root system, no water source that might have nurtured something that could grow that fast, nothing. More puzzled than ever, they moved on to Biome 2.

Biome 2 was a temperate, forested region farther south of the planet's equator, replete with morning mists and warm midday sunlight filtered through the canopy. Ferns and mosses were particularly plentiful; it was in fact difficult to find a patch of soil that wasn't blanketed with a soft layer of moss, though it made natural flooring for their newly arrived shelter.

"It's like a Japanese garden," Cheung remarked, impressed for once.

"Several variant species, though well within the norm for this sector," Saavik was saying, studying her tricorder rather than the landscape, until Mikal reached across and flicked it off.

Before she could object, he said, "Just look at them with your eyes for a moment. Breathe the air, listen to the sound of the leaves."

"It is quite aesthetically pleasing," she admitted after a moment.

Mikal still had his hand over the tricorder screen.

He gestured toward everything around them. "More of that, less of this," he ordered her as the team fanned out to begin their gathering.

There were a surprising number of flowering species despite the tree cover, and some seemed to have luminescent qualities.

"Love to spend the night and see if they really do glow in the dark," Mikal mused.

"We can as easily ascertain that under laboratory conditions," Saavik countered as the sunlight began to fade and the rest of the team gathered at the beam-up point.

"Ah, but where's the fun in that?" Mikal wanted to know.

He suggested as much to Mironova, who thought it was a splendid idea, though *only until the end of beta shift, and only in the interests of scientific observation. If none of you are eaten by carnivorous vines, we may expand the practice for shore leave once you've gathered all your specimens.*

Deema III was moonless, and night at this latitude was immediate; the stars seemed close enough to touch. Almost as quickly, small pools of light began to dot the landscape. The flowers that had absorbed the light during the day now emitted it like multicolored fairy lights. It could hardly be called "darkness" when everywhere one looked there was light.

"It's been three hours, and they show no sign of dimming," Mikal observed almost breathlessly, lying back against the trunk of a tree, peering across an open glade he'd scouted in the daylight for this very purpose. The landing party had set tricorders at intervals around the glade to scan for anomalies, but nothing odd had appeared so far. The others had chosen observation points around the glade, turning ship's rations into a picnic, speaking in whispers if they spoke at all.

"They must start to wane at some point," Jaoui murmured. "Or do they store the light indefinitely?"

No one knew the answer, and no one really cared. They'd already brought samples to the labs for analysis. End of shift came far too fast, and the landing party straggled together reluctantly, beaming up by twos. When only Saavik and Mikal were left, Saavik's communicator beeped.

"*Landing party . . .*" Mironova's voice was half swallowed by static. "*Some sort of interference at this end. Running a diagnostic. Stand by.*"

"Affirmative, Captain."

She could hear Mironova cursing in several languages, then, "*Looks like a bloody ion storm!*" she sputtered. "*Snuck up on us . . . transporter lock unstable . . . breaking orbit . . . ride it out . . . sit tight . . . hear from us . . .*"

Saavik knew the drill. The ship would break orbit, retreat to a safe distance and ride out the storm, whether it took hours or days, then come back and retrieve them. Why then the quickening of her heart rate, a sensation a human might term panic? The last time she had lost contact with her ship—

"*Saavik to* Grissom *. . . come in, please . . .*"

—had been an anomaly. She would not think of the

last time. Ion storms were commonplace; she could expect to experience many in the course of her career. There were rations and sleeping bags in the shelter, luxuries her last planetary stranding hadn't afforded. Even though the temperature in this sector dropped considerably at night, and a sly little wind fluttered the shelter canopy as they settled in beneath it, this was hardly a crisis situation.

"They know where to find us," Mikal said, unrolling the sleeping bags to make a soft place to sit inside the shelter, rummaging through the food packs with a kind of glee. "And if they never come back because they've been sold into slavery by the Ferengi or eaten by a gigantic intergalactic squid, we'll live off the land, hitchhike to the nearest Deemanot settlement—watching out for attack vines, of course—and make first contact, though no one will ever know."

He was talking more than usual. Was he disturbed by their being stranded here as well?

"We'll go native, learn to ingest and egest soil as they do and become productive members of society, emulate their mating rituals if they have any, grow old together . . . that is, if I remembered to pack the *raktajino*. Can't function without my morning *raktajino*. Saavik? You didn't by any chance drink the last of the—?"

She had been standing outside the shelter, ignoring his rambling, staring absently at the swirling pattern of the communicator, as if willing it to respond. When Mikal touched her shoulder, she flinched and whirled on him without thinking. He recoiled even before he saw the knife in her hand.

"Was it something I said?" He tried to joke, keeping his distance just the same. "Fight off many ion storms with that?" Saavik seemed frozen in place and did not respond. "Suppose I should be grateful you didn't go for your phaser, but seriously, this is getting to be a habit—a bad one."

She was staring at the knife as if it were alive and might turn on her. Recovering herself at last, she slipped it back into her boot, and stalked off to the edge of the clearing to collect herself. Mikal followed her.

"What is it?" he pleaded. "It's more than just being stuck here for a few hours. You're trained for situations like this. Saavik, talk to me!"

"I did not have the knife with me on Genesis," she said, more to herself than to him, looking off into the forest and not at him. "If I had . . ."

Genesis. He understood at once. "I wondered if that was you. But there's no reason to think this is anything like—"

"I am aware of that!" she cried, turning on him, cornered, angry, frightened, and more than a little ashamed. She hadn't even realized she had the knife with her until it was in her hand. If she had had it with her on Genesis, it might have saved David's life. Ever since, she had weighed its necessity wherever she went and usually kept it in her quarters but close to hand. Why had she brought it with her this night?

Did she see Mikal as some sort of enemy? Or had Tolek's reappearance in her life, the reminders of Hell-guard and his newfound obsession, triggered some primeval need to protect herself? Everything she had not allowed herself to feel on Genesis, with Spock's life in the balance, she was feeling now.

And what of Tolek? He was aware of the complexities of sending subspace messages at this distance. If *Chaffee* did not return for days, or longer, and she could not reply to his messages . . . even if she could, why had he come to her? What did he expect her to do?

Mikal had a point. As a trained Starfleet officer, she should have gone for her phaser. What was happening to her? It was as if she was reverting to her former feral self . . .

She strode past him to the shelter, retreating into a far corner, reminding herself that he was not the enemy, that there was no enemy, that—

"It's more than Genesis," he observed quietly, sitting on his heels in the doorway, trying to make himself as nonthreatening as possible. The luminescence from the flowers accentuated the paleness of his skin, the contrast of the swirling tattoos across his brow, over the hairless dome of his head, curling under his great bejangled ears, disappearing down his neck into the collar of his field suit, reappearing again on the backs of his surprisingly delicate hands. "Just as you and I quarrel so much for more than ordinary reasons. Tell me what I can do."

Leave me alone! she wanted to scream. *You and your need to watch the night-blooming plants are the reason we are trapped here!*

But while she might have lost Spock forever, she possessed him still. Vulcan logic, Vulcan calm, slowly reasserted themselves, and she drew herself out of the dark corners of her own mind to see the stricken look on Mikal's face, the liquid greenish-brown eyes glowing with concern. And, as he said, there was more behind his look than this moment, some kinship, some recognition.

Was there a Hellguard in his past as well?

"Tell me what I can do," he'd said to her.

Slowing her breathing, she cast about for something that was not of the moment, not about her or this place or this mission or the inchoate fears that defied logic, and said, "Tell me . . . about a scientist . . . offspring of a race of scientists, who abandoned his world and never returned—"

"*My* world!" Mikal snorted in disgust. "It was never mine to abandon. It abandoned me generations before I was born."

"Her name was Preltam," he began. "You'll never have heard of her, but I'm certain you'll have heard of her mentor, Zora. A confluence of circumstance once placed her in a position to stop a genocide, and she failed . . ."

Seven

Someone once said that the true definition of power is to have one's name remembered long after one is dead. Kill or heal, the reason does not matter. No one remembers the names of those you choose to save or slay, but your name is remembered. The fact that Tiburon, a beneficent world, famous for its scientific advancements, produced only two beings whose crimes spread their fame beyond their homeworld made those two all the more noteworthy. When the full extent of Sevrin's crimes came to light, some on Tiburon were almost relieved. The theory was that some might forget Zora because of him. That hope was short-lived. Sevrin's crimes were minor by comparison, limited mostly to the deaths of those who followed him willingly, but Zora . . .

Every schoolchild knows the one-line answer to who Zora was: "Zora, who experimented with the body chemistry of subject tribes on Tiburon." How many step back and say, " 'Subject tribes'? What does that mean, exactly?"

Strictly speaking, there were no subject tribes on Tiburon by the time it joined the Federation. The governing body might call itself a council of tribes, but the populace have not been tribal, in the sense of living in small interconnected families, clans and septs, in many centuries. The remnant of those who survived Zora's atrocities were absorbed rather abruptly into mainstream society. Some adapted, some did not.

But back to Zora. Some tried to claim that she wasn't even a Tiburonian, that she came from offworld, but in fact no one really knew. By the time she became provincial governor, she had already destroyed the paper trail that led her there, and one of her first acts as governor was to eliminate anyone who might say she was anything other than what she claimed to be. And her experiments did not occur in a vacuum. They were carried out with the full knowledge and approval of— some historians said even at the suggestion of—her superiors, though of course they denied it later.

And she had a lot of help, from lesser scientists hoping to make names for themselves, or perhaps naïve enough to accept what became known as Zora's Equation, that if the drugs she developed worked on the subject peoples, they would save millions of more "evolved" citizens, and that was a good thing, wasn't it?

Was the difference between a clinical trial, in which a thousand patients were given an experimental drug and a thousand more given placebo, and the same drug administered to ten thousand unlettered natives anything more than one of scale? Surely if these aboriginals *could* read a consent form, they would sign it, wouldn't they? Half the educated people who gave consent had no idea of the possible side effects of an experimental drug, or they'd never consent. Was this any different?

"Her name was Preltam," Mikal said. "She was my

many-times great-grandmother. She began as a lowly lab assistant, no more skilled than the robot that collects used beakers and stacks them in an autoclave— less, in fact, because a robot's sensors recognize the residues in the beakers and make sure not to mix the volatile ones together. But Zora took a shine to her, taught her, groomed her, and made her a member of the inner circle, one of the Bringers of Medicines to the remote villagers who had no access to the news feeds and didn't realize what was going on. It is both because and in spite of her that I am what I am today . . ."

Tiburon went through a dark phase after Zora's party was overthrown. Long after the toxins had been destroyed, the killing fields covered over with flowers and monuments, the promises that this would never happen again broadcast into everyone's ears planetwide, there persisted a state of fear. It was as if science itself had become the enemy, and the backlash would last for generations in some regions. Sevrin's Eden Movement had many predecessors, all sprung out of that fear.

Eventually society as a whole would recover, and Tiburon would become known for its scientific and technological achievement, frequent host of the conference of the Interspecies Medical Exchange. But that recovery was hard-won and a long time in coming.

In the short term, there was anger and retribution, against not only the perpetrators but also anyone with any connection to them. Friends, acquaintances, and especially kin were, if they were fortunate, rounded up, questioned, and usually released. If they were less fortunate, they were simply dragged out of their houses in the middle of the night and dispatched, as if the four-year-old grandchild of a scientist somehow contained the "bad seed" that would bloom into another. But every society has its witch trials, does it not?

Only by "recanting"—promising to abandon the pursuit of science in perpetuity—could one be spared.

Some refused, and those who survived the purges became the next generation of scientists who would get the culture back on track. But others, Preltam's survivors among them, were only too eager to abandon not only science but all learning.

"I am the descendant of sixteen generations of illiterates," Mikal said quietly.

Saavik did not know what to say.

"Zora herself had no kin, which may have been one of the reasons she lost her way, forgot that her 'subjects' were sentient beings, though that is only conjecture. Her experiments were benign at first, but competition for the revenue she needed to continue was fierce, and at first all she did was cut corners, fiddle her results, exaggerate her findings . . ."

The wind ruffled the flexible sides of the shelter, sending waves of color rippling through the phosphorescing flowers. Saavik tried not to think of David and of protomatter.

"But that was in the beginning. At some point her treatments became less expedient and more toxic. Yet her defenders argued that sometimes a cure may seem like a kill. In ancient times, before gene therapies and anti-inflammatory therapies, cancers were literally burned away with chemicals and radiation. Were those doctors criminals because some of their patients died?

"At least, that was Preltam's defense when she stood before the tribunal. I've read the transcripts. She argued eloquently. But when you compare what she said with the conditions in the camps where these tribes were housed, when you realize they didn't even bother sterilizing the instruments they used, eloquence does not justify her.

"So when she was remanded to the penal colony, she lost all connection to her family. Her spouse divorced her, changed his name and those of their children, but that was not enough. People knew. As the former spouse of a criminal, he was forbidden to go offworld—Tiburon likes to keep its dirty laundry self-contained—and he soon found himself out of work, through guilt by association.

"Thus my many-times great-grandfather signed the Document of Recantation, abandoning the sciences and becoming an itinerant merchant. Whenever the whispers about his identity began in town, he and the children would move somewhere else. The children were denied schooling. They followed in their father's footsteps. Their children and their children's children were not even taught to read.

"Within a generation or two, their identities blurred and the acute pain of the past was forgotten. Preltam's grandchildren might have been quietly enrolled in schools, but past bitterness for everything they had lost gnawed at their parents' souls, and they refused.

"Thus, inhabiting the dark corners of the cities,

among the remnants of the 'subject tribes' who could
not adapt but who instead squander their lives in
chemically induced dreams (some purportedly provided by the very society that once subjugated them),
move the unlettered beggars and tinkers of Tiburon,
kept out of sight of the outworlders who flock to the
planet's renowned medical conferences. No world is
completely free of secrets."

Mindful of Romulans, of Hellguard, and of Vulcan,
Saavik wondered which of "her" worlds had claim to
the most unspoken truths.

"Have you ever gone days, even weeks, without bath-
ing, and then washed at a cold water pump in a public
square whose source is suspect?" Mikal was no longer
speaking to her, was no longer even present so much as
lost in his own reverie.

Saavik thought of pools of stagnant water, if there
was water at all.

"Have you ever lived for weeks on the spoiled food
left over in the family's caravan when the power's failed
and no one will buy it and your father and your uncles
haven't enough credits between them to buy anything
else until the next consignment comes in? Do you know
what it's like to own not a single garment that someone
else hasn't worn before, often until it's in rags?"

Indeed, Saavik thought. Her eyes, reflecting the light
of the flowers, glowed with a light of their own, catch-
ing Mikal's attention in the dark. Their intensity made
him stop, as if he were listening to her thoughts.

"I'm not saying it was always thus. There were flush
times, times we even stayed in one place for more than

a season, and some of those places were posh. There was an inn with featherbeds, I recall, and the inn-keeper's middle daughter taught me things a boy of ten could hardly be expected to learn on his own.

"But that was the real hardship, don't you see? I was forbidden to learn. Oh, I was taught to tap out numbers on a dataslate to add up sales, and to scan any road signs in the rural areas that hadn't yet learned to talk to the slate. But my ignorance was so profound, I didn't even know that there was more.

"So here I am one wretched cold morning before dawn, shoved out of the warm funk of the caravan to make deliveries for my father, wiping snot off my lip with my sleeve, rags wrapped around my feet in the snow—don't ask me why after those experiences, but I still love snow, maybe only because it kept the lice down."

He paused, as if something else had just occurred to him.

"In my . . . in Tiburon culture there is a custom. During the first snowfall of the season, lovers stop whatever they're doing and walk with each other in the snow. It's a beautiful sight, couples of all ages holding hands and strolling day or night through ordinary streets made magical by the falling snow. When the snow stops, everyone goes back inside and resumes their very important scientific work. Except for the pariahs, who returned to our scraps and scrounging. When I was a boy, I wondered if I would ever have the privilege."

He shook off the reverie and looked at Saavik as if seeing her for the first time. "I don't know what made me remember that just now. It never occurred to me at the time that even a pariah can enjoy the snow . . ."

"It's snow! Snow in the same sector. Fantastic!"

Saavik, who had to that point never experienced snow, had observed its properties on *Grissom*'s monitors with the same curiosity with which she examined any new thing and, while she could understand David's surprise at the rapidity of the climatological changes occurring over such a small region of the Genesis planet, she heard something else in his voice and wondered what all the fuss was about. Until they'd beamed down to Genesis and she felt it crunch beneath her boots and blow cold against her face, its crystalline nature was nothing more than an intriguing scientific phenomenon.

"No two snowflakes are alike, Saavik," David said as they pushed against the wind, following what sounded like the cry of a frightened child. "Did you know that?"

Its unexpected presence in what had been designed as a temperate zone undergoing late spring to early summer, its effect on the naked child she and David found hypothermic and shivering, mere hours from death if they had not happened along, had threatened her sense of wonder at this first encounter.

Yet it was beautiful. Under ideal circumstances, she might have walked in it for hours, watching it reshape and soften everything it touched, cupping it in her hands, letting a few of the supposedly unique crystals touch her tongue as she'd seen David do when he thought she wasn't watching, as they tracked the source of the unexplained tricorder reading making child-sized footprints where there should be none.

No two snowflakes were alike? How was it possible to know? Had some Earth scientist cataloged every snowflake in a given storm to verify this statement? Did the hypothesis apply only to that storm, so that the multiplicity of shapes was reincarnated, in a sense, in the next storm, or had no two snowflakes ever been alike since the universe was formed? Even with advanced computer simulations, how was it possible to know?

Humans made such statements as if they were proven hypotheses, then worked backward to verify them after the fact. This behavior had been what destroyed Genesis, nearly destroyed her, yet gave Spock back his life. Out of great harm had come great good, all overseen by coincidence. If Carol Marcus's team had not created Genesis, if Spock's tube had not been jettisoned at precisely the moment it was, if she and David had not noticed the anomalous reading on the planet surface, if Admiral Kirk hadn't stolen the *Enterprise* and come looking for them, if, if, if . . .

There had been no time to ask David how he knew about snowflakes. And in all this time, she had neglected to research it herself.

". . . but anyway, snow, me scratching at the lice, haven't bathed since the warm season, trudging under a pack nearly as big as I was, a consignment I had to deliver to someone in town, and all I was thinking was, Will it be warm in the shop and will they let me stay until my feet stop stinging, or will they take the pack from me, fling the payment on the counter, and shove me back outside before I stink up the place? when I saw a light up ahead, a fire. Someone had made a fire in an old tin barrel and was warming his hands over it . . ."

He'd been warned often enough not to talk to strangers, but the fire drew him like a moth. The boy crept up quietly, saw that there was just one man, elderly and unarmed. His smile was as welcoming as the fire and Mikal almost bolted, especially when he saw how well dressed the stranger was. Why would he be out before dawn in the cold unless he was one of those predators who preyed on vulnerable young boys, out in the cold alone?

But the pack was heavy, and if he dropped it the retribution from his father and his uncles would be almost as dire as what a predator could do to him, and anyway his feet were so numb he wasn't certain he could outrun even an elderly man.

He'd placed the pack at his feet and stood straddling it, ready to heave it back onto his shoulder and move once his hands were thawed. But he stood there in silence beside the stranger, warming himself until the sun came up and the stranger said simply, "It's time," and motioned to Mikal to follow him. For reasons he would never understand, he did.

There was a food shop just opening. It was clear the staff knew the stranger from the way they welcomed him. He told them to bring "the usual" and the same for "my young friend here."

I'll eat, Mikal thought, *and by then my feet will be warm, and I can leave.*

But before he even had time to stow the pack under the table, the stranger had activated the screen in the center between them and began to read aloud.

"It was only the day's events, local news and gossip, global and offworld," Mikal explained, "but I was so ignorant it took me I don't know how many minutes to realize the squiggles in front of him on the screen were the source of the information and not something he was inventing as he went along. I asked him if he was a sorcerer, and could he teach me his magic too? He just laughed and told me he'd be here every day, no matter the weather. And so for the next however many days, I rushed to make the morning deliveries so I could meet him there whenever I could, and we'd continue reading.

"Yes, I said 'we,' because some of those squiggles on the screen reshaped themselves into the words he was speaking, and it *was* a kind of sorcery, even a kind of alchemy. He had given me the greatest gift in all the worlds.

"I was so ignorant, I never even asked his name, and a good thing too, after what happened next. And I'll never know why he did it, though in thinking back, I realize he didn't need to be standing by that fire on that first morning. Perhaps he'd watched me trudging past the food shop every morning and saw something, something that for all the science in the universe I cannot put a name to. But he gave me the gift of that universe, and then I almost forfeited it . . ."

He'd slunk back to the caravan one night and some-thing triggered a suspicion. Perhaps he looked too smug or only too well fed, perhaps the aromas from the food shop clung to his clothes, perhaps a member of the clan had seen him with the stranger, perhaps, with the whole family bundled together for warmth, he'd muttered something in his sleep. But one of his uncles was waiting for him behind the door and grabbed him by the ear so hard he tore three earrings loose, cuffed him on the side of the head, and began to curse him.

"I know what you've been doing!" he kept shouting. "I know!"

"We were just talking, I swear it!" the boy insisted, seeing it through his uncle's eyes. No one gave anything for nothing. The man had to be a predator, plying him with food. What other reason could there be? "Just talking, that's all!"

As the blows rained down, he realized too late what his crime was. He had broken the family taboo. He had dared to *learn*.

When his father returned late that night, he beat him a second time and locked him out in the snow. One of his aunts risked her own life to follow him, giv-ing him a packet of dried meat and one of her bracelets to sell. Battered and confused, Mikal trudged back to the food shop, but it was locked for the night, and he had no idea where the stranger lived or even what his name was.

He thought of waiting until the shop opened again at dawn, but if the wet snow seeping through the rags wrapped around his feet hadn't dissuaded him, the thought of the constables or a true predator finding him did. It also occurred to him that his father and his uncles, while they usually kept family matters within the family, might exact retribution from the stranger if he led them to him.

He didn't even have the means to leave a note to thank the stranger and wish him well, but he did have the gift the stranger had given him, a knowledge of the larger world beyond the neighborhoods he'd prowled on his deliveries.

He slept in a doorway until the pawnshops opened, traded the bracelet for a pair of secondhand boots, hitched a ride to the nearest teleport, found a lavatory and washed the blood off his face, hoping his tattoos would hide most of the bruises, snuck aboard a ferry to the nearest space hub, lied about his age, and for the next several years alternately stowed away or worked his passage on whatever ship of whatever registry would have him.

He learned languages by osmosis and pestered his bunkmates and ships' crews to teach him how things worked and tell him of the worlds they'd visited, acquiring a generalist's knowledge in a variety of subjects. One fellow passenger was a botanist who taught him everything she knew, and not only about plants. In a roundabout way he found himself on Earth.

• • •

"I never looked back, I never went back. Sometimes it occurs to me to wonder what became of them. Is my father still alive? My mother? The uncle who beat me? The aunt who gave me her bracelet? Something stops me from finding out. Some scientist I am, eh?"

"A scientist, self-taught, who made a decision that certain courses of inquiry are not worth pursuing," Saavik said, though she wondered which of them she was speaking of. She remembered the question Mironova had asked during her interview, the question she hadn't been able to answer. "You were not so much running from as running toward. I do not know that, given your path, I would have persevered."

"Yes you would," Mikal contradicted her. "You've survived worse. I saw it the first time I looked at you."

No! she thought, wanting to bolt again. *What you saw, what you said—*

"Oh, I know what I *said* . . ." Was he reading her thoughts? "But that was cover. Galina and I have a past. If she hasn't told you—and knowing Galina, she has, if indirectly—you've intuited that. I could hardly tell you what I really felt while she was standing there. I also assumed, being a Vulcan, that you were already wed or at least betrothed."

"I am neither," Saavik blurted before she could stop herself. Try as she might, she could not quantify what she was feeling right now, except that it *was* a feeling, and feelings were not Vulcan, therefore they must be from that *other* heritage, which was anathema and which—

Stop it! she told herself, realizing that in the split second she had been trapped in that thought loop, Mikal's expression had altered from the haunting of his past to something hopeful.

"It is complicated," she said, realizing this would only inspire more questions.

"I see," Mikal said, though clearly he didn't. "I just assumed the subspace messages were from—"

"An acquaintance . . . from my own past."

"A past that compels a Vulcan to travel with a knife in her boot? Tell me."

Reluctantly at first, she did.

Aboard *Chaffee,* things were not going well. The little ship had been able to outrun the main brunt of the ion storm, but it was still being jounced about by the stray ripple, and the crew was in little better shape. Galina Mironova gripped the arms of the command chair and watched an unwary crewman pick himself up from the deck as the ship surfed over another incoming wave.

"Report," she said evenly, hoping her voice would be enough to calm the handful of new recruits, who were green in more ways than one.

"Scanners and sensors still inoperative," came from the helm. "Shields holding at seventy-nine percent."

"Hold your course."

"Nothing but static, sir," comm volunteered before she even asked.

"Keep trying." Mironova hit the intraship toggle. "Engine room?"

"Engines at eighty-five percent," came her engineer's

voice on speakers. *"Compensating for fluctuations, but I'd like to know how long we're expected to—"*

"As long as it takes," Mironova said, cutting the connection. There was a subliminal shake of the head around the bridge. Engineers! "Transporter room, stand by. Let me know when it's clear enough to get a fix on those two on the surface." She closed that connection as well, took a breath, and said, "Nav, come about forty-three degrees and stop engines."

The navigator turned and gaped at her.

"You heard me. Riding over this thing isn't working. We're going to try sliding under it without rattling any more crockery."

As they made the shift from impulse to dead stop, Mironova looked hopefully toward comm, who shook her head.

"Nothing from the surface, sir. Still hailing."

"Captain?" Helm sounded distinctly alarmed. "I think you need to see this!"

As the forward screen cleared somewhat, they all looked.

"Oh, bloody hell!" Mironova managed between clenched teeth before the screen snowed over with static again.

The wind shook the shelter, and the flower lights showed Mikal's eyes filled with tears. For the first time since Saavik had known him, he had no words. Gently he took her face in his hands, leaned forward, and kissed her—chastely, he thought, not knowing that between her upslanted eyebrows was one of her species' erogenous zones—then released her, settling back into his corner of the shelter, as still and nonthreatening as he knew how to be.

Outside, the fairy lights were beginning to dim. In this world devoid of forest creatures, birds, or even insects, there were no other sounds but the wind and their own breathing, and the occasional crackle of static from Saavik's communicator, still open to the ship's frequency but giving no indication that it was being heard. Could they remain like this, studying each other across a space of only a meter or so, until the sun came up?

Mikal yawned. It brought them both to their senses.

"Colder than I thought it would be," he said, rubbing his arms briskly. "I'd imagine you feel it more than I do."

"I am well able to adapt . . ." she began, but he was busy opening two of the sleeping bags and joining them together as one.

"I'm sure you are," he said, settling himself in on one side and motioning for her to take the other, "but where's the logic in it?"

The wind died down at last, and the fairy lights went out altogether. Two lost children slept chastely in each other's arms, their breathing slow and synchronous, punctuated only by the silence of the tricorders placed now outside the shelter, set to recognize hostile plant life, and the static from Saavik's open communicator, still awaiting a signal that meant their ship had returned.

With the dawn, they were not alone.

Eight

Was it the sound or the touch that woke her? Thinking about it later, she realized it was neither, for while both occurred simultaneously, the sound was lost beneath the sound of Mikal's breathing, not a snore exactly but the deep rhythmic sound of someone at peace after a long day's labor and a long night of the soul. The touch was gentle, velvety, slightly cooler than the surrounding atmosphere, slightly moist, inquisitive. Not strictly the touch of an appendage or that of a snout, it was both and neither. It also seemed to breathe somehow, as if more than nerve endings were engaged in its exploratory process. Through all of this, it simultaneously asked a question in her mind.

Who—?

I am called Saavik, she replied before she had even opened her eyes, then added, *Saavik*—why did she hesitate?—*of Vulcan.*

Even as she thought it, she wondered, Was she? No longer Saavik of Hellguard, and not only because Hellguard no longer existed. Saavik of Romulus? Never! But even as Vulcan held her at arms' length, had she not done the same?

Pay attention! You've been asked a question by another telepath. This is no time for obfuscation!

And your companion? the mind at the other end of the touch asked. *He cannot speak?*

Saavik opened her eyes then to see a great wall of mucoid being looming over her, the very tip of its blind snout still caressing her face, ever so gently despite the size of the being it belonged to, precisely at the temple, one of the contact points of mind-meld. Coincidence, or had it somehow known? Slowly, carefully (*Do not alarm the being, though it is twice your size* . . . even as she thought it she could hear the laughter and realized it understood everything), she eased herself out of the sleeping bag and into a sitting position.

He does not speak as we do, she thought to it.

Orienting herself, she could see that there were several of them, four, to be precise, two smaller ones hanging back a bit, another of the larger ones touching Mikal's face in the same way. Then, as he continued to slumber unaware, one languid tattooed hand brushing vaguely at his face as if something tickled him, the being withdrew its touch as if disappointed and joined its companion in studying her.

All four beings were balanced on the lower third of their bodies, bending at the clitellum—the smooth, thickened portion of their otherwise ridged bodies— just as they'd appeared in the live feeds from their cities that the crew of *Chaffee* couldn't get enough of, forming a kind of S-curve or question mark nearly two meters tall, studying the two interlopers.

We mean you no harm, Saavik thought. *Our intent was to study your world without disturbing you. We did not know your kind ventured this far from your cities.*

Again there was that chuckle in her mind. *We surmised you meant us no harm even before we touched your mind. You could not know we come here whenever the universe aligns itself in this configuration.*

"If I understand you correctly," Saavik said aloud, seeing Mikal stir and hoping he would hear her voice before he saw the Deemanot and did . . . what? He was Mikal first and a scientist second, and while the latter would remain calm in order to study the phenomenon before him, the former might do something impulsive. "You visit this place at a certain time and season?"

We are the forerunners, the being said. *We come to assess, before the others . . .*

Before Saavik could ask what that meant, the caress was withdrawn, and with it the being's mind. All four visitors lowered themselves to the ground and, in a movement quite rapid for beings of their size, began to slither away. Their movement was all but silent, yet the sheer weight of the two larger ones caused a mild tremor that faded along the ground once they were out of sight.

Saavik scrambled to her feet, seeing that a low-lying mist had arisen during the night, obscuring the forest around them and swallowing up the visitors, though traces of the mucus that protected their otherwise vulnerable bodies formed trails in the soft moss. Her impulse was to follow them, but her tricorder indicated they had split off in four directions, moving so quickly that she might barely catch up with one of them at a run.

Suddenly they stopped registering on the tricorder

altogether. Only the mucous trails and the readings she had saved proved that they had been there at all. The mist, meanwhile, hid everything beyond the clearing where she stood.

"So I didn't dream it," came Mikal's voice behind her as he struggled out of the sleeping bag, rubbing his face briskly to wake himself up. "Do you realize what this means, Saavik? They were here!" His voice was as excited as a child's. "*They* approached *us*. That means we're free to reciprocate."

"It means," she said carefully, scanning for tunnels that might explain the Deemanots' arrival but finding none, "that we will report their appearance to Captain Mironova, who will consult with Starfleet Command—"

"—and turn a simple first contact into a bureaucratic horror show." He gestured it away, too excited about the encounter to concern himself just yet with what might happen next. "No, oh, no! We're not letting them spoil this for us. We—"

"Mikal—!"

For a moment she wondered if he intended to go after them, barefoot and befuddled—his sandals had somehow found their way under the sleeping bags, and he could locate only one—but the sharpness of her tone slapped some sense into him.

"I . . . I . . ." He stopped, clapped his hands to his brow in amazement, his eyes wide. "They were here. They spoke to you. What was it like?"

She described it to him as best she could, finding words inadequate to encompass what happened when two very different telepathic species interacted for the first time, even on as light a level as the Deemanot had communicated with her.

"They're telepaths, then? Of course, they'd have to be."

"It is logical. It explains how they were able to overcome such a simple body habitus in order to develop a complex culture."

"I envy you," he said, then quickly amended his words. "I mean, I envy any telepath. When I think of how much is often lost in translation between species who can communicate with only the spoken word . . ."

Indeed, she thought, mindful of the many words that had passed between them the night before, leading now to a kind of awkwardness neither wanted to address. Where before their relationship had been adversarial, as much an opposition of personalities as of research styles—Saavik saw now why Mironova was so eager to have them work together, point and counterpoint—it was now an indefinable dance of elliptical phrases punctuated by nervous silences.

Why did I tell you all of that last night? Mikal wondered, studying Saavik with renewed appreciation even as he finally located his missing sandal. Ordinarily a graceful man, flamboyant of gesture but always calculatedly so, he suddenly didn't know where to put himself. *Was I only trying to distract you, keep you from pulling the knife again? Or did I really mean to comfort you?*

I only wanted to comfort you! Saavik found that thought disturbing. She kept her back to Mikal as she focused with inordinate concentration, even for a

Vulcan, on her tricorder readings, trying to ascertain whether the Deemanot had tunneled here or traveled over ground, and from where? Something about them, possibly the slime, confused the tricorder, which would have to be recalibrated against . . . well, what, exactly, since they didn't have a Deemanot to compare against? *I have never voluntarily told anyone my story until now. Even Amanda had to draw it out of me, based on what Spock told her, over the course of years. What made me decide to trust you? Why you?*

Why you? Mikal was refolding the sleeping bags, fiddling with comm, though truth be told he half hoped the ship would never come back for them. *It's not as if I haven't bared my soul to women before, but the results have been universally disastrous. In fact, it's the quickest way to drive most of them away, and it's not as if I haven't used it for just that reason, but the last thing I want to do is drive you away . . .*

It is essential that we comport ourselves as professional colleagues and nothing more, Saavik told herself, not believing it for a minute, *but I am uncertain of the proper course of action now . . .*

I've never been at such a loss before, Mikal thought, wanting to reach out to her where she stood in the clearing, the mist dissipating now, only a few tendrils coiling about her ankles, rendering her more elfin than ever. He gestured helplessly, the words caught in his throat, grateful there was no one else here to see him behaving this way. *I'm not used to not knowing what to do . . .*

Their thoughts flew past each other; the silence

remained. When it became unbearable, Mikal cleared his throat.

"What was it they said to you again? 'We are the forerunners.' The forerunners for what?"

"Or whom?" Saavik turned toward him at last, though still unable to meet his eyes, grateful for the distraction from the distraction of what she was feeling. It was past time to get back to work. "I do not know. I am more concerned with how they got here. Their nearest metropolis is over one thousand kilometers away, and I find no evidence of tunneling."

"We can ask them when they return, or send these 'others' in their place," Mikal decided, thinking out loud. "And I intend to stay right here until they do."

"Captain Mironova may decide otherwise."

"Then there's no need to tell her just yet, is there?"

"Tell me what?" Mironova's voice issued crisply from Saavik's communicator, left on an open frequency all night. *"Anyway, belay that for now. We've finally got a fix on you. Stand by to beam up . . ."*

Tolek sat at his desk in the adjudicator's office, wondering how long it would be before his activities were detected. He had just enough skill to decode T'Saan's messages and return them on a carrier wave below standard frequencies, but so did most of Vulcan. Sooner or later, someone would wonder why he spent more time than even the most dedicated subaltern working at odd hours, particularly since his output was no better than anyone else's. Only the fact that no one would have reason to suspect him of any clandestine activity had protected him thus far. Not for the first time, he recognized how truly unsuitable he was for this sort of thing and wished there were some way out.

"*Status* ch'kariya?" T'Saan's first message asked. Translation: "Have you heard from Saavik?"

A *ch'kariya* was a small burrowing mammal. Some V'Shar functionary had thought it a suitable code name for someone silently searching Starfleet's files, though Tolek found it as ludicrous as much of the rest of this operation. His own assigned name was *aylak,* a flat, mud-colored reptile adept at camouflage. Also inapt, he thought, since it seemed to him he was acting in plain sight and vulnerable to being caught at any moment.

"No response," Tolek replied to T'Saan's query. "Migrated out of range."

Translation: "Subspace messages take too long; we're communicating with data squirts only, and there haven't been any for several days. She *is* doing fieldwork on a distant world, remember?"

T'Saan's comeback was almost immediate. "*Unacceptable. Communicate to* ch'kariya *that habitat is about to be . . . endangered.*"

What in the Elements was that supposed to mean? Tolek was sweating. Several strings of numerical code followed, giving him precise instructions for what to do next. Before he could even begin to decipher them, much less object to his new orders, T'Saan had not only severed the connection at her end but also rerouted her server, rendering her unreachable until such time as she chose to contact him again.

Helpless, furious, Tolek clenched his fists to keep

from pounding something; only the throbbing in his damaged hand made him stop. He hadn't thought it was possible to hate anyone more than the creature who'd damaged that hand, but in the case of the V'Shar, T'Saan in particular, and his own role in this charade, he might be willing to make an exception.

Even through the ion storm's interference, the crew had seen the unsettling phenomena occurring on the ground, apparently the result of tiny "rips in the fabric of space," as Captain Mironova would describe them in her log. Plants, trees, even rock formations had begun to vanish; some reappeared after a few moments but in different locales, others disappeared entirely, with new varieties appearing in their stead. All of this activity occurred in a circle around a central locus—the clearing where Saavik and Mikal had last been located. Nothing in the clearing, or for a radius of not quite three kilometers, had been disturbed.

"Until the storm cleared, we half wondered if those rips hadn't snatched one or both of you." Mironova wasn't even pretending to keep the concern out of her voice once the two of them were safely on the bridge. "Ensign Graana, bring them up to speed."

Graana had been filling in for Saavik at the science station. "A lot's been happening in your absence, Lieutenant. Some of the material being moved around started showing the same peculiar outputs that the long-range scans showed initially. The same readings as the portulaca did initially."

"Initially?" Mikal asked.

"Died in the lab," Mironova explained, "the best horticultural technology known to Starfleet notwith—"

An alarm went off somewhere.

"Captain!" helm interjected, sounding more than a little alarmed. "More turbulence at seventy-mark-four and two-oh-three-mark-seven."

"Dammit! Back us out of here," Mironova ordered, locking the restraints on the center seat. "Give us some distance until we figure out what this is!"

Chaffee reversed engines and retreated to a safe distance. Spectral analysis revealed that the Deema system was passing through what appeared to be small interspatial black holes too unstable to trace to a point of origin.

"Can we seal them off?" Mironova asked.

"Affirmative, sir," Saavik reported, having relieved Graana at the science station.

With every seat on the bridge taken, Mikal stood uselessly between comm and the science station, feeling left out of the conversation. "Galina, you might not want to—"

"Not now, Mikal! Do it, science officer!"

"Those rips are almost definitely the source of everything that's popping up on the surface!" Mikal watched helplessly, throwing up his hands in disgust. "They could lead anywhere!"

"Exactly right!" Mironova snapped. "A large enough one could grab hold of *us* and drag *us* anywhere. Not in the mood to take that chance just now, thank you."

"Rips contained and sealed off, Captain," Saavik reported after a few tense moments.

All she had done was follow orders. Where was this hypothetical leadership quality Spock insisted she possessed?

"For all you know, you've just shut us off from another quadrant, maybe another galaxy!" Mikal raged.

"Mikal, do shut up. For all we know, we arrived in the nick of time to keep those rifts from endangering the inhabitants."

"They could also be a normal, maybe even essential, part of their environment!" he shot back.

Mironova rotated her chair in his direction.

"And now that we've sealed them off," she said very calmly, enunciating each word precisely, "we have ample time to study them while we notify Starfleet Command and await further instructions. As for you, you can either stop flapping your arms and shouting and participate in that study, or get the hell off my bridge. But before you do either, you can tell me what you found downplanet that Saavik wanted to share with me and you didn't."

They followed Mironova into the ready room, and she heard them out.

"*They* found *us,* Galina," Mikal insisted. "Both Federation law and Starfleet regs state that that constitutes a valid reason to reciprocate. You know I'm right."

Mironova deferred to Saavik. "Science officer?"

"No doubt the Deemanot are discussing us even as we are discussing them," she said carefully. "They did not seem surprised by our presence. In fact, they seemed almost to have been expecting us."

"All the more reason—" Mikal began, but Saavik was not finished.

"There is no immediate danger to the Deemanot from either of the empires or any of the other . . . usual suspects, and we will not know without further study whether or not these rifts pose a danger. Therefore I see no harm in awaiting Starfleet's assessment while we continue the study we came here for."

Mikal threw up his hands in disgust, muttering, "Who's side are you on, anyway?"

Naturally she heard him. "The side of science, obviously."

Mironova had been enjoying the show. She'd already made her decision, anyway. "Your team still has one more biome to study. If we're all very lucky, Starfleet will have gotten back to us by the time you're done. Dismissed."

"No tunnels." Mikal slapped his tricorder shut a little more forcefully than necessary. "And no anomalies, either. Just sand and shale, cactus and creosote. Two of us can cover this biome all by ourselves. We don't even need the rest of the team."

"The better to prolong our study in the hope that either Starfleet or the Deemanot will intervene before we have completed it," Saavik suggested, more than a little irritably. There had been another communiqué from Tolek awaiting her the night before.

"Two more, in the same manner. What little I could glean from the documents available follows. Thank the

Elements you are far removed from whoever is doing this, but I am now more apprehensive than ever. If there is anything, anything you can do . . ."

Was there any remnant of the courageous boy who had defended her under far more dire circumstances in this desperate and illogical adult? What more did he expect her to do?

His message had ended abruptly and, more concerning, her attempt to reply had bounced back almost immediately, indicating that the problem was not one of distance—the squirt should have taken days to reach its intended recipients, as its predecessors had—but that the transmitter Tolek had sent from had been terminated.

It might signify nothing. Perhaps he had been traveling and used a one-time server. Or it might signify that the transmitter was not the only thing terminated.

She had stayed up most of the night perusing the attached documents—such personal information on Saya and Grelek as was available, medical reports indicating "cause of death unknown," even a smattering of local newsfeeds remarking on the deaths and, for the first time, mentioning that the two had not been born on Vulcan but "on a distant colony world destroyed by seismic phenomena."

That last part had given her pause. Had it taken five deaths for at least some acknowledgment that Vulcan was not all logic and truthfulness and respect for diversity, however achieved? Or had regional media simply noted some anomaly in the birth records and remarked on it without realizing its implications?

Whatever sleep she might have gotten for the rest of the night was disturbed by her own knowledge of those implications. In comparison, Mikal's petulance over not being allowed to chat up the Deemanot (*yet,* she reminded herself, growing more angry as she thought about it, *yet*; it was not as if he was being forbidden altogether) seemed most extraordinarily trivial.

In the meantime, there was work. Saavik set down her collecting kit and began to scrape away a thin layer of topsoil in search of the underlying strata.

But Mikal had more to say. "Nice of you to have my back up there."

Saavik sat back on her heels and suppressed a sigh. "Your back? I do not understand."

Mikal crouched beside her, his eyes intense. "It's one thing for us to have scientific differences. That's part of the process, and we can hammer those out on our own. But the minute Galina told you to seal off those rips you complied, without so much as—"

"It was my assessment at the time that—"

"So what we shared the night before meant nothing?"

" 'What we shared'?" Saavik echoed him, on her feet. "If you are suggesting that our acquaintance should in any way influence our scientific judgment—"

" 'Acquaintance'?" Mikal leaped to his feet as well. "Is that what you call it?"

They stood toe to toe, their faces inches from each other. The proximity and the violation of her personal space may have been what distracted her, or she most certainly would have felt the rumbling sooner. She whipped around and retrieved the tricorder from her kit.

"Oh, no you don't. You're not going to duck this and go all scientific on me now!" Mikal, oblivious to anything but his anger, misinterpreted her gesture. "We're going to have this out once and for all!"

"Mikal, this may not be the time . . ." Saavik started to say, but Mironova's voice cut across both of them.

"What are you two squabbling about now?"

There was an awkward silence. Still unaccustomed to the newer communicators, Mikal had left his open since they'd beamed down. Their conversation had apparently been broadcast on the bridge, quite possibly throughout the entire ship.

Beyond embarrassment at the best of times, Mikal was too preoccupied with what was happening around him at the moment to care who'd overheard what. Finally he managed to clear his throat and say, "Squabbling? Us? Not at all, *Chaffee*. Not at all."

This time, there had to be a hundred of them. Some had emerged from the soil in a several-meter-wide circle around the visitors, others were literally shaking the sand off their upper bodies at the two scientists' feet.

As a gesture of politeness, Saavik put the tricorder away. It had already recorded the presence of the newly arrived Deemanot and the maze of tunnels they had created to get here. As if their presence, towering above their visitors, their shimmering bodies showing subtle color variations that might denote thought or mood, were not fascinating enough, she made note of the fact that their nearest metropolis was more than five thousand kilometers distant. How had they been able to get here so quickly?

"Captain," Saavik said with remarkable calm, "I believe we no longer need to wait for Starfleet to answer at least one of our questions."

Nine

___

"Someday," Mironova said quietly, pulling a reluctant Mikal out of the center of the circle, leaving Saavik alone in the midst of the Deemanot, "someone will develop a universal translator sophisticated enough to read brainwaves. Until then, there's a reason why all Starfleet officers, even scientists, need to be diplomats."

She had beamed down alone and at a distance as soon as she understood what was going on, showing up on the scene with as little fanfare as possible, wisely intuiting that her mind and particularly Mikal's would only serve as a disturbance in any telepathic encounter, and removing him from harm's way.

Now the Deemanot began gathering closer around Saavik—slowly, unthreateningly, in a rocking, shuffling almost dance, the lower portion of their gleaming bodies making a sound against the dry soil like fabric rubbing together—until they were all touching. Some draped over each other, others intertwined, but even if it was only the tips of their tails touching, the proximity seemed necessary in order to pass thought from one to the next.

The one who had caressed Saavik's face in the shelter the day before—she was not certain how she was

able to distinguish it from the others, but she did—
gradually wound itself around her and eased her back
until it was completely supporting her weight, its body
essentially one extended muscle, undulating gently
("Like a massage chair?" Mikal would ask later, unable
to keep the envy out of his voice).

Saavik was only vaguely aware of Mikal and Mironova standing off at a distance, their minds far away, as
she gave her own over to the Deemanot mind, recalling
what she had learned—in theory, at least—about how
to explain herself to beings who could neither see nor
hear.

"As you gain experience, Saavik-*kam,* you will find that
life-forms that lack certain senses often have remarkably sophisticated enhanced or alternative senses
that compensate," Spock had said as they began their
instruction. "Taste, vibration, magnetism, electricity—
all are potential avenues of exploration. Intelligent life
cannot evolve to a level of sophistication in the absence
of sensory input. You may in fact find that it is you
whose senses are limited . . ."

Being Saavik, she had at first balked at mastering
more than the most rudimentary telesper skills that
were part of every Vulcan schoolchild's curriculum. She
had known too many forms of violation to welcome
the notion of allowing anyone else to have access to
her thoughts. As head of the household, it had fallen to
Sarek to attempt to reason with her.

"As Vulcans, we are innate telepaths, Saavik. Your

mind must be trained, lest you intrude unwittingly into that of another."

"What if I promise that I will not?"

Saavik no longer found the senior member of her adopted family as daunting as she once had, but his frequent absences on diplomatic missions made her seek his approval in subtle ways whenever he was around. When Sarek spoke, she listened. Nevertheless, she would not be Saavik if she did not raise objections, at least occasionally.

"Do you think it so simple a matter to block one untrained mind with another, my child?" the ambassador had said with not a little tenderness. What he could not show to his own flesh and blood, he could to her. It was not logical, but it was true. "It is not always possible to control one's circumstances. The touch of another is often inadvertent and can bring with it unwelcome thoughts if one is not prepared."

This earned him the characteristic jut of her chin. "Then I will not touch anyone."

It was then that Sarek reached to brush a wayward curl off her brow. "Even as you say this, you know it is not possible," he suggested.

The tips of her ears burned, but she tamped down her anger, and considered.

"Blocking out thoughts I will learn," she offered charily, somewhere between barter and compromise. "It is allowing thoughts to enter that I do not wish."

The slightest trace of a smile softened Sarek's eyes. "One does not always have the luxury of choosing."

Saavik was losing ground and she knew it. *Not fair!* she thought. *He is older, wiser, trained at this and . . .*

. . . and you are essentially making Sarek's argument for him!

Flummoxed, but still unwilling to give in, she tried one more ploy. "Maybe I don't need to learn the discipline. Maybe I'm not a telepath at all."

Because I am half Romulan, she thought but would not say, *and no one knows what skills the Romulans lost in the Sundering.*

Sarek did not need telepathy to see that this road led over a cliff. He would save further discussion for another time.

Nevertheless, though he spent considerable time explaining, bargaining, reasoning on several more occasions, the senior diplomat made no headway. Apparently in his recalcitrant foster daughter he had found at least one being in the universe more stubborn than a Tellarite. And his attempt to bring Amanda into the discussion was equally unsuccessful.

"Oh, no, you don't!" was her response to his request. "I have come by my own very small esper skills only after many years of practice. They are not innate to me, and I'm in no position to judge their rightness in another. Keep me out of this!"

Sarek sighed. He was needed for another round of talks between Eminiar VII and Vendikar and would be leaving in a few days. Even after nearly a decade, negotiations between these two contentious sibling planets could go on for months. The child—more a young woman now than a child—would have passed another birthday by the time he returned home, something he regretted enough in and of itself. He had hoped to win her over before then. But this particular negotiation would have to remain open-ended until his return, unless . . .

Fortunately, Spock was home on leave following *Enterprise*'s second five-year mission under James T. Kirk. Had Sarek not hoped that his son would one day follow in his footsteps? If negotiating with Saavik was not proper training for a diplomat, what was? Was it weakness to ask for his assistance?

"Oh, for heaven's sake, swallow your pride and ask him!" Amanda had said, seeing the struggle on his to-anyone-else-impassive face and nudging him toward the study where Spock was overseeing Saavik's schoolwork.

" 'Very small esper skills,' my wife?"

"Oh, I've always been able to read you."

Spock did not lecture; he did not try to persuade. He simply drew upon the range of his experiences and told Saavik about the Horta.

"Truly?" She had sat up straighter, her dark eyes wide. "A creature resembling living rock? It communicated with you?"

It had been a given since he'd left her with his parents that they would always stay in communication, no matter where his mission took him, and that even as she reported on her schoolwork and the thousand little events that made up her day, he would tell her of his travels and the beings he had encountered without her having to ask. This particular instance was enhanced by his presence in the room with her instead of on a screen. He savored the wonder on her face, which no attempt at Vulcan discipline could obscure.

"Indeed. It said 'No kill I.'"

He watched her arrive at the same questions that Kirk had arrived at at the time.

"But did it mean 'Do not kill me' or 'I will not kill you'?"

"We were uncertain at first," Spock said, holding fast to his own sense of wonder. How bright the child was, how full of promise! "But we *had* communicated on a common ground. The details could be clarified later. What mattered at that moment was that the killing stopped, on both sides."

Again he waited for her to think it through. Having chanced upon the conversation, perhaps not entirely by chance, Sarek observed unseen from the hall. There was pride and not a little envy in his demeanor. The best teacher hopes his student will surpass him. Spock's methods were not Sarek's. Nevertheless, his father was certain at that moment Spock would choose the path of diplomacy someday, if he had not already begun.

"But what if it was a trick?" Saavik asked. "What if it meant to fool you into touching it so it could kill you?"

"A chance I deemed worth taking at the time."

"And if you hadn't . . ." Saavik said cautiously.

"I might not be here to speak to you today. The Horta might have gone on killing, beginning with Captain Kirk and myself. She and her children would most likely have been destroyed as well."

"But instead, they became members of the Federation!" Saavik said brightly. One thing her childhood had not succeeded in destroying—if anything it had honed it all the more sharply—was her need for justice, and a happy ending.

"Indeed."

Sarek smiled faintly and went on his way.

"So a mind-meld can be a weapon . . . more powerful than a starship."

Spock kept his face under more careful control than ever. "Think of it rather as a Rosetta stone, and—"

"—and my next assignment is to look up this term and study its origin," Saavik finished for him, accustomed by now to the drill. With a great sigh, she yielded. "I will continue to study and practice mind-meld. But not because you or my foster father wish it."

"Of course not."

"Because *I* wish it!"

Now it was Spock's turn to allow himself the smallest suggestion of a smile. "As it always should be."

So it was that all these years later, covered with slime, cradled in the embrace of a three-meter-tall annelid and surrounded by a hundred of its peers, she offered herself as a Rosetta stone and wondered where to begin.

Given their need to commune by touch, she anticipated that the Deemanot would share a group mind, at least on some levels, and there was a suggestion of that. But as she entered the realm where there were no words, she realized that this was no collective. Even as she touched only one being, who touched the others, she could "hear" their individual voices.

Feel . . . sun is warmth, energizing. But sun can burn, endangering. Skin is breathing, sensing. Slime is comfort, mobility against friction, sharing with another. Soil is nutrient, shelter, safety, tunnel medium, separation. Touch is thought, sharing. Universe is those-not-like-us. Like you . . . who are Saavik.

Yes, I am Saavik. Do you have a name?

Several. Perhaps too deep in my mind for your primitive skills. You may call me Worm.

Mikal will be pleased . . .

Observing, Mikal and Mironova at first saw only a great stillness. Every one of the creatures, however busy they had been in shuffling about and intertwining in the beginning, stood motionless now, an extraordinary feat if one considered that, if they truly were highly evolved annelids, they had no lungs but breathed through their skin. Were they breathing? If they were, it was so subtle it was not visible. Outwardly, they were a single unmoving entity, with Saavik at their center.

"Jealous, Mikal?" Mironova couldn't resist tweaking him. It might go down in the scientific annals as his first contact, but he was not the one being contacted.

"A little," he admitted, arms folded over his chest in a pose that suggested he was making a mighty effort to control himself.

But what the captain saw on his face was not jealousy. It was an expression she remembered all too well.

• • •

"We're impossible," she'd said, raising herself on one elbow and tracing the tattoos on his chest with one finger. "You know that, don't you?"

He'd yawned and stretched, taking her hand and kissing the palm before he answered. "Of course. That's why we were drawn together. Neither of us can stand the thought of permanence, even if our careers allowed it. Still . . ." He'd sat up and taken both of her hands. "I adore you, Galina. You have to know that."

"What I know," she said, sitting up as well and pulling away, if gently, "is that you are wedded to hyperbole, hate to be alone, and are looking for a mum."

"Relationships are built on less than that," he said, denying none of it.

"True, but then the question becomes, What's in it for me? Aside from the occasional glorious shag. And don't mistake me, they are wonderful, but not wonderful enough to make me want to mother you, Mikal, much as the thought appeals. You'll have to do your growing up on someone else's watch."

That made him angry, as she'd known it would, and he'd scrambled out of bed. "Maybe if you'd occasionally find a man your own age—"

"Oh, cruel!" she'd vamped. Yes, this was going well.

"As if what you said wasn't!"

"Truth hurts."

"Yes. Yes, it does!"

They'd glared at each other for a long moment across the great expanse of the bed they'd just shared, two bits of flotsam on the solar wind, neither capable of permanence or of anchoring the other. Mironova broke the glare first, pursing her lips, sweeping the silver hair up off her brow.

"Right, then." She'd made a shooing motion. "Off you go. I'm due on the bridge in an hour, anyway."

It took him only a moment to slip his rainbow robe over his head and find his sandals where he'd kicked them under the bed in his eagerness the night before. He stopped just short of where the cabin door would have sensed his presence and opened automatically, looking back for one last moment.

"But I still adore you."

Mironova had twinkled at him, her smile like a girl's. "Of course you do, darling. No hard feelings?"

Yes, Galina Mironova thought, watching Mikal watching Saavik. *You do adore women, Mikal, one at a time or as a species. Will this one be enough for you?*

Deep in her meld with Worm, Saavik nevertheless felt something tickling at the edges of her consciousness, something that took the shape of the two humanoids watching and waiting for the outcome of the meld. Not for the first time wishing she had studied the disciplines of the mind more thoroughly, she tried to concentrate, only to discover that it was Worm's curiosity about them that had brought them into the conversation.

Mikal is the null one we touched this morning? s/he asked.

Yes.

The small one does not answer, either. Are they all null except you?

It is theorized, Saavik explained, *that all sentient creatures have telepathy, but only some have learned to use it.*

We know this, Worm replied. *Like many of the others, they do emit a certain kind of . . . static . . . but believe themselves to be null or nearly so.*

Others?

Mikal felt as if he might burst out of his skin. Bad enough Mironova could read his mind better than a telepath, because yes, he was jealous—no, envious; there was a difference. But more than that, watching Saavik, so absorbed, and so beautiful in her absorption that he couldn't take his eyes off her, he wanted to rush to her and wrap himself around her the way the Deemanot were and hold her to him forever.

Look at you! he thought, his thoughts so painful they almost squeaked. *Whatever gods you or I or anyone believes in, look at you! I am so proud of you, so taken by you, I want to . . . I don't even know what I want, except I wish this moment would last forever, even as I can't wait for it to end!*

Again Worm seemed to be listening.

He is not entirely null, the Deemanot reported, one tendril of mind studying Mikal. *One does have to burrow beneath the static, though, and he has much to learn. But for now, tell us about this . . . Horta?*

Saavik realized she had lost concentration, allowing Worm to access that long-ago conversation with Spock.

Clearly, Worm meant no harm, perhaps hadn't realized this was a private memory, and so she let the image flash from her mind to Worm's.

Yes, we know this! Worm thought, hir glee unmistakable. *We have seen its like!*

The link broke abruptly, as did Worm's embrace. Released from the coils that had supported her, Saavik staggered to her feet, bewildered. Had she understood correctly? The Deemanot receded from her, coiling and uncoiling about each other, communing with what seemed a sense of urgency. Carefully stepping over clitella and tails, Saavik made her way toward her companions. Mikal caught her as she stumbled, holding her close in spite of the slime on her uniform.

"Are you all right?"

She rested her head against his shoulder for a moment until her mind cleared and she remembered her dignity, pulling away and gathering herself.

"Report, Lieutenant," Mironova said sharply, focusing her. "What did they say to you?"

"The Horta . . ." Saavik managed. "They say they have seen them, or similar beings. They find us familiar as well . . . and there have been many others."

"It's true they didn't seem terribly surprised to see us the first time," Mikal said, unable to take his eyes off Saavik, who almost seemed to glow. For their part, the Deemanot were still communing with each other, giving off a kind of subaural vibration, or at least that was what it sounded like to Mikal's overlarge ears. "Obviously they've had visitors before."

Mironova shook her head. "We can't be sure of

that. It might be some glitch in our understanding. Saavik . . ."

"Captain, one does not 'misunderstand' in mind-meld. Certain nuances might need clarification, but it is not like learning a spoken language."

Even before she finished her thought, the Deemanot began to unravel from their coil, and Worm came closer, hir three-meter length lowered to half height as s/he moved so as to appear as unthreatening as possible.

"Mikal . . ." Mironova cautioned.

"I'll be good, promise," he replied, finishing her thought.

Slowly, carefully, Worm began to coil about all three of them—first Saavik, whom s/he knew would not feel threatened, then Mironova, and finally Mikal. When s/he had them all in hir embrace, there was a chuckle in hir tone. *Let us show you! Besides, we need to get out of the sun . . .*

The concern about the sun was genuine. Deemanot were no more protected from direct sunlight than was a garden-variety earthworm, and their architecture reflected that, replete with tunnels and arches and over-hangs wherever it rose aboveground. Up close, it was even more fascinating than the holos had suggested.

The central structure Worm led them to could best be described as a museum, an example of Deemanot construction at its finest. The outer walls were as smooth as the finest adobe, carefully encrusted in places with glittering semiprecious gems in swirling geometric patterns reminiscent of Celtic knotwork that suggested the intercoiled shapes of the Deemanot themselves.

"These designs must be visible from every point in the city," Mironova marveled, examining a particularly exquisite mural of marcasite, jade, and turquoise splashed across a façade that loomed easily twenty stories above them. "But why go to all that trouble, if they're blind?"

"To impress offworld visitors?" Mikal suggested. "Also, each variety of stone has a subtly different texture, at least to our calloused fingers. Their tactile sense is obviously much different from ours."

"Which would provide an aesthetic experience we can only imagine," Saavik reported, as always with her gaze more concentrated on the tricorder than the artifact she was examining, until Mikal put his hand over the screen. She scowled at him but closed the tricorder for the moment. "Each variety of stone gives off a different magnetic signature on frequencies that Deemanot physiology can read. While they cannot 'see' as we do, they in fact see in ways we cannot."

As they followed Worm into the interior, along a floor of packed earth worn into a smooth and slightly grooved texture by the slithering passage of countless Deemanot before them, they noted the incredible hardness and sheen of the arched walls rising well above their heads.

"It feels as hard as marble," Mironova said. "It's even cool to the touch."

Saavik shot Mikal a warning glance that suggested she might break his fingers if he prevented her from reopening the tricorder. "And yet it is the same ingested and egested soil that comprises every structure in the city," she reported. "Indications are that the Deemanot secrete and mix different enzymes into different types of soil for different purposes."

However strong their sense of wonder, what they saw in the "museum's" main chamber reduced even the ordinarily garrulous Mikal to silence.

There was barely room to move among the artifacts showcased here, not in any order a humanoid might choose, but following sinuous pathways between displays designed primarily for their tactility, thus lending a rather jumbled, vaguely ordered disorder to the collection, or so it might seem to those who relied primarily upon sight and hearing to study the world around them.

Where someone accustomed to museums constructed by bipeds might expect high, if not vaulted ceilings, looking up one saw spirals leading up to ledges at different levels, each containing still more artifacts arranged in an order that no doubt made sense to Deemanot science and aesthetics but to their three visitors seemed bewildering at first glance.

"For one thing, we'd need climbing gear to reach them," Mikal stage-whispered. "No staircases," he explained off Mironova's glare.

"I know!" she whispered back. "Though you might keep your voice down!"

"But they can't hear—" Mikal started to say, looking to Saavik for affirmation. "Well, they can't. So we aren't being rude if—"

"It is possible they are reading our thoughts even without touching us," Saavik said, which gave him something else to think about. Then something on a ledge just above their heads caught her eye.

"It's a history," Mikal said, once their eyes had grown accustomed to the near darkness, his voice echoing down dim passageways twisting off into mystery. Only Worm had accompanied them into the museum; the others had simply melted away into the general populace moving about the city streets, slipping in and out of doorways, tunnels, spirals moving up or down or sideways. Now their host waited patiently while hir guests studied the images on the walls.

They'd climbed to the ledge and found themselves in a fair-sized kind of rotunda not visible from the ground floor where they'd entered. On the perfectly circular walls (Saavik had of course determined this) was a mural depicting a variety of life-forms from other worlds. Plants, animals, things that might be both or neither, some of them familiar ("Is that a Denebian slime devil?" Mironova wanted to know. "There's your Horta," Mikal pointed out, "though whether they've actually met one, or just seen it in some other visitor's mind . . ."), some not, bipedal humanoids from species no one in the landing party recognized to beings more unusual than the Deemanot themselves.

"Egypt, Babylonia, the Fabrini Book of the People,

the Royal Museum of Epsilon Hydra VII, the lost library of Sarpeidon," Mikal recited. "Every civilization that's been able to draw has something similar, but how—?"

"Unknown," was all Saavik could say, running her fingers—with Worm's encouragement—over one curve of the wall. "The images are partly carved, partly colored in with pigments of an indeterminate composition."

A portion of the wall that had heretofore been unadorned suddenly began to glow, and three holo-images seemed to etch themselves. First was a small, silver-haired female humanoid in a red Starfleet uniform. Flanking her, a taller, dark-haired female and a bald and tattooed male in practical coveralls made themselves evident.

Both the mechanism that created them and the images themselves seemed uncanny. They were almost photographic, yet with artistic flourishes as well. Saavik's eyes, for example, seemed even larger than they were in life, reflecting whole worlds within them. Mironova's cap of silver hair seemed spun of starlight, and Mikal's tattoos were universes of color and energy. Each one's personality was there somehow as well, impossible to describe—a texture, a flavor, a sound.

As they watched in silence, the images impressed themselves into a previously empty curve of the wall, becoming permanent even as the glow faded and the rotunda returned to its natural ambient light, which seemed to come from the material that formed the wall itself, since there was no other light source.

Worm, who while the images were forming had not moved from hir upright, S-shaped posture, now began to sway slightly, as if in time to some inner music. With a slight forward movement, hir "head" rested lightly on Saavik's shoulder.

Does it please you?

"It is . . . extraordinary," Saavik replied, aloud for the benefit of her companions, sensing somehow that Worm was the artist who had captured these images from her mind and imprinted them on the wall. "How—?"

In time, in time. Come, there is more . . .

There were other, lower chambers leading out of the rotunda, which had to be crawled to on hands and knees, if one were burdened with such appurtenances. The Deemanot propelled themselves by way of small attenuated setae on their undersides about a third of the way along their bodies from the mouth or head. When they stood upright, these small palpating hairs almost gave the appearance of chin whiskers, but their ability to propel the beings through any medium was remarkable, and in part explained how they could tunnel from place to place so quickly. Their visitors were considerably less agile.

"Anything for science!" Mikal grumbled, bumping his head, not for the first time, on the low clearance, convinced Mironova was being deliberately perverse in making them crawl instead of beaming them into the inner chambers.

"Come now, Mikal!" she said over her shoulder,

scurrying along at a fairly quick pace ahead of him, a chuckle in her voice, obviously enjoying his discomfort. "You've got your wish. First contact should include immersing yourself in the Deemanot world as they do."

"Indeed," Saavik added behind him, "if I am not mistaken, not all outworlders are permitted into the lower chambers. It is an extraordinary honor."

Surrounded, outnumbered, and needing all of his energy to keep crawling, Mikal conceded the point.

They were led by one of the smaller Deemanot, whom Worm introduced as Scolex (*a nickname*, s/he informed Saavik, who was beginning to think their true names had no analog in spoken language), who had suddenly appeared as if summoned (and most likely was, on a telepathic frequency even Saavik could not sense) from a newly dug tunnel in the side of one wall, and slithered merrily along in the forefront, with Worm bringing up the rear behind Saavik.

"No slime," Mikal was muttering, but before either of the women could ask him what he meant, the tunnel, which through several twists and turns and not for the claustrophobic, had been leading inexorably down, suddenly opened out into one of the innermost chambers.

"Oh, my!" Mironova said, almost in awe, taking the liberty of leaning on Scolex's proffered head to pull herself to her feet, flexing the kinks out of her lower back and allowing herself to drink in their surroundings. For some moments, as they once again waited for their eyes to adapt to the dim light, Saavik's tricorder was the only sound.

"You were right, Saavik," Mikal said at last. "The

rotunda is meant to be a display piece for trusted out-world visitors, but this . . . place is designed for the Deemanot themselves. We're seeing only a fraction of what's really here. I'm guessing it would take years to decipher all of this and interpret it from a humanoid perspective."

"I concur."

"Then look, will you?" he insisted. "Look with your eyes and your heart and put the damned tricorder away!"

For once she did not argue, because for once she had to acknowledge that his was the better way.

Everywhere around them were . . . *experiences* . . . some visual, most tactile, many interactive in that, when they were touched, they moved or made a sound or suggested that they were emitting data designed for senses humanoids didn't possess. Warmth, cold, changing textures, subliminal or hyperaudible movements told stories the visitors could only guess at.

The visuals alone were breathtakingly complex—snarls and tangles and Celtic knots, some even reminiscent of Mikal's tattoos, which Scolex, once hir mission to lead them here was completed, had taken to tracing with hir mouth and the lightest of touches, curious and intrigued. No longer questioning how a blind Deemanot could "see," Mikal stood very still and allowed the little one to explore.

"At a guess, s/he's sensing a difference in the skin texture where the pigment was added," he suggested, a slow smile lighting up his entire face. "Or using some extrasensory ability we don't even have a name for."

The two seemed quite taken with each other ("I swear the little one is purring," Mironova whispered mischievously), and there was a contentedness on Mikal's face, a decorousness in his posture and his movements that neither Saavik nor even Mironova had ever seen before.

Leaving him to his newfound friend, the two women continued their examination of the many rooms within rooms that constituted the Deemanot's annals of their evolution and their history.

"Captain," Saavik whispered, not even trying to contain the wonder in her voice, "I believe the entire history of the Deemanot is contained in these artifacts. It might take years to translate and study it."

"I concur entirely, Lieutenant," Mironova replied, her voice also soft. "Can you convey to our hosts that we wish to initiate such an exchange of information?"

"I have already done so, in our initial meld. Worm tells me it would please them to add us to their 'interconnectedness with the universe,' as s/he describes it. But first they require us to reopen the spatial rifts. Prior to our arrival, these were their point of contact with sources beyond their own system. Everything displayed in the rotunda at one time passed through those rifts or others like them. It is possible the Deemanot themselves did not originate on this world."

"That may very well be, Saavik. But not everything that passes through those rifts is safe. That vine, for example . . ."

At the mention of the vine, Worm seemed to stand up straighter, as if listening, Mironova noticed.

"Can s/he read my thoughts without touching me?"

"For a time," Saavik explained. "Communing with me has left signatures—resonances, if you will—that will fade eventually."

Worm began to sway again, and Saavik seemed to be listening.

"Worm wishes to apologize for the vine. S/he wishes to tell you that . . ." listening ". . . her people accepted it 'on consignment,' found it 'not as advertised,' and 'returned to sender.' I am not certain I understand the meaning, but—"

Mironova laughed. "I do. Humor, Saavik. I'll explain later." She looked directly at Worm then, confident her thoughts would be conveyed, even if her words could not be heard. "You have my word I will reopen the rifts if and only if our instruments determine that they pose no danger to your world. Convey that to hir, will you, Saavik?"

This time Saavik needed only to lay one hand on Worm's head. Worm reciprocated by touching hir mouth lightly to one of Saavik's ears, leaving a slight slime trail in her hair. The movement attracted Mikal's attention and, giving Scolex an affectionate pat, he once again drew closer, mesmerized.

After a long moment, Saavik broke the link.

"As we surmised, the Deemanot's prior visitors have come through the rifts. The concept of space travel in a vessel is unfamiliar to them, as is the ability to take scientific readings in space. Worm will discuss this with hir people, but we are permitted to study the rifts in the meantime. Also . . ."

Again she communed with Worm for a brief moment, to make certain she had understood. Scolex scurried past Mikal and joined them.

". . . Scolex wishes to invite us to hir wedding."

The comm unit in Tolek's spartan apartment beeped unanswered. Waiting for him, unopened, were the last three data bundles Saavik had sent from *Chaffee*. He had not bothered opening them once T'Saan had given him new orders and he had sent his final subspace message to *Chaffee*. Friendless now that Lerius was dead, he had taken leave of his employer several weeks prior, so his absence had gone unnoticed by anyone.

The ubiquitous desert dust of Vulcan settled over the furnishings, and a species of tiny *a'lazb*, near-transparent glass spiders, industriously wove their almost-invisible webs in the corners of the ceiling. Tolek had deactivated the cleaning servitor before his departure. If he never returned, he wanted what little forensic evidence there was to remain in an effort to explain why.

Ten

_____

Captain's Personal Log. Having gathered more data than we could possibly have hoped, our mission is essentially complete. Command has ordered us home pending its decision on what, if anything, is to be done about the interspatial rifts we have discovered in the Deema system. If it were up to me, Chaffee would remain in orbit to conduct further studies while the brass muttered and consulted, which is probably why these things are never left to me. Based on experience, I'm guessing the drama will play out as follows:

Act I: Enter starship, heavily armed and bound for the Deema system, on the assumption that even though these rifts appear to be natural phenomena that have to date neither swallowed the planet nor proved to be the conduit for an invasion from another galaxy, "precautions must be taken."

Act II: Exit Chaffee, reassigned to cataloging algae on some uninhabited waterworld, with advice to forget about Deema III.

Act III: Enter diplomats, complicating.

But I could be mistaken. Sometimes I am. Meanwhile, time to polish my boots. I've a wedding to attend.

• • •

The guests sheltered from the setting sun beneath translucent canopies of some delicate substance that fluttered slightly like sail canvas in the breeze as it stretched from one rock crag to another to another around the natural semicircular basin whose worn stone floor suggested it had been used for these rituals for a very long time.

"Another form of slime, I'll bet!" Mikal whispered, surreptitiously snipping a sample to study later.

Mironova had ordered them to leave their tricorders aboard, though the wedding party had permitted them to record the ceremony from the ship; now she elbowed Mikal in the ribs to silence him.

The focal point of the semicircle was a waterfall, a twisting cataract that was mostly mist by the time it reached the lower level where the betrothed couple waited to begin their joining, in the presence of their respective clans and honored guests.

Scolex and hir mate (*Lumbricina,* Worm had told Saavik in extending the invitation, *though we call hir Cina for short*) stood veiled in the mist from the waterfall in the characteristic Deemanot S-shaped "upright" posture, facing each other—if it could be described in such anthropomorphic terms; mouth to mouth, in any event, close but not quite touching. They seemed to be glowing and, in fact, they were. As the guests watched, their clitella changed color, from an everyday reddish-pink to bright orange. When the transformation was complete, they touched, beginning at the head, gradually intertwining in a slow dance that seemed to resonate through the entire assemblage, for a gentle ripple moved through the gathered Deemanot, even to those separated by rock ledges, all the way up to the heights where the cataract began its tumble from the river that fed it to the pool below.

The three offworld guests, on a ledge of their own in a place of honor where the curve of the basin began and the mist from the waterfall only occasionally reached them, felt something like a mild electric charge pass through them, enough to raise the small hairs on the backs of the women's necks and give the bald-pated Mikal gooseflesh, and cause them to glance at each other as if to say, *Did you feel that, too?*

As the bridal couple began to untwine and lower themselves to the floor of the grotto, Mikal took Saavik's hand, and she did not pull away.

Slowly, sinuously, the bridal couple slithered over each other until they were lying head to tail, joined at the clitella. They then grew very still.

They remained that way throughout the night, and throughout the night the assembled Deemanot continued emitting their subliminal electrical "chant," from which Saavik could detect certain concepts, most directed at the conjoined couple—wishes for health, fertility, longevity, and joy—but some conveying messages to their outworld visitors as well.

The visitors' comfort had been seen to in all regards. Not only had they been given their own ledge, sheltered beneath a canopy, but the ledge had been modified by Deemanot construction (still unhardened in spots when they'd arrived, it was so new) to provide three couchlike forms where the guests could sit or even lie comfortably, should the night prove overlong. The provision of fresh drinking water and some of the native fruit showed a sensitivity to the fact that these creatures might need sustenance other than a mouthful of soil.

The chanting seemed to have a soporific effect on Mironova. Once it became clear that the wedded couple would not move until sunrise, she had barely hidden a yawn behind her hand, curled up like a cat, and fallen into a light doze.

"Deceptive," Mikal whispered, observing her with something out of their former affection. "Sound a Red Alert and she'll be on her feet with her phaser drawn in a nanosecond."

Saavik stopped herself from pointing out that they had left their phasers on the ship along with the tricorders. The chanting was having a strange effect on her as well. For one thing, she did not mind that Mikal was still holding her hand. For another, she was remembering the *fal-tor-pan* . . .

"He is not himself, but he lives," she had told Admiral Kirk, not realizing at the time how much was contained in that simple yet accurate statement.

Her only thought, when she and David found the bewildered child in the snow on Genesis, was to keep him warm, somehow get him to safety even after *Grissom* was destroyed. Watching him age in conjunction with the dangerously unstable planet, almost certain even before their capture by the Klingons that they would all die there, she had nevertheless sought to comfort this stranger who was Spock but not Spock in every way that she knew how. Even grown to adulthood, his understanding of what was happening around him was primitive, yet his trust in her was absolute. He followed her with his eyes wherever she went, a look of puzzlement on his face. If she thought too long about the contrast between him and the Spock who had been the most important person in her life, she would go mad.

So she had blocked all other thought from her mind except the need to stay alive, to keep Spock alive. The sound of Kirk's voice on the Klingon communicator had all but shattered her control. There was no logical reason for him to be here. How? Why?

Even when they were safe at last on the pirated Klingon vessel en route to Vulcan and Doctor McCoy took her aside and explained it all to her, she could not believe it was happening.

"You're in shock, young lady," a haggard-looking McCoy said, two fingers on the pulse at her wrist. The Klingon ship had nothing resembling a sickbay, and he hadn't had any of his instruments with him when he'd been detained on Earth. "No need to say anything," he'd headed her off before she could. "I don't need to know every gory detail of what went on down there to put the pieces together with what's in here."

He'd tapped his temple then, and she'd given him a puzzled look.

"Of course. You have no idea about the *katra*. How could you? We've got some time before we get to Vulcan. Let me explain what's going on, at least as much of it as I understand myself . . ."

How could she, indeed? she'd thought, castigating herself in retrospect. *By paying closer attention, by continuing your studies in the telesper skills, that's how! Had you known, you might have prevented all of this! You might have accompanied Admiral Kirk to the engine room, known that McCoy had been entrusted with Spock's* katra, *and—*

And what? Instructed the admiral to bring McCoy to Vulcan, where Spock's *katra* would have been enshrined in the Hall of Ancient Thought? Would that have been preferable to what happened instead?

"My logic is uncertain where my son is concerned," Sarek had told the high priestess T'Lar before the *fal-tor-pan* began. Saavik's logic had started to fray before they even arrived at Mount Seleya.

Once there, Saavik had never felt more of an outworlder. At first she was angry. Angry with herself for not knowing that a mind could be re-fused into a living body, angry with whoever it was who should have told her. How could the Vulcan Masters keep something so important a secret? After McCoy explained where they were going and why, inasmuch as he understood it, she had rushed out of the improvised sickbay, seething with anger, hoping there was some duty she could fulfill on the bridge of the Klingon ship. Admiral Kirk, his own nerves frayed from the battle with Kruge, had spun the center seat around sharply at the sound of the opening door.

Seeing the anguish in his eyes, the dirt and bruises on his face, Saavik had hesitated, almost turned and run back the way she had come.

"Saavik?" Kirk said, as if uncertain what to say to her. "What is it?"

"I . . . I thought I might be of use . . . on the bridge, Admiral," she said, squaring her shoulders, damping down her distress with as much dignity as she could muster. Her glance quickly took in everyone there: Sulu and Chekov at helm and navigation, Uhura at comm. There was what appeared to be a weapons station where there ought to have been a science station. Clearly there was no place for her. "I see I was mistaken, sir."

"You should get some rest," Kirk said warmly.

So should you! Saavik thought, managing, just barely, not to say it aloud. She accepted his directive as an order. "Aye, sir."

She couldn't return to sickbay; McCoy would mother her to death. She was not about to commandeer some Klingon officer's private quarters, if such there were; she'd heard all but the commander slept in barracks, regardless of rank. The engine room was Scotty's territory, even on a borrowed ship, and he would fuss over her in his way worse than McCoy. She roamed the corridors until she found what appeared to be ship's stores, secreted herself in the darkest corner behind crates of squirming *gagh,* and found she could no longer hold back the tears. They were hot tears, tears of anger, and of shame.

She could barely bring herself to think of what she had done on Genesis, yet how could she have done otherwise? The sight of the trembling, bewildered manchild huddled in pain, not understanding what was happening to him, had moved her to act—beyond logic, out of some primal instinct that had kept his species and hers alive for perhaps a hundred millennia, adapted to their desert environment by needing to mate only once every seven years, but making that need inexorable.

If she had not done what she did, he would have died. Why, then, when it was over, did she feel shame?

She had mastered all of these emotions, she thought—or if not, she was too exhausted to care—by the time the ship touched down on the floor of the valley below the long, narrow path leading up to the place of the *fal-tor-pan*. If she had expected the sight of the dozens of torchbearers, of the dreamlike wraiths of priestesses in their filmy white robes to evoke some ancient species memory, some sense that this was her homeworld, the place where she belonged, she was disappointed. She had no more idea what was transpiring than her human crewmates did.

As the rite began, and Sarek retreated from the gathering place, having made his confession of inadequacy to T'Lar, Saavik saw his eyes pass over the crew of the late *Enterprise* and, in barely masked surprise, fix on her. In her peripheral vision she could see the Lady Amanda, standing apart, her outward calm a careful mask, Saavik knew, for the fear churning inside her.

She had quickly lowered her head and looked away, as if deep in meditation. In fact, she did feel something urging her to enter the landscape within, some conjoining of the minds of the gathered priests and priestesses, focused like a lens upon the red-robed T'Lar, strengthening her powers to do what must be done if Spock and McCoy were to be restored.

At first she hesitated to join her mind with theirs. Would the fact that she was not fully Vulcan impede them somehow? *Neither is Spock,* she reminded herself, *and McCoy is nothing Vulcan!* At first she only feigned meditation so that Sarek would not approach her, not so much as motion to her with the uptick of an eyebrow to say, *Come, child, and be with your family!*

She could not. Not now, perhaps not ever, lest he ask what had transpired on Genesis.

As if he would! she castigated herself. *Have the events of the past two days so rattled your brain that you have lost all reason? Control, control, now as much as on Genesis, now more than on Genesis, lest you disrupt the rite with your chaotic thoughts . . .*

She found herself standing by default with the rest of the crew, if only because she had walked with them up the long path and there did not seem to be anywhere else for her to stand. Admiral Kirk liked to talk about Starfleet as a family, and such it might be for some. But seeing Scotty at a loss and glancing to her for instruction—as if to say, *You're one of these people. Tell me what's the proper protocol here!*—visited her with the thought that she was as much a stranger to them as to "her own kind."

It was with great effort that she had gathered all of these thoughts as they whirled about her, tamping them down with the last shred of control remaining to her. Perhaps Spock was not the only one whose mind needed restoring.

But whether it was the tatters of her own control or the power of the myriad minds surrounding her, she at last found the place where she could meditate, bring her mind into focus with the others, and bowed her head in earnest as the lightning flashed and the two who had been conjoined were returned each to their rightful place—

—and the two beneath the waterfall began to separate from each other as the Deemanot marriage rite concluded.

The wind had changed direction, sending a spray of mist from the cataract toward the guests on their ledge, shaking Saavik out of whatever dream or reverie had taken hold of her. She cleared her thoughts and looked about her.

The wedded couple were separating from each other, and a satisfied almost murmur reverberated through the minds of the gathered guests; even the offworlders experienced it. The ceremony appeared to be coming to an end.

Mironova roused herself from her doze, yawning and stretching and bounding lightly to her feet, straightening her uniform tunic. Mikal had somehow ended up sharing Saavik's couch, and not for the first time she had to extricate herself from his embrace and try to find her dignity. When she dared look at him, he was grinning at her.

A slithering on the rock face below them turned out to be Worm, who slid hir full length upright onto the ledge and greeted Saavik with a light touch above one ear as before.

The rite was successful, s/he explained. *Both are with child.*

"Lovely!" Mironova said, beaming as Saavik translated.

With Worm escorting them, they joined the others on what passed for a receiving line.

"Thanks ever so much to all of you," Mironova said, embracing Scolex and Cina without waiting for the translation, "and blessings on all your children!"

Captain's Personal Log, Supplemental. Brilliant idea, if I may say so, getting the Deemanot's permission to record the wedding ceremony from the ship while it was taking place. Not only will it serve as an excellent proof of concept for the argument that this is a species with whom diplomatic overtures ought to be made, but giving the rest of the crew the opportunity to "attend" the wedding, so to speak, has assuaged some of their feelings of not having been invited. There are, of course, always exceptions . . .

"It's like nothing new or interesting will ever happen again!" Ensign Cheung moaned. "I'm bored! I can't stand it. I wish we were back on Earth already!"

A bit of a whiner at the best of times, Cheung was less than happy with the prospect of spending most of the return trip to Earth cataloging every bit of data the landing party had collected in the Deemanot museum. She'd been weeping openly during the wedding ("Blubbering," Palousek had categorized it, explaining to a puzzled Saavik that it actually meant Cheung was happy), watching the holos again and again, murmuring "Oh, how sweet!" every time and bursting into tears again. Even Jaoui and Graana had rolled their eyes and avoided her. But it was Saavik, uncharacteristically, who'd snapped at her.

"If you are suffering from depression, Ensign, I'd suggest you report to sickbay. Otherwise, I will thank you to spare me and your crewmates further caterwauling!"

Cheung blushed but wisely kept her mouth shut. Ta'oob and Jaoui, who were also in the lab that evening, tiptoed around their superior officer for the rest of their shift. But word quickly spread throughout the small ship that Lieutenant Saavik was in a . . . *mood*.

It was not *Pon farr.* Of that much she was certain.

("It is called Pon farr . . . Pon farr." *There had been no recognition in the boy's face—not of the words, much less of their meaning. She at the time had felt nothing more than the need to help him.)*

As a scientist, she was familiar with the symptoms, even though she had never experienced them. She would know it when it came upon her, and it was not now. Few outworlders knew that the initial stages were actually quite pleasant, resulting in a heightening of all the senses and an augmentation of the innate Vulcan appreciation of all the universe had to offer. This was necessary for the species to survive and procreate. Only unanswered did *Pon farr* become a fearful thing.

Engrossed in supervising the cataloging of the

hundreds of specimens and thousands of tricorder readings they had gathered from the planet, she did not at first notice the subtle changes in sensory input—her normally acute hearing became even more acute, sight and smell and touch, especially touch, became ever more sensitized. But when she found herself distracted, unable to concentrate, she became aware of the rest.

What disturbed her most was the *anger*. Every little thing—Cheung's whining, a ruined tray of slime specimens that Esparza, mooning over Graana now that it was clear he had no chance with Saavik, had dropped, spattering it on his boots in a fit of clumsiness—things that would ordinarily have merited a raised eyebrow and perhaps a mild scolding ("Were those the only specimens of that particular class of slime, Ensign?" "No, sir. There's plenty of slime from the tunnels, sir. I just—" "As you were, Ensign. Just try to be more careful.") suddenly set her teeth on edge and made her want to smash things, perhaps even hurt someone. She had managed to avoid such thoughts since an unfortunate hair-pulling match in art class the first year she came to Vulcan, and a classmate, an intolerable snob named T'Amar, had characterized her first attempt at clay sculpture as "primitive."

What was she so angry about?

Admittedly, she was frustrated. Tolek's complete silence was . . . unsettling, as if after all but begging for her help for all these weeks he had slipped over some sort of personal event horizon and disappeared. Logically, it might mean nothing more than that he was busy gathering more data at his end. Why, then, did she have this feeling of foreboding? In any event, they would be in Earth orbit within six days, their mission truncated by Command's order that they return to report on their findings in the Deema system, and she would no longer need to rely on long-range communication in order to reach him.

And, once on Earth, she could expect Sarek to summon her back to Vulcan to begin the long-overdue process of finding her a mate. Was it that which was making her—to borrow Lieutenant Palousek's word—"cranky"?

Why should it?

"It's all about the slime," Mikal said. He had noticed a streak of it crystallized briefly in the hair above Saavik's ear where Worm had touched her in parting after the wedding, a bright jewel that vanished as he watched.

"It's gone," he said now, his feet up on the desk in the ready room, waiting for Mironova so that, as department heads, they could update her on what he considered their most important finding . . . after the Deemanot themselves, of course. "All of it. You were literally covered with it during the mind-meld, but by the time we got to the museum, it's as if it never existed. There was none on your uniform, and when we were crawling through the tunnels we should have been covered in it, but the floors were dry."

"Traces were found under spectral analysis," Saavik pointed out. Ever since they'd returned from the wedding, she had felt compelled to argue every minor point with him, and she did not know why.

"Traces. Doesn't explain how it's able to sublimate so

quickly!" he shot back, always ready for a good wrangle. "And I'm convinced it's the reason we couldn't detect the tunnels under our feet in all three biomes."

Mironova slid into her chair without a word, glowering at Mikal's feet until he removed them from her desk and sat up straight.

"Go on."

"We've isolated at least twelve different types of slime, varying by chemical composition, degree of viscosity, and the purpose it's used for," he said, handing her the padd he'd been holding. "There's the variety that hardens egested soil into the marblelike consistency we noted on the inner walls of the museum. That's actually very rare. Less rare is the type used as a communication medium, which is what we found traces of on Saavik's uniform and in her hair. It dries very quickly but only *seems* to disappear. Under 3-nitrophthalic acid analysis, it shows up immediately.

"Then there's the most common type of slime, which is what they use to lubricate their bodies against the sun, and also for mobility. And nine other varieties we're still working on. They all seem to evaporate almost immediately once they're no longer in contact with the Deemanot's outer dermis, regardless of ambient humidity, even underground. That's why we were able to crawl through the tunnels with them without getting covered in it. But here's where it gets interesting. We suspect the mobility slime sublimates onto the walls as it dries and has some sort of chemical property that blocks our scanners; Ta'oob and Esparza are still testing it. But just on a hunch, that's probably why our newfound friends seem to be able to move so fast underground. The entire planet is probably riddled with tunnels our equipment just doesn't register. If we can figure out what's causing it and recalibrate for it . . ."

". . . you'll have your next paper for the *Kropasar Journal of Applied Biotechnology*," Mironova finished for him, giving Saavik a bemused look. Usually eager to provide counterpoint for Mikal's monologues, the Vulcan hadn't said a word.

"You seem lost in thought, Lieutenant. Don't you have anything to say?"

"The slime is Doctor Mikal's area of expertise, Captain," she said vaguely. "My team has been cataloging the artifacts from the museum. If you will excuse me"—she was on her feet without even asking to be dismissed—"I should like to continue."

"Permission granted," Mironova said after the fact, refusing to let Mikal see that she was smiling.

It was not *Pon farr*, but she was as mystified as to what it *was* as that bewildered boy on Genesis. Perhaps, she thought, it was some resonance of that event. At the time she had not permitted herself to feel anything, compelled only by her duty—as a Vulcan, as a Starfleet officer—to save Spock's life. Was it possible that only now, so many months later, some neurological remnant of that event, those actions, some chemical signature in her blood remained, causing her to experience . . . what, precisely?

As if I am floating, distracted, strangely euphoric, and yet visited with an illogical sense of . . . need?

How was it possible to have survived Hellguard, alone and without ever feeling a need for the companionship of another? She recalled her early days at the Academy, and her wish that the majority of those surrounding her, their voices piercing the thin walls of the dorm, could be somewhere else. As for the euphoria, there was indeed great satisfaction in their close encounter with the Deemanot, but that satisfaction was purely intellectual, not euphoric.

No, this was something other. Not *Pon farr,* not the elation Mikal was experiencing now that his wish to make first contact with a new species had been fulfilled. What then?

Or who?

There it was again, that indefinable something between thought and impulse that in the past had bubbled into her consciousness and propelled her down paths that led she knew not where. Each time before it had enabled her to save Spock's life.

As far as she knew, Spock was safe aboard *Enterprise,* continuing the studies that would restore his mind, in the company of Admiral Kirk and his crewmates, who would keep him from harm, inasmuch as anyone aboard *Enterprise* was ever safe from harm.

Nevertheless, she felt a shiver that raised gooseflesh on her arms, though the lab was no more chill than most humancentric environments to which she had learned to adapt. Was she ill? Should she report to the ship's tiny sickbay? Or was it her mind that beset her?

It was not *Pon farr.* She had time yet; she was

certain. Before that time came, Sarek had assured her, he would find her a suitable mate.

And why could she not get Tolek out of her mind?

His continued silence troubled her, but perhaps not as much as it should have. It might mean everything or nothing. His arrival in her world had been abrupt; might not his departure be as well? Perhaps he had reached the same conclusions she had, that the death of a handful of survivors was, lacking more concrete data than they between them had gathered, even with the recent deaths, only coincidence, random accident.

Tolek was the last link to her past, a past she would as soon forget. Nevertheless, could this desolation, this sense of loss, have something to do with him?

The pictograph currently on her computer screen, part of a display in one of the many underground rooms of the hidden Deemanot museum, showed an ancient wedding ceremony, no different in form from the one she had just witnessed. Clearly that was the answer. The joining of Scolex and Cina had left resonances in her central nervous system. That was the cause, nothing more.

"You feel it too," Mikal said.

"Indeed. Undoubtedly some as yet indeterminate effect of the electrical and telepathic impulses the Deemanot emitted during the bonding."

"Is that all you think it is?"

"I have eliminated all other possible causes for the sensations I am experiencing, and the fact that you are experiencing them also suggests an explanation."

"Oh, yes it does!" he said, his eyes dancing. "Now follow that thought to its logical conclusion."

Saavik frowned slightly. "I do not—"

"Galina never felt a thing."

"You have asked the captain this?"

"No need. Trust me, I'd know." He seemed to be waiting for her to say something more. When she didn't, he said. "Any theories?"

"Perhaps different species experience different effects."

"Or perhaps it has something to do with you and me."

"You and me?" she repeated.

"You're a scientist. Examine the evidence. What conclusions do you draw?"

Had she never noticed before how beautiful his eyes were? Accentuated by the perfection of his hairless head, framed by the tattoos, they were large and clear and an unusual shade of hazel, fringed by long, thick lashes, framed by whimsically arched brows that expressed whatever emotions his mobile mouth and flamboyant gestures did not.

"You told me you were not betrothed." His hands were on her shoulders, but lightly, as if to let her know he would step back at once if she commanded him. "But if there is someone else, someone important to you, even if you're not spoken for . . ."

The Vulcan pulse was normally quite rapid. Was it possible for it to go faster? For some reason her mouth was dry, and she had difficulty finding her voice.

"There is not," she said. What else could she say? "However, while I am mindful that you and I have shared a bond of mutual trust and respect, I hardly think—"

"Shut up," he said and, his lips on hers, made it so.

She had read Shakespeare's sonnets and the poems of Donne, as well as the love poems and songs of many other worlds, examining them as cultural artifacts whose sentiments had nothing to do with her. What she knew of this most puzzling emotion she had learned from observing Amanda and Sarek. The light she saw in Mikal's eyes was familiar, yet not the same. She had seen its like in Sarek's eyes when he looked at Amanda, but . . .

He held her in his arms and kissed her between her upswept brows and caressed her ears, even as she traced the swirling tattoos from the curl in the center of his brow, down his neck, across his shoulders to the wrists, sensing it would please him. He in turn traced the delicate shape of first one ear and then the other, as she did the same. Even then, however, she could not turn off the thoughts churning in her mind.

I am not betrothed, it is not forbidden. But even if, apart from my foster father's wishes and the Vulcan way, I were free to choose, I could not join my life with that of a nontelepath.

But who is to say that he cannot learn, as Amanda did in joining with Sarek? Was I not aware of his presence in my mind when I was joined with Worm? Do I not feel it now? Do not some scientists postulate that all sentient beings have telesper skills, but only some use them? If anyone can teach him, can it not be I?

Stop overthinking everything! Or if you must think, think of what you know of him and the casual way he falls in and out of relationships. Let this be what it is for the moment, in the moment, and do not fear hurting him when it is ended, if it is ended. For all your pretense, you are not fully Vulcan. To deny the passions that are yours from that . . . other side is . . . illogical.

Mikal is correct, she thought, acknowledging this for the first time in their adversarial relationship, as he entangled his fingers in the luxury of her hair and they tumbled in unison onto the bed, *You really do need to shut up!*

She knew all the biochemical reasons why certain sensations evoked certain responses, knew all the logical reasons why perpetuating a species compelled certain impulses, though why those impulses should occur beyond the need to propagate had been presented philosophically as both arguments for the superiority of certain species as well as a weakness that needed to be overcome by religious sublimation probably since those species had first crawled out of the primordial ooze and stood on their hind legs.

But why should the curve of his earlobe, the flex of the muscles in his forearms, evoke more of an aesthetic response in her than anyone else's? Why should the spangling of freckles across her shoulders be rendered special somehow simply because he had kissed them one by one? Were the sensations they shared in those brief hours enough? Enough for what?

For probably the first time since the moment in

infancy when her eyes had first focused (Focused on what? A face? Stern or smiling? A blank wall? She would never know), she did not *think*. She simply *was*. And he, more practiced in living in the moment, dared to think beyond it, beyond his own need for gratification, to consider, *Do I want this for more than now, possibly . . . for life?*

For a brief and timeless moment two lonelinesses touched, canceled each other out, and then the universe moved on.

After, he was the first to stir, gathering all the pillows and arranging them at the foot of the bed so that they could gaze at the traces of star shine flowing by in the window behind the headboard.

"I'll never understand why anyone would want to sleep facing *away* from the stars," he remarked, drawing the coverlet up over both of them and nestling her head in the crook of his shoulder. "You have to agree this is better."

"It is . . . quite pleasant," she murmured, marveling at herself, at him, at the two of them.

Was this happiness? She could, if called upon, describe precisely the pathways in the brain responsible for sexual response, the release of hormones, plus endorphins and serotonin that resulted in climax and the sense of relaxation and well-being in its wake, even the likelihood that the male would fall asleep before the female, whose responses often included an enhanced wakefulness and sense of contemplation.

She could, but she would not. Instead she laced the

fingers of one hand through the downy hairs on Mikal's chest and felt the slow basso continuo of his heart beneath her hand. If not happiness, at least contentment. It would serve.

For a time they watched the stars, unspeaking, the only sound the ubiquitous hum of the engines beneath the deck plates and the softness of each other's breathing. Far from being sleepy, Mikal took Saavik's hand and kissed her palm, in the same gesture she recalled his greeting the captain with the first day he'd beamed aboard. She closed her eyes to heighten the sensation and allowed herself a smile. He kissed the tips of her fingers one by one, and her smile deepened. But then he joined her first two fingers and absently began caressing them with his own—

(*So, it has come. It is called* Pon farr . . . Pon farr. *Will you trust me?*")

He felt her tense and stopped. "What's wrong?"

You cannot tell him, she thought, forcing herself to relax. *What you know is as much about Spock's privacy as about yours. But what can you tell him that will not be a lie?*

And the Spock you shared that with no longer remembers, may not ever remember what transpired, so where is the harm?

And what of what you have done this night, when you know that as soon as you return to Vulcan, Sarek will be waiting for you and you will have to choose a mate?

"It is . . . nothing," she replied, tracing the extraordinary shape of his mouth, thinking, *Nothing about you, about us, about now. I have lived all my life haunted by*

*the past, uncertain of the future. Now, for now, I will live
in the now . . .*

"Argued like a Romulan!" the man who'd watched her
kill and eat the lizard would say with more than a touch
of pride. "You are your father's daughter in spite of all
attempts at corruption from the other side!"

She'd woken in a cold sweat that morning despite
the desert's heat, knowing somehow that this would be
the day he would come. Mikal, Tolek, Spock, Sarek—all
were lost to her by then. Only the desert remained.

How did the rest of the crew know? She and Mikal
had been discreet, speaking only as colleagues in public, making certain no one saw one leaving the other's
cabin or vice versa. Surely Mikal hadn't said anything
to anyone—or, given his propensity for mischief, had
he? Perhaps then it was the contrast between his usual
behavior and a sudden quietness about him that made
people notice. In any event, she heard the whispering,
saw the knowing looks, and *did not care.*

Was this happiness?

Whatever it was, it seemed to be affecting her innate
Vulcan time sense. While objectively she could count
the time she and Mikal had been together, down to the
minutes and seconds, it seemed somehow that they had
left orbit around Deema III only moments earlier, and
yet Earth's spacedock suddenly loomed on the forward
screen, and everything changed.

Eleven

Sarek was speaking to her and she could not hear him. Her only thought was, *What is he doing here, on Earth, at Starfleet? Surely the matter of my betrothal is not so urgent? The time, the place, are wrong. I cannot do this now, not with Mikal here, not with what I have just learned . . .*

Mikal caught her as she stumbled.

"What is it? Saavik, what's wrong?"

Later, in the long desert nights, she would have more than enough time to sort out the sequence of events, the hows and whys of Sarek's presence and why the message from Tolek had come through on a coded frequency so secret it required her to report to the comm center in person. For now, she recalled it this way:

Chaffee's crew had been debriefed and granted shore leave while Command decided what to do next about the matter of Deema III.

Mikal suggested sightseeing. For all his time on Earth, he had never been to San Francisco. They were crossing the grounds on the way to the tram that would take them into the city when they heard the announcement.

"*Lieutenant Saavik, please report to Comm Center Main immediately. Lieutenant Saavik, please report . . .*"

"Go," Mikal said, squeezing her hand, "I'll wait for you in the tram station."

There were retinal scans and several locked portals and long corridors to traverse before she got to where a perky little human yeoman took a palm print and examined her clearance level on a screen.

"Urgent message for you from Nah'namKir on Vulcan," the yeoman said unnecessarily before pointing her to a booth where she could ostensibly read the message in semiprivacy. Concealing her puzzlement, Saavik remembered to thank the yeoman, then waited for her to go back to whatever it was she had been doing when she had arrived before activating the screen.

She did not recognize the name of the city at first but, recalling a child's long-ago lesson on Vulcan geography, she remembered that it lay within the northern polar region. It could only be the "minor city you've never heard of" that Tolek hailed from. It took her a moment to realize that the communication was not from Tolek at all but from the healer who had performed the autopsy.

Performed the autopsy. The words did not make sense at first. Had Tolek finally managed to find a healer who saw things his way? Somewhere between concern and annoyance, it took Saavik a moment to realize that the victim was Tolek himself.

The healer's message contained the proper Vulcan mix of fact and compassion. *"You were given as his next of kin . . . a search of all databases indicated that there was no one else . . . details follow . . . disposition of the remains upon your reply . . ."*

Somehow she managed to maintain her composure long enough to read through the "details," such as they were. If she'd had any doubt that the previous five dead had been murdered, Tolek's death erased it even before she got to the words "unknown etiology."

If she had believed him initially, would it have made any difference? If she had remained on Vulcan, if, if, if . . .

She was able to divert the pertinent data to her private frequency for later retrieval, deactivate the screen, and somehow find her way back through the maze she'd traveled to get here, back to the sunlight and the tram station and Mikal . . .

. . . who was standing in the waiting area in quiet conversation with Sarek. It made no more sense than the news she had just received. The outside doors had barely closed behind her when Mikal glanced her way. That was where her memory refused to work correctly.

She remembered stumbling. She remembered Mikal taking her arm to steady her. She remembered seeing Sarek's lips move but being unable to hear his words past the sound of her own voice shouting . . .

She awoke in her room in the house in ShiKahr. It was dark. A single lamp in one corner was the only source of light. Somewhere in the house she could hear Amanda and Sarek. They were doing something she had never heard them do before—not as a child, not as recently as before Sarek left for Earth and the trial. They were *quarreling*.

"What were you thinking?" Amanda was saying

softly—Amanda never raised her voice—but passionately. "The impact this could have on her career, her future!"

"The physician who attended her was Vulcan. The matter was handled most discreetly."

"'Discreetly'! You arranged for her to 'lose consciousness'—with the help of a nerve pinch, no doubt; don't try to tell me otherwise—in a public place, on the grounds of Starfleet Academy, then used your diplomatic influence to have her sedated by a private physician and spirited away. You might just as well have . . . I . . . I don't know what else you could have done that would have been crazier."

She paused for breath.

"What were you thinking?" she asked again.

"If you must know, it was my thought that some . . . residual effect of her assistance to our son on Genesis . . ."

Sarek's voice trailed off. Despite the swimming in her head, Saavik tried to sit up, managing finally to prop herself on one elbow, the better to listen. She had never before known the senior diplomat to be at a loss for words.

"Oh, spit it out!" Amanda said. "You can say the words. I've never understood how Vulcans can build an entire culture of secrecy around a perfectly normal biological function! Spock went through *Pon farr* on Genesis, and Saavik saved his life. There! I'm not embarrassed by the words. And you . . ."

Here her tone softened. "You thought there might have been . . . consequences."

"Yes," Sarek said after a time.

Saavik heard Amanda exhale. "Well, then, in that case I suppose you did what you thought was right. But the healers found no . . . residual effect, as you put it. Something else must have triggered her outburst. Poor child! I advised her against taking an assignment again so soon. Legend may have it that Vulcans don't suffer from nervous exhaustion, but whatever label you want to put on it, she needs rest."

"Indeed. She will have it now."

What did that mean? Despite the vertigo, Saavik managed to get to her feet and stagger as far as the doorway before she had to steady herself, vaguely noting that someone had taken care to dress her in one of her favorite sleeping robes and brush out her hair. Amanda, no doubt, tending to her for—how many days? Add that time to the days it had taken Sarek's private shuttle to reach Vulcan. By now *Chaffee* had no doubt sailed without her, and Mikal—

Chaffee *would as easily have sailed without you if Lieutenant Eyris resolved her family problem on Denobula and resumed her rightful place as science officer,* she reminded herself. *And Mikal—*

—no doubt demanded to know where Sarek was taking you, and can find you if he chooses. You have more immediate problems right now.

The vertigo conquered, she followed the voices to the main living area, her senses so heightened she could feel the grain of the polished stone floor beneath her bare feet. What she also felt was a growing rage.

"How *dare* you!" she demanded of Sarek before

either he or Amanda could react to her presence and say a word. "You had no right!"

She did not bother to finish her thought, did not trust herself to speak it, did not trust Sarek's reaction, considering how he had responded the last time she'd raised her voice at him. He had no right to bring her here, assume responsibility for her life, potentially ruin her career as Amanda had pointed out, all for what? To save himself the shame of hearing what had transpired on Genesis? To intervene in her relationship with a male she had chosen for herself without asking his permission? To, in any event, act in loco parentis when he had no such right?

The thoughts whirled around her as she stormed back to her room, sealing the door to protect what little privacy she had left, dressing quickly and finding herself outside the wall, in the public thoroughfare, seeking transport to the place where Tolek's body lay waiting for her to claim it.

It was over quickly.

There is a universal sameness to the places where the unclaimed dead lie in wait, regardless of the planet or the culture, a coldness to the places where they are kept in stasis, regardless of the climate or the ambient temperature the inhabitants find amenable.

Even before she entered the mortuary, Saavik felt chilled, and not only from the weather in Nah'namKir, where the temperature when she arrived was around twenty degrees Celsius. A human would be quite comfortable, but the Vulcans who passed her as she walked from the transport station wore several layers of insulated clothing, something she had not considered in her haste. But that was not what was making her cold.

Why was she overreacting this way? Her contact with Tolek since his reappearance in her life had been so minimal, yet she felt as if she had lost her oldest and dearest friend.

Well, have you not? Until Spock came along, who else was there?

The same healer who had sent her the communiqué met her at the entrance, and again she found herself walking down seemingly endless corridors, though this time there were no retinal scans, and the portals opened to the healer's touch. Even knowing what lay within the hermetically sealed chamber, knowing from having read the other autopsy reports that there would be no marks on the body (though had she not seen enough carnage in her life to be unaffected if there were?), and that he would appear at first to be in repose, merely sleeping, forever.

Seeing him now, a wan, inert thing on the mortuary slab, he who had protected her, rescued her under the most dire circumstances, and only once come to her for help, help that she had given grudgingly and from a distance when, with all the resources at her disposal, she might have, if not helped him solve his mystery, at least prevented this . . .

She recalled the single tear that had trickled down her cheek as she watched Spock's photon tube make its ponderous way down the track before it was jettisoned into space. If they had not been near enough to Genesis for it to be caught in its gravity well . . . Another "if" she could not tolerate.

She couldn't bear it, not again. She *could not*!

This time her breakdown had no words, only sound, a noise that was deep, guttural, animal. It had barely freed her throat before she caught herself at the edge of the table to keep her knees from buckling. Was the room spinning around her or was it she who was moving, flailing around, smashing lab equipment, cursing in every language she knew until the healer managed to summon an assistant and together they were able to restrain her and . . .

This time when she awoke, she was not alone. One minute Tolek was there, alive and speaking to her, explaining that it was all a ploy—albeit a bad one, and he apologized—to get her attention, make her take the matter more seriously. Then Spock replaced him, the Spock she had known before Genesis—wise, patient, the calm that balanced chaos—and he too was speaking, though she could not hear the words, and then . . .

She'd been sedated again, apparently, sequestered in a remote part of the city's main hospice, not imprisoned, exactly—she was certain she would find the door unlocked if she'd been able to reach it—but by implication given to understand that she was not on her own recognizance and someone would have to come for her before she was free to leave. She tried to sit up but couldn't, didn't remember dozing, but she must have, because where first Tolek and then Spock and then emptiness had been, there was Amanda, sitting patiently at her bedside. It took her a moment to realize this was not illusion.

"I cannot . . ." was all she managed to say.

"Of course you can't," Amanda said, one hand on her brow as if feeling for a fever, or perhaps initiating a light meld; for all the human's protestations, Saavik had always suspected that Amanda's esper skills were greater than she let on. "No one but you, and perhaps my son, would expect to push themselves beyond their own endurance."

"Cannot lose . . . anyone else . . ."

"You won't," Amanda said with a touch of steel, stroking Saavik's hair and then withdrawing, hands primly in her lap, willing to wait how ever long it might take.

"Tolek . . ."

"Will be interred among Sarek's kin." When Saavik looked surprised, she added. "He was obviously very important to you. No other reason need be given."

"I am responsible . . ." This time she did sit up, wrapping her arms around her knees to steady herself. "He would not be dead if I had believed him."

The whole story came pouring out then, from the chance meeting in the marketplace that was perhaps not chance at all, to the moment she had lost control in the mortuary. Amanda listened without speaking until she was certain Saavik was done.

"What could you have done to change any of that?" she asked at last.

Saavik scowled. Was it the lingering effect of the sedation that made it impossible for her to think clearly?

"I suppose you feel compelled to blame yourself," Amanda said mildly, studying her hands. "Humans often do that when they can't control a situation. It rather surprises me from you, though."

A flicker of anger swept the fog out of the corners of her mind, but rather than lash out again (At *Amanda*? Was she that much out of control?), she forced herself to calm and said, "Perhaps I should have listened to you. Do you think the savants at Amorak will accept me after . . . after all this?"

"In its time, Amorak has sheltered brigands and reprobates of all stripes and transformed them into sages," Amanda said with a smile. "I think they would welcome one whose only crime was caring."

The food was bland enough to make fasting easy, almost mandatory. The long refectory tables, the bowed heads, each individual lost in his or her own thoughts, the silence punctuated only by the sound of spring water poured from carafe to cup, the scrape of utensil against bowl were all too familiar even as they were alien. Was it her fate to end her life as she had begun it . . . what was the word humans used? Institutionalized?

Was it the thought or the food that brought the wave of nausea that made her set aside her spoon and hope no one noticed? What was the protocol for not finishing the food one had been given? A human classmate at the Academy had told her once of an ancient Earth tradition known as "Eat everything on your plate because there are children starving in China." Vulcans, who had eliminated the climatological and political reasons for hunger in the time of Surak knew that molecules returned to molecules, it was all star stuff, and that which was not eaten would decompose and be born again in the endless recycling of a universe, and there was no guilt attached.

And yet, someone had grown this, harvested it, prepared it, served it. Was the fact that she was expected to rise with the dawn tomorrow and, following the first meditation, to repair to the grain fields or the orchards or the hydroponic gardens to participate in this process, and that over the course of her stay here she would participate in all aspects of this simple life as well—harvesting crops, preparing meals, scrubbing floors, the only material difference between here and the facility on Hellguard that she could see in her first hours here being that the propaganda films had been replaced by meditation—sufficient excuse for leaving the table without finishing?

She watched others finish and return their empty dishes to the kitchen area. What was one to do if one could not finish?

"If thee has not hunger, it is illogical, and perhaps unhealthy, to continue to eat," the ancient beside her said so quietly no one but she could hear him.

Simar, she recalled, and was about to thank him, when with a motion so subtle one would have had to be looking directly at him to see it, his deceptively tremulous hands reached sideways and exchanged his empty bowl for hers, and he said, in the same low voice, "Alternatively, when one is still hungry at the end of a meal, it is logical to seek further sustenance."

His eyes were so pale they were almost white, his face so withered from decades in the desert that his eyes had almost disappeared, and yet he emanated such compassion she found it almost overwhelming. Was it that which caused her to rise perhaps too abruptly from the long table, or was it the memory of Tolek in the marketplace, devouring her unfinished *plaberry* pastry as if he had not eaten for days?

The shrine had originally been a fortress in the violent times, dug directly into a cliff face and expanded over the centuries by means of a honeycomb of corridors and inner chambers. Some of the ancient carvings—friezes of sieges and battles, faces contorted in agony, piles of corpses—had been left in place as a reminder never to return to those times. The walls were anywhere from meters to kilometers thick on the mountain side, hence soundproof, weighty, as if the mountain were a living thing holding the inhabitants in its embrace, warm in places where ancient lava flows still made their sluggish way deep underground, cool in others. Saavik let her hand trail over the stone as she walked, feeling the contrast—warm and cool, warm and cool, warm and cool—so temperate compared to the alternating rage and cold anger she was feeling.

Yes, feeling. She was nothing Vulcan at the moment. But if she was not Vulcan, what was she? The alternative only made her angrier.

"Will you allow yourself to be ruled by mere genetics?"
The voice was Spock's, reminiscent of the many chal-

lenges with which he had honed her logic when she was younger.

"Did you not?" In public she was always deferential to him as a mentor, but when they were alone she confronted him as a peer. "I have seen how you try to deny one-half of your heritage, though it is nurturing. Mine was nothing nurturing. Do I not have the right to do as you do?"

"I had hoped to spare you some of the . . . uneasiness I have experienced."

"'Uneasiness'?" That merited an eyebrow. "One can hardly dismiss Kolinahr as merely 'uneasy.' "

Now he was the one to raise an eyebrow. "Explain."

Her chin was stubborn, and yet it trembled.

"I will not judge that which transpired before I knew you." He had been at Gol while she was still on Hellguard. "But some might say you ran away."

"Do you say that?"

"I only wish to know how one can run away from something that exists inside one."

No! she thought, stopping in her headlong rush to . . . where? She steadied herself against one wall of the shrine that was particularly warm beneath her touch. That conversation had never taken place in the real. *Kolinahr* was not a matter to be discussed lightly. She would not have thrown that in his face.

You are overcompensating, she told herself, *for the emptiness where Spock once was, where Spock may never be again, regardless of the* fal-tor-pan. *But these are daydreams, projections, unworthy of the Spock who went before. You have much work yet to do.*

Amanda is correct about one thing. The answer lies here, where you are, where you can rest and seek the answers in your mind. The shrine, the regimen, the hot springs will heal you. As with Starfleet, you require order, discipline, even a uniform, if one can call traditional Vulcan robes a uniform. Everyone here wears the same, eats the same, follows the same path, even if it is only for a time.

How long will you stay here, and where will you go next? Back to Starfleet—if they'll have you, after the scene in the tram station—or perhaps deeper into the realm of the mind?

Is there a Kolinahr at the crossroads of your future?

"Those are the orders, Mikal," Captain Mironova said, unnecessarily, really, since Mikal had the padd in his hand and could read them for himself. "We're due for departure in three days. That's not enough time for me to replace you if you decide to go walkabout, but it would be nice to have at least one experienced scientist from the original expedition return to Deema III with us. Eyris is back, but she'll need to be brought up to speed. Don't make this any more difficult than it needs to be."

Ordinarily matters like the spatial rifts surrounding the Deema system were batted around at Starfleet Command for weeks or months or longer. The speed with which the order had come down this time seemed to Mikal almost to be mocking him. He didn't usually subscribe to pathetic fallacy—the belief that the universe ordered itself solely to make him miserable—but in this instance he was strongly tempted.

So here were *Chaffee*'s new orders. She was to return to Deema III, reopen the rifts and observe, send unmanned probes into the larger ones to gather data in an attempt to determine point or points of origin and to what extent the exchange of minerals and plant life from point or points unknown had affected the evolution and culture of the Deemanot. They were to leave immediately, and stay for however long it took. Months? A year or more? That was for the universe to decide.

Mikal set the padd down on Mironova's desk none too gently. The look in his eyes was bleak.

"If I could just get some word from her . . ." he said.

Mironova sighed. Mikal was difficult at the best of times, but he would be useless to her and the mission if he didn't pull himself together.

"Ordinarily you'd be ecstatic at being allowed to go back and finish what we started," she reminded him.

"This is not 'ordinarily'!" he said crossly.

"Well? And so what if it isn't?" Mironova said with an edge to her voice. "Officially, Lieutenant Saavik is on medical rest leave. You saw her into the care of Ambassador Sarek. She's with family, she's under the best of care, there isn't anything for you to do except possibly get back to work."

"There's more to it than we've been led to believe. I feel it."

"Ah, well, in that case. Nothing like a solid scientific hypothesis based strictly on the evidence."

He glowered at her. A silent Mikal was even more perturbing than a vociferous one.

"I promise you we'll try to get word through diplomatic channels, if not through Command," she said with more than a little tenderness. "If there's any news . . ."

He wasn't even looking at her now, just hunkered down in his chair, arms folded, staring off into space. Were those tears? Not just another fling, then, but the real thing?

"Right!" she went on. Let him pout; it wasn't her job to baby him. "Back to business. Just so you know, I've put in a request for another telepath—a Vulcan or a Betazoid, if we can manage it—in order to maintain direct communication with the Deemanot. I don't intend to waste that opportunity while we're prowling around in orbit gathering data, but I'll also want you in charge of any landing parties, since Worm and the others have already established a rapport with you—"

"Whatever!" he said, on his way toward the door. "Three days to departure? I'll be there. But I won't be happy about it!"

You were *happy, weren't you?* Mironova thought to his departing back. *For a few days, anyway. Best most of us can hope for sometimes, isn't it?*

Twelve

No one was prepared for what happened next.

James T. Kirk was a changed man. Perhaps it was being demoted to captain again and realizing how much he'd missed the center seat that had rendered him not contemplative, exactly, but more contemplative for him—more observant, more sensitized to the moods of those around him. Then again, any of the after-effects of recent events, not least of which was an inability to mourn the son he'd barely known before losing him forever, might have made him that much more determined to hold on to those who were important to him. Whatever the reason, he had become a tuning fork for every nuance of Spock's behavior.

The reintegration of so complex a mind by a technique all but lost to ancient history had not been without its rough spots—some of them amusing, if there hadn't been so much at stake—and even so many months afterward, there were still gaps and hiccups. With a touch of the old impatience that required him to have answers, and answers *now*, Kirk managed to find a way to check up on Spock at least once a day off shift, "to make sure he's all right."

Most of it was healthy—a game of chess, some casual

conversation—if one ignored the barely disguised expression of anxiety behind the captain's eyes.

"Stop hovering, Jim!" McCoy barked at him. "Leave the man to his thoughts!"

"Easy for you to say," Kirk joked, but McCoy wasn't playing.

"Does it occur to you he might heal faster if you weren't waiting in the wings with a pop quiz every day? Believe me, it's all there. You said yourself it would come back to him."

"The technical expertise, yes. It's the personality that concerns me."

"You trusted him to calibrate a Klingon vessel for time travel in order to save Earth, and you're worried about his *personality*? Godalmighty, Jim, will you listen to yourself? It's a different file drawer in his brain, but he hasn't lost it. He just needs some time to reconnect the neurons."

Nevertheless, on this particular evening, after he'd left the bridge in Uhura's capable hands, an antique two-dimensional chessboard in a fine teakwood case—the latest addition to his collection—tucked under one arm, he made his way down the at once new and yet familiar corridors. ("Never lose you—never!" What was it that he'd meant? Not the deck plates and Jefferies tubes and warp engines that were Scotty's bailiwick, though it had all but torn his heart out to watch her burn like a meteor across the sky, but the essence of her—her *katra,* for want of a better word—was contained in the minds and spirits of those who manned her, not least of whom was his first officer and his friend.) He was aware as soon as he crossed the threshold that something was different.

Spock was just terminating a subspace message on his screen, though not before Kirk noted the Vulcan call signal.

"Greetings from home?" he presumed, knowing Amanda checked up on her son almost as often as he did. "Lady Amanda is well?"

"She is," Spock said vaguely, as if his mind were elsewhere, as it frequently was even so many months following the re-fusion.

"You should have given me a chance to say hello," Kirk said, making polite conversation while he opened the teakwood case and started setting up the board.

"My apologies," Spock said, taking him seriously. "Unfortunately my mother was . . . somewhat preoccupied."

"I hope everything's all right." Kirk was still making small talk but, all the chessmen now in place, he chanced to notice the length of the silence and Spock's continued preoccupation. Despite hearing McCoy's disapproval nagging at the back of his mind, he blundered on. "Spock?"

"There has been a . . . situation."

It was the term Sarek had used when the savants contacted him. The privacy of Amorak's pilgrims was for the most part sacrosanct. But there were occasions when it was necessary to notify next of kin.

"What is it?" Amanda asked, seeing a bleakness in his eyes, a hurriedness to his pace as he terminated the message and announced that he must leave for a few days.

She'd expected it was some offworld crisis, but the brevity of the journey suggested something more local. What possible trouble could there be within their own system that required the ambassador's immediate attention?

She was startled when he said, "It is Saavik. There has been a . . . situation at the shrine."

"What sort of 'situation'?" Amanda followed her husband down the hall to their sleeping quarters. "She's not ill, is she?"

"She was . . . physically whole at the time she took her leave," Sarek said carefully, in full diplomatic mode, which ordinarily made Amanda furious but this time told her just how serious the situation was.

"She's left the shrine? Why? She seemed to have found peace there at first."

"Seeming is not always being, my wife." Sarek was removing garments from their cabinets in his deliberate way. Amanda found herself doing the same, preparing to pack and accompany him.

"Where has she gone? And what can I do?"

Sarek stopped his rummaging and took her hands, gently but with just enough firmness to suggest that she stop what she was doing and hear him out.

"She was last seen walking off into the desert, alone. None followed her. More than that cannot be said until I speak with the savants in person. And before thee asks, no. Thee cannot accompany me. This is a Vulcan matter."

Amanda's impulse was to blurt out, "She's my daughter too!" but over the years she had learned when to negotiate, when to stand her ground, and when, as now, to yield. This was not to say she was content. Sarek saw it in her all-too-human face.

"My wife," he said tenderly, releasing her hands, extending the first two fingers of his right hand as Amanda reciprocated, joining her fingers with his in their familiar gesture of affection. "I will speak with you as soon as I know more. Worry not. Such matters are rarely as they seem. And as we know our daughter . . ."

". . . we must trust that she is not so changed by recent events that her true self has not survived." Amanda turned away and began closing cabinet doors now that it was clear she would not be traveling. Whatever else she might have wanted to say, she only added, "Journey safely, husband."

She waited until the purr of the air car faded into the distance before she took action. She had her own sources of information, not as extensive perhaps as the master diplomat's, but they would serve.

What information they yielded only deepened her concern.

The *Enterprise* family had been aware of Saavik's abrupt departure from Earth several weeks ago in Sarek's care. One could hardly expect a scenario played out in the Command HQ tram station to remain secret for long. Despite the inevitable chatter, to date the only official word was that Spock's young protégé had been granted medical rest leave on Vulcan, which surprised no one who knew even a portion of what she'd gone through on Genesis. Kirk hadn't inquired further until now, but . . .

"I have to ask. Saavik?"

"Indeed."

"She certainly never asked for the hand she was dealt." Kirk settled himself in his usual chair on one side of the chessboard. "How much are you able to tell me?"

Spock seemed to be contemplating his opening gambit. "Only that she has . . . I believe the expression is 'gone off the grid' . . ."

Even Vulcans are not immune to gossip. Not everyone in residence at the shrine was a permanent member of the community. Some stayed for a brief time, others never left. There were stories from ancient times of brigands seeking sanctuary among the first savants and more often than not being converted to the ways of peace, but some had proved incorrigible. Nevertheless, not in the memory of anyone at Amorak in these times had there been such a scene. And some who were in residence only temporarily took the story with them in their departure.

"The more often an event is described, the more easily the details are distorted in the telling," Spock said, his voice devoid of emotion, his gaze very far away. "Therefore it is difficult to know for certain what is truth, what is exaggeration, and what has been left unspoken."

"*Rashomon,*" Kirk suggested.

"A film by Akira Kurasawa, based upon the short story 'In a Grove' by Ryūnosuke Akutagawa, describing a single crime from the point of view of several witnesses, each of whom sees something entirely different," Spock said, and Kirk suppressed a smile. It would come back to him, indeed. "What is known is this: There was an altercation. About what is unclear. What is certain is that Saavik initiated it. It escalated beyond words, and several at the shrine were injured. One, it is said, an elder named Simar who tried to intervene, may even be near death. In the event, having violated the peace of the shrine, Saavik was obliged to leave."

"Just leave?" Kirk asked carefully, rubbing his chest absently, hearing the singing of a blade through the air, feeling the razor's edge against his skin as he struggled to breathe in the thin air, mindful at firsthand of the anger of a Vulcan aroused. Add Romulan ancestry to that mix, and the survival instincts of a once feral child, and . . . "There must have been some penalty."

"Jim, the desert surrounding the shrine is penalty enough."

Kirk tried to picture it, then wished he hadn't. His last encounter with Saavik—highly intelligent if a little too serious, poised, beautiful, soft-spoken, disciplined, impeccable—didn't mesh with the image of some maddened, wild-eyed creature lashing out at those around her, being driven off into a wilderness that, even to a Vulcan, alone and unassisted, inevitably meant death.

"Lord knows we've all had our moments of madness," he managed finally. "McCoy's attempt to use the Vulcan neck pinch on that security guard in his favorite bar has become legend in some circles. As for you and me, between spores, transporter accidents, and general mayhem . . ."

"Indeed."

"There must be something we can do."

"My father has already repaired to the shrine."

"And?"

"The savants allow no technology other than a single comm unit in the prefect's cell with which to communicate with families when there is a death or . . . something untoward such as this. Had they wished to track Saavik once she left the shrine, they would not have had the equipment to do so, even if their precepts did not forbid it. Once the wind swept the sand across her trail, she was no more."

Kirk's impulse was to protest, to offer some reckless suggestion about mounting a rescue mission. A younger Kirk might have done exactly that. But this was the post-Genesis, contemplative Kirk, and what he heard in his old friend's voice said, *Let it alone. Sometimes there's nothing you can do except . . . nothing.*

"I don't know what to say."

"Sometimes, Jim, no words are necessary."

The first time she killed a lizard, she apologized.

Forgive me, little one. I would not do this if I did not have to.

Crouched over her kill, she had bitten off the head, trying unsuccessfully to fight the gag reflex spasming in her throat. It had been so long since she had eaten animal flesh. She managed to brace herself against the ground with one hand without losing her grip on the small dun-scaled body, whose blood oozed from the severed neck and ran over her other hand, dripping into the sand, where it was immediately swarmed over by small, voracious insects, but the retching had caused her to spit the head out into the sand, and the insects claimed that too. When the retching finally stopped, she reclaimed her prize, fighting off the stings of the ants, brushing as much sand off the morsel as she could before crunching it between her molars, grit and all, making a mental note not to be so careless again.

She had kept track of the nights and days since the evening she strode off with the shrine at her back, deliberately heading into the light of the setting sun, lest anyone be foolhardy enough to follow her after what she had done.

Simar, Elder, I never meant you harm. Your spirit knows this. I have violated the peace of this ancient place and will never come this way again.

The stark desert wind had erased her footprints even as she made them. By the time the sun made her shadow long before her the next morning, she was well out of sight of the shrine, and it of her. She never once looked back.

Her inner time sense told her that that had been forty days and forty nights ago. At first she had survived on the fruits of the desert, following the animal trails that led to clumps of cactus and other succulents swollen with sap derived from water sources deep underground and the rare desert rains. Every plant had some portion that was edible, though many were

poisonous as well. Ironically, many were akin to the
sparse vegetation on Hellguard, and her early experiences held her in good stead.

But under these conditions, she could not live on
vegetation alone, and so she had to resort once more
to killing. Eventually she remembered how to bite off
a reptile's head without gagging, how to overturn a
rock and devour everything that squirmed in the shade
beneath before it got away, which parts of a snake's
body to eat first and which to save for later.

She also could not stay in one place very long, and
there were stretches of sand so barren that not even
animals ventured there. No telltale tracks or sand shifts
that meant snakes in their sidewinding traverse or
overflights of predator birds homing in on food or even
the tiny disturbances that meant reptiles dug into the
sand awaiting nightfall, their eyes alone above the surface, indistinguishable from the pebbles surrounding
them unless one happened to see the occasional blink.

Across those barren places, she neither ate nor
drank, but walked with the night, listening for predators, though even a *le-matya* would not waste its time
here where there was no food, seeking shelter behind
rock croppings or even burrowing into the sand like
the lizards for protection from the sun in the daytime.
Plumes of steam—indistinguishable in daylight from
the mirages that plague desert dwellers everywhere
(once an entire ancient city rose to greet her, its cren-
ellated walls as new as the day they were constructed,
the bronze shields of its warriors displayed along the
battlements, throwing the sun back into her eyes; it had

lingered the day long—she could even see the sentries walking the battlements in clockwork regimentation—then shimmered away, whether into time or space she would never know, with nightfall)—became real beneath the starlight, signaling hot springs and some respite from the sweat that made the sand cling to her and rub her skin raw, but they were few and far between and, again, she could not linger.

One time she found a brackish pool, the water undrinkable, but it attracted a strange kind of land fog that formed jewel-like dewdrops nurturing the cacti that ringed the pool, even fostering lichen that grew in long strands between the cactus spines. The presence of moisture brought wildlife—snakes, lizards, even *chiroptera*, their leathery wings batting so quickly they could not be seen, making a kind of eerie wind noise as they came to feed on the night blooms of the cacti, their sonar cries, imperceptible to human ears, mildly irritating to a Vulcan's. Here she made her camp, and waited.

The reopened spatial rifts in the Deema system were proving to be a treasure trove.

Most were tiny, temporary, opening and closing in an eyeblink, able to be recorded by ship's instruments but retaining their mystery, too brief and ephemeral to reveal where they led or what lay on the other side. Others were more stable, able to be threaded with unmanned probes and followed to various previously mapped sectors of the Alpha Quadrant, still others to regions as yet unexplored by Federation vessels. Thorough study, with the possibility that some might be used as shortcuts in the future, was estimated to take decades, and *Chaffee* and her science crew were on point and credited with the discovery.

Most of the anomalous plants and minerals the original landing party had discovered appearing and disappearing on the surface of Deema III turned out to have originated in a far-flung star cluster on the edge of Tholian space. Whether any of the several dozen planets in the cluster were habitable, much less whether they contained intelligent life and, still less likely, whether those hypothetical life-forms were deliberately sending specimens through the rifts or the rifts themselves were somehow scooping up rocks and uprooting greenery from those unmarked worlds, were facts as yet unknown.

Mikal should have been ecstatic, and on one level he was. There was work enough here even for his boundless energies, academic credit enough even for his fragile ego, except that for the first time in his life he didn't want it.

"Divvy it up among the team," he told Mironova when she asked him why he hadn't signed any of his reports. "In fairness it belongs to all of them."

"Generous of you," she said, "if out of character. What you really mean is it should be shared with the entire team, including the missing one."

"Salt in the wound?" Mikal accused her. "Isn't that the Earth expression? Tell me you've heard something."

"No more than you." Mironova shrugged. "In point of fact, probably less than you. Starfleet scuttlebutt goes only so far. You've got a direct line to the Vulcan ambassador."

"Who's been as forthcoming as an Aldebaran shell-mouth," Mikal grumped. "Oh, we chat every few weeks, and we're all so very cordial, but if there's another being in the whole of the Federation who can say as much while saying so little . . ."

"We can credit Lieutenant Saavik with the work she's done on the first mission, and with the initial contact with the Deemanot, but that's it, I'm afraid," Mironova said pragmatically. She hated watching Mikal brood, as much for the sake of wanting him focused for the mission as for his personal welfare. "Lieutenant Loth is making good progress with the Deemanot."

"Right!" Mikal snorted. "If you can filter what Worm and the others are actually saying out of his maudlin drivel. Betazoids can't help ascribing their own feelings to every species they interact with. Saavik—a Vulcan—would have simply reported what was on the Deemanot mind without the emotional frills."

"If only a Vulcan had been available," Mironova reminded him, seeing him wince and regretting her words almost instantly. "Our Betazoid has been instrumental in helping you communicate with Worm and the others. You might thank him for that at least."

He might have, if the first attempt to form a three-way link with Worm and through hir to the entirety of the species hadn't begun with Worm's asking, *Saavik is not among you?*

Gwailim Loth, the Betazoid, had greeted Worm on his first visit to the surface by allowing hir to twine about him and cover him with slime as Saavik had done the first time. The two had communed for what seemed a small eternity while Mikal stood by and fidgeted. He'd disliked the overtall, spindly, slightly walleyed Loth from their first encounter and wished more than ever that he had even the smallest amount of esper ability so that this interloper need not be part of his expedition.

Much to his surprise, when Loth at last opened his eyes and reached out one hand, indicating that Mikal was to take it and join the link he had established, the Tiburonian discovered that he did, in fact, have esper abilities he had never recognized before. The touch of the Betazoid's hand was like an electric shock coursing through him, and he barely had time to brace himself before he heard what could only be Worm's voice in his mind, as distinctly as if the being had spoken aloud, *Saavik is not among you?*

He'd recoiled then, his hand slipping out of Loth's from the slime, as he scrambled inelegantly away from all of them.

"No!" he half shouted, his voice shaking. "No, she's not. She was . . . called away . . . a family matter . . . Oh, explain it, will you?" he ordered Loth gruffly, though Loth had no idea. Mikal had stormed off without another word, feeling like a fool.

So, yes, his latent esper skills had been awakened, but not at all under the circumstances he might have desired. In time he managed to recover his equilibrium and join with Loth and the Deemanot as they struggled

to build a language that nontelepaths could understand, feeling like a toddler learning to speak. In some
respects it was exhilarating, an experience he could not
have imagined before . . . before Saavik. But at the same
time he was aware that it would never have occurred
without his joining with Saavik, and her not being here
seemed so profoundly unfair, to everyone.

"I think he's tragic," Cheung remarked wistfully, watching Mikal striding *Chaffee*'s corridors whenever he
wasn't coordinating starcharts with the ever-changing
rifts or puttering about on the surface cataloging whatever new specimens appeared there. He seemed to
have given up sleeping, or allowing himself to be alone.
"Like something out of a play. He was obviously in love
with her."

"There's dubious wisdom in falling in love with a
Vulcan," Palousek suggested. Older and somewhat
wiser following an ex-wife or two, he could afford to
be cynical. "Might as well develop an infatuation with
a chronometer."

"Just because you're bitter, old man—!" Cheung
snapped, then went back to mooning over Mikal.

"Rebound syndrome," Jaoui, watching all of this,
observed. "I wouldn't if I were you."

"Too late!" Cheung told her. "I've already tried. It
was like I wasn't even in the room."

Days were for sleeping, how ever fitfully, first making a
paste of mud from the sand and the brackish water and
coating oneself with it, even working it into the roots

of one's hair, to protect against insect bites and ward off
the sun. Nights were for watching, waiting, and whatever meditation she could not have accomplished in the
company of others at the shrine.

With sufficient deprivation, there is a fine line
between meditation and hallucination. She was not
surprised that Spock appeared to her, more real than
the bats availing themselves of the cactus fruit in the
air above her, but rather at the manner in which he
appeared.

The last time she had seen him, he had been wearing
the white robe of the *fal-tor-pan*. Now he appeared to
her in a manner she had never seen him, wearing the
gray and dun robes of *Kolinahr*. She knew enough of
psychology to realize this was a projection of her own
subconscious, wanting the kind of peace that Spock
had sought but been denied.

Vanity! was her first thought. *As if you could be more
worthy of such an achievement than he!*

But the vision was not real in the corporeal sense.
What harm was there in indulging it?

"My mentor," she said aloud, "Speak to me of *Kolinahr*."

"What is it that you wish to know?" the vision
answered at once.

"How do you vanquish the anger?"

"Each one's anger is his or her own, Saavik-kam."

"That is a nonanswer!" She challenged him as she
had when she was a child.

"Or an unspoken truth," he countered as quickly,
and she was suffused with memories of that early time,

when everything had seemed so serious, but that in ret-rospect had been simplicity itself compared to what she had encountered since. *"Consider, Saavik. Of what pur-pose is undifferentiated advice on how to manage one's own individual anger? Such answers cannot be given; they must be earned."*

The answer made her angry; she had already known it before she asked. At the same time it filled her with what seemed an inconsolable sorrow at the thought that they might never have such conversations again. The emptiness without him, the bewilderment in his face when she spoke to him aboard *Bounty*, the mix of disappointment, shame, and relief all at once, but most of all sorrow.

Lost in that memory of him, addressing her as "Lieutenant," looking at her as if at a stranger, she did not notice the vision fade until it was gone completely, and for some reason that startled her more than its appearance. How far was she from the nearest sentient being, and what did distance matter? There was a sci-ence that said that all matter was interconnected all the time, in ways that could not yet be understood or mea-sured. Had she been any more or less alone on Hell-guard? Had she simply not known enough then to be frightened?

You chose this, she reminded herself. *You cannot change your mind now. Anyway, it will be ended soon.*

She found herself tracing shapes in the sand with one filthy finger, mandalas out of a thousand cultures that reminded her of the Deemanot cities, and again there was sorrow, but of a different sort. Mikal. Such a brief moment, with no guarantee of other, future moments, but might she not have been permitted a few moments more?

Last, she grieved for Tolek, beginning and end of all of this, his *katra* gone somewhere she could not follow.

Silent tears made tracks in the grime rubbed into her face, and her shoulders shook with sobs she would not voice. Somehow she knew that *he* was watching.

When it was time, she gathered herself, physically and spiritually. Usually she waited until almost sunrise to bathe in the brackish pool and coat herself with a new layer of mud, because nightfall signaled hunting, and if the previous morning's mud cracked and crumbled off her as she moved, it did not matter. But this evening, as the last rays of 40 Eridani stretched long shadows over the sands before winking out over the horizon, she altered her routine.

Stripping off the ragged remnants of the dun-colored garment in which she had left the shrine, she stepped into the water—ankle-deep, knee-deep, up to her shoulders, slipping under the surface to feel the individual grains of fine sand work their way out of the roots of her hair and float away. When she was as clean as such primitive ablutions could render her, she stepped out onto the shore, the silty water sliding off her limbs as, with a Vulcan's disdain for human shame about the body one had been born into, she allowed the rising night breeze to dry her skin before seeking out the spare robe she had secreted with her that night so many nights ago, and put it on.

It was wrinkled from having been crammed in haste

into a small carry bag, but the wrinkles would shake out in time, and the sheer cleanness of it against her skin was palpable after so many weeks of filth; she imagined she could feel the individual threads in the weave wherever fabric touched flesh and suppressed a small shudder against the sheer luxury of it.

She had saved her sandals against the wear of desert travel, and now slipped them on to feet hardened yet at the same time smoothed by barefoot traverse across weeks of time and a variety of sand and stone, and slipped her oldest companion, the knife she had salvaged from Hellguard, into her sash. As for her hair . . .

Logically, she ought to have cut it short when she'd first come to the shrine, as a symbol, perhaps, of her having chosen a new way of life. Barring that, she ought at least to have hacked off the sun-scorched, tangled length of it as she made her way across the desert. It was now frowzed and matted beyond redemption; she could not so much as run her fingers through it at the scalp. No matter. She would not let so minor a thing detract from what little dignity the Elements had allowed her thus far.

Remembering that dignity, she pulled the mass of hair back into a loose knot at the nape of her neck, straightened her spine, reseated herself on the flat rock wherefrom she had been drawing out the history of the universe in the sand, and waited.

Suddenly, he was there.

Thirteen

At first glance, a Vulcan. No brow ridges, none of the characteristic hauteur one expected of the distant cousins, at least in her limited experience. She had heard no vehicle approach, so he must have concealed it and walked a distance, though his boots still retained some of their shine against the ubiquitous scouring sand, so it could not have been that far. Wisely he had waited for nightfall, so that not only was he spared the day's heat, but he had not been visible through the heat shimmer from a distance but was simply *there*.

She had made a point of establishing her camp with a maximal view toward the horizon at all turns of the compass, but the same cacti that provided sustenance for her and the small creatures she subsisted on did have a tendency to clump, providing cover for someone trained in desert concealment, especially at night. Nevertheless, his arrival did not startle her. The bats' hypersonic chittering had stilled suddenly while he was yet more than a kilometer away. It was credit to her survival skills that the night wings had become so accustomed to her presence after the first few days that they'd ceased to notice her.

Startled or not, she would not have let him see it.

How had she been so certain he would come? For

that matter, how had she known her stalker would be a single individual, and "he"? It was not something logic could answer.

He stood there in the open, hands tucked fastidiously into his belt. Dark clothing, she noted, including a traditional Vulcan travel cloak, all of good quality, all designed to render one inconspicuous in urban settings, but he'd have stood out markedly against the sand in daylight. An interesting choice, if not necessarily a wise one. Perhaps he'd never been to the desert before. That might prove useful. She also assumed that there was an Honor Blade concealed somewhere on his person—wearing it openly would have given him away—but she was reasonably certain he carried no phaser or other advanced weaponry. Also useful.

He waited without speaking, boots planted firmly, an air of confidence about him, as if he was certain this half-mad desert creature crouched protectively over the designs she drew in the sand would not attack him outright or, if she did, the attack would be random and unorganized and he could defend himself. A small sarcastic smile seemed to be trying to work its way onto his otherwise sensuous lips. The way the shadows fell, she could not see his eyes.

She let him wait.

"It took you long enough," she said finally, when an almost imperceptible shift in his stance told her she had gotten her point across. If her own voice, raspy with disuse, seemed alien to her, she gave no sign.

"I had to make certain you were alone."

His voice was not unpleasant but a touch impatient,

as if he feigned a Vulcan's deliberation of speech with difficulty and perhaps had a tendency to become shrill when he was angry. She would test that soon enough. As for his statement, she dismissed it with a gesture that marked it as ridiculous. Surely he had pinpointed her location with some manner of scanner—the strictures set forth by an ancient Vulcan shrine would have no hold on him—and knew she had been alone from the moment she left the shrine. Could he see the arch of her eyebrow beneath the grime?

"Because you find me so formidable an opponent, or simply to leave no witnesses?"

That made him laugh, as she'd known it would. She found she could anticipate his every gesture, almost write his dialogue for him. He must have claimed his other victims unawares. Surely if they had exchanged a single word with him, they'd have seen him for the fraud he was. After all she had put herself through to lure him here, was this part to be so easy?

"'Formidable'? Can you see yourself? Bedraggled, half starved, virtually unarmed?"

As you and your kind abandoned me the first time! she wanted to shout but held her anger back. *Do not let him get to you from the outset, or all is lost!*

"Have you a name?" she asked calmly. If nothing else, she had played a Vulcan far longer than he, and she would not let him see through the veneer. "I presume you know mine, unless you lack the courage to know whom it is you kill."

"I am not here to kill you. I am here to talk. In fact, if the outcome of our talk is fruitful, I need not kill again."

Again she made him wait, continuing to trace mystic figures in the sand, which the night breeze almost as quickly blew away. In ancient times, she'd read somewhere, the shamans had written prayers in the sand, interpreting the wind as the breath of gods taking the prayers with them as they moved.

Would he ask her permission to enter her camp, such as it was, or would he cross the invisible line separating their two worlds without bothering to ask? Without looking up, she saw his boots shift in the sand again. He had not a Vulcan's patience. This was useful.

"So, not quite as mad as you pretend to be," he observed, trying to sound conversational, but she heard the note of strain. "Quite a scene you made at the shrine. Did you really kill the old man?"

"You know all that you will know from me."

"A complete character transformation, and in such a short amount of time. Had I a suspicious nature, I'd wonder if it weren't all a trap."

She did look up at him now, under a stray lock of hair she did not bother sweeping out of her eyes.

"Have you a suspicious nature?"

Again he laughed. "I am Romulan. What do you think?"

"I think you have not yet told me your name."

"Why does it matter?"

"Common courtesy?"

"She says, not having yet invited me to sit down."

She shrugged. "Under the terms of our common heritage, I ought to have killed you the moment you violated my space."

He shifted his feet. She waited. Finally he said, "At home I am called Narak. On Vulcan I am known by another name. There, now. What do you know now that you did not know before?"

She stood then, her ankle joints cracking slightly and, deliberately turning away from him, leaving herself vulnerable—no need for undetectable methods of killing out here; he need only leave her to the predators—slowly withdrew the blade from where she had concealed it at her waist, using it to cut a section from a cactus taller than her head whose trunk showed recent regrowth where she had cut segments before. Carefully trimming away the spines, she began to carve out the pulp, sucking the juice, eating fastidiously. The entire process took several minutes, during which time she either had her back to him or the knife was engaged. Her wordless message was unmistakable. *I am not afraid of you. Go or stay or die where you stand; it matters not to me!*

"I have brought food and water," he said only after she'd begun to eat, raising his voice slightly, as if he felt he had to speak loudly to hold her attention, though they were only a few meters apart. "I'm willing to partake of both first to assure you none of it's poisoned."

"Or that you have built up an immunity to the poison over time." She shrugged, still chewing. "Food need not be actually poisoned to be tainted."

"Ah. So everything about me is tainted? How dramatic!" It was his turn to raise an eyebrow, and slowly, his gestures elaborate, almost mimetic, so she'd know he wasn't reaching for a weapon, to remove a water flask from a carry bag concealed beneath his cloak.

She ignored him, finished the segment of cactus as if it were the most delectable thing she'd ever eaten. When there was nothing left but the tough outer skin, she walked a distance—again with her back to him—and buried this near the edge of the pool. Let the insects have it, but not too near her camp. Returning to her flat rock, she drove the knife blade into the sand several times to clean it, then put it away, continuing to watch him, but as she might have watched one of the bats, with mild curiosity but no genuine engagement.

"You're so certain I am responsible for the deaths of your . . . compatriots." He seemed to find this amusing, shaking his head slightly, as if at some private joke. "And I suppose you think I'll stand here until the sun comes up. I won't, you know, and if I leave, I won't return. Say I did kill them. What do you think I'll do when I depart? Do you want more deaths on your conscience?"

His twisted morality intrigued her. By his reasoning, either she would do what he wanted, or he would return to killing, and the blame would be hers.

"And, no, I'm confident you won't kill me, not yet, anyway," he said to her unasked question, putting away the flask when it was clear she wasn't interested, and presuming to sit uninvited on a boulder slightly higher than where she was seated, just at the edge of what she might consider her personal space. Did he think this gave him the advantage, or did he sense she had planned it this way? "If you'd wanted to kill me outright, you'd have done that the moment I appeared. And you won't kill me now, because you need to know *why*. Who am I, other than a name? Why did I kill the others? Did they possess some secret that needed to be silenced? Other than the terrible secret of their origins, of course. Do you also possess that secret, you wonder, without even being aware of it? Nothing so complicated, I'm afraid. I sought them out only as a way of getting to you.

"Still not interested?" he asked off her silent stare. "Pity."

He shifted his weight on the rock as if settling in for the duration. Saavik could see him more clearly now, though the shadows still concealed his eyes. He seemed familiar, though that did not surprise her. It was logical that his masters would have selected him because the shape of his face so closely resembled the one she saw in the mirror on the rare occasion when she indulged such vanity.

Focus! Do not let anything about him distract you!

"Let me tell you a story," he began. "You may listen or not as you choose . . ."

Romulan scientists had devoted generations of research to weeding out "undesirable" genetic traits in their populations and fostering desirable ones, and extensive ancestral and biogenetic records were kept on every Romulan from birth. It was for this reason that a young nonentity named Narak found himself summoned to the Bureau of Sciences and offered what his summoners referred to as an "opportunity."

At the time, he was an enlisted man with an undistinguished career, no family connections, and thus, essentially no future. In addition, had he refused the "opportunity" without so much as learning what it was, it was doubtful that once he'd left the building—assuming he'd been permitted to leave—he'd have gotten halfway across the public square without meeting with an unfortunate accident. Cautiously, weighing his limited options, he had indicated an interest in this "opportunity."

All that was required of him, he was informed by the panel of anonymous scientists who had summoned him—he was almost certain he recognized the voice of one from public broadcasts, though in retrospect her voice might have been as easily disguised as the face hidden in shadow as they all were—was the donation of tissue samples and other "genetic material," and his silence. The procedures were painless, he was assured, could be performed immediately, and he would be on his way back to his unit before his superior officer had noticed his absence. The panel would give him a moment to decide.

What was there to decide? For the first time in his undistinguished life, he had something that someone else wanted. If the gods had chosen to provide him with an ideal genetic array and the chance to use it to his advantage, who was he to refuse such largesse?

"It's always easy to cast blame when one does not know the whole story," he said, his voice still too loud. "Is it logical to blame someone for what is done in his name when he does not know about it? For all I knew, they would use my blood and tissue to cure illness or prolong life. Would you not have done the same? Oh, I'm sure within your Federation such things are a matter of choice, so you wouldn't have any idea what it's like not to have the option of refusal."

What did he expect from her? she wondered. *Pity, understanding, acceptance?* Whatever it was, it was not hers to give. She thought of Tolek, refusing to accept the bullying of a proctor, refusing to cry out as his fingers were crushed in the cabinet door, thought of Spock and his personal *Kobayashi Maru.* There was always the option of refusal. She damped down the urge to ask him if he'd have been drugged, his tissues taken by force, if he'd refused. She was afraid he might say yes, and she might be tempted to forgive him.

Having made his "donation," he had suddenly found doors opened for him that had been closed before. His lack of family no longer mattered. Able now to choose any career path he wished, he chose a safe one as a bureaucrat, little more than a bookkeeper at first, but a keeper of secrets as well. Those secrets, he hoped, would one day make him powerful. Leave the posturing and flamboyance, the challenges and duals and assassinations, to others. Information would be his weapon.

He was bright, thorough, unobtrusive, yet able to say the right things to his superiors in a way that made them nod and smile when he was speaking but forget he existed as soon as he had left the room. As he rose through careful promotion, never drawing attention to himself but always moving upward, he began to be entrusted with highly classified material. That was where he learned of what could only be called a Romulan *Lebensborn* program.

"Are you familiar with the term? It's from some Earther language—don't ask me which one—and while Earthers didn't invent the concept, they have tried more perhaps than any other species to perfect it. In fact, as I understand it, several survivors of the last known human eugenics program caused your mentor's death not too long ago."

How was it possible he knew about Khan? Had she no secrets? Or was it simply that Spock and *Enterprise* were so well known that news of his death had traveled as far as the empires?

"Children were bred and born, some to volunteers, some by way of prisoners—Romulan criminals and Vulcan captives like the ones on the misbegotten planetoid where you spent your early years—who had desirable genetic traits. Those who 'bred true,' that is, those who possessed whatever particular traits the scientists were seeking at the time, were adopted into important families. Those who were deemed 'flawed' . . . am I boring you?"

For a second time she had turned her back on him. Conveying that she cared not whether he continued talking or lapsed into silence, went or stayed or was eaten by a *le-matya,* she had begun to gather reeds from the edges of the pool, cutting only the driest ones with the intention of making a fire. At the same time, still not entirely convinced he wasn't trying to lull her into complacency, her message was clear, *My back may be to you, and you may think me off guard, but the knife and the skills with which I use it are equally sharp!*

Behind her, she heard him laugh again. It was a humorless sound, more disdain than amusement, but even his disdain rang hollow. She knew where his narrative was going and wished he'd get on with it.

"Living like an animal all this time, and now you choose to undergo some ritual of civilization? What are you trying to prove?"

She ignored him, hearing him drink from the water flask again before he went on.

"By now you've intuited something of what this narrative has to do with you," he said wetly. Without looking she could picture him wiping those full lips with the back of his hand, perhaps even spilling a few precious drops into the sand, and she wondered if what was in the flask was only water. "I'll be brief. Offspring who proved less than optimal were eliminated—some euthanized, some dumped on colony worlds, though Hellguard was the worst of those."

She had scooped a depression in the sand and lined it with stones. Now she arranged the reeds so that the fire would be sheltered from the desultory wind and reached into her sash—her gestures almost as elaborate as his had been in reaching for the water flask, to show she was not going for a weapon—and retrieved a palm-sized fire starter. Suddenly she was aware that he was on his feet, moving toward her. She gritted her teeth to keep from reaching for the knife. Not yet.

"So, not quite mad after all," he observed. "A madwoman wouldn't have had the presence of mind to bring a fire starter with her when she stormed away from the shrine. You planned this meeting almost as carefully as I did."

She glanced up to find him standing quite close by, looking down at her in a way that made her flesh crawl. At last she could see his eyes, as large and dark and luminous as her own. Almost convincing.

"Looking at you, one cannot imagine what those who rejected you were thinking," he mused. "What possible imperfection did they think they saw under their microscopes? Whatever it was, it caused them not to kill you outright. Perhaps in addition to all the other perversities perpetuated on Hellguard, they allowed you to live in order to test your endurance. Had they not abandoned the colony when they did . . . Say something, anything, please."

Intriguing, she thought, how he vacillated between mockery and what seemed to be a need for her approval. She glowered at him.

"It is an interesting fairy tale," she suggested. "Far more palatable than 'I raped your mother and abandoned you to starve.' "

He started visibly then, the careful mask slipping before he remembered who was supposed to have the upper hand here.

"Oh, you're good!" he said, recovering himself, though not easily. "Grown to adulthood without knowing who your parents are, but you accept the revelation so casually?"

She'd been concentrating on getting the fire started.

By now the first few wisps of smoke revealed a small flame, which she nurtured into permanence.

"You do accept that I'm your father?" he reiterated against her silence, and she thought, *Good!*

"If one fairy tale, why not another?"

Carefully, she fed the fire. She had given considerable thought to what gesture she would make when he arrived, and making a fire seemed the best choice. Not necessary for warmth so long after she'd acclimated herself to the cold desert nights, certainly not necessary for cooking now that she was accustomed to eating animal flesh, and raw, once more. Not even necessary to ward off predators, since nothing larger than a *gli* snake had threatened her in all this time. Why then?

Because there was something common to their ancestry that caused long-civilized Vulcans to retain firepots in their homes and gave Romulans an affectation toward lighting the corridors of public buildings with flaming torches. Something about fire made a Vulcanoid want to sit and talk. And despite her disclaimer, she needed him to keep talking.

So, he claimed to be her biological father. Not a very original ploy. Neither was his attempt to make her empathize with the hapless young soldier all but force-marched to the sperm bank to make his "donation."

He sighed and retreated to his rock. "This is taking longer than I'd hoped. You don't mind if I continue?"

But she was looking past him suddenly and, as suddenly, the knife left her hand (how it got from her sash to her hand to begin with he never saw, focused as he was on trying to read her thoughts in her careful face)

and sailed past his left ear, causing him to scramble to
his feet, his own weapon—a small Romulan disruptor,
if she were to judge correctly from this distance—at the
ready, too late.

She'd thrown the knife from where she'd been
crouched over the fire. Now she got to her feet and
strode past him as casually as if he were just another
of the tall cacti gathered in a clump behind him, where
her knife had fixed itself, pinning a variety of very large
lepidoptera attracted by the firelight. Its palm-sized
body was mostly liquid, but that liquid contained a
few trace nutrients that long-ago desert dwellers had
prized.

Twisting off the wings as she returned to the fire,
she allowed them to flutter toward her visitor who now,
realizing the knife had not been aimed at him, had put
the disruptor away and was trying to recover his equilibrium. One colorful wing clung to his travel cloak, the
other came to rest on one of his boots as Saavik sucked
the moisture out of the moth's body and dropped the
remaining exoskeleton casually into the fire, where it
flamed blue for a moment before disintegrating.

Her point had been made, and quite literally driven
home. Now she knew how heavily he was armed and
where he had secreted the disruptor. The fact that he'd
reached for that meant he hadn't brought an Honor
Blade. Just so, she had the measure of him. Trium-
phant, she busied herself with gutting a *gli* snake she
had killed the night before, preparing to roast it over
the fire.

"Go on," she challenged him as the snake meat began

to sizzle. "You were about to tell your daughter another fairy tale . . ."

Doubtless the authorities had never intended him to discover what disposition had been made of his genetic material. Indeed, having required him to donate it, they'd quickly forgotten about him, leaving him free to use his employment for research purposes. As he worked his way up in the hierarchy, acquiring higher and higher clearances and access to greater and greater secrets, he learned the details of the program to breed superior offspring, and its various failures.

He began at great risk to himself to delve ever deeper into the files until he found that, indeed, his DNA had produced a single female offspring who, having been found "unacceptable" for reasons even his clearance level did not permit him to learn, had been spared elimination but relegated, along with a handful of others, to a distant colony world where their presence was only one of several horrors.

"From then on I became driven to find you. You cannot know the risks I incurred, burrowing through files, following one lead after another, hacking databases whose very existence should have been denied me. I will tell you only that it took the better part of a year to learn the name and location of the place where you and the others had been left in the care of those who were charged with keeping you fed and healthy until such time as . . . well, even the most hidden of files did not specify what was in store for you. I was haunted by the thought that I might not be in time. How I was to gain access to this place, much less retrieve you, was not something I could even postulate. My thought was that I could somehow alter the files to indicate that there had been an error, and that Specimen 8390923 must be returned at once to the homeworld. Had I thought it through further, I'd have realized . . ."

His voice had become a monotone, soothing almost, if one did not heed the words, background noise like the chittering of the chiroptera lurking in the forks of the cacti ringing the clearing, curious but not daring to come too close because of the fire, whose light was reflected in the glowing coals of their eyes. Saavik busied herself with turning the spit on which the snake was roasting, the aroma of the meat, and that time in her life when it was a regular part of her diet evoking memories of Tolek and the others that she wished would go away. More than ever she wondered if there had been anything she might have done to prevent their deaths, since it was clear they'd been murdered on her account.

". . . ultimately it did not matter because the colony had been abandoned and the planet eventually destroyed itself. Were I not in a position to learn more, I might have despaired, thinking you were dead. But I continued my search, based only on a sense that if you had died, blood of my blood, I would somehow have known."

By that logic, how could you not have known I existed from the beginning? Saavik thought, not for the first time clenching her teeth to hold in the words. She wanted to lash out at him, make him stop speaking, but he was correct about one thing: Her curiosity would not allow it. She had to *know*.

Feigning a calm she did not feel, she lifted the spit from the fire and waited for the meat to cool enough to eat. Should she offer him some? The desert dweller's traditional courtesy was the thought foremost in her mind as other parts of her brain hummed with the permutations of what would happen if he ever stopped temporizing and got to his real reasons for being here.

"Something told me you still lived, but how? I kept searching but found nothing."

"Yet, you are here," she said, meeting his eyes. Dark, like hers. Was he truly her father? He could be anyone. Did it matter? Was biology alone sufficient?

"Yes, I am here. And now at last your curiosity is piqued, because no mere coincidence can explain my presence. Perhaps it's the very convenience of my presence and the neatness of my story that make you doubt me. Am I right?"

"Doubt that you are here to eliminate all trace of the survivors of this . . . *Lebensborn* program? No, that I do not doubt."

"Not all," he said. "I was given permission to spare one of that number. You see, as careful as I was, they found me . . ."

At last the bleeding had finally stopped, but what was left of his tunic, tossed into a corner by his interrogator, was so saturated it left virid smears on the terrazzo floor, and Narak wondered with an odd sort of clinical detachment (the first signs of shock, perhaps?) just how much blood he had lost.

He was never to learn the interrogator's name, though her voice would worm its way into his brain more insidiously than a Ceti eel, painless but insistent, an echo behind every move he made until this exercise was concluded and he—perhaps—exonerated.

"My superiors initially instructed me to execute you," the interrogator said as the Uhlan released him from his restraints at her nod, and he tried to remember what it felt like to have the use of one's hands. "I spent considerable time persuading them that someone of your . . . skills could be of more use to us alive. Here is what you will do to earn your life back . . ."

"I confess I had to ask her to repeat my orders several times," Narak said now, biting fastidiously into the portion of snake meat Saavik had offered him. At her gesture he had also been given permission to sit with her on the opposite side of the fire, and she studied his features—almost too familiar yet not in a way that resonated with her on some visceral level—as he ate and continued to talk. "I apologized, telling her the blood loss made me dizzy, but in truth I was so elated at the thought that you were still alive, and that I was in effect being sent to seek you out—"

"—in order to kill me." *Gli* snake flesh was greasy, and she wiped her chin with the back of her hand.

He stopped chewing and sighed. "Only if you did not see the wisdom of the alternative. You're still alive, are you not? You don't suppose I'd have simply strolled into your camp if I'd intended to kill you? Or are you so sure of your own skills that you think you'd have sensed my presence, hm? Indulge me a while longer and ask yourself this: What would you have done in my place?"

Ever since the *Kobayashi Maru* she had plagued herself with questions like that, postulating countless no-win scenarios, studying the histories of the leaders of several worlds to learn what they had done against untenable situations. Terms like "Pyrrhic victory"— mental exercises for her classmates, an acknowledgment of reality for her—became ingrained in her vocabulary. Tolek's crushed fingers had spared her punishment, Spock's exaggerations had skirted the bounds of Vulcan integrity in order to mislead Khan and save the ship.

She had never lived on Narak's world. How did she know what situational ethics she might have employed to stay alive there?

She shook her head, suddenly sated with the roasted meat, her senses dulled, her thoughts muddled. His words were like a drug, inducing her to see the universe through his eyes.

"I suppose," she said, "I'd have done what I could to survive, so that I could find my offspring and spare her before someone else was sent in my place."

His smile was benevolent. "Precisely!" he said.

The fire had died down somewhat by now, and the surface of the pool at her back had begun to shimmer as it did almost nightly, breeding the low-lying fog peculiar to this place and the reason she had chosen it. Her visitor seemed surprised to encounter fog in the desert and drew his cloak about him, apparently disconcerted.

"Does it always do this?"

"More often than not," she replied, almost conversational by now, making note of the fact that he had not noticed the fog before, confirming her assumption that he had come to this place only hours and not days earlier. From where? she wondered, and where would he go when he left? Assuming, of course, that she allowed him to leave. Knife against disruptor, who would survive? Time to find out. "What do you want?"

"Succinct and to the point, hm?" He got to his feet a little too abruptly, so that again she almost went for the knife. But she saw that it was only because he felt the need to brush the sand off his garments, and relaxed. "I imagine you get that from your mother. Surely not from me, because as you've noticed, I have a tendency to talk too much. Do I see a glimmer of interest in those dark eyes? Surely you want to know who she was?"

"What do you want?" she said again, beginning to seethe. Would a knife to the throat be the only thing that would make him stop talking?

He sighed. "I thought we might take some time to get to know each other before we got down to work, but very well. I need an ally. I want it to be you."

"An ally? For what purpose?"

"The discredit, disgrace, and ultimate dismissal as ambassador of Sarek of Vulcan."

Fourteen

Her knife was at his throat.

"Excellent reflexes," he observed. "Think carefully now."

She'd recalled a simple trick taught her by a human martial arts instructor at the Academy.

"Catch them in midsentence," Commander Nodurft had said. When the cadets had shifted their feet on the mats and exchanged glances, none wanting to be the first to ask her what she meant, she'd laughed at them.

"Think about every action movie you've ever seen. When does the fight start? After the Bad Guy says something that makes the Good Guy see red and he lunges at him. Why wait for him to get to the end of the sentence?"

There'd been nervous laughter, mutters of, "Yeah, I knew that!" until Cadet Saavik politely raised her hand.

"Yes, Cadet?" Nodurft had acknowledged her.

"Your suggestion is logical, Commander, but I submit it is incomplete."

Nodurft had stood there with her hands on her hips, feet planted firmly, exuding the kind of confidence that enjoyed a challenge.

"Explain."

"Logic suggests, sir"—in the flick of an eyclash she

had pinned Nodurft to the mat—"that the Good Guy can also launch an attack while in the middle of her own sentence."

A ripple of sound reverberated around the gym. Ordinarily Cadet Saavik was quiet to a fault. Once the male cadets realized there was no point in flirting with her, she went largely unnoticed in training classes, just as she'd learned the hard way not to dominate all of the academic classes. Murmurs from surprise to amusement to, "Oh, she's gonna catch it now!" reached her sensitive ears as Nodurft picked herself up from the mat and made an elaborate ritual of dusting herself off.

"Not bad, Cadet." She'd grinned, no harm done. "Not bad at all. I'll take your observation under"—now it was Saavik's turn to hit the mat—"consideration from now on."

And she did.

So did Saavik. Narak had no sooner mentioned Sarek's name than she reacted as he'd expected her to, with one variation.

"You cannot be serious!" she had cried with just the right amount of outrage. "You expect me to betray the one who took me into his home and"—without so much as taking a deep breath, she became a whirlwind, knocking him facedown in the sand and straddling him, pinning his arms at his sides, her knife at his throat as she relieved him of his disruptor, flinging it into the thicket of cacti. She grabbed a handful of his hair and pulled his head back to give the knife a better purchase against his throat. Only then did she finish her sentence—"and made me a member of his family?"

Narak spat sand out of his mouth and did something extraordinary for someone in his position. He yawned.

"Did you really think I came all this way just for you?" He laughed, though his inability to draw a full breath with her sitting on him made it difficult. "Excellent reflexes. Think carefully, now."

She did, tying his hands behind him with her sash and his ankles with his own belt before dragging him across the sand to the stand of cacti and propping him against one.

"Strong as well as quick," he commented, flexing his shoulders, feeling the cactus spines finding their way through the fabric of his cloak and deciding he was better off sitting still. "What do you suppose happens now? What if I'm not alone?"

She stood over him, hefting the knife from hand to hand, waiting for the anger to subside. "Then your companions apparently consider you expendable, or they'd have intervened when it appeared as if I might cut your throat."

He gifted her with his best sardonic smile. "Of course I'm expendable, but so are you. If you do not hear me out and follow through, someone else will. That someone else might not have the same . . . compassion for the ambassador that you do. Not content merely to compromise his career, they might choose a quicker course of action."

Suddenly drained of energy—the weeks of desert living and the stressors that had come before had taken their toll—Saavik allowed herself to return to her seat on the flat rock, though she kept the knife at the ready.

She breathed deeply. "Start from the beginning."

Narak shifted his weight again, found a position where the cactus spines didn't poke him. "I am but one of many on Vulcan. Some of us have been here for decades—"

"Sleeper agents," Saavik supplied.

"'Sleeper agents,'" he repeated, canting his head to one side as if to study the concept. "This is not a term I have heard before, but then I have not been on this side of the Marches for very long. Very well, then, sleeper agents, who watch and wait for opportunities to undermine Vulcan, and the Federation, whenever we can. Those who set the greatest store by honesty are those most easily misled. We are drawn here by the gullibility of Vulcan authorities, who think that peace is a real possibility, despite the fact that the innate forces of the universe dictate otherwise."

"You subscribe to the Elements, then," she observed. "I did not take you for the religious type."

"Say rather I am the pragmatic type. If there are gods who intervene in mortal endeavors, it doesn't hurt to stay on their good side. If there aren't, there's no harm in ingratiating oneself among those who believe there are."

"Go on."

"As you might surmise, Ambassador Sarek has been of interest to us throughout his distinguished career. But word of his preliminary negotiations with the Klingons on behalf of the Federation has of course reached the Romulan Senate, causing much consternation. If anyone can bring the Klingon Empire and the Federation to the same table, it is Sarek, and the threat that these two powerful entities, combined in an alliance, would pose to the Romulan Empire is simply not acceptable."

"You intend to assassinate Sarek?" Saavik asked with far more equanimity than she felt.

Narak's smile widened. "Of course not. Any overt action—a military or terrorist attack, an attempt on Sarek's life—would be obvious and could lead to war. But if Sarek himself proved to be not what the Klingons, or even his own people, thought him to be, negotiations could be called off indefinitely."

Saavik seemed to be weighing this. "As you say, however, we are all expendable. Even Sarek can be replaced."

"But not easily. And not by another with such finely honed skills. In the inevitable search for a replacement, other actions can be implemented."

Saavik had a glimpse of it then, a plot as elaborate and full of twists and turns as the mandalas she had been drawing in the sand. How many sleeper agents, at what levels of Vulcan society, assigned to wreak what havoc? And all of it, right now, hinging on whether or not she gave consent to her assigned role.

The smell of the fire, which had long since died to ashes, lingered in her nostrils. To the east, the false dawn brightened the horizon. Whatever decisions were made would have to be made soon, before the day's heat made them moot. Narak seemed to be thinking the same thing.

"Time to get down to business. You'll find a listening device in my left boot," he said casually. "You see what I mean about Vulcan trust and gullibility? Well-trained Starfleet officer that you are, you relieved me of the weapon you saw, but it never occurred to you to search for others."

It was smaller than an earring and irregularly shaped. At first glance it might have been taken for a small, flat stone, which was of course the point. It could be dropped in a flowerbed or lost in the desert, depending on the circumstances.

So. Their entire conversation had been overheard, or at least that was what he wanted her to believe.

"I wouldn't destroy it if I were you," Narak advised mildly. "If you do, you won't get out of the desert alive. May I?"

At his nod, she brought it closer to his face. He spoke what sounded like a code into it, then nodded again. "Now. A good whack with a rock should do it, but stepping on it is usually best."

The whole rigmarole was so ludicrous she might have laughed. Instead, she did as he'd suggested, feeling a bizarre satisfaction at hearing it crunch between the flat rock and the heel of her sandal.

"Now what?" she demanded, after first retrieving the disruptor from among the cacti and searching him more thoroughly for weapons this time, finding nothing further.

"You might start by untying me."

"I might," she acknowledged.

Instead, she went about building up the fire. She

could see the puzzlement on his face. False dawn had faded, and the genuine predawn blush meant 40 Eridani would shortly loom over the horizon. There would be no need for a fire's heat then, and if it were meant as a signal, it would not be seen in sunlight. What was she up to?

Seeing that she could continue to surprise him was strangely satisfying. When the fire was crackling pleasantly, she drew her knife once more and studied him. His expression of puzzlement had changed to one of mild alarm. He was still bound, she had all the weapons, he'd destroyed the listening device by prearranged signal. If she killed him now, the others in his cell would eventually track her down and destroy her and the mission would go forward, but he would still be dead.

Had he misjudged her? he was wondering. *Was she desperate enough to destroy them both?*

She watched him consider his error—perhaps accountants did not make good spies after all—and cherished it far longer than a Vulcan would.

"I can tell you your mother's name."

Did she only imagine a tremor in his voice?

She shrugged, once more hefting the knife from hand to hand, as if wondering where she might begin if she chose to eviscerate him instead of making a clean kill.

"Perhaps you can. Assuming you weren't lying. And I am not prepared to make that assumption yet."

With that she took a handful of her own hair where it was most damaged from sun, dirt, exposure, and lack of grooming, and began to hack it off, tossing the shorn locks methodically into the fire where they hissed and vanished, giving off a ritual smoke not unlike incense. When there was nothing left but the practical cap of curls with which she'd first appeared in Sarek's household as a child, she ran her fingers through it and seemed transformed, another person entirely from the one who had crossed the desert. Only then did she untie her captive.

"What happens now?" she asked.

Access to Sarek's office in the Enclave at Vulcan High Command had been granted far too readily. Impressed as she was with the technology that allowed Narak to alter her palm prints, ear prints, even retinal patterns, she wondered how it was possible that no one had so much as hesitated, much less questioned her presence. Was it true, as he'd told her, that those like him were leavened everywhere throughout Vulcan society?

She had not, of course, simply accepted her role in this mission without numerous questions, which she saved for when they were both strapped in to the two-person skimmer he'd left amid a scattering of boulders half a day's walk from her camp.

"The rocks in this region show high amounts of titanium," he informed her.

"Clever," she acknowledged. "Long-range scans would likely not detect a craft of this size obscured by the background metals."

"I am nothing if not thorough," he said with a touch of pride.

Able to study him at close range, Saavik was again

struck by the physical resemblance between them, whether real or contrived. Still, she felt nothing other than a mild annoyance at the smugness she sensed would easily transform itself into obsequiousness in the presence of those he saw as his "betters."

"Say everything you have told me is true, and I have no choice but to follow your instructions," she said over the whine of the skimmer's powering-up. It was a standard rented skimmer, she noted, unlocked by thumbprint scan, so she was unable to learn what name her captor, now coconspirator, used while he was on Vulcan. "What happens to me when I have done?"

"I must confess the idea of taking down a Starfleet officer, especially such a visible one, at the same time as the ambassador was enticing," Narak mused, almost to himself, his gaze focused on the windscreen as the skimmer rose only high enough to clear the ground, following the contours of the terrain. (*Also clever*, Saavik acknowledged silently. Unless someone were actively looking for him, their flight would also go unnoticed.) "But I had to remind myself that you and I are family. That had to count for something, after all, and it was the one point I was able to negotiate with my superiors. As it turned out"—here he made a face that might be sincere chagrin or not—"they did not trust me to manage two such feats in a single mission. I am, after all, only an accountant at heart.

"So, as it stands, my limitation works to your advantage. You'll be given a false identity—let's call her an avatar—for the first phase. Once that phase is completed, your avatar will conveniently journey offworld for an unspecified time, while shortly thereafter Lieutenant Saavik, late of Starfleet, may emerge from the desert freed of the demons that drove her there, subject herself to medical examination, and be cleared to resume her life and her career."

"Unless, of course, the empire needs her for additional missions," Saavik observed dryly. She had not given him back his disruptor, and he hadn't seemed to care. Not for the first time, she wondered if he truly was protected by a vast network of fellow agents, or operating alone. "It is said that there is only one way out of the life of a spy."

Narak's smug little smile widened. "Largely exaggerated, I'm afraid. Seriously, you will be allowed to go on your way, for now. We may need you, after all, when the Federation's peace feelers to the Klingons fail and the two sides go to war."

Thus with the augmentations Narak provided (applied in a safe house whose location she was unable to determine with any exactitude), a tall, attractive young Vulcan civilian female named T'Vaakis took up residence in a block of flats within walking distance of the Enclave that enclosed Vulcan High Command, having ostensibly relocated from the remote polar city of Nah'namKir, where she had earned her degrees in linguistics and communications, in search of employment. All of her documents were in order, and the rental agent barely glanced at her as he let her into the flat.

Saavik found herself torn between amazement at the thoroughness with which Narak and his handlers

had accomplished this, and annoyance at their obvi-
ousness.

"T'Vaakis? Could you find a more obvious rear-
rangement of the letters of my true name?" she wanted
to know. "As for giving my point of origin as the very
city where you murdered Tolek—"

"Ah, careful now!" Narak said, not for the first time.
"The dearly departed may or may not have met an
untimely end, but you would be hard-pressed to connect me with the instrumentality."

*At present I am hard-pressed to do anything other
than yield to your instructions!* Saavik thought, seething.

"At least give me credit for a well-honed sense of
irony. No? As for your name, the thought was that it
would be easier for you to remember than something
more obscure. Trust me, no one will notice. Everyone
from your landlord to the gatekeepers at Vulcan High
Command will scan your documentation, see that it is
in order and, expecting nothing less, grant you complete autonomy. You'll see."

The fact that he proved correct only made her
angrier. Had Vulcan truly grown so complacent?

Having assumed her new identity, she had expected
explicit instructions.

"There will be none," Narak had told her, his breath
on her face as he admired the lens implants that would
alter her retinal patterns. "It is assumed you're clever
enough to figure out how best to destroy Sarek's reputation on your own. All you need do is report to one of
your contacts periodically and update your progress."

"'One of my contacts'? Not you?"

"Alas, no. To be truthful, this assignment was assembled somewhat hastily. It's as if my superiors are testing me as much as you." He handed her a small memory chip. "This is time-coded. It will tell you whom you're to contact and where when the time comes. Oh, and don't try to tamper with it." Had he studied her so well? "It has a built-in self-destruct. For the rest, you know Sarek better than any of us, for all our years of observation. Follow your instincts."

"Why is it necessary for me to visit the Enclave in person? Surely whatever 'evidence' I manufacture can be planted by remote."

"And tracked back to the source," Narak said, shaking his head at her naïveté. "Vulcan may be complacent, but it's not ignorant. I'm afraid you'll have to risk being caught on the premises. But you'll see I'm right."

Again she'd had to grit her teeth to keep from lunging at him, ripping out his throat, and throwing herself on the mercy of the nearest authorities. But who, exactly, would she be at that point? Former Lieutenant Saavik, late of Starfleet, who, following a series of emotional outbursts, had ostensibly lashed out and killed an old man at a sacred shrine? Or a cipher named T'Vaakis who had sprung into existence only a few hours earlier, and whose "burn identity" had not yet been confirmed by the handler currently violating her personal space in order to transform her into something she was not? T'Vaakis would be detained as a spy. Saavik's fate was less certain. How did she know the authorities she was turning herself over to were not also part of the Romulan plan?

Keeping still as Narak puttered with the syntheskin on her ears and not letting her thoughts seep through to her face took up all her energy. There had to be a way out of this. She simply had not found it yet.

Perhaps, once she gained entrance to the Enclave, it would find her.

She had occasionally accompanied Sarek to his office as a child—not often, but often enough. While she had not been there in years, surely, she thought, someone would recognize her now.

No one did. She had strode through the massive bronze entrance doors, across the echoing marble foyer ("art deco," she'd heard Commander Uhura refer to it once, and simultaneously wondered what that meant and when Uhura had had opportunity to be here), and through the security zones with ease—again, more attention was paid to her credentials than to her face—and moved among the staff, ostensibly inquiring about a minor clerk's position that had conveniently opened up in an ancillary department (had Narak's people arranged that too?), tamping down memories of walking beside the ambassador, dressed in her best clothes, a new tunic bought especially for the occasion, as a sudden adolescent growth spurt had made her taller than Amanda all but overnight, an expression of great solemnity on her face as Sarek introduced her to those with whom he worked whenever he was on Vulcan.

According to the laws of physics, there was a sense by which the very molecules of the walls and floors "remembered" her because she had passed this way before. Saavik wished with a child's passion that they would cry out and give her away so that she did not have to do this thing.

Barring that, she might wish that Sarek himself would pass her in the corridor and, not even trying to disguise the warmth in his eyes, inquire pleasantly why she was here, so that she could pour her heart out to him and throw herself on his mercies.

But she had been away so long she did not even know where Sarek was, where any of those most important to her were. Here in the throbbing heart of the universe as she knew it, she was more alone than she had been on Hellguard. At least there she had had the stars.

With a start, she saw someone approaching her in the corridor, someone who had known her in the life she had left behind. Surely now this charade would be ended.

The ancient one Simar rose from his simple pallet as he did daily, to greet the dawn with optimism and a glad heart, for the eighty thousand three hundred and fourth time. Having performed his ablutions and his morning meditation and partaken of a simple breakfast, he repaired to the orchards to see to the gathering of fruit, which was his particular pleasure. The young ones no longer permitted him to climb to the highest branches, but what he could reach from the ground was his to gather. The simple task pleased him, leaving his mind clear to explore the mysteries of the universe. This morning, however, before his gathering basket was even half full, he became aware of the presence of someone who had glided up silently beside him.

"Another day, Old One," T'Saan of the V'Shar greeted him pleasantly, joining him in the picking.

"And a glorious one," he responded, his pale eyes sparkling. "Especially to one so recently recalled to life."

It was how he greeted his superior whenever they spoke following the event that had sent Saavik into the desert some months before. Call it a story with a humorous climax.

In a place as devoid of technology as Amorak, it had been simplicity itself to fake the old one's death and allow the rumor of it to ripple throughout Vulcan society on the say-so of a handful of temporary guests at the shrine once they returned to their routine lives.

T'Saan had at first considered throwing in a few more "deaths" to make the story more convincing. She had done this before, using the names of Vulcans who had died as infants and building lives for them in the archives, but this time it had seemed quite literally like overkill. It would be difficult enough rehabilitating Saavik when this was over, and besides, she owed one of the V'Shar's eldest operatives his own moment of glory.

Thus Simar, very much alive, suppressed a smile as he remembered how he and Saavik had "struggled" before he fell to the tiled floor in a reasonable facsimile of violent death, giving credence to the young woman's "madness" for the benefit of the person or persons who were stalking her. Now that it was assumed those persons no longer had eyes on Amorak, it was safe for Simar to live once more.

"Was it wise for you to come here in person?" he asked T'Saan now, thinking her presence might renew the interest of the watchers.

She had thrown back the hood of her travel cloak then, and he saw that she wore a face different from the one he'd seen the last time they'd met. It had been her voice by which he'd recognized her.

"None but you knows who I truly am. I thought you deserved to hear my gratitude in person."

"A long journey for an unnecessary indulgence," the old one remarked dryly. "Most illogical."

"So you used to tell me when I was your student," T'Saan mused. "Nevertheless, that wasn't my only reason."

Simar set down the picking basket and tried to read T'Saan's face, no easy task even for someone who had known her since she was younger than Saavik.

"She has been successful, then?"

T'Saan nodded. "With the first phase, yes. She has earned the infiltrator's trust and gained access to the Enclave."

Simar looked thoughtful. "Was it this dangerous when we were that age?"

T'Saan thought about this. "Doubtless it was. We were simply too young to realize it."

Simar carried the picking basket to the gathering place. When he looked back, T'Saan was never there.

Saavik's steps faltered. The elder coming toward her was none other than T'Lores, who had been Sarek's aide for as long as anyone could remember. She had in fact

been a part of the Enclave before Sarek's tenure, helping the green young diplomat find his way when he
first arrived. It was as if T'Lores had been there from
the time of the beginning. If anyone would recognize
Saavik for who she was, it would be this one.

But T'Lores, her step sprightly despite her great age,
simply glanced at the young woman's visitor's badge,
then at her face, and nodded in greeting as was only
polite among strangers. Barely recovering herself in
time, T'Vaakis did the same. Finding the correct turn
in the corridor, and the office to which she needed
access unlocked and devoid of personnel, she set about
leaving the first of a series of data triggers.

There was much to remember. During their time in
the safe house, Narak had had her memorize a plethora of information—dates and times and places where
Sarek had purportedly met with Romulan agents and
persons of interest, to exchange information for finan-
cial considerations and other perquisites, his goal being
to undermine the very peace initiative with the Klingons that he claimed to espouse.

Memorization was essential for this first phase of the
endeavor. Potential employee T'Vaakis had entered the
Enclave empty-handed. It was doubtful she would give
anyone any reason to have her searched, but Narak's
masters had been thorough. Everything T'Vaakis
needed to enter into the main database within the
Enclave was contained in her memory. Hard data such
as holographic "evidence" and supposedly intercepted
communications would be supplied in later phases.

Doing it this way would be time-consuming, hence

dangerous. She would have to gain access to a computer away from prying eyes and sensitive ears and enter key words and strings of code manually into several secured levels without triggering alarms or firewalls.

Narak had chosen the ideal candidate for the task. Even the most thorough spies outside the walls would not know in detail what she knew, right down to where the least used data entry areas were, and which codes to use to access them.

"That went well," she heard Narak's voice in her ear, courtesy of a cochlear implant no larger than an eyelash, as she seated herself at a data console within sight of the door, in case someone entered unexpectedly and she had to do a data dump. *"You were hoping the old one would recognize you, weren't you?"*

"Pure supposition on your part," T'Vaakis barely whispered, beginning to tap in the requisite codes. As invasive as Narak's procedures had been, even he could not monitor the increase in her heart rate as the old one had passed her without recognition. Still, how in the hells did he know what had just transpired in the corridor? Was there more to the corneal implants—cameras as well as retinal reorganizers—than she'd suspected?

"Call it hope," Narak said. *"If you hadn't been wishing she'd recognize you and blow your cover, I'd have thought you'd given in too easily."*

"Do you wish me to proceed, or will you continue to distract me?" she demanded tightly.

"My apologies," Narak said with a chuckle. *"Just one question. How do you feel?"*

Saavik hesitated. "Strangely exhilarated."

. . .

"Subject has entered data room in Sector V as expected," T'Lores said quietly into the personal communicator within the jeweled family crest that decorated the left lapel of her tunic.

"Excellent!" came T'Saan's voice in return.

"Instructions, Lady?"

"At present, observe only."

"Do you wish me to quarantine her inputs when she has finished?"

"Negative. Let them venture where they may, that we may ascertain the extent of the journey before we terminate it."

Fifteen

———

Infiltrating the Enclave and implanting the trigger codes was the first phase and the simplest. Having been given no instructions for the next phase, Saavik was not overly surprised when she returned to her rooms that evening to find that the door code had been activated, the door left slightly open, and someone was waiting for her inside.

She had been told to expect the appearance of handlers at all stages of this venture, but she had not expected to encounter a mirror image of herself.

Obviously another Romulan sleeper agent, was her first thought as she studied the young woman—on closer examination, not her literal twin; the look was identical, but something about the way she moved said she was not yet out of that awkward adolescent stage— examining the decor in the sitting room. *Obvious, for one, because a Vulcan would not presume to touch another's belongings without permission.*

Inwardly she scowled. Why did the interloper's actions irritate her more than her presence? They weren't *her* belongings to begin with but had been provided by another of Narak's cohort in the unlikely event that T'Vaakis chose to entertain visitors, or even that

her landlord might become curious enough to gain
entry to the flat.

That, Saavik decided, was Romulan thinking, just as
what her twin was doing was Romulan behavior. *Curious how they can live among us for years but still not
grasp the nuance. Hold that thought; it may prove useful!*

"Who are you, and what are you doing here?" she
demanded. She had a fair idea, but she wanted to hear
the words.

"I am called T'Vaakis," her doppelgänger said, "and
I am considering which of my belongings to put into
storage and which to send on ahead to my destination."

"Which is . . . ?"

". . . not something a Vulcan, out of respect for
another's privacy, would ask." The interloper set down
the vase she had been examining and rewarded Saavik with a look as unwavering as her own. Her eyes
were luminous, dark, as large as Saavik's . . . or Narak's.
Almost as if she could read Saavik's thoughts, the
stranger sighed and looked away. "Probably unwise to
send anything onward, lest you be tempted to trace my
whereabouts."

This was interesting. "Do you doubt my commit-
ment to the mission?"

"Better to doubt and be mistaken than to trust and
be betrayed."

Saavik had a sense, then, of how Narak must have
felt when he was grooming her to enter the Enclave,
and the thought that occurred there was, *If he had
this one, why did he need me? No doubt the identity he*

provided me, or at least the palm print that opened the door, is hers.

"Spoken like a true Romulan," she said wryly. A lifetime of near obsession with truthfulness had made her particularly unprepared for the layers of duplicity she was now required to participate in.

Think! She may look the part, but only you knew where to go within the Enclave, how to access the mainframe, and where exactly to plant the data triggers. Tread cautiously. Just as you have passed as T'Vaakis to this point, from here forward she might as easily be altered to pass as Saavik. If you are to survive to complete this mission, you must keep your head clear!

"I will take that as a compliment," T'Vaakis said, returning the wry smile. "Come. We have much to do and not much time . . ."

It has always been easier to destroy than to create. Removing the augmentations that had transformed Saavik into T'Vaakis took far less time than Narak had needed to add them. The real T'Vaakis worked quickly and silently to destroy all trace of the palm prints, ear prints, and retinal distorters. The cochlear implant remained. Narak's voice nagging in Saavik's ear would persist, with the added annoyance that she could not answer him.

"So T'Vaakis departs her rented rooms just as she arrived," she mused as, with a snap of her fingers, the real T'Vaakis indicated that Saavik was to exchange clothing with her to complete the ruse. "Leaving Saavik with a conundrum. How am I to explain my sudden appearance in ShiKahr when my last known whereabouts was the shrine, and there is no record of my having reentered the city of my childhood?"

T'Vaakis, knowing she was meant to convey these thoughts to their mutual handler, declined to answer. She was more intent on gathering a datapadd, several garments from the wardrobe, and some toiletries, which she placed in a small travel bag, the better to appear authentic in her resumed identity if she were questioned for any reason. Saavik could almost admire her.

Doubtless, Saavik thought, *Narak will transport her out of the city the same way he had brought her in.* Without the corneal implants, Narak could no longer see what she saw. If she were to follow the real T'Vaakis from a discreet distance . . .

"You're to remain in the flat until your twin is safely on her way," Narak said even as she considered it. "I may not be able to see through your eyes, but there are others watching."

Was he still watching and listening somehow? Perhaps the real T'Vaakis had also been transformed into a seeing and listening device.

"Tell your father I am most impressed," Saavik said as her twin prepared to leave.

There was no indication that Narak had overheard. But T'Vaakis, who had been almost out the door, went motionless. Then she turned, slowly, as if to counter with some snide remark, but physiology did not lie. The dark eyes had widened perceptibly, a quick flick of the tongue over dry lips revealed the truth—at least as

T'Vaakis knew it. Saavik had succeeded in startling her, and now she was trying to think. The physical resemblance was deliberate, in order to make it possible for her to pass herself off as Saavik's twin, but now she was wondering how Saavik had guessed so accurately.

If she wasn't just bluffing. If it was even true. If T'Vaakis knew one way or the other. Had Narak also appeared in her life out of nowhere with a similar sorry tale designed to win her over?

T'Vaakis processed all of these options, then chose to answer by not answering, merely raising an eyebrow as any Vulcan might, an expression that could mean anything in context, and took her leave as if she had never been there.

Well? What if she was your half sibling? Saavik thought. Nothing else to do but wait here until Narak gave her further instructions. *Examine this from every possible angle. Say Narak is your father. Say you have at least one half sibling, raised within the empire. Would she not, out of some adulation for a father who gave the pretense of loving her, as well as her sense of duty as a loyal Romulan, go along with this charade?*

The scientist's impulse was to scan the room for any trace of the interloper—a strand of hair, a remnant of a fingerprint (no need to search for the latter; were there not sufficient objects that Saavik-as-T'Vaakis had touched before the false palm prints had been removed?)—that could be used to verify whether or not this startlingly familiar avatar was in fact connected to her by genetics, if nothing else.

But the damaged child of Hellguard stopped the scientist in her tracks. *If you do not wish to know who your father was, you must not seek to know this answer, either.*

What was the last thing he had said before taking his leave of her?

"Disavow me if you wish. But I can tell you who your mother is."

He had brought the skimmer to rest on one of the numerous landing pads in the park ring encircling the city of ShiKahr, indicating that she was to walk from there to the flat he had arranged for her near the Enclave. Before he released the door lock to allow her to depart, he had secured her promise that she would do as he had instructed.

"Though unwillingly," she added.

"I'd be disappointed if it were otherwise," he'd said. "If you gave in too easily, it would mean I couldn't trust you."

He seemed to be searching for something more to say. The expression on his face was that of someone struggling with irreconcilable emotions. Saavik knew it well. She had seen it in the mirror on the rare occasions when she looked there. Again his sheer effrontery made her seethe inside, though nothing showed on her carefully controlled face. If he wasn't her father, he was a damn good actor. The gestures, the facial expressions were hers, and if she had subscribed to a belief in nature versus nurture, she would have to concede that there was a kinship here. On some wordless level, she *recognized* him. Still, there was no way of knowing how long he and his kind had had her under observation. Easy enough to study her gestures and emulate them.

She had sat in the skimmer with him, hearing the seconds tick by as he seemed to be searching for the right words. But even this could have been feigned.

"When this is done, it would please me to get to know you under less . . . expedient circumstances."

She stopped herself from lashing out at him. "That opportunity is lost to the childhood I never had," she said, her own poetry surprising her.

"I cannot say I blame you for such an emotional response," he said, as if to try her patience. "Disavow me if you wish. But I can tell you who your mother is."

Is? Meaning that she still lives? No, that I will not accept!

Silently, she had sat with her hands in her lap and stared him down until he yielded and unlocked the door. She strode away from the skimmer without looking back.

How much of that had been the truth? Everything he'd told her to this point had had the ring of truth, but she was so unused to duplicity she could not know for sure.

Once again, the memory of Spock served as her touchstone.

"You lied," she had accused him even in the midst of crisis as he beamed Admiral Kirk and the survivors up from the space station at Regula I, Khan Noonien Singh's need for vengeance making every second count.

Spock's expression had been benign. *Who, me?* "I exaggerated."

In retrospect, she could certainly understand the need for duplicity. How else could *Enterprise* have bought time in order to escape from Khan and his intentions? Her reaction at the time—yes, a purely emotional reaction—had been anger, and hurt, hurt that her mentor had not told her the truth.

Later, when she'd calmed down, she'd recalled the knowing looks of the rest of the bridge crew and realized that it was not only old familiarity with the ways of their commanding officers but also an intimate knowledge of the ship and its engineering crew that made it possible for them to retranslate days into hours.

Had Saavik been less emotional at the time, she might have done the same calculations and arrived at the same conclusions. The event taught her one thing: Never take anything on face value, not even a Vulcan's word.

It had also reminded her, as if she needed reminding, of just how naïve she truly was.

How simple life had seemed then, nothing but one *Kobayashi Maru* scenario after another to be solved and encapsulated, the time between filled with duties to perform and expectations to be met. The days and weeks and months that followed had taught her otherwise.

So T'Vaakis would rendezvous with Narak and return to wherever she had come from, and Saavik would wait, an interloper in the very place where only moments ago she had belonged, awaiting further instructions. The waiting gave her time to think and to entertain a fleeting regret.

Say T'Vaakis really was her sister, or not. Would it have cost her anything to make conversation, form a bond, perhaps ask her in some coded way, whether Narak could hear them or not, if she was happy with the role assigned her, if she ever had doubts, if in a different reality they could have called each other friend?

One thought led to another. Mikal, alone in all the universe, denying the family he had left behind on Tiburon, even those who had shown him kindness, seeking temporary solace in the arms of women, the morning light leaving him with the taste of ashes.

At least, she thought, angry with him, he had had the luxury of a family to turn away from. She had been denied that. Even if Narak truly was her father, he had not troubled himself with paternal responsibility until he wanted something. Better to have no family at all.

Mikal. Don't distract yourself with thoughts of Mikal now. He is lost to you. Even if you were ever to meet again, what could you possibly say to him?

Captain's Personal Log, Galina Mironova reporting. Data gathering's almost complete, and we'll soon be on our way home. Meanwhile, my chief scientist looks like hell. Maybe it's not just lovesickness after all. If I can't goad him into shaping up, I'll have to remand him to sickbay for a thorough going-over.

• • •

"How much longer, Mikal?" Mironova asked, study-ing the most recent data on the padd in front of her to avoid looking at him.

"We're moving out of that part of the sky," was Mikal's answer.

Poetry, Mironova thought, glancing up at him with a worried frown. *This is new!*

"What I mean is . . ." he began, reading her mind out of long habit, perhaps augmented by his telepathic interactions with Worm and Gwailim Loth, ". . . the rifts occur only in this region of near space. Deema III's orbit took it out of their path three days ago. There won't be any new appearances or disappearances until this time next year."

"Deema III's 'year' being four hundred seventeen days and change, am I correct?" Mironova said.

"Exactly. So we've located them, counted them, and gathered as much telemetry as we can on the stable ones. The astrometric data's complete, unless we want to wait around for a very long year."

"So that leaves only the work downplanet to com-plete. Estimate?"

"Since I put Palousek in charge of the base camp, the kids have been doing a bang-up job. Between Esparza's obsessive-compulsiveness and Jaoui's hyperfocus and Cheung's determination to be better than either of them, they've probably cataloged every blade of grass in the designated biomes."

"Clever of you to put someone else in charge so all

you have to do is drop by and oversee every few days," Mironova teased him, but he wasn't playing.

"I'm just saying, since there probably won't be anything new suddenly appearing on the surface, we can probably wrap up the geosciences surveys in another few days," he reported humorlessly. "Look, Galina—"

"Which leaves only the interpersonal interaction," Mironova said pointedly, folding her hands on the desktop and holding Mikal's gaze. "Call it sociology, call it diplomacy, call it making friends. How's it going?"

"You'd have to ask Loth," Mikal said a little too quickly.

"So you've been slacking off on that as well." It was a statement, not a question. "Remind me exactly what it is you're doing on this mission? Aside from hogging the glory when it comes to awards and additional entries in your CV, I mean."

"I'm doing what I signed on to do—supervising. Loth's the telepath; I'm only in the way. Things go much more smoothly when I'm not around. He says my 'vibe is disruptive,' whatever that means."

"I could have told him that," Mironova said sotto voce. Before Mikal could use his civilian prerogative to bark at her, she added. "So I guess I'm to consult with Loth about linguistics and that sort of thing before I put in an appearance and start nation building?"

"Please," Mikal suggested. "He'll tell you he's been compiling a linguistics database in order to construct a lexicon before the diplomats are sent here."

"Are they wanted here, though?" Mironova asked

incisively. "The diplomats, I mean? As part of the first-contact team for Worm and the others, it was incumbent upon you to determine that."

"Loth can just as easily—"

"Practically speaking, yes. Loth *can*, but it was understood that you would participate. It's a matter of protocol, if not basic good manners. Worm's expecting you. If you offend hir, you could jeopardize everything else."

Mikal shifted his feet. Strictly speaking, Mironova couldn't order him to talk to Worm and the others, but he'd have to do some fancy tap dancing to explain why he was loath to do so.

Every time we speak, s/he asks about Saavik, and I have no answer. That would be bad enough if it were just Worm and me talking, but with Loth and half the planet listening in, it's . . . embarrassing. I haven't felt this vulnerable since . . . since the old man beat me and sent me packing when I was barely old enough to shave. Is that sufficient reason to risk losing the Deemanot's trust?

The scientist knew the answer. Mikal sighed.

"I'll talk to them," he said.

Mironova beamed at him. "I thought you might."

"What does it say about my confidence in you if I make it too easy for you?" Narak's voice insinuated in Saavik's ear. *"Surely a survivor like you can find a way to return to the desert undetected?"*

She had managed to leave the flat near the Enclave and make her way to the park ring, blending in with the foot traffic along the pedestrian streets, as nervous about being recognized now as she had been under-cover. By all accounts she was still at Amorak, half a continent away. While the citizens of ShiKahr might have been kept from the knowledge of her sudden departure from that shrine, her seeming sudden reap-pearance in the city would stir rumor. Vulcans did not subscribe to gossip per se, but somehow they knew things. Thus by managing to be invisible in her very visibility, Saavik had reached the outskirts without run-ning into anyone who knew her.

She wore the same desert robe and sandals she had arrived in several weeks earlier. She had also had the presence of mind to eat and drink before leaving the flat since she had no means with which to buy food. It had never before occurred to her that it was actually easier, lacking credits, to find sustenance in the desert than in the heart of civilization.

"Good choice of location," Narak said in her ear, let-ting her know that at least one of his watchers was watching her. *"I'd wondered if you'd choose a little-trafficked point at which to slip back into the desert or a busy thoroughfare where you'd as likely go unnoticed. My instinct would have been the latter, but it's intriguing that you chose the former. Fortunately, there were enough watchers to watch both."*

Did that minuscule difference in their approach sig-nify? Saavik wondered. What she wouldn't give to be able to answer him in language he would understand . . .

"Oh, and there's no need to rush," he went on, sounding a little too confident. *"Sarek's offworld at the moment. Ostensibly on a routine visit to Coridan, but we*

have reason to believe he'll manage to make contact with his Klingon masters at the same time."

His words were deliberate. Sarek had no masters, Klingon or otherwise, but the false clues Saavik was planting would make it seem as if he was taking bribes from certain interested Klingon parties as well as Romulans. Whoever had planned this operation had been judicious. The charges leveled against Sarek would be just outrageous enough to destroy his career and, with it, any trust between the Federation and the Klingon Empire, but not so outrageous as to lack credibility.

Saavik scanned the few passersby in this part of the ring, not expecting any to stand out as a watcher but curious whether one of them would give something away. None did. She waited.

Did she hear Narak yawn? *"Feel free to improvise. Take as much time as you need, but don't make it obvious that you're dragging your heels. Prolonging this will neither make it easier nor increase your chances of detection."*

So he still assumed she would run to the Vulcan authorities, given the opportunity. Which meant she should assume she was under surveillance at all times, even in the desert. Just how many sleepers had been assigned to this operation? That knowledge might tell her how important it was to them and, more to the point, how important her part of it. If there were any way she could make herself expendable without making matters worse . . .

Focus! she told herself, not for the first time. If only doing were as easy as saying.

She had taken refuge in a grove of trees, one of many in the park ring where one could meditate or simply savor the surrounding beauty. Here she would remain until nightfall, knowing none would presume to disturb her, before making her move. The night would be especially dark during this season, the sister planet remaining below the ecliptic, hiding her light. Narak or his masters had thought of everything. While Vulcans had excellent night vision, this little detail would make it that much easier for her to move about undetected.

As the traditional tocsin sounded from temple to temple throughout the city, signaling that the majority of citizens would by habit be off the streets and in their dwellings or, if they worked at night, reporting to their place of business, Saavik approached a place on the outer ring where the motion sensors faced outward toward the desert to warn of predators, and slipped through.

One would have to be a citizen of ShiKahr to be familiar with the fact that only the major thoroughfares were marked by sensors facing inward, many of them centuries old, from a time when smuggling was commonplace, designed to detect anyone leaving the city without official sanction. At least, Saavik had assumed only a citizen would know, but apparently Narak's sleepers did as well. In any event, it pleased her that there was at least one thing about her he hadn't known. She would avoid the inward-looking sensors and slip through where she would go unnoticed, as long as she kept to a straight path between two outward-looking sensors until she was beyond their range.

Vulcan had indeed grown soft, assuming that the only predators who might enter from the desert would have more than two legs. Purposefully, Saavik walked. Her destination was at some distance, and she needed to be there before sunrise, not only to avoid the heat.

"This may have been unwise," the figure in the shadows murmured as a momentary image of Saavik, really only a nanosecond's glimpse of the top of her head and one ear tip where she had been less than perfect in eluding one of the corridor sensors, flashed on the screen in T'Saan's private office. "Are we certain she will not succumb under the pressure?"

"In her former life, she was Vulcan disciplined and Starfleet trained," T'Saan replied. "We are confident she will lead us to the others."

"And then? What is to become of her?"

T'Saan gave no answer, and the shadow's silence acknowledged that the question should not have been asked.

"The state of her mind . . ." the shadow ventured.

". . . is unknown at present," T'Saan acknowledged. "Only time will answer."

It took far longer than she'd calculated to return to the desert, though at least this time she entered from a point less than a day's walk from the shrine. No need now to traverse the wastelands for forty days and forty nights to make certain whoever was watching her took her self-imposed exile seriously.

Her first stop beyond the outskirts of the city had

been an unmanned heavy-transport switching station that did not rise out of the sand so much as simply hunker in low profile on the horizon, unlit as well as unmanned. While most transport on the planet was airborne, large, bulky nonessentials were still moved about by ground transport via a network of transit stations like this one, designed to look like nothing so much as a natural rock formation, part of the landscape, obscuring the pneumatic tubes and even, in the case of some of the oldest nodes, like this one, monorail systems moving automated trams about the planet.

Unmanned, of course, did not mean unwatched and, lacking any opportunity to access the schematics beforehand (*Some spy you are!* she'd chided herself on the long walk here. *You should have prevented T'Vaakis from taking that padd!*), Saavik had approached the facility with caution, scanning for motion sensors in the outer structure, knowing that if detected she would not be stopped, but her presence would be recorded and questions would be raised.

As Narak had suggested, this would be a good place for her to risk detection, surrender, tell everything she knew. But by the time the automated system recorded her and the record reached an actual person who would listen to her story and accept its veracity despite its improbability, someone, perhaps even T'Vaakis, would have replaced her, and the mission would go forward.

Thus she took her time, skirting the perimeter, noting every crevice in the outer walls that might conceal a sensor, before she found a blind spot and walked a narrow tightrope between safety and detection. She could feel the rumble of incoming and outgoing trams beneath her feet, and made them her destination.

The interior of the station was much as she'd expected—sterile, almost airless, immaculately clean, echoingly empty. Atmospheric controls kept the temperature within the optimal range for cargo, but there was no need to consider the comfort of living beings, since ordinarily no one came here. Cargo was loaded and unloaded within cities. This place was a switching node, nothing more, the intersection of one set of transit tubes with another. Shunting and reloading were entirely automated, as was every other function. Sonic cyclers kept the long, dim, echoing corridors clean, using high-frequency sound waves to reduce the least amount of dust or debris to the molecular level, to be drawn away by pneumatic cyclers set into the floor. Saavik's first step, upon reaching the interior, was to time the cyclers exactly, lest she be caught up in an active cycle and treated as so much debris.

Still another point at which I might end my participation in this charade, she thought, dismissing the notion immediately, not only because the idea of being shaken down to molecules and swept into oblivion was less than comforting. Again she was reminded of how much worse things could be if she did not follow through.

Hearing the cyclers whine down into the audible range and then turn off, she made her next move.

There were sensors only at the junctures of the corridors, fairly easy to elude if one could accurately gauge their range and possess the sangfroid to align oneself with the wall of the corridor and slip under them. After that, it was only a matter of bypassing the pneumatic tubes—where bulk cargo was shot through at speeds that would crush a living thing attempting to slip between them, though not before the absence of oxygen had collapsed his or her lungs—and locating the tramways.

The goal was to find a tram heading in approximately the direction she needed to go that was not, with typical Vulcan efficiency, packed so tightly that there wasn't at least a little space for her to slip in and conceal herself. Several blind transfers later, if the combination of her innate geolocator ability and a schoolgirl's memory of a lesson on planetary transportation was as accurate as she hoped, she would reach her desired destination.

A manned tram station would have a digital manifest at the access port to each tramway, indicating, for the convenience of its users, where the tram had originated and where it was bound. No such manifests were necessary here, since the trams themselves knew their destination. Saavik would have to call upon a Vulcan's greatest weakness. She would have to guess.

For a second time, she cursed herself for not preventing T'Vaakis from walking off with her dataslate. Her doppelgänger hadn't needed it as anything more than a prop. For Saavik, its absence could result in miscalculations that would leave her half a continent off course.

Doubtless Narak had thought of that. It was likely he had instructed T'Vaakis to take the slate. Surely he would not risk the mission's going awry because his agent lost her way. His constant presence in the cochlear implant would no doubt provide the necessary direction . . . before the sonic cyclers cycled on again, she hoped.

Once again, as if reading her thoughts, he made himself known. *"I have the tram schedule before me as we speak. I'll be happy to share."*

As you *speak!* she thought, thinking of all the curses out of Hellguard she would rain down on him if he were here.

"*Third corridor east, fifth corridor south,*" he was saying. *"A tram will arrive on the northbound track in approximately seven point four minutes. Cargo is predominantly surgical supplies, including containers of* Hirudo medicinalis *leeches and live beneficial bacteria for certain applications, meaning there will be atmosphere. Several cars, flex-couplings. You're nimble; you can slip between cars and even find a way to poke into the onboard computer so you can find the rest of your way by yourself."*

She found the requisite corridor, with ample time to await the passing tram. Narak was still nattering in her ear.

"I must say you've made this entertaining. I hadn't expected that. Truly, when we've finished, I would welcome the opportunity to know you better. I don't expect it will compensate for your lost childhood, but I would enjoy it immeasurably . . ."

Was he *trying* to distract her? What if the cyclers turned on again before the tram arrived? *Calm!* she told herself. *They won't cycle on anywhere near the tram until after it passes. There are no passenger platforms here;*

you'll have to stand on the clearance between the tram and the curve of the wall anyway. Do it now!

"*Surely you realize that once Sarek is disgraced, everything you once knew as a family life will be no more?*" Narak echoed in her head as she eased herself onto the narrow lip of clearance, barely wider than the length of her sandal, that a seldom-needed maintenance crew might stand on to lower themselves to the single track between passing trams. "*Lady Amanda will no doubt accompany him into whatever fate awaits him . . .*"

The rush of air ahead of the arriving tram brushed her face and ruffled her hair as she flattened herself against the side of the tunnel, readying herself to jump.

"*And while Spock will be scrutinized, he will as usual escape unscathed, though I expect his relationship with you will be challenged by unfolding events. Perhaps then you'll be more amenable to my presence in your life . . .*"

Only long enough to rip your throat out so that I never need to hear your voice again!

The tram appeared at the turnout point in the tunnel, slowing as it entered the transfer node. Saavik called upon everything she had in terms of focus, timing, and reflexes and, in the space of a breath and with a leeway of only millimeters, she leaped from the narrow ledge and grabbed a tenuous purchase on one of the flexible junctures that allowed the cars to navigate turns, insinuating herself between two cars as Narak had suggested, and eventually inside the forward car.

Everything was as Narak had said it would be, and as she caught her breath and waited for her pulse to normalize, she was grudgingly impressed with the drill-down detail of his information. Was the entire planet riddled with Romulan watchers?

Narak had gone silent, for which she was grateful at first. As the journey progressed, however, the silence grew oppressive; the assumption that he could at any moment disrupt her thoughts with his pointless parentheticals kept her on edge.

As he'd suggested, she did in fact tap into the onboard computer, learn this tram's ultimate destination and where and how to transfer to the two subsequent trams she would need to get as close as possible to Amorak. This left her long hours between transfers to contemplate just how pervasive the Romulan presence on her world might be.

Her world? Only ever tenuously, and now perhaps nevermore.

It was night once more as she made her rather abrupt departure from the final tram. It had slowed enough before entering the tunnel beneath an ancient city on the outskirts of the desert for her to leap clear, landing in a tuck and roll down a gradually sloping embankment. Crouching low until she had ascertained that no one was observing her from the millennia-old city, whose cliff dwellings were still occupied, she shook the dust from the folds of her robe and set off once more in the direction of the shrine. The night wind erased her footprints even as she made them.

Sixteen

There had been an exercise at the Academy known as Blind Helm. Precursor to the *Kobayashi Maru,* a requirement for all third-year students, it was based on the premise that the candidate was the last able-bodied crewman on a vessel that had lost all visual and was running on sensors only. There were various scenarios—gravitic mine, asteroid field, enemy attack, and so on—and as the candidate survived each level, subsequent levels grew more challenging. The goal was as much to measure calm under duress as piloting skills.

Saavik had inevitably rated in the top two percent of her class. The test threw everything from meteors to wormholes to Klingon battleships at her, and she simply piloted her ship with the data she had and refused to flap.

She had departed the shrine some months ago via a seldom-used tunnel in an ancient part of the western wall, walking deliberately into the setting sun. Now as she approached the eastern gate, the rising sun at her back, she was mindful of the Academy and that test. Though the slanting sunlight made it difficult for those at the shrine to see her clearly, it was she who was flying blind.

Narak had said something about her "killing the old man." She had shoved Simar aside when he'd tried to stop her from leaving, but only to make her rage and her departure seem authentic, in case the watchers were watching. She had not pushed him any harder than necessary, and she had surely never meant him any harm.

Now she had returned to face the consequences.

Had she been acting on her own, she was confident she'd have found some way to emerge from the desert and reclaim her place in Vulcan society without returning to the shrine, though even as she announced herself at the portal, she had no idea what that way might have been. But Narak had insisted she return to the shrine as part of his plan, and so she must face whatever awaited her there. Inadvertent Simar's death may have been, but some accounting would have had to be made.

Not for the first time she thought, *Perhaps this is how it will end. Narak doesn't really need me anymore. The savants at the shrine will try me and require some atonement, even if it is only that I never leave the shrine again. Events will unfold without me, will I, nil I.*

The portal opened to her voice, and without challenge she made her way to the chambers of the high priestess to request an audience. Though many passed her, raising their eyes momentarily from their thoughts, no one stopped her, no one questioned her right to be there and, once there, she was granted entrée without question.

"The old one had a premonition," the high priestess T'Leng said mildly, contemplating the carefully tended garden beyond the tall window of her study. Many of those who devoted their lives to meditation had a kind of agelessness about them, and T'Leng was among them. The face she turned toward Saavik now could have been that of a young woman or an ancient. "There are meditative depths that are beyond the reach of logic. He knew the time of his own death. You were not the cause."

Her wording seemed deliberately ambiguous, causing Saavik to frown and wonder what import lay behind them. But she suspected whatever questions she might ask would not be answered.

"What disposition is to be made of me now, Lady?" she asked.

T'Leng raised an eyebrow. "None. You are free to stay or go as you wish. This time none will attempt to dissuade you. One might suggest you rest for a time. Sleep, take sustenance, compose your thoughts. Your time away from us has not been kind to you."

All was forgiven, just like that? It was too easy. Almost easy enough to make her wonder if T'Leng was part of Narak's network. Glanced at in a certain light, did she not have a rather pronounced forehead, one that might have heretofore sported brow ridges?

Stop it! You're exhausted. Your judgment cannot be trusted. You're seeing shadows everywhere!

She was given a windowless cell with a shelf to sleep on, the same cell that had been hers when she first arrived, and an acolyte brought her refreshment there, lest she have to face a refectory where an empty space still marked Simar's departure, though she suspected even there none would judge her by word or glance. Indeed, when, more exhausted than even she could have imagined, she'd slept through a day and a night to rise with the new day and bathe in the hot springs, she was greeted with mild expressions and no whisper of gossip spoken or even thought.

As she lowered herself to the earlobes in water that was almost painfully hot, she closed her eyes and sighed. *Let me stay here this time! When is enough enough?* But after a day and night of silence, there was still the voice in her ear.

"Three days, no more. You'll hitch a ride on the weekly transport, and then back to civilization."

Once a week, a great lumbering air car arrived at the shrine, bringing in the few necessities the savants could not provide for themselves, transporting out the surplus fruits of their fields and orchards, and a particular type of fine cloth woven on hand looms from the soft fibers of the *a'morak* bush that grew nowhere else and gave the place its name. Riding in the back with the cargo was an unconventional way to leave the shrine, but if she asked, it would be granted.

She wasn't certain what she'd expected to find at the shrine, but this . . . anticlimax was not it.

"It must be the Vulcan part of her that has such patience. Were she wholly ours, she would have snapped by now."

Narak too had a voice forever in his ear. This one came from far away, on the homeworld, and the necessary coding and scrambling gave it a choppy, un-real-time quality. Unlike Saavik, he had the means to answer back, but it was time-consuming to wait until he was certain his source had finished speaking. In the beginning he'd made the mistake of interrupting, and it had cost him.

He was never quite sure who his source was. He'd guessed it was the one who'd interrogated him and offered him a chance to live, but he could not be sure. The processing that made it impossible to make a voice-print rendered the voice in his ear genderless, mechanical; for all he knew it was completely artificial. The orders it gave, however, were not to be second-guessed.

"*I* haven't snapped yet," he presumed to remind it. "Despite what you've put me through. Perhaps it's me she takes after."

Was that a laugh? "*You have one outstanding quality, Narak, and that is doggedness. You are not smart, nor even clever, but you are persistent. We have counted on that in the past. Don't disappoint us now.*"

Silence, ended, to be taken up again at probably the most awkward of times, when he was in a crowded place and his masters knew he could not answer. So even as he had Saavik watched, he was being watched, everyone testing everyone else. This was what it meant to be a Romulan.

As certain as he could be that, at the moment at least, his thoughts were his own, Narak allowed himself the luxury of a genuine emotion. He wept. Silently, all but motionlessly, he stared into the middle distance as tears flowed down a face that might otherwise have been stone, not for the first time regretting that it had come to this.

He had been halfway across the Outmarches on his way to Vulcan before it occurred to him that perhaps Saavik wasn't his daughter after all. Perhaps he had been set up from the beginning. Had the ease with which his interrogator had acquiesced to showing him the Y chromosome markers in the two samples, obviously identical even to his accountant's eyes, been a trick? Did the "offspring match" in fact belong to Saavik, or to some other female, perhaps even the operative now going by the code name T'Vaakis? Ironic indeed if the "daughter" appointed to accompany him on his journey was genuine, and the one he had been sent to groom for treachery was false.

Unless both were false, and he had no offspring, or occult offspring he would never know, and all the data he had ostensibly stumbled upon had been planted expressly with the intention that he find it.

But the possibility that everything he knew was nothing but sham was not what made him weep. He did not mourn for the universe he had been given but for the one he had been denied.

Despite what he'd told Saavik, he doubted his masters would spare her life once she had done what he had directed her to do. The risk that the unspoken truth she carried would betray them both was too great. Once she had completed her mission, she was expendable and so, very likely, was he.

It was why he had tried to prolong their initial encounter, perhaps longer than was wise (the memory of her rising from the lake, water streaming from her hair, of the care with which she had dressed herself, offered him food, ritually cut her hair as if to confirm her purpose before setting off with him, her exquisite face in profile as she contemplated the view beyond the windscreen rather than make eye contact as she asked her careful questions, was bittersweet for its brevity and the likelihood that it would never recur), uncertain if he would ever find a way to see her face-to-face again. It was why he had told her one single, outright lie. Whatever else he'd said had contained at least a portion of embedded true, at least the truth as he knew it, considering who had told it to him in the first place. But in a desperate ploy that could yet harm them both, he had said, "I can tell you who your mother is."

In truth, he had no idea which Vulcan female in all the universe had borne this extraordinary child. He'd claimed that knowledge only in the hope that Saavik would seek him out when this was over and ask to know.

If that time came, what would he tell her? He had no idea. But he would accept whatever consequences of his lie, if only to see that exquisite face, even contorted in rage, one more time.

Was that love? Romulan literature was replete with as many poems and songs and sagas about the love between parent and child as about more conventional types of love. It was almost as if, as much as its institutional forms strove mightily to destroy that bond— encouraging children to spy on their parents and report unpatriotic thoughts, parents to hand their children over to the authorities to be banished for crimes as grave a threat to the state as minor vandalism or breaking curfew—something in the Romulan heart still craved it.

No wonder Vulcan had been glad to see the back of them during the Sundering, Narak thought. Perhaps the distant brothers had not so secretly hoped the contentious ones would all be swallowed up by a nebula or destroy each other with bickering.

Yes, if it was possible to love, he had come to love this stranger, this alien, offspring or not, for being what he could not be—too honest for her own good and as free as any thinking being could be within the constraints she had set for herself. And having spent mere moments with her, he did not want to lose her.

He'd goaded her during her *hegira* from ShiKahr to the desert as much in fear for her safety as in a need to impress those listening to him. If it had been up to him, he'd have found an easier way.

He might have lost her at every step of the way then, and might lose her still, and thus he wept in anticipation of that loss. Were he to ask for a little time to spend with her before the end, his masters would know how much he desired it and deny it to him just because they could. Perhaps he could find something else to bargain with at least to spare her life if not his own, but if there were such a thing, he had not found it yet.

As precipitously as the mood had come upon him, so it ended. The desert air of Vulcan dried his tears as if they had never been, leaving only a trace of bitterness at the corners of his mouth.

• • •

In its way, returning to Sarek's household, recommitting herself to that way of life, was more dangerous, Saavik thought, than anything that had gone before.

The trick was to embed the false data in Sarek's personal files, then activate the triggers she had planted in the files in the Enclave. Backtracking would make it appear as if everything—memos, notes, subspace communiqués with sources within both empires—had in fact originated from Sarek's home and, by implication, had originated with Sarek himself.

All of that would take considerably more time than infiltrating the Enclave, and with no burn identity to mask her intentions. And while Sarek might be off-world, Amanda was here. And she was not alone.

"Saavik!" Amanda cried, making no secret of her joy at the sight of the prodigal. "Child, you've come home. Let me look at you!"

She had been reading, curled up on a divan in the main parlor, a pair of half-glasses perched on the bridge of her small human nose. Like Admiral Kirk, Saavik recalled, Amanda was allergic to Retnax and needed the glasses for close work. They made her fine-boned face seem vulnerable, until she glanced over the tops of them, her face lit up, and she was on her feet at once, the glasses and the padd set aside.

Rapid steps brought her across the room, her hands on Saavik's shoulders, the closest she dared to an embrace. There were no questions, no accusations— "Why didn't you contact us first? How could you have gone off into the desert without letting us know? We were so worried about you!"—only warmth and welcome.

Which made what Saavik was about to do all the more difficult.

The exchange of pleasantries, the obligatory tea and small talk, would forever remain a blur in her memory. Only when she and Amanda walked in the garden afterward did her focus come clear.

". . . and the *echinopsis* cacti bloomed last month," Amanda was saying beside her. "I'm sorry you missed them! But I've started a bed of mosses on one side of the fountain that . . . what is it, dear?"

They were making the circuit of the garden arm in arm, the only sounds the trilling of lizards—safe from predators here, they were free to trill; in the desert they had been silent—and the sough of the midday breeze. As they neared the open casements of Sarek's study, Saavik's steps faltered, a look of alarm flitting briefly across her face. A moment later Amanda heard what had drawn her attention.

"Yes." The human beamed. "Spock is here. I'm not entirely certain of the circumstances, but he's on leave and so much improved since the last time you saw him! He and Sarek have been on a conference call all morning; don't ask me what about . . ."

Her human ears heard only the tone of her son's voice, not the words, and she wouldn't have eavesdropped if she could, but Saavik had heard the words "Klingons" and "peace feelers" well before they turned away from the house and continued down the path

toward the fountain. The colors of the multiple varieties of mosses from a dozen worlds that Amanda
had planted where the prevailing breeze sent the mist
from the fountain wafting over the soil so that it never
needed watering swam before her eyes.

*No! Not Spock! Do not force me to enmesh him in this
thing as well!*

How could she have forgotten that for years Sarek
had been cultivating his son's natural gift for diplomacy? Whether or not Spock chose to follow in his
father's footsteps someday, the pursuit of such knowledge for its own sake, and as a useful skill for the first
officer of a starship that was often the first ambassador
to new species, was always desirable.

Saavik had simply not expected Spock to be directly
involved in Sarek's interactions with the Klingons so
soon. Whatever false information she sowed about
Sarek would embroil him as well.

Little wonder she had no appetite for the extraordinary midday meal that Amanda had prepared. As if
it were not difficult enough to sit across the table from
the adult avatar of the Spock she had known on Genesis, this new dimension only made matters worse.

Surely by now he remembers everything! she thought,
her eyes on her plate as Spock took his place at the
table. *And while surely he will no more speak of it than I
will, it will always remain an unspoken truth between us!*

*Which matters little now, in view of what you must
do, whether or not he is here and, more likely than not,
in conversation with Sarek, in Sarek's study, for as long
as he is here. If you thought the process of planting data*

undetected was daunting before, to do so without arous-
ing the suspicions of an A7 computer expert . . .

"How long will you be on leave, Captain?" she managed to say as Spock reached for the basket of *krei'la* at
the center of the table. Her question evoked one of his
milder expressions.

"Surely we need not rely on Starfleet formalities
here, Saavik-*kam*." As always with her, his face was
somber, but his tone was mild. "Or would you be more
at ease if I addressed you as 'Lieutenant'?"

This was the Spock she knew, recalled to life in time
for her to betray him. "As you wish, C—Spock."

Spock's eyes danced. "Because I am your superior
officer, or because it is what you wish as well?"

"Stop teasing her!" Amanda said sharply, taking the
basket from his hands and serving herself. She knew
him too well.

"Mother—" Saavik started to say, but Amanda cut
her off.

"No, if the two of you are going to be under my roof,
I need to say this." She turned to Spock. "You have no
idea how pleased I am that your sense of humor has
returned as well, but you might remember where Saavik has been since you've been away. Attention must be
paid."

With that she summoned soft string music from the
sound system to punctuate the silence that ensued for
the rest of the meal.

"*Macbeth,* Act one, Scene seven, the soliloquy," she
heard Spock say, followed by Amanda's laughter.

"You're too good! All right, now it's your turn . . ."

Lurking like an assassin—was she not?—Saavik slipped past the parlor where the two were playing a familiar game. Amanda had used it as a teaching tool to expand her own knowledge when she was a child, as she no doubt had when Spock was small, and later to fill in the gaps in his memory when she visited Mount Seleya following the *fal-tor-pan*. Now it served as a pastime in which mother and son could savor each other's company, and it could go on for hours.

Time enough, Saavik hoped, to set the first of the trails of cyber breadcrumbs that would connect Sarek with agents inside both the empires.

Breadcrumbs . . . Hansel and Gretel, she recalled involuntarily, courtesy of Amanda and a childhood that had informed a certain respect for the two resourceful human children who had vanquished the wicked witch. Perhaps, she had thought at the time, if she'd been strong enough to heave the proctor into an oven before she'd crushed Tolek's fingers . . .

Enough! she chided herself as she crept into Sarek's study and went to work.

There was only so much she could do in a single night, meticulously deleting the signatures once she had done so, then forcing herself to sit with her hands in her lap and listen carefully to every sound in the house before retracing her steps. Narak had said to take her time. Part of her wished her role were ended, that she might begin to face the lifetime of regret that would follow.

The house was silent. She rose from the chair,

returning it to precisely the position Spock had left it in hours earlier. A small device that Narak had provided removed all trace of her DNA from the room while somehow leaving Spock's. Too clean a removal of fingerprints from the toggles, the chair arms, the desktop, a complete absence of hairs or fibers would have been suspicious . . . if anyone for any reason happened to be suspicious enough to gather forensic evidence. Doubtless the inquest that would follow Sarek's detainment would include such a gathering.

By the time she passed the parlor a second time, Spock and Amanda had abandoned their game and were having a very different conversation indeed.

". . . spoken to her about this?" she heard Spock ask.

"She's only been back for a day," Amanda answered. "I didn't want her to feel as if she was being interrogated."

Hidden, Saavik could not see either of them, but she imagined Spock nodding. "That is wise. She is still on leave. There is plenty of time."

"I wonder." Amanda's tone was wistful. "I wonder if it isn't too late after all. We tried, your father and I, when you brought her to us, but nothing will ever compensate for those early years. The studies—"

"Studies done on human children," Spock interjected. "A Vulcan child—"

"Is still a child. We're all mammals at base. A kitten needs more nurture than a turtle."

"Mother—"

"Am I wrong?"

How many times had she overheard some variation

on this conversation? Saavik found herself shivering. It was all so wrong, so very wrong, and yet . . .

She heard Spock sigh. "You are not wrong. Hyperbolic, but not wrong."

Amanda's all too human laughter was the last sound in her ears as Saavik crept back to her part of the house, dreading the dawn.

Over the course of the next several nights, she completed her task. The false trails were laid in, the triggers set to cascade. Now all she had to do was wait for Narak to give her the go-ahead for the final phase. The waiting proved the most difficult part of all.

Daily Spock conferred with Sarek, repairing to the senior diplomat's study at a prearranged time that fit with Sarek's travel schedule, and for the hour precisely that they spoke, Saavik lived in agony. Spock frequently referred to Sarek's files as they compared knowledge and strategy for the basic overtures they would make to certain officials within the Klingon Empire, with the Federation's sanction, but on an entirely deniable basis, should things go wrong.

That those same files were adjacent to, sometimes even referenced by and interwoven with, the false data Saavik had implanted increased the likelihood that either her tampering would be discovered, or at least one of the triggers would activate too soon, with each passing day. Once again torn between wishing to be found out so as to end this, regardless of the cost to herself, and the knowledge that only she could prevent worse consequences, she had never had need to act more Vulcan—not even Spock, especially not Spock, could be allowed to sense the internal turmoil she struggled with—while at the same time feeling less.

Life had become an elaborate game of *kal-toh*, the outcome of failure quite literally the collapse of the sphere around her. Starship captains might save planets; she could not save a single being.

So she lurked, seeing Sarek's face on the comscreen, hearing his voice, certain that the next time they met face-to-face, the face he turned to her, the voice with which he addressed her, would no longer have the calm and confidence he exuded now. She lurked, thinking, illogically, *'Twere well it were done quickly!*

But Spock and Sarek completed their daily meetings, and on the day Spock got back into uniform and returned to duty, Narak's voice in Saavik's ear, silent since the shrine, now asked a single question.

"You know what to do next?"

As before, she had no way of answering him, but of course he knew she knew. Even as the official Starfleet air car whisked Spock away, she slipped into Sarek's study for the final time and, by remote, activated the triggers she had embedded in the files in the Enclave.

Even as the data flew through cyberspace, Saavik put her travel cloak on over her Starfleet uniform and set about enacting the final phase.

Seventeen

She passed Mikal by without seeing him.

He stood like a forlorn troubadour in the pedestrian street across the way from the high wall surrounding Sarek's household, lacking the courage to take the next step. *Chaffee,* her mission to Deema III completed, had made orbit around Vulcan some days ago, and as a civilian with no orders once he'd filed all the data they'd gathered, he'd been the first one off the ship.

Impulsive, he had no plan beyond announcing himself and hoping someone was at home who could tell him Saavik's whereabouts, or at least get a message to her. He'd had plenty of opportunity to follow the rumors, had in fact had to bellow at Cheung and Jaoui more than once for gossiping in the labs, but true or false, there were details he simply did not want to know.

Some scientist you are! he chided himself as he shifted his feet and wondered if it was too early to knock on the door. Only the last words Worm had said to him prevented him from giving up and walking away.

As reluctant as ever to communicate with the Deemanot without Saavik with him, he'd left all that to the Betazoid, Gwailim Loth, and to Captain Mironova, who enjoyed visiting with their newfound friends as often as she could. But the day before they were due to leave orbit, Worm had requested his presence specifically.

Before, he'd required Loth to serve as go-between, but on this day, Worm bypassed the Betazoid and wound hirself solely around Mikal.

You will not be returning to this place, s/he began, *there is too much else in the universe that needs your attention.*

Mikal had not been overly surprised that the being knew this much about him. He still wasn't entirely sure how telepathy worked but figured anyone who'd accessed his mind for more than a moment could see his thoughts simmering right on the surface.

"Then I guess this is farewell," he'd said. He always spoke aloud, even with the Deemanot voice in his mind. He might have learned some esper skills but didn't really trust his thoughts to convey themselves clearly without the spoken word.

But it need not be sad, Worm pointed out. *All works out as it should, even you and Saavik.*

Tensing, Mikal wanted to pull away. He hadn't been expecting that.

"I wish you wouldn't do that!" he said a little too loudly. Around him, the science team was packing up, having done a final survey and collection in the Deemanot metropolis, and Esparza, for one, had looked at him oddly. Perhaps a dozen of Scolex and Cina's children were quite literally underfoot as well, and Mikal could swear he heard them making giggling noises in his head. At least, unlike the humans, they could hear both sides of the conversation. Surrounded, defeated, Mikal sighed.

"All right, you win. Tell me what you know."

Only that. It is all interconnected. You and she will meet again, and it will be as it should.

With that Worm had withdrawn hir embrace and, the children in hir train, moved on to say hir farewells to Mironova and the rest. Feeling dismissed, Mikal had beamed up alone.

Now he stood in the Vulcan street, passed by pedestrians who glanced at him without comment, finding nothing untoward, in this cosmopolitan city, at the sight of a bald and tattooed Tiburonian waiting outside Ambassador Sarek's house.

He'd almost found the courage to cross the street and announce himself, when the door in the wall opened, and the last person he'd expected to see emerged. He'd blurted her name before he could stop himself.

"Saavik?"

But, head down, the hood of her cloak limiting her vision, she did not look up or sideways but only at the cobbles at her feet, and kept walking as if she did not hear.

Mikal started to move toward her, started to shout her name, but stopped himself on both counts. She had to have seen him, had to have heard him speak. She had chosen not to acknowledge him, and that was the end of it.

At a loss to know what to do with himself, he too began to walk, in the opposite direction from where she had vanished around a corner. He did not know where he was going and did not care.

One might expect the offices of the intelligence service of a world as wrapped around in propriety and protocol as Vulcan to be all but impenetrable, but Saavik found her access to the head of station unimpeded. T'Saan had prepared tea and gestured her toward a seating area of low, comfortable chairs before Saavik even identified herself.

The matriarch who had replaced T'Pau in this office was unremarkable in appearance, neither tall nor short, of an indeterminate age, a touch of gray at her temples all that was visible of hair swept up inside a wimplelike headdress that had not been in fashion for more than a decade. The best spies, it is said, are invisible, and Saavik allowed herself the luxury of wondering if T'Saan had worn the wimple when she was "on the job." She suspected not.

Pay attention! she cautioned herself. *You don't have time for trivia. Every word you speak in this room must be precisely correct or it all collapses.*

At their final meeting, she had argued with Narak about this part.

"I am to go to the offices of the V'Shar and announce that I have 'come across' sensitive material indicating that Ambassador Sarek is a traitor," she'd repeated his instructions. "I am unskilled in lying. How am I to convince them? In what manner am I supposed to have 'come across' this information? How—?"

Narak had laughed and placed one finger on her lips. Of all the violations, this one angered her the most. Not for the first time, she wanted to rip his throat out, though first, she thought, she would break his fingers one by one.

"In addition to being treacherous, Sarek is careless," Narak said, sounding as if he were reciting from a script. "He has made the mistake of occasionally allowing you to be in the room when he speaks to his contacts. It's a form of psychopathology, a need to flaunt his accomplishments, and also a credit to his confidence in you and your loyalty."

"No one will believe that of Sarek," she had protested. "No one."

Narak had sighed and shaken his head. "Poor naïf! People will believe anything of anyone if it's spoken with enough confidence. I will tell you what to say when the time comes. You need merely repeat what you hear, but with the utmost sincerity."

So she sat on the edge of the too-comfortable chair and, her untouched tea growing cold on the table before her, studied her hands and recited the script as Narak whispered it in her ear, telling T'Saan precisely where to find the incriminating data, both in Sarek's personal files and in the archives at the Enclave. Her voice was low, her speech hesitant, as if it took all her courage to say the words, and in truth it did. It was doubtless that ring of truth that made the words believable.

T'Saan heard her out in silence. When Saavik was done, she said, "These charges are quite grave. You realize what will happen if they are verified?"

Saavik's eyes met hers. "I do."

T'Saan crossed to her desk, logging in the entry codes that allowed the V'Shar access to even the most private files of any Vulcan official, up to and including the ambassadorial level, and scanned the files Saavik had indicated, a slight frown bringing her upslanted brows closer together. When she had finished, she looked at Saavik thoughtfully.

Now, Saavik thought, *it is ended.*

She waited for T'Saan to speak, but the matriarch's next words were not for her. Touching the comm toggle on her desk, she made a series of inquiries. When all of them had apparently been answered in the affirmative, she gathered her thoughts for a moment, then turned back to Saavik.

"I regret it took so long, but we wanted to be certain there were no loose ends. We have backtracked all of the trails you set and pinpointed the entire network, down to an ancient in the Ministry of Records who has passed for Vulcan for over a century, and has been issuing false documents to fellow operatives in all that time. There will be some green faces in the inner chambers of the Tal Shiar when this is over. You have done well, better than could be hoped. *Kal-toh!*"

Saavik exhaled in what might have been a sigh. It seemed as if she had been holding her breath since the day Tolek first accosted her in the market.

"This was no chance meeting," he had said. "I sought you out."

"For what purpose?"

"Because you and I were once close," Tolek had said, and for the briefest moment Saavik had wished for that closeness again, no matter the adversity that had forged it. "And I wanted to warn you . . ."

. . . and simultaneously recruit me, she had thought.

She had left the market and, still carrying her basket, immediately repaired to the address Tolek had conveyed to her, finding herself face-to-face with T'Pau's successor.

Unlike her predecessor who, while she might deny it as illogical, had cherished her place in the spotlight, T'Saan, like the operatives she ran, preferred to remain unobtrusive, and the average Vulcan would not have known who she was. But the complicated relationship between Sarek and T'Pau gave all of Sarek's kin a specialized knowledge. Saavik had known immediately whom she was dealing with.

"There is no obligation on thee at this moment," T'Saan had said at that first meeting, speaking formally, seeing the barely masked resentment in the younger woman's dark eyes. "Thee knows nothing other than what thy friend has told thee in casual conversation. Thee are free to leave and give the matter no further thought."

If anyone but Tolek had come to her, would she have done precisely that, or would innate curiosity have overcome her desire to avoid any such entanglement?

"I have not much time," Saavik had said, then stopped herself.

Logically she should have told T'Saan what she had told Tolek, that she was leaving Vulcan with the dawn and could likely be of little use to the assignment, whatever it might be. But something—was it only her implied duty to Tolek?—made her decide quickly, perhaps recklessly, and she finished her thought not at all as she'd begun it.

"I have not much time," she repeated, and T'Saan seemed not to notice the hesitation. "Lady Amanda knows I have gone to the market. I can perhaps tell her I encountered an . . . acquaintance . . . and stopped for tea, but too long away will raise questions."

"Thinking like a spy already!" T'Saan was clearly pleased, and she dropped her formal tone. "Very well, then, there is something you must know that even Tolek does not. We believe this is about far more than a few unexplained deaths . . ."

She had thought it odd that T'Saan seemed pleased that she was going offworld. Unaccustomed to the ways of espionage, she had accepted it at the time. Since she was needed only to do research, was it not logical?

It was only at Tolek's death that she began to see it in another light. The rage she had experienced when asked to confirm the identity of his body had been only partly feigned. It was not until then that she was told the full extent of the operation.

For, yes, she had received instructions from T'Saan or another senior operative even on Deema III. At first she'd assumed that everything she knew Tolek also knew, but gradually she became aware that each of them had knowledge that the other did not, and there were others along the skein who knew other things,

each operative's knowledge carefully compartmentalized from the others, in case there was a breach.

And, yes, her rage at Sarek at Starfleet HQ had been
feigned, acting under instructions, because by then
it was clear not only that she was to be a target of the
killer or killers but also that she was but a stepping-
stone on the path to get to Sarek.

Thus, her every action taken, from at first taking
herself out of harm's way by leaving for Deema III to
setting herself out as bait by the brackish pond in the
desert, and every step along the way, had been deliberate. The only glitch had been Tolek's murder.

"He overstepped his instructions," T'Saan explained
now. "He understood that we could provide protection
only to a certain point—every operative onworld had
backup; you were the only one, because we had vetted
every member of *Chaffee*'s crew, including the civilian,
who was out on the rim alone, and it appears Tolek calculatedly stepped beyond that point.

"He came to realize we intended to use you as bait,
so to speak, and he resented it. His tendency to protect
you in childhood, often to his own detriment—oh, yes,
we knew about that—muddled his thinking. We will
not disgrace his memory by calling it illogical, but it
was unclear."

"Is there anything about us that the V'Shar does not
know?" Saavik presumed to ask.

It was obvious her role in this was not ended. Even as
they spoke, T'Saan busied herself about the room, sending communiqués, locking down files, as if she planned
to be away from the office, which she seldom left, for an

undetermined amount of time. She and Saavik would be traveling . . . to apprehend Narak, apparently.

T'Saan responded to her question not unkindly. "It is a sad commentary on even the most evolved of societies that there will always be a need for our kind. The polite Vulcan pretends we do not exist and yet is grateful for our service and equally grateful not to have to examine our methods too closely.

"As for outworlders, they cannot begin to understand the complexities entailed in subscribing to a tradition of truthfulness while yet retaining possession of certain truths that are more powerful when unspoken. Yes, of course we vetted you prior to bringing you into our midst. And when it was ascertained that you had chosen to return to your duties with Starfleet, we at first considered sending another operative with you, but there was no time. Instead, we assured ourselves, inasmuch as we could, that no one aboard your vessel, including the civilian scientist, was a danger to you."

Even before they met, Saavik had been made aware of Mikal's hazy past, his ability to disappear for long periods of his personal history, his quixotic approach to his work and to his life. Perhaps that had colored their relationship even before it began. She would never know.

But when she had seen him loitering outside the wall this morning, she had not stopped. She could not. She had to see this through and done before she could see him clearly, unencumbered by the roles she had been playing these past months. Only then would she know what future, if any, lay in store.

* * *

Mikal, meanwhile, had found the one human-run bar on Vulcan that never closed and was getting himself drunk. Mironova tracked him down.

"That didn't take long," she remarked, stepping daintily over a Thermian's tentacles and settling in beside Mikal, elbows on the bar. "Single malt, neat," she told the bartender. "Jameson, if you've got it. Now, then," she said after her drink had arrived and Mikal hadn't said a word. "Lovers' quarrel, or did she just not speak to you? Which was it?"

"What it is, is none of your business!" Mikal growled, hunched over his drink like a dog with a bone, and Mironova wondered if he'd snap at her if she tried to take it away from him.

"Right. Assumption: It did not go well, and here you are."

"Never so much as knocked on the door," he mumbled, "but after she breezed past me like I was invisible, I walked back to the port. Was going to just beam back up to the ship and lick my wounds, but guess who's just beaming down? Sarek his own self, just back from Coridan. Trading pleasantries, must come for dinner sometime, talk about my work, blah blah blah."

"Oh, I doubt he was that talky. That's just you extrapolating." Mironova sipped her Jameson. "Maybe he just doesn't want you dating his daughter."

Mikal gave her a sour look, finished his drink, motioned to the bartender for another.

"On me," Mironova said. "And it's his last. Mikal," she said before he could object, "there's something you should know. Everything that's happened . . . it may not have been her fault. In fact, I'm almost completely certain it wasn't."

She gave him a brief précis of what she knew, that "certain authorities, which shall not be named," had meticulously gone over her crew manifest and Mikal's background and her own as soon as Saavik had accepted her assignment. Mironova had thought at first that it was because of the importance of Sarek's family and let it go. Hers not to question why, and so on. As events had unfolded over the ensuing months, and she'd followed Saavik's course of action as best she could through Starfleet scuttlebutt, she'd drawn very different conclusions, and she shared those conclusions with Mikal now.

When she'd finished, his shoulders were shaking.

She'd expected rage, cursing, and throwing things, was prepared to make it up to the bartender for whatever damages were incurred, but it didn't come. Instead he pounded his fist once on the bar, hard enough to rattle glasses on the back bar, then relaxed his hand and put his head down on his folded arms. When the bartender set a fresh drink down and crept away, he didn't even notice.

"You might have told me!" he accused Mironova after a long moment, wiping his nose inelegantly on one multicolored sleeve.

"I couldn't until now, and you know it. It's still all speculation," she said crisply, motioning to the bartender that she would pay for the drinks, and slipped one arm around Mikal's shoulders. "Come on, baby," she said, pulling him unsteadily to his feet. "Mum will see you home . . ."

At T'Saan's signal, Saavik followed her down a passage that had opened out of the wall behind her desk, amid much sliding and rotating, at the touch of a button. The passage led to a turbolift that took them down a considerable depth to a network of tram tunnels deep beneath the city of ShiKahr.

"Begun in ancient times," T'Saan answered the unasked question. "Originally as shelters during the bombing. Extant beneath every major metropolis where the seismic profile is sufficiently stable. Expanded and interconnected over the centuries. One never knows when one will need to get somewhere quickly without drawing undue attention."

"Where are we going?" Saavik wanted to know as a single tram whooshed into view with uncanny quietness, given its speed, and its doors slipped open to admit them.

"Back to the beginning," T'Saan said mysteriously, buckling the shoulder harness that would keep her from being squeezed up against the bulkheads on the curves, and indicating that Saavik was to do the same.

The best way to roll up a network such as Narak's, the V'Shar had learned from generations of experience, was to first trace it out to its farthest ends, noting as many of the smaller operatives as possible and assigning a watcher to each, surreptitiously moving up the nodes until the spider at the center of the *kal-toh* sphere was reached.

Even as they traveled beneath the surface of Vulcan at incredible speeds, T'Saan stayed in communication with her operatives from time to time, speaking in a coded language Saavik could not begin to understand. The strength of a signal that could reach beneath kilometers of rock and not fade or break up even when maintained under such speeds was impressive.

And stronger than the signal of her own cochlear implant, Saavik realized almost immediately. Narak would assume his signal would be blocked once she'd entered T'Saan's office, but was he trying to communicate with her even now?

"It is not possible to remove the implant just yet," T'Saan had told her as they'd stood in the lift going down to the tram platform. "It is hoped that the spider will assume we are skeptical of your information and are subjecting you to interrogation, so he will not expect to hear from you for at least a day. Have you any idea what he had planned for you if his 'mission' were successful?"

"I have not. Only that he intended me to resume my duties in Starfleet as if none of this had happened."

"He really is quite fond of you," T'Saan said, watching the younger woman carefully as the lift deposited them at their destination. "We've intercepted some of his comms to his other operatives, particularly T'Vaakis. He addresses her as his daughter much as he does you, but he always speaks of you with affection, no matter whom he is speaking to. It is quite possible that this much is true."

Saavik, perhaps thinking of the sneer in his voice when he spoke to her, said nothing.

"Once he is captured, we will be able to ascertain this for certain. Do you wish to know?"

"I will address it when he is captured," Saavik said tersely, thinking, *perhaps not even then.* "It is better for now that nothing cloud my judgment."

"Indeed."

As rapid as the underground tram was, there was still a considerable distance to travel. It was not long before Saavik's inner directional sense gave her an idea of where they were going.

"May I assume that you are using the signal from the cochlear implant to backtrack him?" She could not bring herself to say his name.

"Negative," T'Saan said. "We did attempt that at first, but the device is too sophisticated. There are numerous switchbacks, and they alter over time. Just as we ascertain one location, it switches to another."

"Nevertheless, we are headed in the direction of the shrine at Amorak."

T'Saan's glance was appreciative. "You are perceptive. It grieves me that we cannot make you a full-time operative, but I know better than to ask. Your first, best destiny lies elsewhere. We are returning you to Amorak only because there is less surface-to-surface signal noise that far out in the desert. We are hoping it will help us narrow the radius of his likely location."

"No need," Saavik said. "I know where he will be."

At her suggestion, T'Saan altered the tram's course.

It was sunset, and the bats were beginning to stir. It would be some hours before the mist rose from the surface of the lake, but the cactus blossoms, their circadian rhythms unaltered for a million years, began inexorably to open, at a pace so slow it could not be observed by the naked eye and yet, if one looked away and then glanced back, one could swear each furled trumpet had altered in that eyeblink, if only a little.

In all his life, Narak had never known such tranquility. For one mad moment he wished he could undo everything he had done in the past year or more, leave Sarek unmolested, throw himself on the mercy of Vulcan authorities, explain why he had been sent here, and hope he would be believed. But the moment passed and, alone in the climate controlled shelter he had brought with him this time for what he assumed would be a long wait, he poured some mineral water and reminded himself that he should have thought of all that at the beginning. Too late now.

And too soon for her to be here? She stood in the doorway of his shelter, unannounced. He hadn't heard her approach. Startled, he rose abruptly, hand on his weapon, sending the flagon of mineral water tottering in his haste.

"Father," she said softly. "It is done."

Eighteen

The first time, Narak had brought very little with him in the small skimmer he'd concealed among the titanium-bearing boulders a half-day's walk away. This time, confident that soon there would be news emanating from the city of ShiKahr that would occupy the media and security services from here to the Klingon Empire so thoroughly that they would never notice him, he'd brought not only all of the creature comforts he felt he deserved, but everything else in the various spider holes he had inhabited in his peripatetic way across Vulcan, including his weapons and a scanner at least as good as a Starfleet-issue tricorder.

It confirmed what Saavik told him once he'd recovered from his shock and offered her a seat at his table, pouring mineral water for both of them after wiping up the few drops he'd spilled: a damaged and still smoldering small hovercraft of the kind favored by the Vulcan High Command, nose down in the sand an hour's walk distant. Inside, a single newly dead life-form—Vulcan, female, charred down to bones and teeth.

Of all the things Saavik had been required to do since the day she'd encountered Tolek in the market, this was the most distasteful. She almost wished the V'Shar as well as Narak had an avatar to replace her, a T'Vaakis to perform the task of leaving bodies in her wake.

Offering her water, Narak could see that she was visibly shaken. Of everything he had required of her, killing T'Saan had finally been one thing too many. The hand that held the cup to her lips trembled violently. He took it from her and wrapped her in his embrace as the torrent loosed and she clung to him, shaking with sobs.

After some moments, she quieted and pulled away, composing herself.

"We cannot stay here now," he said, not impatiently but with a sense of urgency. "Invisible the V'Shar may be, but once one of its important operatives goes missing, there will be a search. Just let me scan the nets to learn what is being said of Sarek, and then we will go."

But he scanned in vain. After some moments, he raised his eyes from the scanner, frowning.

"Perhaps they will wait until they've rounded up all of his accomplices," he said, more to himself than to Saavik.

"Or perhaps," she said, a phaser in her hand, "all of yours."

She would remain embarrassed about the crying jag for some time. Even arguing that it had been necessary to distract Narak so that T'Saan's backup could move in, even telling herself that she had drawn from the Romulan side for such a disgraceful display of emotion, did not entirely quiet her self-disgust. Add it to the many sequelae of this mission, though. She did not have time for it now.

T'Saan had resorted to an old V'Shar trick, placing the body of a Vulcan female of about her age—who had in fact died of smoke inhalation following a hovercraft accident—in a damaged craft where Narak's scanner would find it, to make it seem as if she and Saavik had quarreled and Saavik had crashed the craft in a show of loyalty to her newfound father.

Saavik's sudden appearance, and her outburst, had thrown Narak sufficiently off guard that he did not hear the churning of sand as another official hovercraft set down on the shore of the brackish pond. The expression on his face as Saavik relieved him of his weapons and led him outside to confront his fate was something she would remember for the rest of her life.

T'Saan, alive and well and flanked by two armed aides, was quietly issuing instructions into a comm unit. She glanced up at Narak with mild interest as she said, "Hold the one called T'Vaakis for my personal attention," and closed the comm. Her glance moved from Narak to Saavik and back to Narak.

"Indeed, there is a resemblance," was all she said. "Lieutenant, he is ours now."

To his credit, Narak recovered quickly. As he began to understand the full extent to which his own plot had been used against him, he threw back his head and laughed.

"Oh, this is magnificent!" He looked at Saavik with pure, unadulterated affection. "Blood will out! You knew where to find me."

"It was logical," Saavik said diffidently, not entirely convinced herself. "You provided no meeting place, yet you expected me to find you."

But Narak was having none of it. "Say what you will, you are completely mine! No Vulcan could lie and scheme as effectively as you have!"

The hand that held the phaser trembled. Aware that T'Saan's aides had Narak covered, Saavik returned it to her belt and steadied herself.

"One cannot lie to a liar," she said with all the calmness she could muster. "I am myself and nothing of yours."

The laughter in his eyes faded. His face fell. Almost his shoulders slumped, but he kept his dignity.

"Pity," he said. "I never had anything but affection for you. Well, keep the Honor Blade, at least."

She almost gave it back to him, confident that two drawn phasers and whatever other skills T'Saan and her cohort had would be more than a match for an accountant and his ornate knife, but she never had the chance.

As he turned his back on her to face his captors, he burst into flames.

The flare lit up the moonless night and might have been mistaken for a meteorite, for many fell in this hemisphere at this time of year. In less time than it took the four surrounding him to react, he was transformed from living flesh first into matter so hot the others were driven back in spite of themselves, and then to ashes. As with all the devices he'd carried with him at their first meeting, the fire starter had been well concealed and had gone unnoticed.

"Subcutaneous and minuscule, with leads implanted in the major arteries to induce rapid immolation," the healer who examined the remains, if remains they could be called, reported afterward. "Even if one had had time to examine him, it would have been difficult to detect. Quite sophisticated as well, as one can see from the outcome. Pity it left only trace elements in its wake."

"And therefore, one assumes, no DNA." T'Saan did not so much as ask. "Dentition?"

"That's the curious thing," the healer explained. "He had no natural teeth, only implants. One assumes this was done to make identification impossible."

"Unfortunate" was T'Saan's opinion.

If Saavik had an opinion, she kept it to herself.

Over the next several days, nineteen operatives were pulled in along the spider strands Narak had laid across a planet, including a young female who bore a remarkable resemblance to Saavik herself.

"There will be trials, of course," T'Saan informed her, in what Saavik hoped would be their final encounter. "One had hoped in camera, but that is for the High Council to determine. You will be asked to give depositions, but these can be written only."

In camera, yes, Saavik thought. *One* would *hope to protect the ambassador's privacy, not to mention Vulcan pride.*

"And then?"

"Then thee are free to go," T'Saan said, relapsing into the old formality. "With no obligation on thyself. A reluctant spy is an unreliable spy, as perhaps the empire has learned through Narak, if that part of his tale is true."

"My inquiry was about the prisoners," Saavik clarified, steadfastly refusing to allow this to be about herself.

"Logically one has to wait for the determination of the trials," T'Saan said, though she knew what Saavik was asking. "If any are found guilty, they will likely be offered in exchange for prisoners the Romulans hold for just such eventualities."

"If they are returned to the empire, having failed in their mission, they will most likely forfeit their lives," Saavik suggested. She did not know how she knew this, but she knew.

"That is not for thy concern," T'Saan said not unkindly, but with a coolness to her tone that said there was no logic in asking further questions.

Saavik returned briefly to Amorak, primarily, once she was informed that he was in fact alive, to visit Simar and thank him for his service. The old spy allowed himself the shadow of a smile and then, as everyone looked the other way, embraced her to show that he was proud. Then an unmarked vehicle returned her to ShiKahr without fanfare, as she would have wished. Logically there was no other way to be the hero of an event that had not happened.

Amanda was far less shy than Simar about her feelings. She also had plans to whisk Saavik away for the rest she had not had time for before this whole thing began, but Sarek intervened.

"My wife, it is I who need to speak to her," he said quietly, and Amanda yielded.

But confronted by the young woman who had risked so much, the master diplomat found himself at a loss, and said as much.

"No words are adequate to thank you for what you have done," he said, and stopped.

"I did only what was necessary, Father."

"But to risk your career, and the enmity of those who trusted you . . ."

"I had hoped that, as a member of the family, T'Saan would have briefed you, at least in part. Barring that, I assumed you would acquire what information you could through diplomatic channels," Saavik said.

In fact, Sarek had had to wrest the information from T'Saan in spite of, not because of, the family connection.

He had not told Amanda everything about the "situation" at Amorak, most notably that it was reported an elder had died, quite possibly at Saavik's hands. For one thing, even given Saavik's irrational outbursts over the past year, Sarek had refused to accept this as truth. Journeying immediately to the shrine, he'd been told little more in person than had been imparted to him in the initial communiqué. Had he not encountered Simar in the corridor following his rather fruitless dialogue with T'Leng, he might have remained in the dark until the entire mission was ended.

Simar did not speak, merely reached one gnarled hand to Sarek's brow, as was his right as an adept, conveying, with not a little humor, that the report of his death was an exaggeration.

"Where is my daughter?" Sarek had asked aloud, and Simar had withdrawn his hand, though not before conveying an additional thought: *Family knows what family knows.*

The return journey to ShiKahr gave Sarek ample time to ascertain that Simar had at one time been something other than an adept at Amorak. Sarek's next visit was closer to home. Reaching T'Saan at her residence, he was succinct.

"Where is my daughter?"

"As you were informed at Amorak, she has gone to the desert."

"For what purpose?"

"I submit that her purpose was known only to her," T'Saan suggested mildly.

"And I submit that you are being less than truthful."

Lesser beings than T'Saan had been intimidated into revealing much beneath Sarek's gaze. Even one larger-than-life Starfleet officer had been known to find himself making excuses in the Vulcan's presence. While tact might be a diplomat's greatest skill, there was much to be said for psychological arm-twisting.

But T'Saan and Sarek were kin and of an age. They

had spent time in childhood under T'Pau's watchful gaze, and even that old battle-ax would not have been able to say with any certainty which could outstubborn the other.

This time, Sarek broke the silence. "Thee have put her at risk, and thee will not tell me why. Logic suggests I am somehow implicated."

"Only a logic that can leap chasms without looking down," T'Saan replied.

"It is my right to know that which is done in my name."

"Only if thee are prepared to accept consequences over which thee has no control!"

Impasse. Sarek considered the many diplomatic threads he had cast across a quadrant or two, and which of them might intersect whatever multiplicity of threads the V'Shar might have in parallel. It was possible that the V'Shar knew everything he was up to, including most particularly the overtures to the Klingons; it was equally impossible for him to know everything the V'Shar knew. Nor did he want to know, except where Saavik was concerned.

"'My logic is uncertain where my son is concerned,'" T'Saan said now, her tone an exact imitation of his, an annoying way she'd taunted him when they were children. "Yes, of course I heard. All of Vulcan heard the words you spoke on Mount Seleya."

"And so my judgment is suspect hereafter?" Sarek demanded. Was that anger in his voice, or only righteous indignation?

"Say rather that it is taken under advisement,"

T'Saan replied, and not for the first time Sarek was reminded that it had been he who first taught her how to play *kal-toh,* only to have her beat him at every game they played thereafter.

Very well, then. She might have him physically removed from her office but, barring that, he was here on his own time, and she would have tasks that called her away. Eventually her comm would sound and she would have to go back to work. Sarek would use that to his advantage.

He waited. She did not blink. But she knew, as he knew, that this time she would have to break the silence. Eventually she said, "Thee must give me thy word that no matter what I tell thee, thee will take no action, make no further inquiries, leave the matter entirely to us regardless of possible outcomes."

"Without knowing the nature of—"

"Thy word, or nothing."

Sarek exhaled, running permutations in his head. Could he trust that the entirety of the V'Shar was better equipped to solve this, whatever it was, than he alone? That Simar's death had been nothing more than a contrivance argued in the affirmative?

But more to the point, he had to trust that Saavik, whatever beset her at present, would not waver from her true self. If he could not trust her, no action he might take would matter.

He trusted her.

"My word," he told T'Saan.

Again, keeping all parties involved compartmentalized, she had told him only enough to confirm his faith in Saavik and to keep him safely removed from whatever happened next. Not until Narak's network had been successfully rolled up and his operatives detained was Sarek told everything.

And, in fact, Saavik had not even considered whether or not T'Saan had briefed him, until now. She had simply thrown herself in the path of this thing, at first for Tolek, and later, when she understood the enormity of the plot, for Sarek. Logically, there was nothing else she could have done.

"Nevertheless, you took a great risk," Sarek said now. "The rigors of the desert, the likelihood of death at any time . . ."

". . . were preferable to the alternative," Saavik pointed out. "Had the plot succeeded, far more would have been lost." *Take that to mean, Father, that the optimal outcome of your conversations with the Klingons are of greater value to me than any one life or career. To say I feared losing you and Amanda and Spock would be to admit to emotion. That I will not do, even to you.* "Better such temporary risks than a lifetime of regret."

"Indeed."

It was the closest either could come to saying, "I could not bear to lose you." The senior diplomat looked upon his adopted daughter with a new appreciation. His expression softened.

"You have no idea how difficult it was to keep what little knowledge I had from your mother," he said longsufferingly.

"Then it would seem we have both survived the

Kobayashi Maru," Saavik suggested with a new appreciation for the concept of humor.

It was at this point that Amanda intervened before they both embarrassed themselves.

It has been said on Earth that if more women ruled, fewer men would die, this despite the fact that for much of Earth's history, women who ruled frequently did so at least as ruthlessly as their male counterparts. This neglects consideration of the fact that women who rise to power in male-dominated societies more often than not do so having emulated the most cold-blooded tactics of the menfolk in order to achieve that leadership. Where rule is benevolent, the gender of the ruler need not signify.

That aside, when two women put their heads together, the conversation is likely to be very different from the conversations of men.

Amanda was there for her when Saavik finally allowed herself to feel.

"Whatever you tell me does not go beyond this time and place," was how the human began the conversation.

Lying scattered like a strand of rare emeralds tossed carelessly against a bed of red and dun sands, the oases of PirAelim, constructed along a series of freshwater springs drawing from numerous underground sources, had offered refuge to Vulcan's nomad populations from the time of the beginning. Nowhere else on the planet was there so much variation in the type and source of water, from the iciest mineral springs, to sulfur-laden pools so hot they bubbled, to those tolerable to the skin and replete with phytoplankton that glowed in the dark. Trees and grasses of every native variety fed on the waters and flourished only meters from sands so dry that nothing grew. The contrast and the choice of waters offered a haven to even the most restive of souls.

Saavik had not visited here since she was a child, when Amanda had spirited her away on school holidays for what she'd called a "just us girls escape." Ever so serious, Saavik had of course had to ask what they were escaping from, to be rewarded with only a wink, as if it were some great secret. Now, with maturity, she thought she understood. Nevertheless, she had been reluctant at first, consenting only because she knew it would please her foster mother. Surely, Saavik thought, the pristine sanctuary she recalled would seem somehow less than perfect to her adult eyes.

But so far it had proved to be exactly as she remembered it, and just as the healing waters gradually loosened the knots in a body tautened at Red Alert for far too long, the companionship of one who did not judge but merely listened began to loose the knots in her soul.

Weary of keeping secrets for the greater part of a year, Saavik finally let go. She poured out her heart, told Amanda everything, from the moment Tolek had called out her name in the market, to the moment she recoiled from the conflagration that was Narak, the heat so intense it had singed her hair and left the stench of burning flesh in her nostrils for days . . .

"It's the hair that smells the worst," she'd overheard Doctor McCoy say. They were on their way to Regula I at

best speed following their first battle with *Reliant*. Time
enough to count the casualties and mop up.

McCoy was doing the requisite autopsy that would
confirm Midshipman Peter Preston's cause of death,
talking half to himself and half to the three cadets
aboard—one RN and two paramedic trainees—just
qualified enough to serve as fill-in sickbay staff.

Saavik, at loose ends, had waited until Kirk was back
in the command chair and fielding a dozen decisions at
once and finally glanced up to see her standing at attention barely inches from his elbow.

"Orders, sir?"

"Make yourself useful," Kirk had said, and she'd
taken that to mean, "Go somewhere else and see what
needs doing."

She'd stopped at sickbay first, simply because it was
on the way to engineering, but McCoy had seen her and
waved her off. He knew she and Peter had been close.

"You kind of expect burned human flesh to smell
like barbecue, but it doesn't . . ." he'd gone on as she
lingered in the doorway, unable to look away from the
oddly peaceful expression on Peter's face. Of all the
ways one could die on Hellguard, she'd never seen anyone burned before. "We rarely cook a whole animal,
except maybe at a luau, and even then we remove the
internal organs first and singe off the hair . . ."

"Doc, does this have to be done right now?" one of
the cadets had piped up squeamishly, concerned at seeing the old man steady himself against the table before
beginning.

"No better time!" McCoy had barked. "Don't know

but there may be a lot more casualties before this is over. If you don't have the stomach for it, just say so and stand down!"

He'd glowered at each of them in turn, and they'd resumed cutting the scorched uniform away from flesh and preparing the body under the harsh, unrelenting light.

"As I was saying," McCoy continued, "it's the smell of the hair that stays in the back of your throat for days. Hair and nails, as I'm sure you learned in Anatomy 101, are made of keratin, which is loaded with cysteine, a sulfur-based amino acid. Closest thing to fire and brimstone you'll smell on this side of the Styx. Cerebrospinal fluid, now, that gives off a sickly-sweet smell . . ."

Was the present nothing more than a fulcrum between past and future? Saavik wondered. And wasn't the release of emotion supposed to make one feel better?

"I do not understand," she said when she could breathe again. She swept away the disgrace of tears that no one but Amanda would ever see. "It should be of comfort to me that no more of the Hellguard survivors will die. There should be great satisfaction in knowing that Sarek's career and reputation are undamaged, and that his overtures to the Klingons can proceed apace. Why then—?"

"—do you feel so awful?" Amanda supplied. "I don't hear anything about Saavik in that conversation."

The two had taken shelter from the midday sun beneath an ancient *Kamor* tree, which had defied a thousand years of adversity to spread its roots and branches a hundred meters in all directions. The shade it provided was a realm away from the heat beyond, cool and inviting. Local legend had it that an entire tribe had sheltered here for a season when the sandstorms were particularly bad. One of their number had left behind a stone plaque marked with the ancient runes of a lost language in homage to the tree. For now, the overarching branches offered safety to a tribe of only two, protecting them from a metaphysical danger.

"I do not understand," Saavik said again.

"I think you do," Amanda replied. "You've lost a dear friend in Tolek, and you'll spend a great deal of time second-guessing whether you could have done anything to save him. In time I'm hoping you will come to terms with the fact that what happened to him and the others was not your fault. You've devoted almost a year of your life to a mission that might have ended badly, through no fault of yours. The anxiety of that alone, added to everything that went before. When do you give yourself credit for what you have done and allow yourself time to grieve?"

"I still do not know what killed Tolek and the others. If it is some bioweapon that the Romulans will use again, my task is not complete."

"There are some tasks that even you must acknowledge you cannot complete alone," Amanda said with a mysterious smile.

It wasn't until they'd returned to ShiKahr that Saavik understood what she meant. She was almost beyond surprise to find Sarek in the main parlor in quiet conversation with Mikal.

* * *

Seeing her standing in the pool of late afternoon light from one of the high clerestory windows in the parlor, Mikal found himself on his feet, speechless for once in his life.

With everything you've been through, he thought, *have you never wondered, even for a moment, what's become of me in all the time you were away? You'd be well within your rights to assume I'd returned to Deema III without you, and with what you know of me, of my restlessness, my impatience, my often rash assumptions, you'd expect nothing less than that, in the absence of any explanation from me, I'd long since have categorized those few magic days as an aberration and consigned them to memory. If you thought of me at all, I hope it was at least a little fondly.*

But as for false assumptions . . .

Yes, to all appearances I'd been slacking off—assigning more and more of the workload on Deema III to my team, the task of building a language base to the Belazed Loth, stepping aside for Mironova to lay the diplomatic groundwork. What was I doing in those long hours alone in my quarters or sequestered in one of the lesser-used labs? they all wondered. Brooding, most of them thought, and left me alone.

Chaffee's comm officer might have told you about the coded communiqués flying back and forth from my personal comm to the far-flung corners of the quadrant, corners where, if one were curious, and comm officers usually were, one might make note of the fact that Ambassador Sarek was in the vicinity.

So it seems Sarek and I have been in communication for quite some time. What might that mean? It might mean no more than a shared interest in science, or as much as a particular interest in a Vulcan scientist of our acquaintance.

I will tell you, if I find the courage to open my mouth, about how, more than once, mysterious parcels arrived for me aboard Chaffee, *having made their circuitous way round about the quadrant in diplomatic pouches, which exempted them from the usual scans and security precautions. As a matter of protocol, these parcels landed on Mironova's desk, but if she expected an explanation whenever I came to retrieve them, there was none forthcoming.*

That's only one of the many things I will tell you, if only I can find the courage to open my mouth.

Saavik knew none of what passed through Mikal's mind in the few seconds it took him to spring to his feet and cross the room to her, seconds that subjectively felt like minutes to him. She only wondered why Mikal was here, and what it was she was feeling.

Yes, feeling. There was no logic in his presence here, after she had snubbed him in the street, and no logic to the flutter somewhere in the vicinity of her heart when they made eye contact. Something passed across the space between them, something ineffable, perhaps undefinable. Both began to speak at once.

"I'm sorry—" each said, then stopped.

"I did not mean to pass you in the street," she said. "I—"

"I never meant to doubt you. I should have—" he said.

They stopped. Discreetly, Amanda took Sarek's arm and led him away. Mikal shared the pool of light now, arms' length from her. They might have touched, but didn't. Dust motes danced in the chasm.

Mikal sighed, tugged at his ears, setting the earrings jangling, tried again. "When you went off suddenly, without explanation, I—"

"As logically you should have." She was as motionless as he was animated, hands at her sides, all but at attention. "Whereas I should have found a way to tell you—"

"How could you, without giving away your mission? I understand now."

"But you did not at the time."

"Can you blame me?" Silence. "No, I didn't mean it that way. There should be no blame on either side." He threw up his hands in exasperation. "This isn't working! Come with me—" He took her hand, and she did not protest. "There's something I have to show you."

Chaffee hung in drydock above Vulcan, work crews in pressure suits going over her exterior, the conn at station keeping, no one else aboard. The labs, of course, were kept running at all times, analyzing data, preserving samples, awaiting the next mission. Saavik and Mikal, their heads together as they pored over data, were using the labs to solve a mystery.

"Rapamycin," Saavik said at last, remembering a conversation with Mikal a lifetime ago, about how an anomaly found in the soil on a remote island in Earth's South Pacific had been cultivated into a powerful antibiotic, only one of countless examples in the medical armamentarium.

"Pretty much," Mikal agreed. Anyone listening in on their conversation would have had no clue what they were talking about.

"But how did you get access to all of this data?" Saavik wondered.

"Not easily. The first thing I had to do was try to read your mind from half a quadrant away, so I could get into your files. I pooled all the data you and Tolek had amassed, and went looking for things you might have overlooked. That's when I found that all of the victims had three distinct alleles in common, but they varied just enough from X to Y chromosomes to make them difficult to detect, particularly by a scientist up to her pretty pointed ears on an important Starfleet mission being pestered almost daily not only by a layman on the verge of hysteria—yes, I know, never speak ill of the dead, but if Tolek hadn't been so insistent . . . And then there was that other pest, that bald-headed guy who had other motives in mind—"

"Mikal—"

"Quiet, please. Not finished. So first I isolated the three alleles, just on a hunch. Then I did some pestering of my own. That's where Sarek came in."

"Sarek?"

"He was the only person I could think of with enough clout to get actual tissue samples from the three dead. Well, four. I was able to get samples from Tolek on my own. Don't ask!" he said, when it looked as if she was about to. "Let's just say the biggest flaw in Vulcan logic is honesty. A species that spends its life trying not to lie is very easily lied to. Okay, fast-forward, Sarek used his clout with T'Saan—not that I knew her name at the time, much less that they were cousins—and got me the tissue samples. That's what was in those diplomatic pouches Galina was so curious about. I wonder if I'll ever tell her the whole story . . ."

Saavik found herself strangely exhilarated. Listening to Mikal, watching the animation in his face as he described the process by which he'd solved the mystery, was as fascinating as seeing the puzzle pieces fit together beneath the microscope, on the spectrograph, on the screens surrounding them, as he explained.

"I could let her figure it out on her own, but I'll probably tell her. Any other ship's captain would have tossed me in the brig, civilian or no, for being so lazy on this run, but I trusted my team, and I needed every spare minute to crack this thing. For all I knew, you were meant to be the next victim. That part was true, wasn't it?"

"If I had not followed Narak's instructions, I have no doubt he would have had me killed," Saavik said, though even as she said it, she would never be entirely sure. She still wondered whether he'd immolated himself solely to rob the V'Shar of proof as to her paternity, or if the look she'd seen in his eyes in his last moment truly was one of despair.

"I couldn't let that happen!" Mikal stopped his mad peregrinations around the lab long enough to take her hands in his. "And not just because we'd come to be more than friends. This"—he indicated the readouts—"wasn't the only puzzle to be solved. You do realize that?"

She hadn't, and was about to say so, but he was off again.

"So, okay, step one, try to read Saavik's mind and guess her pass codes so I could access her data. Wangle tissue samples from the V'Shar by way of Sarek. Isolate the three alleles and note how they'd mutated from the healthy body to the dead one. Then figure out what substance or process in the known universe could affect that mutation and leave no trace when it was done. Simple, right?"

"Rapamycin," Saavik said again.

"And a leap of faith," Mikal added.

"'Nothing that is, is unimportant.' Worm kept telling me the same thing, but I wasn't paying attention."

Saavik took a seat, if only to stay out of Mikal's way as he continued to careen about the lab.

"You do know the V'Shar vetted every one of us before allowing you to go on the original mission to Deema III?" Saavik nodded. "Pure coincidence, if you believe in such things. They might just as easily have secreted you away somewhere on Vulcan for safekeeping and tried to figure this thing out on their own. Then you and I would never have met, and I'd have had no . . . emotional investment in figuring out what killed the others. Oh, somebody would have figured it out eventually, if only by secreting a scientist or two into the empire, but it might have taken years or even decades.

"But there's Sagan's 'star stuff' theory, that everything in this universe, at least, is in harmony with everything else. Some scientists extend that to medicine—if there's a disease, there's also a concomitant cure. Why does a common yew tree yield tamoxifen, a primitive cure for certain cancers? Why does a wildflower yield a substance that controls heart rate? Why does a substance found in the soil of the Romulan homeworld interact with those three alleles to cause an overgrowth in copper-based platelet cells that literally clog up every major organ and cause death? And why does the enantiomer for that substance—"

"Wait," Saavik pleaded. Ordinarily she could follow any scientific explanation if sufficient facts were present, but Mikal's rapid-fire delivery, or perhaps the time she had spent away from a world in which things proceeded in an orderly fashion, gave her a sense that she was missing something. "Repeated examination of the bodies from crude autopsy to submolecular sampling found no such clotting."

Mikal's grin was almost feral. "That's the beauty of this thing. While the blood is circulating, it proliferates. As soon as a clot large enough to impact a major organ system—heart, lung, brain—causes infarction and death, the anomalous cells literally evanesce away. You'd have to be in the room at the moment the person died and perform an autopsy immediately in order to catch these little demons in the act."

Saavik considered. "And the likelihood of medical personnel being on hand at that precise moment . . ."

"Much less willing to say to the relatives, 'Hey, your

adopted son is dead, time of death such-and-such; I'm cutting now.' "

"Indeed. Then how did you—?"

"I didn't at first. I was looking at only half of the puzzle. The soil in the Kiral Valley on Deema III was the other half. Watch this."

Using a scanning electron microscope, Mikal selected a tissue sample marked TOLEK, growing autonomously on an agar substrate, and added a purplish granular-looking substance one cell at a time. Within seconds, the sample had been transformed into a single massive green clot. As he separated the clot from the growth medium, it began to dissipate.

"Nevertheless," Saavik said, impressed but still skeptical, "the time involved in a single clot, multiplied by every major organ system . . ."

". . . would be several hours. Which is why . . ."

Choosing a second sample, he treated it the same way, only this time, before removing it from the growth medium, he treated it with a second substance that, under maximum magnification, Saavik could see was an enantiomer, an almost mirror image or "left-handed" version of the original molecule.

The silence that ensued was palpable, as electrically charged as the silence in the parlor when the two of them had stood in a pool of light, wondering what would happen next. That time it had been a silence of emotion. This time it was a silence of discovery.

"I suppose," Saavik said carefully, "that if I asked you how you obtained the killer molecule, which you say is found only on the Romulan homeworld—"

"Known to be found on the Romulan homeworld," he corrected her. "It might be extant throughout the empire, but this much we know about."

"I stand corrected. But you will not tell me how you acquired this?"

Mikal grinned. "I would if I could, but I don't actually know. Sarek might, though. You can ask him. As for your next question, it was Worm who told me about the Kiral Valley."

It seemed almost too easy, and Saavik said as much.

"Easy for you to say. Worm kept trying to tell me, and I wouldn't listen, because s/he kept asking about you and I didn't want to hear. But when the team came to me and said there was one last place on the maps where anomalies had been appearing and disappearing for centuries, and why hadn't we gone there yet? I sent them on their own, Jaoui and Cheung, with Graana in charge. They brought back several dozen plant specimens, complete with root systems, and examination of the soil around the root systems revealed traces of this stuff.

"The rifts had closed by then. We'd have to go back this time next year to try to trace those soil samples and find out if they're native, if they come from somewhere in Romulan space, or from somewhere else entirely. I've already submitted the paperwork; this one's not getting away from me. We can't stop the Romulans from continuing to develop killer organisms, but we can try to have something on hand to counteract them when they do."

Nineteen

The trials of the Romulan prisoners were swift and enacted with little fanfare. The charges against them were a masterwork of balance between justice and truth unspoken. At no point were their intended targets specifically mentioned.

Saavik submitted the required depositions anonymously. Though she was not required to testify in person, she nevertheless found herself in attendance at the hearing that determined T'Vaakis's fate.

Of the other eighteen taken into custody, the two who had assisted Narak in murdering the four Hellguard survivors managed to commit ritual suicide while Vulcan authorities conveniently looked the other way. Twelve others, not surprisingly, elected to remain on Vulcan and serve out terms for espionage of varying degrees of severity. The remaining four, essentially middlemen along the web, were exchanged for Federation prisoners held by the empire. An unsettling light in their eyes suggested they were trusting enough to believe that this would, if not necessarily make them heroes to their people, at least guarantee them some sort of safety when they returned home.

Of those four, only one made a public statement. She had extended family, including two young children, and it was for them she had agreed to return to the empire. She made it sound as if she looked forward to returning to the arms of her loved ones, but the implication was that she was sacrificing herself for the family name. Her name would be stricken from the public record, so that theirs might be redeemed.

"It's lunacy!" was Galina Mironova's opinion, as the crew of *Chaffee* followed the proceedings on the public feeds. "It's a wonder they haven't gone extinct as a species with all their different codes of honor and reasons to die for them."

"Maybe that's why they have such large families," Esparza muttered under his breath. "The eldest go into the star service, the middle ones are thrown to the wolves so that the youngest can inherit the estate."

Mironova eyed him with a new appreciation. He gave the impression of being a bumbler, but there was considerable insight at work beneath that unruly thatch of hair.

There was no such light in T'Vaakis's eyes, but rather a disconcerting lack of affect. She said little during her hearing, other than to answer the questions put to her in as few words as possible. It became quite clear that she'd known nothing more about the operation than that another would be sent to perform certain actions while using her name and her identifying characteristics. Wisely, or perhaps only naïvely, she had asked no questions, merely followed instructions. Under intense questioning, including a mind-meld to which she gave assent, neither the name "Sarek" nor even "Saavik" evidenced any recognition. When given a choice between detention on Vulcan and return to the empire, her answer was succinct.

"It matters not."

It was not a holding cell in the strictest sense. Yes, there was a force field and a guard beyond it, but the accommodations within were as pleasant as they could be to one who knew she could not step beyond them. From the look in T'Vaakis's eyes, it did not matter either way.

Saavik removed Narak's Honor Blade from her belt. She had not submitted it with the other weapons she had relieved him of in the desert and, curiously, no one seemed to have noticed. She would not, of course, give it to T'Vaakis as long as she was detained, but she wanted her to know what had become of it.

"As I understand your culture, it would be illogical for you to return to the empire," Saavik began. "Nevertheless, the charges against you—"

"—give me the choice of a brief detention between these walls and then 'freedom' to go where I wish," T'Vaakis finished with a baleful look. But she was very young and could not hold her emotions in for long. The dark eyes filled with tears. "He groomed me for this, from the time I was a child. I have known no other life. That is hardly 'freedom.'"

Saavik, more skilled at masks, revealed no trace of the anger, the envy gnawing at her. How dare this pampered child complain of having a father who, whatever his motives, at least was there for her?

"It must seem as if he has abandoned you," Saavik managed to say past the constriction in her throat.

"What would you know of it?" the girl demanded, dashing the tears off her face, grief turned to rage in an instant.

More than you can possibly imagine! Saavik thought but did not trust herself to say.

"I am completely alone," T'Vaakis went on. "What does it matter whether I live or die?"

What would adolescence be without self-absorption? Saavik wondered, slipping the Honor Blade back into her belt. Until the green haze cleared from her vision, she did not entirely know what she might do with it if it were still in her hand.

"Dead you will at least be freed of self-pity," she said when she could control her voice.

It was like a splash of cold water. Saavik marveled at the play of emotions across a face that was the mirror image of her own. It was as if for the first time T'Vaakis was stepping outside herself, allowing that someone else's life might be more arduous than her own, considering what it might have been like to have no father at all.

"W-what was your life like, growing up without him?"

Oh, no, little one! You don't get access to that so easily! Saavik thought. What she said was, "Live, and someday I might tell you."

With that she motioned to the guard outside to release the force field. She ought not to have looked back, but she did.

"I will keep the Honor Blade against that eventuality" were her parting words.

Tough love, a human might call it. Then again, a human might have wrapped the girl in an embrace, called her "little sister," assured her that she was not alone "as long as we have each other." Humans!

Apparently Saavik was not to leave the facility unimpeded. T'Saan met her in the outer courtyard.

"Nicely played," she said, a touch of admiration in her tone.

Inwardly Saavik cursed herself in all the languages she knew.

"Of course. I should have realized the cell was monitored. Further proof I would be of poor service as a spy."

"Starfleet's gain, our loss, though you can always change your mind," T'Saan said diffidently.

"If that is all . . ." Saavik eyed the outer gate, and the impression it gave that once she was clear of this place, she would be free.

"You *are* kin, by the way, you and she," T'Saan said to her retreating back. "We've done the blood work."

The green haze again crossed her vision. She turned, seething, her hand inadvertently on the Honor Blade, set in the place where her own primitive Hellguard blade usually rested. "You had no right!"

"She is our prisoner; that gave us the right. And Starfleet has your records," T'Saan said with unassailable logic. "Whether or not Narak was the source, you share the same father. And logically, given that he raised her, groomed her, then came seeking you—"

"*Kroykah!*"

There was only so much one person could bear. As soon as the word was out of her mouth, Saavik found a dozen ways to apologize for it, but stopped. How was she to read the expression on T'Saan's face? Had no one ever told her to be silent before? Surely not anyone younger, surely not since she had found her place in the V'Shar. In any event, she said nothing further and made no move to stop Saavik from leaving.

She passed through the outer gate unmolested, her heels clicking furiously on the paving stones beyond. She would walk unseeing for the better part of an hour before she accepted the possibility that, given who it was who had made the suggestion, it might as easily be another V'Shar trick as truth.

In time she would inquire further, only to discover that there was no record of the nineteenth detainee in any database, under any name or designation, at least not to someone with her computer skills. Someday, perhaps, she would ask Spock to assist her. For now, T'Vaakis had ceased to exist. Had she made a choice, or had it been made for her? Returned to the empire, absorbed into the V'Shar—who better to be transformed into a mole?—or, like her purported sibling, allowed nominally to go free? It was not for Saavik to know.

Captain's Personal Log, Galina Mironova recording. Dress uniforms, ship scrubbed and polished down to the last bolt and rivet. We are entertaining guests tonight. As we began and ended this mission from Vulcan space, most will be Vulcan scien-

tists and diplomats, including Ambassador Sarek and his wife, though we will also have a live feed to Federation HQ on Earth to discuss the future of Deema III. I shall be hosting a small reception, along with Doctor Mikal, Lieutenant Loth, and as many of the science team as can be trusted not to fall into the punch bowl, as we introduce the Federation Council to Worm and hir people, prefatory to setting up a permanent scientific presence, and an at least temporary consulate on hir world.

"You're blushing," Mikal stage-whispered shamelessly when Mironova finally managed to tear herself away from Sarek's aura with the excuse that she needed to give her other guests equal time.

"I am not!" she retorted, glowering at him. "The reds and oranges in your robe are so damn bright they're reflecting on my face."

"Does that explain the giggling too?"

Yes, she had been giggling. Sarek tended to have that effect on the females of several species. It had been said that a good part of his success as a diplomat rested in precisely that innate ability. Despite feeling like a schoolgirl again, however, Mironova had managed to be completely professional when it came to discussing the science of the thing.

There was, indeed, to be a permanent scientific presence on Deema III, led by Lieutenant Commander Palousek, senior member of the original science team after Doctor Mikal and Lieutenant Saavik, which would do a thorough study once the interspatial rifts opened again in approximately three hundred seventy-five days.

"The goal," Doctor Mikal explained during his presentation to the gathering, "will be to ascertain how many of the rifts are fixed, that is to say, opening at the same time and leading to the same point of origin, and how many are variable. While it would be premature to speculate just how valuable the fixed ones may prove in terms of perhaps finding a shortcut or shortcuts to distant regions of our space or unexplored regions, their measurements will be taken in exhaustive detail . . ."

And so on and so forth. While the guests were attentive, Mikal's presentation was mercifully brief. Everyone knew that the highlight of the evening was to be the communiqué from Worm.

The distance to Deema III made live communication impossible. This had been explained to Worm by Lieutenant Loth before *Chaffee* departed Deema III. At least, Loth had begun to explain, but Worm had interrupted him.

Yes, we know this. Thus it must be, for now. In time, we will communicate by means less primitive than your technology. This is not a judgment, merely an observation.

More of a linguist than a scientist, Loth was at first not certain he understood. But when he allowed himself, as a telepath can, to see the universe through Worm's perspective . . .

"I was tempted initially, ma'am, to say 'through Worm's eyes,'" he explained, managing not to stutter despite his nervousness in the presence of such luminaries when Amanda, always interested in language in all its forms, had asked him, "except of course that the being doesn't have eyes. Through Worm's *perspective*, then. The Deemanot don't exactly see the universe as absent time, but the *passage* of time is less important to them, apparently, than it is to us. I'm making a muddle of this, aren't I, ma'am?"

"You're doing splendidly, Lieutenant," Amanda said, an encouraging hand on his arm. "Do continue."

Drunk on her words without ever having gone near the punch bowl, Loth blithered blissfully on in the intermission between Mikal's presentation and Worm's.

The reception was being held in *Chaffee*'s cargo bay, the largest open space in the small ship, which had been cleared of cargo (the junior crew's grumbling about sharing their already cramped quarters with relocated ship's stores had been resolved by granting shore leave to everyone but the science team and a handful of cadets drafted to mingle with trays of champagne and hors d'oeuvres) and tastefully decorated for the occasion. Viewscreens had been placed about at intervals and, as it turned out that prior to switching to sciences, Lieutenant Ta'oob had held a degree in acoustics, the sound system was flawless. When at last Worm's transmission came onscreen, there was a barely suppressed gasp from the audience, even the Vulcans, and the crew who had met and interacted with the Deemanot in person.

The acoustics, it should be explained, had required the synchronization of several technologies. First was a mind-link between Worm and Loth where Loth, connected to the latest in electroencephalopathy technology, had allowed his brain waves to be monitored and transcribed into electronic impulses, which were then encoded as sound waves, which were subsequently translated into the spoken word. Small wonder that Amanda, linguist, etymologist, and teacher, was fascinated. Saavik, meanwhile, was almost envious.

It was fair to say *almost*. In a different reality, it would have been she, not Loth, who had served as interlocutor this time as well as the first. But envy was illogical. She watched and listened to the transmission, as intrigued as everyone else.

"Persons of the United Federation of Planets," Worm's "speech" began, "we greet you with respect and hope."

Onscreen, the being was a looming presence, tastefully framed and lit by the best existing technology, resplendently iridescent, hir colors changing with hir speech, from the basic Deemanot earthworm-reddish-brown through a rainbow of golds, greens, blues, and violets, each color representing a nuance of mood. The voice, while computer generated, possessed warmth and a touch of the dry humor those who had met Worm in person recognized immediately.

"Ours has been an outlier's existence, awaiting contact from our brethren in the larger universe," the voice continued, as the being undulated slightly, hir body language synchronous with the words. "Whether it was you or someone other was not for us to determine and, defenseless as we are, such an encounter with beings who were not like us might have had a very different outcome. In brief, we are grateful it was your kind that got here first.

"Our world in and of itself offers nothing that innumerable other worlds cannot offer in greater volume and specificity. Mineral wealth, interesting scenery, plant life, essential location in a quadrant buzzing with ever-shifting hostilities—these things are not all that important, after all. Our value as a member of your Federation lies in a certain curiosity about our species—intelligent worms, imagine that!—but primarily because what happens in the space surrounding our otherwise unremarkable little planet intrigues the explorers in you.

"We do not judge. We, rather, say that the first of your members who have made themselves known to us have piqued our curiosity, and thus we welcome your presence in our system, on our world. Most important, reaching into the minds of those named Saavik, Mikal, Mironova, and, finally, Loth tells us that we can trust you and your kind. As you continue to study our artifacts, which will tell you of our connectedness with the universe, you will understand that all of this was foretold, and so we look forward to your presence in our future. Yes."

With that final word, the being nodded. A human gesture? No one from *Chaffee* had seen Worm or any of the other Deemanot nod before. There was still so much to learn.

"I sometimes wonder," Amanda said, "just how many worlds the Federation can encompass before it becomes unwieldy. But then I listen to something like this and

I think it's not necessarily only about physics or even politics, but about some overarching interconnectedness. But then, my husband will tell you I'm a hopeless romantic."

"Husbands are like that," Mironova agreed. "I had one once. Useless appendage, in my case. You've been luckier."

"Indeed," Amanda agreed.

The two women had bonded immediately, not only in their admiration of Sarek. At the moment they were watching Saavik making her way through the crowd, congratulating "the kids," as Mikal had taken to calling them, on their meticulous work, introducing herself to Loth, who'd begun to stutter again, asking him detailed questions about his sequential melds with Worm and the other Deemanot. Finally, as the two older women watched, her path crossed Mikal's.

"Interesting young man," Amanda observed. "Sarek seems quite taken with him."

"He has his moments," Mironova acknowledged. "But, honestly, she deserves better."

Amanda eyed her appraisingly. "You're not a telepath," she said.

Mironova twinkled at her. "One doesn't necessarily have to be."

The science team gathered around Saavik, universally glad to see her again, eager to tell her what they'd accomplished on the return to Deema III. If any of them were tempted to ask her about the rumors flying through subspace in her absence, the awareness that Captain

Mironova would have their hides if they stepped over that line kept those questions unasked.

Not for the first time, Saavik was simultaneously gratified and puzzled by their attention. When one has lacked a sense of place in the formative years, one is never certain of one's welcome later on.

"They adore you," Mikal said, sidling up beside her—a signal to the others to go play somewhere else—and offering her a champagne flute, which she took out of general politeness; the substance it contained had not, in her experience, ever had any effect on her mood. "The women see you as a role model; the men all want to bed you. Maybe some of the women do as well, but at least—"

"And you, I note, remain as incorrigible as ever," she said dryly.

"Not true! You haven't read my most recent paper, have you?"

She confessed she had not, which compelled him to escort her to the nearest console to show her.

" 'Observations of Interspatial Rifts Recorded in the Deema System and Artifacts Gathered Therefrom' by Mikal, Palousek, Graana, Jaoui, Ta'oob, Esparza, and Cheung," she read, scanning the content in less time than it took Mikal to finish his champagne. "Impressive."

"What? That we were able to gather so much data, or that for once I credited everyone involved instead of hogging all the glory myself?"

"Yes," she said without the slightest hesitation.

"It's good to see you smile."

"Is that what you perceive I was doing?"

"In your particularly Vulcan way. Sarek gave the V'Shar our data on the substance we found in the Kiral Valley."

"That *you* found in the Kiral Valley."

Mikal dismissed this with a gesture. "That *we* formulated as an antidote to the Romulans' latest tricks. Your name's going on that paper in tandem with mine."

Her expression said it did not matter. Nevertheless, she was finding the conversation pleasing.

"Captain Mironova was correct," she said as Mikal accepted another glass of champagne from a passing cadet, gesturing inquiringly toward hers, though she had not drunk from it.

Mikal gave her a puzzled look. "Correct about what?"

"At our first interview, she suggested a certain synchronicity in the contrasts between your scientific method and mine. This would suggest the potential for similar synergies in the future."

Mikal laughed, turning heads at least in their immediate vicinity. Now it was Saavik's turn to look puzzled.

"Is there something . . . humorous in what I just said?"

"I think I've just been propositioned." Mikal finished his champagne in a single swallow, set down the empty glass, took her hand. "Walk with me . . ."

With no one pressing to speak with him at the moment, Ambassador Sarek watched them go. It had been in his mind to speak to Saavik, if not this evening, then soon, about her future. He had no doubt that, her sojourn with the V'Shar now complete, she would soon be leaving Vulcan and returning to Starfleet, where, he could more easily acknowledge now than he had with Spock so many years ago, she did in fact belong. Despite the many . . . interruptions, his intention to see her suitably bonded remained stronger than ever.

He could never repay her for what she had done for him. At the very least, could he not assist her in resolving this matter? He stopped himself. Had she not, in walking away in private, hand in hand with Mikal, indicated a determination, as she had since she was a child, to make her own choices?

"You're pensive," Amanda said quietly beside him.

"I have reached a decision," he said in his characteristically abrupt manner, which had a tendency to startle those who did not know how much internal monologue accompanied it, and which he had found most effective in his career.

"Have you?"

"Childhood betrothal had its place in Vulcan's past. It does not necessarily serve the present. Saavik must be free to choose for herself."

"Good for you!" Amanda said in a tone that might be mistaken for sarcasm if one didn't know the lifetime of affection that lay behind it. "Now may we say our good-byes? I have *got* to get out of these shoes."

"We'll be gone for a long time," Mikal said. "More than two years, maybe three, maybe longer."

Captain Mironova had announced earlier that

Chaffee had just received new orders for an open-ended mission to the Beta Quadrant to backtrack the point of origin of what was believed to be the most significant of the Deema III rifts. The journey alone would take the better part of an Earth year.

Saavik had assumed Mikal would either return once more to Deema III or, in his restless manner, move on to the next project. She had given considerable thought to how she would respond when he told her where he was going next but was still uncertain what she would say.

"It should prove to be an extraordinary opportunity for you as a scientist," was what she did say.

"We leave at the end of Tasmeen. Before that, though, I wanted you to know that I'm returning to Simeran for the first time since . . . since I left."

"I do not believe I have heard you refer to your home planet by its true name before."

"My home planet," he repeated thoughtfully, as if the concept of a home had just now occurred to him. "I've never thought of it that way before. Not just as another dot on a starmap, not a nightmare of the past frozen in time, but a process, an evolving thing. You taught me that."

"I?"

"I've never met anyone so free of self-pity. It helped me put my own into perspective. Come with?"

"To Simeran? I would be honored, but—"

"To the Beta Quadrant. Galina can pull some strings with Command. You started on this mission; it's only logical that you follow through."

She had assumed they would be going their separate ways after tonight. Spending the next several years together, living and working at close quarters with their contrasting personalities and methodologies had not occurred to her. Was this what she wanted?

"Galina's right, you know," he was saying. "You and I are a perfect balance for each other."

"Scientifically, of course."

"Of course."

She hesitated. "I shall consider it."

"That means no."

"If I had meant no, I would have said—"

He waved away her objection, becoming a restless blur of movement, pacing, robes swirling, earrings jangling, eyes scanning everywhere except into her eyes.

"I don't believe in coincidence," he was saying. "I also don't believe that the future is written. There are so many reasons why you and I should never have met, and almost as many events that conspired to see that we did. Yes, I know," he interrupted himself before she did. "That's a completely unscientific assessment, but it's all I've got. That and the fact that I never expected to fall in love with you."

"Mikal—"

"No!" He stopped flailing about and came to rest, took her face gently between his hands. "If you were anyone else, I'd have been furious with you for going off into the desert, maybe even dying there, without telling me. But where I should have been angry, I was only frightened. Frightened for you, for us . . ."

"Mikal . . ."

How was she to put this? There were emotions she knew too well, primarily rage, and after that fear. But this one, this seeming most complex, inexplicable, and as potentially harmful as beneficial one, eluded her. Perhaps by the time Mikal returned from the Beta Quadrant, she would understand it better.

She held his hands between her own. "If I am to subscribe to your theory, there are also numerous reasons why it was necessary for me to go off into the desert at precisely the time I did. Without being able to tell you."

"Flawlessly argued." He sighed. "You'll always have secrets, and that's as it should be. That's not the part that bothered me, but—"

"But it is not yet time," she said, and whatever else he might have said, he didn't. In that one moment, they understood each other completely.

He squeezed her hands, then released them, giving her his best winsome smile. "It's a small universe. Is it logical to assume our paths will cross again?"

"Scientifically, of course."

"Of course."

Twenty

———

"Logic is the cement of our civilization with which we ascend from chaos using reason as our guide," wrote T'plana-Hath in the before-time.

Spock had returned to Mount Seleya to pay a courtesy call on the priestess T'Lar. Isolated as she was within the realms of thought, she might not be aware of how well the re-fusion of his mind had succeeded, and he wanted her to know. Following their encounter, he thought he might revisit the computers in the training room, just to test himself against his last session and see how far he had progressed. He had not expected to find someone else there before him.

For reasons she could not explain, Saavik had returned to Mount Seleya as well. She was doing much as Spock had done following the re-fusion—looking for answers. She had the computers on silent mode, yet she spoke her answers aloud. Curious, Spock observed his protégé without making his presence known.

"Gottfried Leibniz," he heard Saavik say. "Seventeenth-century human philosopher, who perceived time as neither an event nor a thing, hence neither measurable in and of itself nor able to be traveled."

Spock smiled. Had Leibniz had children? If so, he might have arrived at a different conclusion. Surely there was no better arbiter of time than watching a child come of age, this child in particular.

Hovering in the archway, Spock made no sound, yet somehow Saavik sensed his presence. She turned.

"My mentor, I did not expect . . ."

His gesture suggested that it was he, not she, who was the intruder here. And there was something more.

"Surely we no longer have need of titles, do we, Saavik?" Not Saavik-*kam*, she noted. "Where I might at one time have attempted to mentor you, it has been my experience that I have learned just as much from you. We are peers."

As a child she had stood up to him, even defied him, making clear where the boundaries were. Why, as an adult, was she suddenly shy around him? This would not do.

He had crossed the threshold, stood beside her at the three computer consoles, contemplating the answers she had been seeking.

"One can only wonder what Leibniz would have thought if he had had the opportunity to travel aboard a starship," he mused.

This whimsical way of looking at the universe was, Spock thought, something new, perhaps a resonance of Doctor McCoy's mind in juxtaposition with his own. Then again, as his mother frequently pointed out, he *was* half human.

"Indeed," Saavik ventured. "There is the temptation to consider his philosophy primitive, if one takes it out of context. Centuries from now, how primitive will our philosophy seem to those who follow?"

"Thus why it is necessary to leave oneself open to new thoughts, new ideas."

"You are yourself again," she observed. "This pleases me."

"Perhaps almost as much as it pleases me?"

Humor, she thought, and together they left the training room to contemplate the stars from the promontory outside.

Neither spoke, neither touched, yet somehow their thoughts were the same. When she had first been accepted to the Academy, she had hoped for nothing more than the quiet life of a research scientist. But from the beginning Spock had seen in her a natural leadership ability and urged her to take command training in addition to the sciences. At the time, her sense of gratitude and not a little hero worship had led her to reluctantly agree.

Following the events on Genesis, having seen the kinds of decisions starship captains were sometimes forced to make and the terrible consequences if things went wrong, she had wanted to distance herself from command as much as possible.

Now, looking back on the decisions she had made—some by choice, some by necessity—she acknowledged Spock's wisdom, his ability to see what she had at the time been unable to see for herself.

Enterprise, the new *Enterprise,* would retrieve Spock shortly, return him to where he knew, without any hesitation, that he belonged. While she was far less certain of her place in the universe, Saavik was certain that there was at least one place out there where she was always welcome.

This time she would leave Mount Seleya with more confidence. She would report to Starfleet HQ Vulcan and request clearance from Starfleet medical to return to duty. If *Enterprise* would have her, she would go, and take her place among the stars.

ACKNOWLEDGMENTS

My thanks to Margaret Clark, for swift and merciful editing. May the wind be at your back. Special thanks to Diacanu, for calling Mikal "a swashbuckler," and thus making him visible. Homage to Robin Curtis, Susan Schwartz, and all Romulans, cloaked and visible. And of course, to Jack, ever and always.

ABOUT THE AUTHOR

Margaret Wander Bonanno is the author of *Dwellers in the Crucible*, *Strangers from the Sky*, *Catalyst of Sorrows*, *Burning Dreams*, and *Unspoken Truth*, as well as *Its Hour Come Round* in the *Mere Anarchy* series, and "The Greater Good" in the *Shards and Shadows* anthology. She lives on the Left Coast.